Prize Stories 1970:

THE O. HENRY AWARDS

Prize Stories 1970:

THE O. HENRY AWARDS

Edited and with an Introduction by

WILLIAM ABRAHAMS

27729

Doubleday & Company, Inc., Garden City, New York

1970

CONTENTS

PUBLISHER'S NOTE

This volume is the fiftieth in the O. Henry Memorial Award series.

In 1918, the Society of Arts and Sciences met to vote upon a monument to the master of the short story, O. Henry. They decided that this memorial should be in the form of two prizes for the best short stories published by American authors in American magazines during the year 1919. From this beginning, the memorial developed into an annual anthology of outstanding short stories by American authors published, with the exception of the years 1952 and 1953, by Doubleday & Company, Inc.

Blanche Colton Williams, one of the founders of the awards, was editor from 1919 to 1932; Harry Hansen from 1933 to 1940; Herschel Brickell from 1941 to 1951. The annual collection did not appear in 1952 and 1953, when the continuity of the series was interrupted by the death of Herschel Brickell, who had been the editor for ten years. Paul Engle was editor from 1954 to 1959 with Hanson Martin co-editor in the years 1954 to 1956; Mary Stegner in 1960; Richard Poirier from 1961 to 1966, with assistance from and co-editorship with William Abrahams from 1964 to 1966. William Abrahams became editor of the series in 1967.

Doubleday also publishes *First-Prize Stories from the O. Henry Memorial Awards* in editions which are brought up to date at intervals. This year Doubleday will also publish, under Mr. Abrahams' editorship, a fifty-year selection from the series.

The stories chosen for this volume were published in the period from the summer of 1968 to the summer of 1969. A list of the magazines consulted appears at the back of the book. The choice of stories and the selection of prize winners are exclusively the responsibility of the editor. Biographical material is based on information provided by the contributors.

INTRODUCTION: PRIZE STORIES 1970

We have arrived at the end of the decade and the easy temptation to speak of the 1960s as a "period" in our writing. Where the short story is concerned—as a part of the period—I am reluctant to generalize, if only because one is so likely to be contradicted (each generalization containing its built-in repudiation), but more seriously, because art doesn't occur by the decade or undergo radical change as one decade ends and another begins. Marking off ten years of achievement is a convenience, not a definition; and I am reminded of Richard Poirier's complaint, in his introduction to *Prize Stories 1961*, "We are constantly hearing . . . that current fiction is so hopping with life that we can already tell, barely into the second year of the decade, how fiction of the 60s differs from fiction of the 50s. Of course there is necessarily some difference: Calvin Coolidge's second term was necessarily different from his first."

The truth would seem to be that we have come to the end of a decade but are in the middle of a period—the period of the Vietnam war. It is this terrible fact, terrible in itself and calling into being or augmenting like a chain reaction so much else that is terrible, that determines the spirit of the age in which we live, in which stories, good, bad, and mediocre alike, are written. Which is not to say that they reflect it directly; most do not, it is more a matter of tone and sensibility than subject matter; and each year, inevitably, there will be complaints from readers who confuse stories with news bulletins and believe contemporary writers are escapist or trivial in their concern. (It is worth remembering that stories dealing with the war itself have only recently begun to be published. Two examples are in the present volume: David Grinstead's "A Day in Operations" and William Eastlake's "The Biggest Thing Since Custer," as powerful in its way as a Goya "Disaster of War.")

William Abrahams

Period or not, having reread the ten volumes in this series that account for the decade, I am relieved to discover how fine so many of the stories are, how fine so many of them have continued to be. Some have not, of course; and leaving aside the question of editorial frailty (no small thing!), it would seem that some stories, like wines, don't age well. Brilliant in their year, they tend to go off . . . one wonders what one saw in them in the first place. But I hasten to add that such stories constitute a very small minority. On the whole, the level is reassuringly high. The American short story has come through the 1960s in good health; and though its health is endangered—as it has been through the decade—I have no doubt that it will survive.

The ten volumes for the 1960s contain 157 stories by 117 writers (some of whom have been represented by one or more stories). There has been no set figure agreed upon for a given year: the number chosen has ranged from 10 (in 1961) to 18 (in 1965); this year there are 17. Of the 117 writers, some were old and famous, others young and unknown, at the time their stories were chosen—from the latter group have emerged some of the best-known and most admired writers of the period; some have fallen silent, one hopes temporarily; and some—among them, Flannery O'Connor, Carson McCullers, David Stacton—are dead. They make an impressive group, these 117 writers of the 1960s, and merely to list their names supports better than any generalization a claim for the quality of the American short story in the past decade.

The list, which follows, has been arranged chronologically, in the order in which the writers first appeared in the collection in the 1960s (their subsequent appearances aren't shown; and it must be kept in mind that many of the older writers had appeared in the collection before, some of them making a first appearance two or three decades earlier).

1961—Tillie Olsen, Ivan Gold, Reynolds Price, Jackson Burgess, Ellen Currie, Jesse Hill Ford, Ervin Krause, Jack Ludwig, Arthur Miller, David Shaber, Peter Taylor, John Updike. 1962—Katherine Anne Porter, Thomas Pynchon, Tom Cole, Shirley W. Schoonover, Mary Deasy, Shirley Ann Grau, David Jackson, John Graves, Thomas E. Adams, Miriam McKenzie, Maureen Howard, Thomas Whitbread. 1963—Flannery O'Connor, Thalia Selz, William Saroyan, Ben Maddow, Sylvia Berkman, Norma Klein, Terry South-

ern, Jessamyn West, J. G. McClure, Helen Essary Ansell, James
Trammell Cox, Joyce Carol Oates (as J. C. Oates; she did not
appear as Joyce Carol Oates until 1967), Ellen Douglas. 1964—
John Cheever, Margaret Shedd, Bernard Malamud, Sallie Bing-
ham, Lillian Ross, David Stacton, Irwin Shaw, Hortense Calisher,
George Lanning, George A. Zorn, "Sara" Philip Roth, Wallace
Stegner. 1965—Sanford Friedman, William Humphrey, Tom
Mayer, Eva Manoff, Nancy A. J. Potter, Donald Barthelme, Leon
Rooke, Peter S. Beagle, Leonard Wolf, Carson McCullers, Daniel
Curley, Arthur Cavanaugh, Mary McCarthy, Warren Miller.
1966—Leonard Michaels, Elizabeth Spencer, Harry Mark Petrakis,
Vera Randal; Philip L. Greene, Nancy Hale, Joy Williams, Chris-
topher Davis, Gina Berriault, Georgia McKinley. 1967—Jonathan
Strong, Marvin Mudrick, Miriam Goldman, Josephine Jacobsen,
James Buechler, Ernest J. Finney, Diane Oliver, M. R. Kurtz,
Conrad Knickerbocker, Robie Macauley, Allen Wheelis, Richard
Yates. 1968—Eudora Welty, E. M. Broner, Shlomo Katz, Calvin
Kentfield, Gwen Gration, F. K. Franklin, Brock Brower, Jay
Neugeboren, James Baker Hall, Eldon Branda, Paul Tyner,
Marilyn Harris. 1969—John Barth, Nancy Huddleston Packer, Leo
Litwak, Anne Tyler, Evelyn Shefner, Eunice Luccock Corfman,
Thomas Sterling, Michael Rubin, Grace Paley, Max Steele, H. L.
Montzoures, Susan Engberg. 1970—Robert Hemenway ("Stephen
Patch"), William Eastlake, Norval Rindfleisch, Perdita Buchan,
George Blake, H. E. F. Donohue, James Salter, Patricia Browning
Griffith, David Grinstead, Nancy Willard, James Alan McPherson.
   And what of their stories? Since limitations of space preclude
naming all 157 that have appeared in the collection through the
decade, and since I would prefer not to have to pick and choose
among them for a "representative" group, I will offer simply a list
of First Prize stories: 1961, "Tell Me a Riddle" by Tillie Olsen;
1962, "Holiday" by Katherine Anne Porter; 1963, "Everything that
Rises Must Converge" by Flannery O'Connor; 1964, "The Em-
barkment for Cythera" by John Cheever; 1965, "Revelation" by
Flannery O'Connor; 1966, "The Bulgarian Poetess" by John Updike; 1967, "In the Region of Ice" by Joyce Carol Oates; 1968,
"The Demonstrators" by Eudora Welty; 1969, "Man in the
Drawer" by Bernard Malamud; 1970, "The Girl Who Sang with
the Beatles" by Robert Hemenway.

It may seem perverse in the face of such splendid accomplishments to speak of the health of the short story as endangered; yet I believe this to be the case. I am not thinking now of the writing of stories—which is at as high a level as it has ever been —but of the publication and audience for stories, a situation that threatens to reduce the form to a minority art. In my introduction to *Prize Stories 1967*, I wrote that "serious cause for alarm lies in the indifference, or even the hostility, toward the short story that is evident in a number of magazines that used to publish fiction regularly, but now no longer do so. . . . We are living in the heyday of the article. At the present time, there's hardly a magazine, whatever its category, that doesn't offer its readers articles in abundance. They are wanted and in a way that stories are not. Perhaps in an anxiety-ridden age like ours, when certainties aren't easily come by, there is a peculiar reassurance in the factuality of the article.

"Consider the article: it describes brilliantly; it analyzes convincingly; it informs you, and at the same time it never asks that you be implicated in its situation; it makes no demand except to be read—*once*. Reading an article is like looking through a pane of glass, never into a mirror.

"Obviously this is very different from what the short story does, and demands of us. . . . The two forms are so different that there ought to be a place for both. But apparently this is not possible. In far too many magazines the preponderance of space is given to articles. Meanwhile the number of stories such magazines publish grows fewer each year; one can foresee a time when even the token gesture will no longer be made, on the palpably false pretext that good stories aren't being written."

Certainly the situation has not improved since that was written; actually it has worsened. What I failed to foresee, however, was that magazines themselves might eventually fall into the category of a minority interest, might prove, no matter how ostensibly popular, a dispensable phenomenon. The recent disappearance of *The Saturday Evening Post* serves as an ominous instance. (For the record: five stories from the *Post* appeared in this collection through the decade.) As I suggested above, magazines, crammed full of articles as they are, are meant to be read. But we are arriving (it would seem) at a time when watching and listening will take primacy over reading as a function even of the literate and educated. The incursions and effects of TV upon our lives are only dimly recognized as yet. We are made aware of them, frighteningly aware perhaps, not in sociological or polemical articles, but in a story with quite different intentions like "The Girl Who Sang with the Beatles," which, quite apart from its exceptional qualities as a particular story of the disintegration and paralysis of a particular marriage, has a more generalized emblematic value—of American life in the 1960s—that even readers hostile to symbolism cannot fail to recognize. In a world of earphones shutting out all but electronic noises and a screen flickering with images—of the moon?—how long, one wonders gloomily, will the reading and writing, let alone the publication, of short stories matter?

But I do not want to end on so gloomy a note. It is a great pleasure to announce that the publishers of the series have established this year a new prize in connection with it: a Special Award for continuing achievement by a writer of established reputation. The award will be made at the discretion of the editor at such times as seem appropriate; and I am very pleased that it should be given for the first time to Joyce Carol Oates, a gifted writer whose achievements and reputation are a part of the history of the American short story in the 1960s.

—*William Abrahams*

Prize Stories 1970:

THE O. HENRY AWARDS

ROBERT HEMENWAY was born in South Haven, Michigan, in 1921. He attended the University of Chicago. He is on the staff of *The New Yorker* and lives, with his wife, in New York City. The story here was originally published under the pseudonym "Stephen Patch."

The Girl Who Sang with the Beatles

OF course, their tastes turned out to be different. Cynthia was twenty-eight when they married, and looked younger, in the way small, very pretty women can—so much younger sometimes that bartenders would ask for her I.D. Larry was close to forty and gray, a heavy man who, when he moved, moved slowly. He had been an English instructor once, though now he wrote market-research reports, and there was still something bookish about him. Cynthia, who was working as an interviewer for Larry's company when he met her, had been a vocalist with several dance bands for a while in the fifties before she quit to marry her first husband. She had left high school when she was a junior to take her first singing job. She and Larry were from different cultures, practically, and yet when they were married they both liked the same things. That was what brought them together. Thirties movies. Old bars—not the instant-tradition places but what was left of the old ones, what Cynthia called the bar bars. Double features in the loge of the Orpheum, eating hot dogs and drinking smuggled beer. Gibsons before dinner and Scotch after. Their TV nights, eating delicatessen while they watched "Mr. Lucky" or "Route 66" or "Ben Casey," and then the eleven-o'clock news and the Late and Late Late Shows, while they drank and necked and sometimes made love. And listening to Cynthia's records—old Sinatras and Judy Garlands, and Steve Lawrence and Eydie Gorme, or "The Fantasticks" or "Candide." They even agreed on redecorating Cynthia's apartment, which was full of leftovers from her first marriage. They agreed on all of it—the worn (but genuine) Oriental rugs; the low carved Spanish tables; the dusky colors, grays and mauve and rose; the damask sofa with its down pillows; and, in the bedroom, the twin beds, nearly joined but held separate by an ornate brass bedstead. When they came back from their Aruba honeymoon, Cynthia said, "God, Larry, I *love* it. This place is pure 'Sunset Boulevard' now."

Their apartment made Larry remember Hyde Park Boulevard in Chicago, where he had grown up in a mock-Spanish apartment filled with the wrought iron and walnut of an earlier fad. Entering the new place was like entering his childhood. "Valencia!" sang in his head. "Valencia! In my dreams it always seems I hear you softly call to me. Valencia!"

They were married early in the summer of 1961, and by the spring of 1963 the things they had bought no longer looked quite right. Everyone seemed to be buying Spanish now. Larry and Cynthia found themselves in a dowdy apartment full of things that had begun to look as if they dated from the twenties. It was depressing. They began to ask each other what they had done. Not that either of them wanted out exactly, but what had they done? Why had they married? Why couldn't they have gone on with their affair? Neither had married the other for money, that was certain. Larry had made Cynthia quit work (not that she minded) and now they had only his salary, which was barely enough.

"We still love each other, don't we? I mean, I know I love you." Cynthia was in Larry's bed and Larry was talking. It was three in the morning, and they had come back from their usual Saturday-night tour of the neighborhood bars. "I love you," Larry said.

"You don't like me."

"I *love* you, Cynthia."

"You don't like me." Propped up by pillows, she stared red-eyed at a great paper daisy on the wall.

"I love you, Cindy."

"So? Big deal. Men have been telling me they loved me since I was fourteen. I thought you were different."

Larry lay flat on his back. "Don't be tough. It's not like you," he said.

"I *am* tough. That's what you won't understand. You didn't marry *me*. You married some nutty idea of your own. I was your secret fantasy. You told me so." Cynthia, naked, was shivering.

"Lie down," Larry said. "I'll rub your back."

"You won't get around me that way," Cynthia said. "You tricked me. I thought you liked the things I liked. You won't even watch TV with me anymore."

Larry reached up and began to rub the back of Cynthia's neck and play with the soft hairs behind one ear. "I can't stand your programs anymore," he said.

"You don't like me," Cynthia said. "If you really liked me, you'd watch. You'd *like* being bored."

Larry sat up. "That isn't it," he said. "You know what it is? It's the noise. All the things you like make noise."

"I read."

"Sure. With the radio or the stereo or the TV on. I can't. I have to do one thing at a time," Larry said. "What if I want to sit home at night and read a book?"

"So read."

"When you have these programs you quote have to watch unquote?"

"Get me headphones. That's what my first husband did. Or go in the bedroom and shut the door. I don't mind."

And so it went, on many nights. Everything was tainted by their disagreements—especially their times in bed. They would slip again and again into these exchanges, on and on.

What Cynthia seemed to resent most was that Larry had not been straightforward with her. Why had he let her think he cared for her world of song and dance? She knew it was trivial. She had never tried to make him think she was deep. Why had he pretended he was something he wasn't?

How was Larry to tell her the truth without making her think he was either a snob or a fool? There was no way. When they met, he *did* like what she liked, just because she liked it. What was wrong with that? He wanted to see her enjoying herself, so they did what she wanted to do—went to Radio City to see the new Doris Day, or to Basin Street East to hear Peggy Lee or Trini Lopez, or to revivals of those fifties movie musicals Cynthia liked so much. Forget the things *he* liked—foreign movies and chamber music and walks in Central Park—for a while, if she didn't like them. She must have known his tastes, after all. She had been in his apartment often enough before they were married. She had seen his books and records.

"I thought you gave all that up," Cynthia said. "I thought you'd changed."

"I thought you *would* change," Larry said. "I thought you wanted to. I thought if you wanted to marry me you must want to change."

"Be an *intellectual?*" Cynthia said. "You must be kidding."

No, he was serious. Why didn't she get bored with the stuff she watched and the junk she read? He did. When you had seen three Perry Masons, you had seen them all, and that went for Doris Day movies, the eleven-o'clock news, and "What's My Line?"

"I know all that," Cynthia said. She liked to be bored. God, you couldn't keep thinking about *reality* all the time. You'd go out of your mind. She liked stories and actors that she knew, liked movies she had seen a dozen times and the books she reread once each year. Larry took his reading so seriously, as if reading were life.

Larry tried to persuade himself that Cynthia was teasing him, but he could not. She meant what she said. She *liked* "East of Eden," "Marjorie Morningstar," "Giant," and "Gone with the Wind." She liked Elizabeth Taylor movies. She found nourishment in that Styrofoam. He could see it in her childlike face, which sometimes shone as if she were regarding the beatific vision when she was under the spell of the sorriest trash. What repelled him moved her. He could feel it when, after she had seen one of her favorite movies, they made love. How odd that he should have married her! And yet he loved her, he thought, and he thought she loved him—needed him, anyway.

Sometimes they talked of having a child, or of Cynthia's going back to work, or of attending night classes together at Columbia or the New School, but nothing came of it. They were both drinking too much, perhaps, and getting too little exercise, yet it was easier to let things go on much as they were. Larry did set out to read Camus, the first serious reading he had done since their marriage, and in the evenings after dinner he would go into the bedroom, shut the door, turn on WNCN to muffle the sounds from the living room, put Flents in his ears, and read. Although the meaningless noises from the TV set—the not quite comprehensible voices, the sudden surges of music—still reached him, he was reluctant to give Cynthia the headphones she had suggested. They would be too clear a sign of defeat.

Cynthia often stayed up until three or four watching the late movies or playing her records, and Larry, who usually fell asleep around midnight, would sometimes wake after two or three hours and come out of the bedroom shouting "Do you know what *time* it is?" and frighten her. Sometimes, though, he would make a drink for himself and watch her movie, too, necking with her the way they used to do, without saying much.

When it was very late, usually on Saturday nights after they both had had quite a lot to drink, Cynthia would stand before the full-length mirror in their bedroom and admire herself. "I'm beautiful," she would say. "Right now, I'm really beautiful, and who can see me?" Larry would watch her from the bed. Something slack in her would grow taut as she looked in the mirror. She would draw her underpants down low on her hips, then place her hands on her shoulders, her crossed arms covering her bare breasts, and smile at her reflection. "I'm a narcissist," she would say, looking at Larry in the mirror. "How can you bear it?" Then she would join Larry in his bed.

Larry couldn't deny Cynthia anything for long. If he insisted on it, she would turn off the set, but then she would sulk until he felt he had imposed upon her, and he would turn the set back on or take her out for a drink.

One Saturday night when they came home from the bars, Cynthia changed clothes and came out of the bedroom wearing a twenties black dress and black net stockings and pumps. The dress was banded with several rows of fringe and stopped above her knees. She danced for Larry (a Charleston, a shimmy, a Watusi) and after that she sang. She had sung to him before—just a few bars, in a soft, almost inaudible voice—but tonight her voice seemed full and moving to Larry, and with a timbre and sadness different from any voice he had ever heard. "*Like* me. Please like me," the voice seemed to say. "Just like me. That's all I need. I'll be nice then." She *could* have been the star she wanted to be, Larry thought. She had the charm and the need for love, though perhaps the voice was too slight and the need too great. She had once told him that twice while she was singing with a band in Las Vegas she had been "discovered" by assistant directors and offered a movie audition, and that each time she had been sick, literally sick to her stomach, in the studio and unable to go on. She was just too scared. Yet she might have a career again, Larry thought. He would encourage her to practice. It would be an interest for her—something to do. She was barely past thirty and looked less. There was still time.

Larry decided to read Camus in French and to translate some of the untranslated essays, just for practice, into English. One night, he came home with the headphones Cynthia wanted —the old-fashioned kind made of black Bakelite—and hooked them up to the TV set through a control box that had an off-on switch for the speaker. Now that he could blank out the commercials, Larry would watch with Cynthia now and then—some of the news specials, and the Wide World of Sports, and the late-night reruns of President Kennedy's press conferences, one of the few things they both enjoyed.

Cynthia was happier now, because with the headphones on and the speaker off she could watch as late as she pleased. And as she became more wrapped up in her programs, Larry became more wrapped up in Camus. She would sit on the sofa for hours, dressed as if for company, her eyes made up to look even larger than they were, wearing one of the at-home hostessy things from Bergdorf's she had bought just before they were married that hardly anyone but she and Larry had seen, and with those radio operator's black headphones on her ears.

The sight of her made Larry melancholy, and he continued to work lying on his bed, propped up with a writing board on his lap. He would hear Cynthia laughing sometimes in the silent living room, and now and then, hearing thin sounds from her headphones, he would come out to find her crying, the phones on her lap and the final credits of a movie on the screen. "I always cry at this one," she would say. With the headphones, Cynthia was spending more time before the set than ever. Larry encouraged her to sing—to take lessons again if she wanted. But she did sing, she said, in the afternoons. She sang with her records, usually. There were a few songs of Eydie's and Peggy's and Judy's she liked. She sang along with those.

When Larry compared his life now with his first marriage or with the years after that, he could not say that this was worse. Cynthia was almost content, and left him free to think or read what he pleased. There were many nights, though, when he put his book aside and lay on his bed, hearing Cynthia laugh now and then or get up to make herself another drink, and asked himself why he was there. Little, in his job or in his life, seemed reasonable or real.

How could he have fallen in love with Cynthia? It was just because she was so *American*, he decided. She *liked* canned chili and corned-beef hash, the Academy Awards, Chicken Delight, the Miss America contest, head lettuce with Russian dressing, *Modern Screen*, takeout pizza pies. She liked them and would make faces at them at the same time, looking up at him and saying, "Oh God, isn't this awful? Isn't this vile?" Everything he had renounced in the name of the Bauhaus and Consumers Union, of Irma Rombauer, D. H. Lawrence, and Frank Lloyd Wright—here it all was dished up in Cynthia, all the things that he could see now he had never had enough of. He had lost out on them in high school, when he had wanted them, because he was studious and shy. He had rejected them in college, where it was a matter of principle among his friends to reject them, before he could find out what they were like. At thirty-eight, when he met Cynthia, what did he know? Weren't there vast areas of the American experience that he had missed? Why, until Cynthia he had never shacked up in a motel. Nor had he ever seen a barroom fight, or smoked pot, or been ticketed for speeding, or blacked out from booze.

And how glittering Cynthia's world had seemed to him. The sixties—this is what they *were!* Thruways, motels, Point Pleasant on a Saturday night, twisting to the juke! That trip to Atlantic City in winter when he and Cynthia wandered through the cold deserted corridors and public rooms of those great stucco

hotels like actors in a shabby "Marienbad." And the music! Miles,
Monk, Chico, Mingus, the M.J.Q., Sinatra and Nelson Riddle,
Belafonte, Elvis, Ray Charles, Dion, Lena Horne—all new to
him. He had stopped listening to music before bop, and with Cynthia he listened to everything. Did he like it all—how was it possible to like it *all*—because Cynthia did, or had he fallen in love
with Cynthia because she liked it all? What difference did it make?
It was all new—a gorgeous blur of enthusiasms. For the first time
in his life he had given himself away. How wonderful, at thirty-
eight, on the edge of middle age—*in* middle age—to play the
fool.

And how he had been taken in by it all! Cynthia never had.
She knew show business from the inside, and dug it, and liked it,
and laughed at herself for liking it. She knew how shabby it was,
even though it did something for her—that trumpery, that sincere
corn. Once Larry found out something was bad, how could he
care for it any longer? It was impossible. He had gone overboard
at first because pop culture was new to him and he saw fresh
energy there. But how spurious that energy had turned out to
be—how slick, how manufactured, how dead. And yet something
in it rubbed off on Cynthia and made her attractive to him still.
He still wanted her. Wasn't it just that fakery he despised which
shone in Cynthia and drew him to her? Then what in their marriage was real? He felt as detached from his life as a dreamer
at times feels detached from his dream.

Quiet and sedentary as it had become, Larry's life continued
to be charged with a forced excitement. The popular love songs,
the photographs of beautiful men and women in the magazines
Cynthia read, the romantic movies, Cynthia herself—changing her
clothes three or four times a day as if she were the star in a play
and Larry the audience—all stimulated him. He recognized in
himself an extravagant lust that was never quite spent when he
and Cynthia made love.

"We shouldn't have got married," Cynthia said one hot Saturday night in the summer of 1963 as they were lying in their
beds trying to fall asleep.

"Maybe not," Larry said.

"Marriage turns me off. Something happens. I told you."

"I didn't believe you," Larry said. "And anyway we're married."

"We sure are."

"I picked a lemon in the garden of love," Larry said. Cynthia laughed and moved into Larry's bed.

Later that night, though, he said something else. "We're like the Catholics and their sacrament," he said. "When you're married for the second time, you're practically stuck with each other. You've almost got to work it out."

"You may think you're stuck, but I'm not," Cynthia said.

A few nights later she brought up what Larry had said about being stuck. Why had he said it? Didn't he know her at all? Whenever she felt bound she had to break free—right out the door, sooner or later. That was what had always happened. Was he trying to drive her away? He knew she'd been a rolling stone. That's what he liked about her, he'd said once. All that talk about protecting each other's freedom! What a lot of crap. Look at them now. Two birds in a cage, a filthy cage.

Cynthia's anger frightened Larry, and, to his surprise, the thought of her leaving frightened him, too. But nothing changed. There wasn't much chance of her breaking away, after all. They didn't have enough money to separate, and neither of them really wanted to—not *that* routine, not again.

Now and then Larry sat in the living room reading while Cynthia watched her programs, and when he looked over at her, knowing that at that moment she was content, he felt at peace. At times, he would lie with his head on Cynthia's lap while she watched, and she would stroke his hair.

One day, Larry came home with a second pair of headphones, made of green plastic and padded with foam rubber, the sort disc jockeys and astronauts wear, and plugged them into the stereo through a box that permitted turning off the speakers. Now he, like Cynthia, could listen in silence. He stacked some of his records on the turntable—the Mozart horn concertos, a Bach cantata, Gluck. It was eerie, Larry thought, for them both to be so completely absorbed, sitting twenty feet apart in that silent living room, and on the first night he found himself watching Cynthia's picture on the TV screen as the music in his ears seemed to fade away. Finally, he took off his earphones, joined Cynthia on the sofa, and asked her to turn on the sound. After a few nights, however, the sense of eeriness wore off, and Larry was as caught up in his music as Cynthia was in her shows. The stereo sound was so rich and pure; unmixed with other noises, the music carried directly into his brain, surrounding and penetrating him. It was so intense, so mindless. He felt endowed with a superior sense, as if he were a god. Yet there was something illicit about their both finding so intense a pleasure in isolation. He was troubled, off and on, by what they were falling into, but their life was tranquil and that was almost enough.

One night, when Larry was reading (something he rarely did now) and there was nothing on TV she cared for, Cynthia put some of her records on the turntable and Larry's headphones on her ears and listened to Eydie and Judy and Frank, dancing a few steps now and then and singing the words softly. "Why didn't you tell me!" she said. It was *fantastic*. She could hear all the bass, and the color of the voices, and things in some of the arrangements she had never known were there. More and more often as the summer wore on, Cynthia would listen to her music instead of watching the tube, and Larry, thinking this a step in the right direction—toward her singing, perhaps—turned the stereo over to her several evenings a week and tried to concentrate again on his reading. But music had held him in a way books no longer could, and after a few weeks he bought a second stereo phonograph and a second set of headphones. By the fall of 1963, he and Cynthia had begun to listen, each to his own music, together.

On the day President Kennedy was assassinated, Larry and Cynthia were having one of their rare lunches in midtown at an Italian place near Bloomingdale's, where Cynthia planned to go shopping afterward. People stood before the small television set above the restaurant bar waiting for definite news after the first word of the shooting, and Larry and Cynthia stood with them. When it was clear that the President was dead, they went back to their apartment, watched television together that afternoon and evening, and then went to bed and began to weep. When Larry stopped, Cynthia would sob, and then Larry would start again. So it went until after four in the morning, when they fell asleep. Until the funeral was over, Cynthia sat before the set most of

the day and night. Much of the time she was crying, and every
night when she came to bed the tears would start. Larry, dry-
eyed sooner than she was, was at first sympathetic, then impatient,
then annoyed.

"He was such a *good* man," Cynthia would say, or "He was
ours. He was all we had," and after the burial she said, half smiling, "He was a wonderful star." Nothing in her actual life could
ever move her so deeply, Larry thought. How strange, to feel real
sorrow and weep real tears for an unreal loss. But she was suffering, no question of that, and she could not stop crying. The
Christmas season came and went, and she still wept. She had
begun to drink heavily, and often Larry would put her to bed.
On the edge of unconsciousness, she would continue to cry.

What was she, he thought, but a transmitter of electronic sen-
sations? First she had conveyed the nation's erotic fantasies to
him, and now it was the national sorrow, and one was as unreal as
the other. John Kennedy had figured in her fantasies—Cynthia
had once told Larry so—and she wept for him as a woman would
for her dead lover. She was like a woman betrayed by Death, Larry
thought, when what had betrayed her was the television set she
had counted upon to shield her from the real. It had always told
her stories of terror and passion that, because they were fictitious,
might be endured, and now it had shown her actual death and
actual sorrow. And there was no way to console her, because her
loss was not an actual loss.

Cynthia read little during the weeks after the assassination but
articles on it, and she did not hear of the Beatles until Larry, hoping to distract her, brought home their first album. She thought
little of it at first, but after the Beatles appeared on the "Ed Sullivan Show" in February she became an admirer and then a devo-
tee. Larry brought her the new Beatles 45s as they came out, and
he stood in line with teen-age girls at the newsstands on Forty-
second Street to buy the Beatles fan magazines. "I guess the period
of mourning is over," Cynthia said one Saturday night. She still
saved articles about the assassination, though, and photographs
of Jacqueline in black.

When Cynthia began to sing as she listened to the Beatles late
at night, Larry, listening from the bedroom, was pleased. She

would play their records over and over, accompanying them in a voice that seemed flat and unresonant, perhaps because with the headphones on she could not hear the sounds she made. She no longer wept, or Larry was asleep when she did.

One night, Larry woke around three to the tinny noise of "I Want to Hold Your Hand" spilling from Cynthia's phones and found he was hungry. On his way to the kitchen, he stopped in the dark hall to watch Cynthia, who stood in the center of the living room with the astronaut headphones on, singing what sounded like a harmonizing part, a little off-key, holding an imaginary guitar, swaying jerkily, and smiling as if she were before an audience. Her performance, empty as it was, seemed oddly polished and professional. Afraid of startling her, he stood watching until the end of the song before he entered the room.

"How much did you see?" Cynthia said.

"Nothing," Larry said. "I was just going to get a glass of milk, that's all." The look on Cynthia's face troubled him, as if he had discovered her in some indecency better forgotten. "After this I'll flick the lights and warn you," he said.

And he said no more, though often now he awoke during the night to the faint sounds from Cynthia's headphones and wondered what she was doing that held her so fast. He was jealous of it, in a way. She was rarely in bed before four, and always in bed when he left for work in the morning. In the evening, though, as she watched television, she seemed happy enough, and much as she had been before Kennedy's death.

For some time after the assassination, they gave up their Saturday nights in the bars, but by April they were again making their rounds. Once, when they came home higher and happier than usual, Cynthia danced and sang for Larry as she had before, and Larry joined her—something he did not do often. They had a pleasant time, and when Larry put on a Beatles album and Cynthia began her performance for him she explained. "We're at the Palladium in London, you see," she said. "The place is mobbed. . . . The Beatles are onstage. . . . I'm singing with them, and naturally everybody loves us. I work through the whole show . . . playing second guitar. I back up George." And then she sang, a third or so below the melody, "She was just seventeen if you know what I mean. . . ."

"I never sing lead," Cynthia said when the number was over.

"Is this what you do every night?" Larry asked her.

Cynthia was breathing heavily. "Sure," she said. "It may sound silly but it's not. Besides, it's possible, isn't it? It *could* happen. I can sing." She looked at Larry, her eyes candid and kind. "Don't worry," she said. "I'm not losing my grip."

"It's a nice game," Larry said later when they were in bed.

"Oh, it's more than a game," Cynthia said. "When I'm with them in the Palladium, I'm really *there*. It's more real than here. I know it's a fantasy, though."

"How did you meet the Beatles?" Larry asked her.

"D'you really want to hear?" Cynthia said. She seemed pleased at his interest, Larry thought, but then she was drunk. They both were.

"It's not much of a story," she said. "The details vary, but basically I am standing on Fifth Avenue there near the Plaza in the snow waiting for a cab at three in the afternoon, dressed in my black flared coat and black pants and the black boots you gave me, and I'm *cold*. You know how cold I get. And then this Carey Cad stops with a couple of guys in front and in back is George Harrison all alone, though sometimes it's Paul. He gives me a lift and we talk. He's completely polite and sincere, and I can see he likes me. It seems the Beatles are rehearsing for a television special at Central Plaza and they'll be there the next day, so he asks me to come up and bring my guitar. I go, naturally, and it turns out they are auditioning girls, and I'm the winner. What would be the point if I wasn't? They want a girl for just one number, but when they see how terrific I am, naturally they love me, and when they find out I've already worked up all their songs I'm in."

"You join them."

"Sure. They insist. I have to leave you, but you don't mind, not anymore. In one year, we're The Beatles and Cynthia and we're playing the Palladium, and Princess Margaret and Tony are there, and Frank, and Peter O'Toole, and David McCallum, and Steve McQueen, and Bobby Kennedy. And all those men *want* me. And I'm going to meet them afterward at the Savoy in our suite."

" 'Our'?"

"I'm married to a rich diamond merchant who lets me do whatever I want. Played by George Sanders."

"I thought you were married to me," Larry said.

"Oh, no. You divorced me, alleging mental cruelty. Maybe I was cruel once, but I'm not anymore, because the Beatles love me. They're like brothers to me."

"Are you putting me on?" Larry said.

"No. Why should I? I made it all up, if that's what you mean, but I *really* made it up."

"Do you believe any of it?" Larry said.

Cynthia smiled at him. "Don't you? You used to say that I had a good voice and you used to say I was pretty. Anyway, I don't have fantasies about things that couldn't possibly happen. I could get a job tomorrow if you'd let me."

Cynthia's voice had a lilt Larry remembered from the days before their marriage. It was all so convincing and so insane. She had begun to amuse him again, and he indulged her in her illusions. "I'm going to Beatle now," Cynthia would say nearly every night after dinner, and Larry would go into the bedroom. Whenever he came out, he would flick the hall lights and she would stop. She was shy and did not let him watch often at first. She seemed embarrassed that she had told him as much as she had—if, indeed, she remembered telling him anything at all.

Larry liked the Beatles more and more as the nights went by, and often he would listen to their records with the speakers on before Cynthia began her performance. "Listen, Cynthia," he said one Saturday night. "The Beatles are filled with the Holy Ghost." He was really quite drunk. "Do you know that? They came to bring us back to life! Out of the old nightmare. Dallas, Oswald, Ruby, all of it, cops, reporters, thruways, lies, crises, missiles, heroes, cameras, fear—all that mishmash. Look at *you*. They've brought you back to life. I couldn't—not after November. Nothing could."

"You're right," Cynthia said. "I didn't want to tell you. I thought you'd be jealous."

"Jealous? Of the Beatles?"

"They're very real to me, you know."

"I'm not jealous," Larry said.

"Then will you read to me the way you used to? Read me to sleep?"

"Sure."

"Can I get in your bed?"

"Sure."

Before Larry had finished a page, he was asleep, and Cynthia was asleep before him.

For her birthday in September, Larry gave Cynthia an electric guitar. Though she could not really play it and rarely even plugged it in, she used the guitar now in her performances, pretending to pluck the strings. She began to dress more elaborately for her Beatling, too, making up as if for the stage. What if she were a little mad, Larry thought; it did no harm. She was prettier than she had been since their honeymoon. Perhaps he no longer loved her, but she had grown likable enough, and he cared for her. She *should* have been a performer. She needed applause and admirers and whatever it was she gave herself in her fantasies. It seemed to be something he could not provide. By now he and Cynthia rarely touched or embraced; they were like old friends—fellow-conspirators, even, for who knew of Cynthia's Beatle world but him?

Cynthia discussed her performances with Larry now, telling him of the additions to her repertoire and of the new places she and the Beatles played—Kezar Stadium, the Hollywood Bowl, Philharmonic Hall. She began to permit him in the living room with her, and he would lie on the sofa listening to his music while her Beatling went on. He felt sometimes that by sharing her fantasies he might be sharing her madness, but it seemed better for them both to be innocently deranged than to be as separate as they had been before. All of it tired Larry, though. He was past forty. He felt himself growing old, and his tastes changing. Now he listened to the things he had liked in college—the familiar Beethoven and Mozart symphonies, and Schubert, and Brahms, in new stereophonic recordings. Often, as he listened, he would fall asleep and be awakened by the silence when the last of the records stacked on the turntable had been played. Cynthia's performance would still be going on, and he would rise, take off his headphones, and go to bed.

One night, Larry fell asleep toward the end of the "Messiah," with the bass singing "The trumpet shall sound . . ." and the trumpet responding, and woke as usual in silence, the headphones still on his ears. This time, he lay on the sofa looking at Cynthia, his eyes barely open. She had changed clothes again, he saw, and was wearing the silver lamé pants suit, left over from her singing days, that she had worn the first night he had come to her apartment. He saw her bow, prettily and lightly in spite of the headphones on her ears, and extend her arms to her imaginary audience. Then he watched her begin a slow, confined dance, moving no more than a step to the side or forward and then back. She seemed to be singing, but with his headphones on Larry could not hear. She raised her arms again, this time in a gesture of invitation, and although she could not know he was awake it seemed to Larry that she was beckoning to him and not to an imaginary partner—that this dance, one he had never seen, was for him, and Cynthia was asking him to join her in that slow and self-contained step.

Larry rose and sat looking at her, his head by now nearly clear. "Come," she beckoned. "Come." He saw her lips form the word. Was it he to whom she spoke or one of her fantasies? Did it matter in the end? She stood waiting for her partner—for him—and Larry got up, unplugged his headphones, and walked across the room to her. The movement seemed to him a movement of love. He plugged his headphones in next to Cynthia's and stood before her. Then, together, in silence, not quite touching, in that silent room, with the sound of the Beatles loud in their ears, they began to dance their little dance.

WILLIAM EASTLAKE is the author of many short stories and two novels, *Castle Keep* and *The Bamboo Bed*, the latter published last fall. He is married and lives in Arizona.

The Biggest Thing Since Custer

THE chopper came in low over the remains of Clancy's outfit. Everyone below seemed very dead. They were as quiet as lambs. Sometimes you could see what looked like smoke coming up from a fire, but it was only ground fog. Everyone with Clancy was dead. All of Alpha Company. It was the biggest thing since Custer.

Mike, the correspondent, had to watch himself. The correspondent tended to take the side of the Indians. You got to remember that this is not the Little Big Horn. This is Vietnam. Vietnam. Vietnam. They all died in Vietnam. A long way from home. What were the Americans doing here? The same thing they were doing in Indian Country. In Sioux Territory. They were protecting Americans. They were protecting Americans from the Red Hordes. God help Clancy. You could tell here from above how Clancy blundered. Clancy blundered by being in Vietnam. That's a speech.

The chopper circled now low over the dead battle. Clancy had blundered by not holding the ridge. Clancy had blundered by being forced into a valley, a declivity in the hills. It was the classic American blunder in Vietnam of giving the Indians the cover. The enemy was fighting from the protection of the jungle. The first thing the Americans did in America was clear a forest and plant the cities.

Concentrate on the battle below. Do not always take the side of the Indians. You could see here clearly from above how Clancy blew it. In the part of the highlands of Vietnam near the Cambodian-Laos bunch-up, there is no true open country. Everything is in patches. You could see where Clancy's point squad had made contact with the enemy. You could see, you could tell by all the shit of war, where Clancy had made, where Clancy had tried to make, his first stand on the ridge and then allowed his perimeter to be bent by the hostiles attacking down the ridge. Then Clancy's final regrouping in the draw where all the bodies were.

Clancy should have held that ridge at all costs. If you must fight in the open, fight high. Then the only way the enemy can kill you is with arching fire. Mortar fire. You can dig in against mortar fire. When they force you in the valley, you are duck soup. They can hit you with everything from above. From the way the bodies lie Clancy had mounted three counterattacks to get the ridge back he had too early conceded. The attacks were not in concert. He did not hit them all at once. There should have been more American bodies on the ridge. Clancy should have paid any price to get back the ridge. The ridge was the only opportunity. The valley was death. Ah, but the valley is comfortable. The hill is tough, and the men are all give out and dragging ass, tired and leaking blood. See where they stumbled up and were shot down. See where they failed. See where they tried again and again and again. Where they were shot down. See the paths of bright they made with their blood. See Clancy pointing them on with his sword. War is kind. See Clancy pointing them on with his sword. The son of a bitch had one, like in an old movie. See Clancy pointing them on up the ridge. Once more into the breach. Once more, men, for God and Country and Alpha Company. I blew the ridge. Get it back. Get it back. Get it back for Clancy. Go Smith, go Donovitch, go Lewis, get that —— back! I need it. Now Shaplen, now Marshall, now Irvine, get me the —— back. I will lead this charge. Every man behind me. Where has every young man gone? Why is that native killing me? Why, Shaplen? Why, Marshall? Why, Irvine? All dead. The valley is beautiful, warm, and in this season of Vietnam, soft in the monsoon wet. Contemplative, withdrawn, silent, and now bepatched, bequilted with all of the dead. Alive with scarlet color. Gay with the dead.

The helicopter that carried the correspondent made one more big circle to see if it would pick up ground fire, then came in and hit down in the middle of Clancy's dead with a smooth chonk noise.

The grave registration people got out first. They ejected in the manner of all soldiers from an alighting chopper, jumping out before it quite touched the ground, then running as fast as they could go to escape the giant wind. When they got to the perimeter of Alpha's dead, they stopped abruptly as though they had come to a cliff, and then they came back slowly, picking their way among Alpha's dead, embarrassed and wondering what to do about all this. The lieutenant got out and told the body people not to touch any of the bodies until the army photographers had shot all the positions in which they had fallen. This was important, he said, so Intelligence could tell how the battle was lost. Or won, he said. We are not here to draw conclusions right now. The lieutenant was very young and had red hair. The grave registration people just stood now quiet among the dead, holding their bags in which they would place the dead folded over their arms, like waiters.

The army photographers alighted now holding their cameras at high port like weapons, and began to shoot away at the dead it seemed at random, but they began at the concentric of the perimeter and worked outward in ever widening waves of shooting so that there was a method to their shots. The young lieutenant kept telling them not to touch. The photographers kept having trouble with the angle of repose in which many of the Alpha bodies lay. They had not fallen so that the army photographers could shoot them properly. It was important that they be shot so Intelligence could tell the direction they were pointing when they were hit, how many bodies had jammed guns, how many bodies ran out of ammo. What was the configuration of each body in relation to the configuration of the neighbor body, and then to the configuration of the immediate group of bodies in which the body rests? What relation does said group of bodies have to neighbor groups? To all groups? Bodies should be shot in such a way so that patterns of final action of dead are clear and manifest to establish Alpha's response, if possible, to loss of ridge. Does bodies' configuration show aggressive or regressive response to ridge objective? Where body position of men and commissioned officers? Does body position of noncommissioned officers manifest immediate body group leadership? Neighbor body group's leadership? Photographer should manifest if possible commissioned officer's response to command situation. Does command officer placement of body manifest command presence? Lack of same? Does placement of commissioned officer's body manifest battle plan? Lack of same? Find Clancy. Photographers should shoot all mutilations. Does Captain Clancy's body show normal kill? Planned mutilations? Do commissioned officers' bodies show more mutilation than ear men? When battle situation became negative did ear men attempt to throw away ears? Hide ears? Display ears?

"Don't touch," the lieutenant said.

The correspondent was examining the bodies. He had never seen it so bad.

"Don't touch," the lieutenant said.

"What's this about ears?" the correspondent said.

"Ears?" the lieutenant said.

"Yes."

"You must mean years," the lieutenant said. "We have some five-year men, some ten-year men."

"I see them," the correspondent said.

"I wouldn't write about it if I were you," the lieutenant said.

"You'd pull my credentials?"

"Yes."

"I'll have a look-see," the correspondent said.

"Don't touch," the lieutenant said.

The correspondent leaned over a soft-face boy whose M-16 had jammed. The boy body had never shaved. He was that young. The boy had something stuck in his mouth.

"Jesus," the correspondent said.

The young lieutenant knelt down alongside the correspondent now.

"You see how bad the enemy can be."

"Yes," the correspondent said. "Why has it got a condom on it?"

"Because Alpha was traveling through jungle swamp. There's an organism that gets in the penis opening and travels up to the liver. The condom protects the penis."

The correspondent made a move to remove it.

"Don't touch," the lieutenant said.

"Why don't you bag him?"

"Intelligence wants pictures."

"Bag all of them," the correspondent said, "and let's get out of here."

"It won't be long," the lieutenant said.

"If I report this you'll lift my credentials?"

"I don't know what the brass will do," the lieutenant said. "I do know the people at home can't take it."

"They might stop your war," the correspondent said.

"They don't understand guerrilla war," the lieutenant said.

"You're tough," the correspondent said.

"Listen," the lieutenant said, and touched the correspondent.

"Don't touch," the correspondent said.

"Listen," the lieutenant said, "it makes me sick. I hope it always makes me sick."

The correspondent stood up. There was an odor in the jungle now from the bodies that the correspondent had not noticed when the chopper rotor was turning. Now the chopper was dead. It was very quiet in the jungle.

"How did Clancy get into this?"

"He asked for it," the lieutenant said.

"I heard different."

"You heard wrong," the lieutenant said.

"I heard he was ordered out here."

"He ordered himself out. Clancy's an old ear collector. Alpha Company always had that reputation. Clancy's an old ear collector."

When the lieutenant became angry, his white skin that could not tolerate the sun became red like his hair. His red hair was clipped short under his green helmet, and when the young lieutenant became angry, his white skin matched the hair.

"Clancy wanted to provoke the VC, Victor Charlie. Clancy wanted to collect more ears."

"I don't believe that."

The lieutenant kicked something with his boot.

"Why not scalps?" the correspondent said.

"Because they're too difficult to take. Did you ever try to take a scalp?"

"No."

"It's difficult," the lieutenant said.

"What makes you think Alpha Company asked for this?"

"Because Clancy could have made it up the hill," the lieutenant said pointing. "But he stayed down here on the narrow ridge hoping Charlie would hit him. You see," the lieutenant said carefully. "Look. It's only a hundred more meters up the ridge to the top of the hill. That makes a perfect defense up there, you can see that. And Clancy knew Charlie could see that too, and he wouldn't hit. That's why Clancy stayed down here. Clancy wanted Charlie to try to take him."

"A full battalion?"

"Clancy didn't know Charlie had a full battalion."

"How do you know that?"

"We had contact with Appelfinger, his RTO man, before radio went dead. Clancy guessed the Unfriendlies as maybe an overstrength company."

"Unfriendlies?"

"NVA. North Vietnamese Army. Clancy knew that. They are quite good." The lieutenant almost mused now, looking over the dead, reflective and sad.

"We got a man alive here, Lieutenant," someone called.

The jungle had been most quiet, and everyone had been moving through the bodies with caution, almost soundlessly, so that the announcement was abrupt, peremptory, and rude, almost uncalled for.

"Don't touch," the lieutenant said. The lieutenant raised his arm for a medic and moved toward the call, sinuously winding through the bodies with a snakelike silent grace. The man who had called, the man who made the discovery, was a body man, one of the grave registration people. He had been standing gently with his bag over one arm waiting patiently for the others to finish when he noticed a movement where there should have been none.

"Don't touch," the lieutenant said, standing over the alive. "See what you can do," he said to the medic.

Each of the American dead had received a bullet through the

head, carefully administered to each soldier by the enemy after they had overrun the position, to make absolutely certain that each was dead. The soldier who was alive had received his bullet too, but it had been deflected by the helmet, and you could see when the medic removed the helmet from the head of the young Mexican soldier that it had only torn through the very black, very thick hair and lodged in the head bone. The soldier was dying of natural causes of battle. You could see this when the medic removed the boy Mexican's shirt, which he did skillfully now with a knife. The boy Mexican had been sprayed with hostile machine-gun fire, eight bullets entering the olive-colored body just above the pelvis. The boy Mexican with the olive body in the American olive-colored jungle uniform was cut in half. But he lived for now, taking in sudden gusts of air terrifically as though each were his last.

"Nothing can be done," the medic said without saying anything. The medic's hands were just frozen over the body, not moving to succor, just antic and motionless like a stalled marionette's.

"Water?" the lieutenant asked.

The medic shook his head no.

"If he's going, it could make it easier," the lieutenant said. "He seems to be looking at us for water."

The medic shook his head OK. Nothing would make any difference.

When one of the photographers tried to give the boy Mexican water from his canteen, the water would not run in the mouth; it just poured down the Mexican's chin and down his chest till it reached his belly and mixed with the blood that was there.

"I think the son of a bitch is dead," one of the army photographers who was not pouring the water said.

"No," one of the body men said. "Let me try it."

"That's enough," the medic said, letting the body down. "I think he's dead now."

"How could the son of a bitch last so long when he was cut in half?"

"We have funny things like this all the time," the medic said. "Another funny thing is I've seen guys dead without a mark on them."

"Concussion? But there's always a little blood from the ears or something, isn't there?"

"No, I've seen them dead without any reason at all," the medic said, wiping clean the face of the Mexican boy with the water the Mexican could not drink. "If you look good at the guys around here I bet you'll find at least one that doesn't have a mark on him that's dead. It's funny. Some guys will die without any reason at all, and some guys will live without any reason at all." The medic looked perplexed. Then the medic allowed the boy's head to rest on his smashed helmet. "You'll find some guys with just that one bullet in the head given by the Unfriendlies after they overran Alpha."

"Some guys will play dead," the army photographer said, "hoping to pass for dead among the dead."

"They don't get away with it though too much," the medic said. But the medic was not listening to himself. He was still perplexed that the Mexican boy could have lived so long when he was cut in half. "It's funny, that's all," the medic said.

"You want them to die?"

"I don't want them to suffer," the medic said.

"There's another live one over here," someone called.

"Don't touch," the lieutenant said.

No one moved. There was a hiatus in the movement in the jungle, as though, the correspondent thought, no one here wanted to be deceived again, no one wanted to be taken in by another illusion. The problem was that Alpha was all dead. You could tell that with a glance. Anyone could see that they were ready to be photographed and placed in bags. It wasn't planned for anyone to come back to life. It made all the dead seem too much like people. The dead should stay dead.

"Maybe this one's real," someone said.

That started a drift toward the caller.

"Don't touch," the lieutenant said.

The correspondent got there early. It was a Negro. It did not seem as though the boy were hit. He was lying in a bed of bamboo. He looked comfortable. The Negro boy had a beginning half-smile on his face, but the smile was frozen. The eyes too were immobile. The Negro boy's eyes looked up, past the correspondent and on up to the hole at the top of the jungle canopy. There were two elongated fronds that crossed way up there at the apex of the canopy. Maybe that's what he was looking at. Maybe he was staring at nothing. The Negro boy said something, but nothing came out. His lips moved, and words seemed to be forming, but nothing came out. Maybe he was saying, the correspondent thought, that he had come a long way since he was dragged up with the rats in the ghetto. He had never been close to white people before, except relief workers. Now he had joined the club. In death do us join.

The young Negro stopped breathing. The white medic was on top of the Negro like a lover. In one sudden deft movement the white medic was down on the bed of bamboo with his white arms around the black boy, his white lips to the black lips, breathing in white life to black death. The Negro lover did not respond. It was too late. The white boy was late. The eyes were all shut. Then abruptly the young Negro's chest began to heave. The eyes opened. But not to life, the correspondent thought, but to outrage, a kind of wild surmise and amaze at all this. As though he had gone to death, to some kind of mute acceptance of no life and now come back to this, the lover's embrace, the lover lips of the white medic.

The white medic ceased now, withdrew his lips from the young Negro's and tried to catch the erratic breathing of the Negro in his hand to give it a life rhythm. He was astraddle the boy now, up from the bamboo bed, and administering a regular beat with his hands to the young Negro's chest.

"Ah," the Negro said.

"Ah," the white boy said.

"Ah ah ah," they both said.

Now the medic allowed the boy beneath to breathe on his own.

"Ah," the lieutenant said.

"Ah-h-h-h . . ." everyone said.

Now the jungle made sounds. The awful silence had given way to the noises that usually accompany an American motion picture. The cry of gaudy birds seemed fake. The complaints of small animals, distant, were remote like some sound track that had blurred, some other mix for a different cinema, so that you not only expected that the next reel would announce the mistake, that this war would have to start all over again, but that the whole damn thing would be thrown out with whoever was responsible for this

disaster here at Dak To, this unacceptable nightmare, this horror, this unmentionable destruction of Clancy and all his men.
But more, the correspondent thought, this is the finis, the end of
man in this clearing, this opening in the jungle, the end of human-
kind itself and the planet earth on which it abides. And shit, the
correspondent thought—and Ah— He found himself saying it
too now, celebrating the rebirth, the resurrection of the black
man and the rebirth and resurrection after the crucifixion of hu-
mankind itself. And shit, he reflected, they, Alpha Company, are
the ear hunters, and maybe not shit because all of Alpha were
standing in for us, surrogate, and all of us are collectors of ears.

"Will he make it?" the young lieutenant said.

The medic looked perplexed. It was his favorite and especial
expression. Then he went down in the bamboo bed in lover attitude to listen to the heart.

"No," he said from the black heart. "No."

"No?"

"Because," the medic said from the black heart. "No. Because
they were supposed to be all dead here, and we needed body
room in the chopper, and there was no room for my shit."

"Blood plasma?"

"We didn't bring any," the medic said.

"Can he talk?"

"Yes." The medic passed a white hand in front of the black face.
The black eyes did not follow it.

"Ask him what happened to Clancy's body. Clancy is missing."

The medic made a gentle movement with his hands along the
throat of the Negro and whispered to him with lover closeness,
"What happened to the captain?"

"He dead."

"Where is the body?"

"The RTO man," the Negro pronounced slowly.

"Appelfinger carried him off," the medic said to the lieutenant.

"Can you give the boy some morphine?" the lieutenant said to
the medic.

"I don't like his heart."

"Risky?"

"Yes."

"Can he talk more?"

"I don't think it would be good," the medic said.

"All right, keep him quiet," the lieutenant said.

"They was so nice," the Negro said.

"Keep him quiet," the lieutenant said.

"They gave us each one shot," the Negro said. "They was so nice."

"Keep him quiet."

"They was so nice—"

"I said keep him quiet," the lieutenant said. And the lieutenant thought, war is so nice. Looking over all the dead, he thought ROTC was never like this, and he thought in this war everything is permitted so that there is nothing to be forgiven. And he thought about the ears that Clancy took, and he thought a man can read and read and read and think and think and still be a villain, and he thought there are no villains, there are only wars. And he said, "If the photographers are finished, put the men in the bags."

And then there was that goddamn jungle silence again, this awful and stern admonition and threat of the retribution of Asia to white trespassers. But that is metaphysical, the lieutenant thought, and it is only the VC you have to fear. More, it is only yourself you have to fear. It is only Clancy you have to fear. Clancy is dead.

"When you find pieces of body," the lieutenant said, "try to match them and put the matched pieces into one separate bag. Remember a man has only two arms and two legs and one head each. I don't want to find two heads in one bag."

And the lieutenant thought, Clancy is dead but the crimes that Clancy did live after him. Custer too. Custer liked to destroy the villages and shoot up the natives too. Listen to this, the lieutenant told Captain Clancy silently. I did not spend all my time in the ROTC. I spent some of the time in the library. What you did in the villages is not new. Collecting ears is not new. Listen, Clancy, to Lieutenant James D. Connors after the massacre of the Indians at Sand Creek, "The next day I did not see a body of a man, woman or Indian child that was not scalped by us, and in many instances the bodies were mutilated in the most horrible manner. Men's, women's and children's private parts cut out. I saw one of our men who had cut out a woman's private parts and had them for exhibition on a stick. Some of our men had cut out the private parts of females and wore them in their hats." I don't think you can top that, Clancy. I don't think war has come very far since then. I don't think your ears can top that, Clancy.

"What's happening, Lieutenant?" the correspondent said.

"Happening?" the lieutenant said. "I was thinking."

"This man is dead," the medic said, pointing to the Negro.

"Bag him," the lieutenant said.

"What were you thinking?" the correspondent said.

"That this makes me sick. Awful sick."

"Have you ever seen it this bad?"

"No, I have never seen it this bad," the lieutenant said, spacing his words as though the correspondent were taking each separate word down. "No, I have never seen it this bad in my whole short life. I have never seen it this bad. No, I have never seen it this bad. Is that what you want me to say?"

"Take it easy," the correspondent said.

"OK," the lieutenant said. "I'm sorry." And then the lieutenant heard something. It was the sound of a mortar shell dropping into a mortar tube in the jungle. It was the sound the lieutenant had heard too many times before, then the poof, as the enemy mortar came out of the tube, then the whine as it traveled to their company. The symphony. The music of Vietnam. Incoming! The lieutenant hollered as loud as he could make it. "Incoming!"

Incoming? Where? Who? Why? The shell hit their helicopter, and it all exploded in a towering orange hot pillar of fire in the jungle.

"Pull the bodies around you, men, and try to dig in. Use the bodies as a perimeter!" the lieutenant hollered. Then the lieutenant said quietly to the correspondent, "I'm sorry I got you into this."

"You didn't," the correspondent said.

"I'll try to get Search and Rescue on the radio."

"You do that," the correspondent said.

NORVAL RINDFLEISCH teaches English at Phillips Exeter Academy in New Hampshire, where he lives with his wife and four children. He has written many short stories which have been published in *The Literary Review*, *Yale Literary Magazine* and *Epoch* and is currently working on a novel.

A Cliff of Fall

"O the mind, mind has mountains; cliffs of fall
Frightful, sheer no-man-fathomed."

HOPKINS

FATHER SCHAUF was up and dressed and ready for mass before six o'clock. He had moved a chair away from the dresser into the hallway to be closer to the heat from the stove. Using the edge of the light from his room as it splashed over into the hall, he read aloud in Latin from his breviary articulating each word and stopping occasionally to listen to the quality of a pronunciation as it resonated for a moment after he had stopped speaking. He was usually pleased with what he heard.

He looked from his breviary down the hall to the flames that flickered behind the isinglassed door. The stove had been left in the hallway near the head of the stairs and the doors of the other bedrooms had been closed off when the first priest had moved into what was then a farmhouse. It had been his impractical speculation (and one of his most enduring legacies) that the heat would be channeled into the open bedroom, thus leaving more room in the bedroom and spreading the heat over a larger serviceable area. It seemed to reach the door and hang vaguely and indecisively upon the threshold. It rarely entered. In colder weather Father Schauf undressed in the hallway and danced across the icy linoleum rug to his bed. Whenever he wished to read, he moved a chair into the hall or crawled into bed.

He marked his place in the breviary with a ribbon, closed the book, and leaned forward out of the chair to return to the bedroom. As he entered the room, he felt the wall of chilled air. He placed the breviary on the dresser top along with the other dozen or so books and pamphlets, each carefully marked for future reference and each deferred to some later time for closer examination.

Father Schauf had finally reconciled himself to the coldness of the room. He had inherited it along with a score of other miscalculations from the priests who had preceded him at St. Joseph's. In the enthusiasm of his first months he was going to have the parish house remodeled and the church redecorated, but his ardor cooled as other more pressing matters took precedence until he finally decided to defer the remodeling because he just didn't have enough money. He simply accepted the inconveniences as part of the tradition of the parish, the temporal signs, the heritage of the spiritual struggles of one of his predecessors with the "facts" of the human condition.

Now it was time for the morning unveiling. He went to the window, opened the curtain, and raised the shade. Father Schauf gazed once again at the flat Dakota farmland. He stooped and rested himself, suspended his body on stiffened arms and the balls of his hands pressed against the sash. In the blear light of early morning, he could see the low rain clouds. The gray and black patched farmland stretched to the horizon. Occasionally, an island of trees, a windbreak of uniformly spaced cottonwoods protecting a house or barnyard, interrupted the endless flow of land. In the distance a cattle truck moved slowly, marking (tracing as it moved) one of the plane dimensions of an ordered, static, Euclidian universe.

The land and weather permitted no excesses. Season moved into season gradually. Within a week of winter, fall was forgotten; within a week of summer, spring was forgotten. True, the land grew green in summer but only briefly. The black and brown and gray fields were covered with growing verdure by June, but by the end of July at the height of summer, the oat and wheat beards mounting above the green stems had already begun to return the earth to its natural color. Then the oats, flax and barley were harvested and fields were already being plowed again. By Labor Day even the corn fields were dominated by the brown tassels and the leaves were fading into pale yellow. There was no time for nature to experiment in brilliance. The earth did not flame out with violent oranges and reds.

Father Schauf felt that his parishioners had been formed by a corollary of that law that had cast the land into its bland and homogeneous mold. His flock, centered at Amburg but with two mission congregations at Ravinia and Salemn, was uniformly flat and gray like the land. There were no extremes. There seemed to be a singular incapacity among his people for great virtue or great evil. Only the trivial, the slight offenses (even the serious sins were relatively unimportant except, of course, in the eyes of a perfect God) managed to accumulate, to gather gradually but slowly into a force of moral attrition.

It was this undifferentiated venial world that was his enemy. Experience had taught him that his greatest struggle was to keep his sense of proportion, not to lose his powers of discrimination. The great temptation was to reduce everything, to see everything in his boredom as trivial and trite. (The confessional alone had taught him the overwhelming logic of Purgatory.)

He looked across the room with pain and gnawing anxiety at the galley proofs of the diocesan newspaper hanging over the back of his bedside chair. They were to be returned by noon to the printer seventy miles away. He still had three of the long sheets to read and correct by ten o'clock if he hoped to make it on time. He sat, turned the shade of the wall lamp to direct the light to his lap, and took up his reading where he had left off at midnight the night before. There was still a half hour before he would have to leave for church.

Although he had expected some kind of diocesan "intellectual" responsibility to supplement his parish duties when he was first transferred to St. Joseph's, his appointment as proofreader came ironically. His assignment to the post of assistant copy editor by the Bishop had a twist to it that reflected Father Schauf's failure from the very beginning.

It happened soon after he arrived and because he had made a

fool of himself. He had been invited to the Bishop's for dinner as was the Bishop's custom with priests newly appointed to his diocese. He had heard little about the Bishop. He knew that he was called the "Owl" by some of the younger priests in the diocese. Father Schauf had not yet discovered whether or not it was a term of approbation. He had also learned that the Bishop was somewhat pompous and formal (because his predecessor had been most informal) and that he had an incredible reputation for fund raising.

Father Schauf arrived at the Bishop's residence punctually at six o'clock. He had, in fact, arrived fifteen minutes earlier, but he drove around the neighborhood and then into the commercial center of the city and back again before he parked.

He was admitted by the housekeeper and sent to the library where he found another priest, a Father Cullen, mixing a drink from a portable bar. Father Cullen was attached to the Bishop's residence. He was in charge of the Newman Club at the State University and taught English and religion at Sullivan High School. The two priests introduced themselves and shook hands.

"Have a drink, Father," Father Cullen said as he introduced the bar with a toss of his hand. "If you don't mind, I have to finish reading an assignment for class tomorrow."

"I have to admit I am happy to see somebody else," Father Schauf laughed nervously. "I've never been here before."

Father Cullen nodded, crossed the room to the sofa, and resumed reading a book he had apparently put down prior to Father Schauf's arrival. Father Schauf sipped his drink and then asked: "What's he like?"

"Who? The Owl? Oh! He's O.K. He won't bite you," Father Cullen said. "Drink up! Don't worry, he's not as bad as everyone says," he added with a smile and returned to his book.

"Thanks a lot," Father Schauf laughed and drank his highball quickly and mixed another. He walked about the room, casually examining the contents of the library. He looked across the room occasionally at his fellow priest. Father Cullen wore his reddish blond hair in a crew cut style. His body was thick, muscular, and his face was beginning to accumulate the flesh of his thirty to thirty-five years of maturity. An athlete going soft, Father Schauf decided. It took another drink and two tours of the room before

Father Schauf ventured to interrupt the uncommunicative Father Cullen.

"If you don't mind my asking, where is our host?"

"Probably fund raising," Father Cullen answered flatly, without irony and without looking up from his reading. Then he cocked his head toward the doorway. There were footsteps on the carpet.

"Speaking of the ———," Father Cullen said, closed his book, and stood up as the Bishop hurried into the library. The Bishop smiled an insipid greeting as Father Schauf knelt to kiss his ring.

The Bishop's face was round and plump. He wore rimless glasses, the kind Father Schauf had always associated in his mind with bankers and accountants. Most of his hair was gone on top except for a faint remnant, a wisp of hair that stuck up intensifying his hurried manner. The Bishop poured a glass of sherry and said:

"I hope you don't mind that I have neglected you so notoriously, Father Schauf, but I have been gone and since you are a Midwesterner, I didn't think you'd have any trouble. It's the Bostonians I worry about. I get one every so often." He paused and smiled faintly. "They think this is mission country like Africa or China. No one understands them with their 'idear' and 'heah' and 'feah'. The parishioners think their priest speaks Latin as a native tongue for a month or so, and our Boston priests think the faithful out here are all Indians—genuine, unadulterated aborigines."

The Bishop walked to the window and back as he talked. Father Schauf smiled ambiguously. He decided the Owl wasn't so bad after all. He seemed to have a sense of humor.

There were several priests from Boston currently in the diocese. Father Schauf had met one, Father Donohoe at St. James in Covington. To Father Schauf's ear Father Donohoe spoke like the Brooklynese he had heard in the "Bowery Boys" movies of his childhood, but he judiciously refrained from commenting and let the Bishop ramble, uninterrupted, until a dinner bell chimed.

When they entered the dining room, Father Schauf noticed its conspicuous elegance. The room was carpeted from wall to wall. There was a huge floor to ceiling window that overlooked a flower garden. From the ceiling hung a sparkling chandelier showering its light on a long mahogany dinner table set with expensive linen and china. He did not know the meal was to be so formal. Although Father Cullen seemed to accept everything as normal, Father Schauf could not avoid a growing apprehension. He was impressed but he withheld his opinion for fear he would seem a gusher or a false flatterer. The Bishop continued his talk, his light meaningless banter as they seated themselves for grace. Father Schauf decided the Bishop was a paradox: a rare combination of conversational superficiality and rigid formality of manner.

After the prayer the Bishop pressed a button on the floor with his foot which signalled the pantry for the first course and which also prompted someone to turn on a stereophonic phonograph flooding the room with a Tschaikovsky symphony from loud speakers concealed somewhere in the walls or ceiling.

"You are in the musical position, Father Schauf," the Bishop said. "The multi-directional effect is maximal in your seat."

Father Schauf felt conspicuous and uncomfortable. He felt he should get up and offer his seat to the Bishop.

"Father Cullen and I are off center," he continued. "He gets mostly strings and I get the brass."

Father Schauf nodded but said nothing again. Then the housekeeper brought in a tureen of soup and bowls which the Bishop began to ladle, serving Father Schauf first.

"I am modern, too," the Bishop said pointing to the ceiling with the ladle.

"Do you mean the music, Your Excellency?" Father Schauf said.

"No, I don't," the Bishop said with a frown. "I meant the stereophonic equipment. I meant the electronic aspect." The Bishop began to spoon his soup. Then it seemed, as Father Schauf recalled it all later, that the Bishop suddenly turned upon him without provocation.

"What do you think of the music, then? I suppose it is too old-fashioned for you?" he asked.

"It is good dinner music, Your Excellency," Father Schauf answered ambiguously.

"It is Tschaikovsky," the Bishop said testily.

"I know," answered Father Schauf.

"I take it, in your judgment, that Tschaikovsky is only dinner music?" he demanded.

Father Schauf blundered an answer.

"Some of Tschaikovsky is all right, but frankly I find much of it boring in its sentimentality, Your Excellency."

The Bishop was clearly irritated.

"I suppose you prefer Stravinsky or one of those noisemakers. What's his name?" He hesitated trying to remember. "Bartok. Yes. Bartok. I can't see he makes anything but noise."

Now Father Schauf was irritated too, for the Bishop had translated his simple disagreement of taste into a split between generations, as a split between tradition and progress—an oversimplified dialectic of opposites that did violence to the truth and turned a simple discussion into an argument of blacks and whites.

"Actually I prefer Prokofiev and Shostakovich," he answered as benignly as he could. He knew he had taken the Bishop beyond his musical depth. Apparently the Bishop thought the music of the turn of the century was still radical and experimental.

The housekeeper cleared the table and served the main course. As the Bishop began to eat, he smiled as he struck upon what he thought was an irrefutable argument.

"They were both communists, weren't they?" he asked. Then he exploded. "Reds!"

Father Schauf answered calmly in the voice and manner of a teacher in serious discussion, not angry, but concerned with the truth. He disregarded the Bishop's baiting rhetoric.

"That is perhaps true, but I don't think that has any bearing on the music. The political opinions, the philosophy, even the disposition of a composer are not necessarily reflected in the art object." He paused for a moment and then clinched his argument. "Take Tschaikovsky, for example. He was a neurotic and latent pederast."

The Bishop looked confused. Father Cullen almost slid under the table from shock.

"Pederast . . . pederast?"

Father Schauf knew that he had won, but propriety, common courtesy, the spirit of love demanded delicacy. He could not blurt

out a "homosexual" with the same almost cruel, vicious explosive-
ness that the Bishop had flung the word "reds" in his face.

"A pederast is a man . . . who is not quite normal." He decided
a negative definition was the least offensive.

"I see," the Bishop said, with a nod acknowledging that Father
Schauf had trapped him.

He changed the subject and shifted the conversation to Father
Cullen. For the rest of the meal he avoided Father Schauf and
then dismissed both priests abruptly after dessert. The Bishop had
an appointment with a professional fund raiser.

Father Schauf had won a battle but lost the war.

It wasn't until the next morning in the cold, critical light of
day that Father Schauf realized fully what a fool he had been.
Anxiety and a few drinks had resulted in acts of arrogance and
pride. What did he care one way or the other if the Bishop liked
sentimental music? In his heart he knew he had been dishonest
in evoking composers beyond the Bishop's grasp of appreciation,
and in his heart he knew that there was disobedience in his manner and voice. He wanted to go on his knees before the Bishop
and beg his forgiveness, but time and space did not allow such a
dramatic mitigation of his guilt. He made a vow to cultivate humility in everything he did.

A week later Father Schauf received a short and characteris-
tically formal letter from the Bishop. He was informed that "in
order to put his great vocabulary to practical use" he was to assume, immediately, responsibilities as assistant copy editor of the
diocesan newspaper. It had amounted to little more than a proofreading job, and although it had been Father Schauf's bitterest
and most frustrating duty, he accepted it without complaint in
the spirit of humility he had vowed to practice.

Now he sat reading the long, uncut columns, checking the set
type against the thin, yellow, onionskin sheets of typed copy. It
was growing lighter outside. Soon he would go downstairs and
get ready to leave for the church to prepare the altar for seven
o'clock mass.

As he sat proofreading, he was startled by the sudden whir of
an electric motor from somewhere downstairs. He looked at his
watch. It was only six thirty-five. Mrs. Johnson, his housekeeper,
usually arrived at seven-thirty to prepare his breakfast and clean

the house. He bolted from his chair and hurried across the room and down the hall to the stairway.

At the bottom of the stairs he turned to his right toward the noise. In his study he discovered Mrs. Johnson vacuuming. He watched her short, squat body working like a piston driving the wand into the corners. Mrs. Johnson loved her vacuum cleaner. It seemed to Father Schauf that all she did was vacuum, vacuum, vacuum. Every day without fail. It was a wonder there was any nap left on the rugs.

He cupped his hands around his mouth and shouted:

"Good morning, Mrs. Johnson."

He felt he was struggling against a great wind. She could not hear him and he refused to shout louder, to lose his dignity before a vacuum cleaner. It suddenly struck him that, from behind, Mrs. Johnson looked like a sausage—fat, round, nondescript.

The whir of the motor drowned his voice again. His eye caught the electric cord, trailing behind her to the plug. He took a step into the room and bent to the floor with his knee, reached forward with his right hand and grasped the cord. He stood up in a single motion, pulling the plug from the socket. The motor stopped instantly, but Mrs. Johnson kept right on working, pumping the nozzle into the rug, for several seconds before she realized the power was off.

It occurred to Father Schauf that had someone been watching, his action might have appeared like a genuflection, one of those sloppy, hurried genuflections characteristic of his careless, incompetent altar boys. When she finally turned around grumbling, he assumed a casual attitude by leaning against the door, crossing his legs, and twirling the plug nonchalantly in a lazy arc.

He sensed a certain humor in the scene. He knew that she would tell everyone, by way of illustrating her industriousness and diligence, and the effect of his action would heighten his reputation for humor and wit. They would laugh and talk about him with the pride they usually reserved for their children who had gone away to college to become clever, and intelligent, and incomprehensible.

He could not help but feel that they regarded him, as a person that is, as a kind of prize bit of livestock, a genuine blue ribbon pet in which they took great paternalistic delight. He knew that, in conversations, they flung him in the teeth of their Protestant friends who could hardly retaliate with an amusing story about the slow, somber, plodding Rev. Peterson, the Lutheran minister.

There was no question about it. What little success he had was the result of the "class," the urban sophistication they attributed to him, but it made his distance from them even greater. It ruled out any intimacy between equals. The inequality was sharp and clear. The irony of it all was that he wondered who patronized whom. He often felt that they with their practical intelligence laughed at him. Certainly they took great pains to explain the mechanical workings of the parish house and church as if anything prosaic was beyond his ken.

Mrs. Johnson put her hand over her mouth and squealed.

"Father," she blurted when she recovered from her surprise, in a scolding tone as if he were a naughty child. He had difficulty pretending to be angry, restraining the self-mocking undertone of his seriousness; he had difficulty taking Mrs. Johnson seriously under any circumstances. He had inherited her along with a cold bedroom and a defunct toilet when he came to the parish. She kept the house clean and cooked breakfast and dinner. Supper he had to make for himself or eat out.

Mrs. Johnson was an uncertain fifty to sixty years of age. Father Schauf decided she did look most exactly like a sausage, the fat layers folded under her chin minimizing the separateness of her head. Her hair was streaked with gray unevenly and cut high in back in the masculine style of the Twenties. She had a permanent reddish purple color high on her cheeks. Only her glasses—modern, sophisticated, intelligent—belied the fact that she might well have been a sausage.

Father Schauf never doubted the humanity, the essential dignity of his parishioners, but he often doubted, or rather wondered in awe, how a person like the bland and venial Mrs. Johnson had ever been sexually viable. His imagination, his charitable willingness to believe anything good about his fellow creatures was hard put to visualize Mrs. Johnson as sufficiently attractive even to a completely indiscriminate Mr. Johnson to result in six children. But six children she had and eight grandchildren. Humanity was capable of far more outlandish accomplishments than Father Schauf had ever dreamt of in his meager experience, and this he knew was his central limitation. Too much of his life had been vicarious, by word of mouth. Too much had to be guessed at through the facade of words that were rarely adequate, rarely direct. His whole life had been lived by the word not the deed.

He tried to appear stern. He looked at his watch and then held his wrist out to her, pointing to the hands.

"It is six thirty-five. You are approximately one hour early."

Mrs. Johnson shrugged. She had never paid any serious attention to him. He had suggested changes when he first arrived, but she continued the old habits after dutifully acknowledging his new orders with the ceremonial and meaningless "Yes, Father." He had made mistakes in the beginning too. He had been too jovial, too playful in his early attempts to win her over. He had wanted immediate popularity too eagerly. Once before in the first few months she had frightened him silly and to cover his embarrassment and fright he responded in comic exaggeration.

He was reading in the study one morning when she entered behind him in her silent way and suddenly turned on the infernal vacuum cleaner. He jumped up, whirled around, and crossed the room in a feigned stagger, grasping his heart with both hands and panting for breath. Her jaw dropped and her eyes opened wide. He collapsed into a stuffed chair across the room, took out a handkerchief and began to wipe his forehead. When he looked at her gaping at him, he could not suppress an open laugh. From that moment on Mrs. Johnson was never certain whether he was serious or joking, and so she continued to do just about what she had always done. The tone of their relationship was set with that incident, and he could not help but temper even his most serious orders with some joking or self-mockery.

Besides, he had come to feel that Mrs. Johnson regarded him as a fool, as an utter incompetent that God in his mysteriousness had endowed with the ultimate power. There were a hundred incidents that Father Schauf preferred not to recall that seemed evidence of her attitude. She seemed a silent critic whose expressionless gaze and complete indifference stood as continual reminders of his failure to understand or be understood.

In her phlegmatic way, she explained to Father Schauf why she had come so early. She had a chance to earn a little extra money at the Co-op cleaning pheasants. The morning shift began at

seven. Because the hunting had been excellent, there were over
two thousand birds waiting to be cleaned from yesterday's kill.
And what was she going to do about his breakfast and dinner?
Well, she thought he could have cold cereal for breakfast and she
was just about to ask him about dinner. But why didn't she ask
him before? She didn't think he minded. Then *he* shrugged indif-
ferently. He certainly wasn't going to make an issue of such a superficial matter.

She left to vacuum the living room as he sat at his desk. He
removed the sacramental wine from the lower right-hand drawer
and poured some into the tubular vial he used to fill the cruet.
On his desk were two sheets of paper: one with the notes he had
made for announcements on Sunday, and the other blank—the
total result of three days of thoughtful consideration of next Sunday's sermon.

From the beginning the sermons had been difficult. The reluctance of anyone to speak at length was exasperating. They
shrugged, they grunted in monosyllables, but they rarely carried
on a conversation. They lived in a world of action where husband
and wife and children responded to the rhythm of habit and
work, where vague suggestion was taken as statement of intent.
He couldn't even think out loud anymore.

Once at a card party he had suggested that the brushing of an
elm branch on his roof over the bedroom was distracting. He was
only half serious and he mentioned it in a joking context. One
evening about a week later and without any forewarning, three
men in a pickup truck drove up in front of the rectory and un-
loaded a ladder. They went around to the rear and placed the
ladder against the house under the elm. It was nine-thirty at night
and Father Schauf was reading in his room.

Later, whenever he told the story, he confessed he had never
been so frightened in his life. He heard bumps outside the window and footsteps across the roof. Then he heard the saw followed
by an enormous clump on the roof. For a moment he thought
someone was dismantling the rectory right about his ears. At that
time he couldn't remember having ever mentioned the elm
branch. When his desperation and curiosity had overcome his fear,
he pulled up the shade and threw open the window.

Out on the lawn was the President of the Holy Name Society

directing two other members, one on the roof and the other in the tree. "Sorry, Father," he said taking off his hat in respect. "Didn't mean to disturb you." Then they all apologized and briefly explained that because of cultivating they couldn't get by any earlier. As their flashlights danced in his eyes, he realized they meant earlier in the week as well as in the evening. He thanked them and withdrew still trembling half in rage, half in fright.

How was he ever going to communicate? They lived in a world of action and he had been prepared to cope only with a world of ideas. All of his studies had been ultimately and essentially linguistic disciplines. *In the beginning was the Word,* but also in the beginning was the light—the light of energy expended in gigantic creation, the energy of grace and love. He understood the Word, but they knew the Light.

What good was the language of philosophy or theology? How could he possibly find some common ground of understanding without compromising himself and implicitly patronizing them? Analogy was the answer, but his experience was so meager. In three years he had barely begun to immerse himself in their world. Oh, they understood the planting and reaping metaphor. Whatever you sow, thus also will you reap. Unless you get hailed out, of course. He didn't believe their stories of hail the size of baseballs until he walked into a corn field shredded to bits by round clumps of ice still lying in the furrows hours later.

Oh, Lord. He had tried to learn their way of life. In his first year, he had dutifully accepted every invitation to Sunday dinner. Wherever he went it was always the same—a heavy meal which he overate out of kindness, a seat close to the heater set at eighty degrees, and two hours of polite questions on his part and polite grunts and nudges on theirs. Until once out of sheer boredom, to escape the stares of the stone chorus of nodding heads, he volunteered to help the farmer and the vet, who had been called in the emergency to treat the frothy bloat in a young steer.

Outside the cold air was a welcome relief. He stood on the fringe of the action as they cut the Hereford calf from the others in the feed lot and into the barn. The vet was a huge, young, crewcut Kansan who had been educated in Texas. Father Schauf guessed he was six feet three and two hundred twenty pounds at least. He spoke a twang with a drawl, but what endeared him to

Father Schauf was that he spoke—incessantly to the animals, to the farmer, and to Father Schauf.

They had given Father Schauf an old jacket to cover his clothes, so he ventured close and even helped swing a gate when they ran the animal into an empty stall. He began to ask questions and instead of the usual one syllable answer, he got intelligent and detailed responses. They put a ring halter into its nostrils, ran the rope over a rafter and then down the outside of the stall where the farmer pulled down on the rope yanking the head of the steer high into the corner. He watched their crude efficiency with fascination, asking questions each step of the way.

The animal's sides were swollen and it was frothing. He learned from the vet that the cause of the symptoms was unknown but that death was imminent unless treated immediately. Why did it hit only one animal out of twenty, each with the same food and environment? Nobody seemed to know. There was no question that the killing gas that was pressing against the heart and lungs came from wet, newcut alfalfa or green corn. There was probably a virus involved somewhere but it had never been isolated. The treatment was simple enough: relieve the gas pressure and neutralize, with dextrose, the thickened green sputum that blocked the canals of egress.

Father Schauf stood a little distance from the work. He listened with pleasure to the jargon as it rolled from the vet's lips. The vet jammed the steer with his hip against the wall as the farmer pulled down on the rope, stretching the head and neck of the animal straight up in the corner. Then he punched a needle into what Father Schauf thought was the region of the kidneys.

"What's that for?" Father Schauf asked.

"I'm lettin' the gas out of its stomach," the vet answered.

"What is the stomach doing way back there and up so high?"

"Well, that's where the good Lord put it."

The steer gave a violent lurch and the vet jammed it with his shoulder and drove it back, tight against the wall. As he spoke, he leaned against the animal and talked over his shoulder.

"I can tell you've been educated somewhere, but you never had a good course in animal anatomy. No sir." He smiled over his shoulder. Father Schauf realized that they had never been introduced and that the vet did not know he was a priest because his collar was covered.

"No, I haven't, but I think I might recommend just such a course for the curriculum." He paused and asked, "What's happening now?"

"Why, gas is comin' out of this end of the needle almost asphyxiating me. Whew!" He shook his head. Father Schauf listened closely and heard the hissing sound. The needle looked like one of those Father Schauf had used to pump up footballs when he was a child.

"What do you do next?" Father Schauf asked. The steer lurched again and the vet lost his footing.

"I don't think I'll do anything if you just stand there with your hands in your pockets trying to get my education for nothing."

Father Schauf laughed. "What can I do? This is as close as I've ever been to a cow." The vet reset his feet and drove his shoulder into the steer again.

"Well, first of all this is one helluva strange cow, and secondly all I need is unskilled labor. No specialist required." Father Schauf stepped forward and the vet eased off the steer.

"I want you to step around here on the other side of this *ole cow*," and he pointed to the spot on the wall-side just forward of the hind legs.

"I won't get kicked, will I?" Father Schauf asked apprehensively.

"Not if you stand in front of his leg," the vet answered sarcastically. Father Schauf took the position.

"Now," the vet said with a wide smile, "*this* is the tail."

"I *know* that *much*," Father Schauf said with nervous laughter.

"Your job will be to grasp the tail like this, twist it, and shove it forward driving the steer's head into the corner, there."

"Oh, it's a steer," Father Schauf said. "I know what that is, too."

"Why, you'll be gettin' your Ph.D. in no time. Now you all grab on here and use a little weight to keep this *ole cow* still."

Father Schauf was surprised to discover that what he had been told to do worked. The steer was caught in a vise of cross pressures.

Once Father Schauf was set, the vet attached a tube to the needle and to the end of a bottle of dextrose. When he inverted the bottle the amber fluid flowed slowly into the steer's stomach. Then the vet shoved a long black rubber hose down the gullet of the animal and eased it back and forth pumping the thickened mucous out and releasing the gas that had built up behind the lungs and heart. An acrid stench filled the stall. Father Schauf's eyes began to water.

Then he was told they were all done. As he eased off the steer it seemed to Father Schauf that the animal almost politely stepped aside to allow him to pass. But the steer's weight shifted and it stepped backwards onto Father Schauf's foot, all seven hundred pounds.

As Father Schauf limped to the farm house for coffee and lunch, he noticed his trousers were spattered with manure. Later he threw them out rather than have them cleaned. In that first year he was overly fastidious. The vet and the farmer preceded him into the kitchen. He paused to wash up in the entry. When he entered the kitchen without a jacket, the vet stared at his collar and then jumped up from the table in respect.

"Why, Gawd a'mighty, a preacher," he exclaimed in astonishment. Father Schauf limped to the table and managed a wan smile.

"No, only a crippled priest."

There was no doubt that the incident helped him. The story of his injury circulated rapidly. The next morning the high school football coach called and wondered if Father Schauf would like to use the whirlpool for treatment. Complete strangers smiled hello as he limped down the street. But that was the last time Father Schauf went out to Sunday dinner. He discontinued the practice by politely refusing all invitations. He confined his "immersion" into local experience to occasional visits after confessions on Saturday night to the vet's office on Main Street. There he listened to the farmers, all neatly scrubbed and dressed, complaining—forever complaining—to the loquacious young vet and then listening shrewdly in hopes the vet in his great love of talk would inadvertently outline a treatment they could administer themselves.

But his difficulties didn't arise only because of the disparity between his background and theirs. It was partially the result of his own temperament. He simply disliked the language and devices of persuasion, of rhetoric, as manipulative and deceptive. In Father Schauf's mind they were tantamount to lying. Once his theology instructor had entered the classroom late. He walked to the front of the class, whirled around toward the students, paused deliberately, and then detached his collar and with care placed it on the corner of his desk. Then he announced dramatically and with great emotion in his voice, "There is no God." Father Schauf, repulsed by the artificiality of the device, refused to engage in the discussion although he would normally have been one of the most articulate debaters.

Whatever effectiveness he had as a speaker or a teacher had resulted from his natural, unaffected delivery of what he believed to be true and logical. Fortunately, before coming to Amburg, his audiences had been more responsive. His first sermons in Amburg, however, had been received with cold indifference. His first effective sermon, or at least the one upon which several of his congregation had commented, had been a shameful compromise according to his standards.

The Bishop had requested that a sermon on the evils of communism be delivered sometime during the month of September. Father Schauf wrestled the whole month with the language he believed relevant. He wanted to do his best job. He wrote and rewrote, and then at the last minute he threw the whole thing out. It was too historical, too philosophical even though he had grounded the sermon on a well-known parable and quoted liberally several of the more popular Catholic radio and television speakers.

Finally, in last minute panic he reduced his entire argument to terms he knew they would understand: *Thou Shalt not Steal.* He proceeded to elaborate upon the infringements of totalitarian states upon the rights and freedoms of individuals, especially upon the rights of private ownership of property which he used as a concrete illustration. They could at least understand the loss of property; perhaps, he hoped, they might understand how the state could "steal" such precious rights and freedoms as worship and speech.

They understood *that* sermon all right, but *he* didn't believe his own argument. He knew that his entire position could be demolished and he felt sick and angry at himself for the snobbism implicit in his compromise of logic and language. He was appalled when several of the men of the parish commented favorably on the sermon at the Tuesday Holy Name meeting. Then a farm wife, a nervous, shrewish woman who had said little or nothing to him since he had arrived, called unexpectedly at the rectory one evening and used his sermon as a pretext to unload upon Father Schauf an hysterical harangue of the most confused and frighteningly incredible political sentiments he had ever heard. Apparently she thought he held the same apprehensions about government, labor, Negroes, taxes, and foreign aid as she held. The only response he could give was to gently lessen her fears and sympathetically qualify her rambling and chaotic assertions and then to diplomatically change the topic of conversation.

Since then Father Schauf had limited his sermons to obvious comments on the gospel, but even these simple commentaries were becoming more excruciatingly difficult. He no longer tried to guess how they might respond. His rhetoric, whatever he did, invariably had ambiguous or unpredictable results.

He was ready now, to leave for church. He opened the closet door in his study and slected his heavy winter coat and overshoes. For some reason his feet were always cold. He slipped the tubular bottle of wine into the outside pocket of his coat and left the house through the kitchen. He opened the side door just off the pantry, leaving Mrs. Johnson to her last chores and her day of pheasant plucking.

Outside the wind was blowing. The low rain clouds had vaulted high. It would be colder now, but it seemed as though the rain was over. Bending into the wind, he walked across the yard, really only a closely cut empty lot of weeds that separated the rectory from the church and which Father Schauf whimsically called his "farm," and around the back of the church to the sacristy door.

After he turned on the church lights, he set about immediately preparing the altar. Of one thing he was certain: his altar boy would be late. He removed the green felt altar cloth and stood the framed prayer cards up in their proper places. He fixed the cruets, put the missal on its stand on the epistle side of the altar, and then lit the candles for low mass. Then he prepared the chalice in the sacristy and began to put on his vestments.

Father Schauf's altar boys were deplorably bad, but try as he would it was simply impossible to find time for practice. It was difficult enough for religious instructions. His parish covered three school districts and the bus schedule which served each precluded any early morning or late afternoon classes or practice.

He had managed to schedule religious instruction classes but not without dissent and grumbling. He tried to be democratic, but first one group objected to Saturday, then another group didn't want Sunday, and nobody wanted the evenings. Sunday was impossible for him anyway because he had to say mass at two locations and wouldn't have time to supervise the instructors. They finally accepted one week night for the high school students and Saturday morning for the grammar school children. He knew that those who lived on the farms were angry for some time because of the schedule. He heard by way of rumor that they believed he had favored the town folks unfairly.

He abandoned his plans for altar boy practice for fear of aggravating his already strained relations with the rural parishioners. He used the boys from Amburg as much as possible for daily mass, but they were few and in order not to overburden those who were adequately prepared, he had to use boys who were careless and irresponsible. Often he said mass without a server. Sometimes old Raymond Madsen, one of the few daily communicants, would volunteer to serve, hacking and spitting phlegm throughout mass and requiring oral instructions each step of the way. Father Schauf preferred an incompetent server or no server at all to old Raymond.

At five to seven his sleepy and disheveled altar boy arrived. After dressing slowly, the boy wandered onto the altar to prepare for mass. He wandered back into the sacristy when he discovered that his duties had already been done. His surplice was bunched high in back. Father Schauf pulled it down, then took the boy over to the sink, wet his hair, and combed it with his own comb.

He was ready to enter the altar for mass. Now, all his petty triumphs and failures were peripheral in the light of the eternal sacrifice. Father Schauf may have doubted himself, but never Christ or the grace which flowed from the mass. He did not feel he was unreasonable in demanding at least a simple dignity in its execution. He was not overly concerned with an elaborate and formal exactitude. He did not expect perfection. He smiled with

others at the standing joke about a certain wealthy parish in the
Cities where four altar boys in colorful cassocks were used even
for the daily low mass and where on Sunday there was such an
elaborate use of bells and altar lights which chimed and dimmed
so often that it was rumored they employed a stage manager to
keep everything straight.

Introibo ad altare dei. He articulated the prayers at the foot of
the altar with deliberate accuracy, trying to convey in the tone
and inflection of his voice the exact meaning and feeling of each.
Because this particular altar boy was almost worthless in his responses, Father Schauf answered each of his spoken prayers silently with the words the altar boy was supposed to say aloud.
Once when he was depressed and short tempered, he lost his patience with a server and answered every response himself, loudly
drowning out the boy's feeble attempts.

As he ascended the steps to the altar, he was distracted by one
of Mr. Madsen's coughing fits. It seemed the old man would never
catch his breath. Father Schauf continued his prayers with a conscious effort to keep his mind on the meaning—the Kyrie, the
Gloria, and then the Epistle. He extended his left hand to signal
the change of the missal and was surprised to hear the altar boy
scrambling behind his back to remove the book on the proper cue.
Then the Gospel and the Credo.

The boy missed the cue for the cruets, so Father Schauf stood
with the chalice at the top step of the epistle side until the boy realized that it was the Offertory. At the center of the altar he
faced the congregation and said in Latin, "Pray brethren, that your
prayer and mine be acceptable unto God," and he answered himself silently, for he knew the boy couldn't even pronounce the response reading from the altar card let alone memorize it.

The altar boy missed the first two responses of the Preface and
slurred the last two. "Lift up your minds and your hearts," the
priest said. "We have lifted them unto the Lord," he responded
for the congregation. The boy picked up the bell in anticipation
and then rang the "Sanctus" correctly which suggested to the
priest that perhaps the boy's performance might be an improve-
ment over the effort of the day before.

In the intention of the mass Father Schauf remembered his
parents as usual and prayed for the special intentions of Father

Willet, the pastor of one of Father Schauf's neighboring parishes. It was the geographical proximity of their assignments which had brought the two priests together. Over the past year Father Willet had become his closest and most frequent companion. But just a week before, they had had an argument which had cooled their friendship.

Father Willet was not the kind of friend Father Schauf was drawn to naturally. He was thin and nervous. Everyone called him "twitchy fingers" in description of his continual wringing of hands. Father Willet was precise and exacting in his speech, prissy and shrewish in temperament, timid and distant in his relationships with everyone, fellow priest or parishioner. But friends they had become, drawn to each other out of isolation and loneliness.

The argument was petty. It was about a new holy day that had been added to the liturgical calendar. Father Schauf argued that qualitative additions might be significant but simply to *add* another opportunity for grace to the liturgical year was like trying to measure God out in buckets, quantitatively. Poor, timid Father Willet was shocked by the analogy. Father Schauf felt sick at heart for being so argumentative and so insensitive. He prayed for the virtues of patience and self-control.

The boy did not see the priest extend his hands over the chalice as the last bell cue before the Consecration. He craned his neck looking for the signal that had already passed. He did not know that when the priest blessed the host and then leaned over the words of consecration were about to be pronounced. He did not hear the words "Hoc est enim corpus meum," and he did not hear the priest, after a moment of silent terror, repeat the words. He did not see the trembling hands, nor did he see the contorted face fighting the tears of self-pity and despair. His eye caught the reflection of light when the chalice was raised for adoration. He grasped the bell and with six quick, short, late bursts rang the Presence of God upon the altar.

PERDITA BUCHAN grew up in Philadelphia. After college she lived and worked at various jobs in New York, London and Florence. She now lives in Marlboro, Vermont, with her husband and baby daughter. Her first novel, *Girl with a Zebra*, was published in 1966.

It's Cold Out There

"Keep america beautiful," the sign read, "cut your hair." It was pasted on the mirror between "deluxe hamburger special" and "things go better with coke" and beneath "ask for sealtest ice cream." There were two other homemade signs: "please pay when served" and "all sandwitches on toast 10¢ extra."

"Look how 'sandwich' is spelled," Cressie whispered, hooking her finger under Paul's belt and tugging to get his attention.

The old man behind the saltwater-taffy bin limped into the open as if he thought they were about to do something obscene or dangerous. He scowled at Paul.

Cressie fingered the face guard on her football helmet. Paul had taken his helmet, an orthodox motorcycle helmet, off and was running his fingers through the wild red hair that tangled below his ears and down the back of his neck. He added six cents for a pack of Juicy Fruit to the money he had put down for a bunch of green grapes and two cans of beer.

"Do you want to eat yet?" he asked.

Cressie shook her head.

"Not hungry."

After they had gone out through the springless screen door, the old man locked it.

"Did you see the sign?" Cressie said.

Paul shook his head.

"On the mirror behind the counter. You didn't see it?"

"What did it say?"

"'Keep America beautiful, cut your hair.'"

Paul laughed and dropped the helmet onto his head. "Hop on," he said.

The Honda started after seven tries.

"I think it's broken," Cressie said.

"I can't hear you."

Cressie snapped the chin strap on the football helmet.

The bike spluttered as Paul wheeled it across the cement parking strip. There were four boys in white T-shirts on the corner. Two were fat and two were thin, and they had crewcuts.

"Cut your hair!" one of them yelled.

Paul pressed the accelerator and the bike stalled.

"I think it's broken," Cressie said again.

The four boys on the corner jeered.

"Better make sure it's running before you get on the road," another of them said.

"Gun it!"

"Torque out!"

Paul's shoulders set. He jumped on the starter three times before it caught. They screeched out onto the road across the marshes. Speed seemed to make the muddy salt smell stronger, and Cressie leaned happily into the curves.

"They were punks," she said, but Paul did not hear.

"Punks," she said again to herself, hugging the beer and the grapes in the paper bag against the front of her leather jacket.

A high bulwark of pebbles ran between the road and the beach, like the discard of some giant construction. Cressie scrambled up them, holding her hand out to Paul; she was more surefooted in sneakers than he in sandals. The tide had risen, leaving only a thin strip of sand crowded with radios and sunbathers. Boys, like the ones on the corner but bare-chested, were feinting with footballs, tennis balls, and Frisbees. Girls in flowered bikinis lay in sun-imposed stillness. The army blanket was still there where they had left it, with the New York *Times* and Paul's notebooks and their other belongings rolled up in it. Paul spread it out and threw himself down on his stomach.

"It's that aggressiveness," he said.

Cressie leaned over and rubbed his shoulder.

"I hate college kids," he said.

"I thought they were younger than that."

He rolled over quickly, pinning her hand. "No. They were around nineteen."

Cressie withdrew her hand and picked up "Selected American Short Stories."

"Have you found a good one yet?" Paul asked.

"No," she said, "they're all pretty sentimental."

"Did you read that one I said was good?"

"Not yet."

"Well, read it."

Cressie twisted her hands in his hair. "O.K.," she said, and stood up. She unzipped her leather jacket and threw it off, hitching at the bottom of her bikini. She kicked off her sneakers, bracing one foot against the other, and lay down close to him, pressing into the curve of his side. He was reading the *Times* again, mauling it as he always did in his frustration at the Vietnam battle reports.

Cressie read three stories and went for a walk, as near as she dared to the beach club beyond the breakwater, where people were drinking Martinis. Paul relentlessly destroyed the newspaper as he read. For a while, they slept side by side. Then they ate grapes and drank their beer. Paul picked up one of his notebooks and began to write, frowning. Slowly the beach cleared of people, who took their radios, their footballs and Frisbees, and retreated over the pebble hills. Paul and Cressie lay there alone till a policeman came and stood above them on the pebble hill, his hand on his gun. He beckoned to Paul, who got up and went to him—ran, because he feared the police. Cressie watched him run, dispassionately. She only felt that the policeman, feeling fear like an animal, would react nastily. He was an old man, and, despite Paul's courtesy, kept his hand on his gun. She did not hear their conversation.

"What did he say?" she asked when he had gone and Paul slowly descended the hill. Paul shrugged and began to fold up the *Times* as if he were afraid of repeating the policeman's words.

"What did he *say?*"

Paul sighed. "Get up," he said.

"Paul, what did he *say?*"

"To get off the *beach*. It's private or something."

"Well, is there a public beach?"

"Down the road. Where all the cars are parked."

"Oh," said Cressie, and turned to gather up her own things—baby oil, sunglasses, and the book of short stories. She put the sunglasses on her nose.

"Are we going there?"

"Yes," Paul said. There was some exasperation in his voice, as if she were interrupting him in a mental wrestling with things of more consequence. He folded the blanket as well as the *Times* and stuffed the empty beer cans and grapes into the paper bag.

"It's the bike," he said. "He probably wouldn't have bothered to see who was here if we'd had a car."

"I guess it's all those riots they had in Crystal Beach. They're scared that'll happen again. Maybe they think we're the advance guard." She zipped up her leather jacket.

There were no pebble hills at the public beach; its perimeter had been graded for a parking lot, and the beach itself was wide. They left the stuff on the bike and walked down the beach. Paul put his arm around Cressie and hugged her every so often, pulling her off stride.

The beach was nearly empty. An old couple sat near the parking lot in deck chairs, and out near the sandbar a Labrador whirled around a group of castle-building children.

"Let's find out the time," Paul said.

He went to ask the old man, who clutched nervously at the arms of his chair. Cressie watched at a distance. The Labrador streaked past her with one of the children, a red-headed child, behind. She watched them run down to the end of the parking lot and back.

Paul and the old man had discussed the weather.

"He says it's been a lousy summer," Paul told her, "up until this weekend. We're lucky."

He smiled and hugged her again.

"In most big things," Cressie said.

"It's six o'clock. Let's eat."

"We have to go to the drugstore, remember."

"Oh, Cress. We don't need those."

Cressie frowned, rubbing one foot with the other.

"Cress." He hugged her. "Will you worry?"

"Of course."

"All right. We'll go into Crystal Beach. We can change on the way."

The motel room looked dishevelled, though Paul and Cressie had only arrived in the morning. Cressie thought motel rooms had a built-in dishevelment factor, just as they always smelled of unseasoned wood.

"You know we made it from Boston in two hours?" Paul said.

Cressie sighed. "We're that much farther from the Cape," she said. "It's going to take forever to get to the island."

"Don't you want to go see her, Cress?"

Cressie shook her head. "Fortune-tellers scare me."

"She may tell me something that will help," Paul said. "I've got to know about writing. I can't waste any more time."

Cressie watched him tossing things out of his bag and thought about the island. She thought of the cherry tree behind the summer house, its fruit scattered and spoiled by birds long before they arrived each summer. From its branches, the whole topography of the cove was clear.

"You'll like the island, Paul," she said. "There's an amusement park on the north shore. With a penny arcade."

Paul paid no attention. "The lady in the junk shop said she went to Mrs. Blake not believing in it. And what she told her happened."

"I could probably prophesy," Cressie said. "I go into a trance on the back of the motorcycle. I go into another world back there. I made up a great poem this morning."

"Let's hear it."

"I forgot it as soon as we stopped. I can only remember one stanza."

"Say it for me."

"Oh, Paul, I don't remember. It just seemed great at the time."

"I'd like to sit on the back and work," Paul said morosely. "Driving takes up all my concentration."

"It wasn't work, Paul. It was nonsense."

"All that time lost," Paul muttered. "A whole summer wasted on that stupid theatre workshop. Acting's the wrong life."

"It wasn't as stupid as summer school," Cressie said. "Nothing's as stupid as that."

Cressie pulled on a sweater and blue jeans but threw her sneakers into the corner, though the gravel hurt her bare feet when they went out to the motorcycle. The wind on the road was cold, too, and her toes were numb by the time they got to Crystal Beach.

"What a honky-tonk place," Paul said as they coasted down the main, cement-divided street. Amber lights flashed at every intersection. Street lights mottled the pastel façades of gingerbread frame houses. Every other one had a "GUESTS" or "ROOMS" sign. To Cressie there was something sinister in it, as if she and Paul were Hansel and Gretel to a hundred witches. They passed the arched complex of movie theatre, bowling alley, and discothèque —closed now that Labor Day was past. The empty showcases and shredded posters seemed natural as turning leaves, made autumn near. Cressie inched her arms farther around Paul and held on to him for more balance. He reached down and let his hand rest for a moment on her knee. She moved her head and their helmets knocked sharply.

They stopped opposite the all-night drugstore. Children, jackets over pajamas, were still swinging on the playground swings.

"Go on," Cressie said.

Paul took off his helmet.

"Why don't you go, Cress? Every time I go, the place is filled with little old ladies. It's a real trauma."

"No," Cressie said, and pressed her face as close against his sleeve as the face guard would allow. He went reluctantly.

Groups of teen-agers wandered back and forth across the street, looking seedy and abandoned. Some of them came within a few yards of the bike and stared. Cressie rested her foot on the handlebars, working the numb toes, and gazed up at the top stories of the buildings across the street. There were more signs for rooms and for haircutting and dressmaking and one that read "MADAME NETTIE * FORTUNE-TELLER." The sign was sprinkled with stars, like the knockout scene in a comic strip. She pointed this out to Paul when he came back. He wasn't impressed.

"She wouldn't be any good. Just a resort fortune-teller for tourists. Mrs. Blake is a seer. She goes into a trance."

"Were there a lot of old ladies?"

"They didn't have them."

"Did you ask?"

"Yes."

"Liar."

"Cressie, I wish you wouldn't say things like that. It makes me wonder what kind of person you think I am."

"I don't know you," Cressie said. "How could I tell?"

Paul ignored this.

"It was funny anyway," he said. "There was a young kid behind the counter and he was very nice. He said the man who runs the place doesn't carry dirty books or contraceptives. He said some guy came in really desperate the other night—he must have had the girl in the car—and he was screaming, *Man,* you've *got* to have them!"

"That is funny," Cressie said after some deliberation.

Paul laughed and patted her football helmet.

"Cress," he said, "Cress. We'll ride on into Harbor Centre."

The road to Harbor Centre was flat, unlit and empty, and gave Cressie the feeling that the whole world really was flat, that it dropped sharply away on either side just at the perimeter of vision. They were stopped by a motorcycle policeman.

"Goggles," he said.

"She had them in her hand," Paul said, and Cressie held them out mutely.

"Put 'em on," said the motorcycle policeman. "I won't give you a fine, but next time you may not be so lucky."

"I can't see anything," Paul said wryly once he'd put on the goggles.

The drugstore in Harbor Centre was more liberal. Cressie stuffed the package down the front of her jacket.

They ate in a seafood diner on the main street. There was a hundred-year-old lobster floating around in a tank, but the food wasn't very good.

"Those fried clams aren't so great for your stomach."

"They'll give me pains," Paul agreed.

Back at the motel, Cressie had to rub his stomach while he planned their route on the map.

"I wish you wouldn't get sick," she said. "It makes me scared."

He smiled and caught her hands with his.

"My stomach's O.K. now. Why don't you lie down?"

Cressie lay with her head on his stomach. He rested the map in her hair and it made loud crackling noises in her ear as if her hair were some metallic substance. His skin smelled of baby oil and tobacco and was very smooth and soft—smoother and softer, Cressie thought, than her own. Absently he stroked her shoulder.

"We'll have to get up at eight," he said.

"O.K.," said Cressie. "It's you that can't get up, not me."

Paul threw the map on the floor and turned over.

"Ow," Cressie said.

"Well, I'm going to read you a poem."

He pulled all the notebooks off the night table—fat notebooks filled with loose pieces of paper that he had carried with him all summer long, scribbling in the subway, in Cambridge coffee shops, and lying under the trees of the Common. Now he sorted through them and read her a poem about rain on Beacon Hill; but she was only really conscious of his warmth and the way the scent of his skin filled her nostrils to the exclusion of the unseasoned wood.

Mayville was divided by the Sadagwa River. It began with a textile mill that was still, surprisingly, active. Other factory buildings occurred among derelict balconied houses as the outskirts thickened into Main Street.

"A tannery," Paul cried. "There's a tannery here. Can you smell it?"

Cressie had noticed a thin, acrid chemical smell.

"It's like the town I grew up in," Paul exulted. "There was a tannery. It was a town just like this."

They had slowed down, within the city limits, so that conversation was possible.

"Maybe that's what Mrs. Blake is," Cressie said. "Maybe she doesn't tell futures at all. Maybe she is your past."

Paul laughed.

"We're early, too," said Cressie. "I told you that we didn't have to get up at eight."

They went to have coffee in one of the drugstores. Paul made Cressie take off the football helmet before they went inside. Even so they were stared at.

"Do you have cigarettes?" Paul asked.

"No," said the man behind the counter happily.

"Do you have a ladies' room?" asked Cressie.

"No," he said with triumph.

The coffee was instant and Paul began to look gloomy. Cressie poured a lot of milk into her cup. There was no cream.

"I hope it'll be worth it," she said. "I hope she doesn't tell us that we're going to be killed between here and the Cape."

"I don't think they ever tell you that kind of thing," Paul said vaguely.

"Why not? It's certainly your future and your fate."

"You're morbid, Cressie."

The drugstore owner had gone back to the front of the store, where he eyed them over the cash register.

"I can't see why he's staring," Cressie said in annoyance. "I'm wearing shoes and the helmet's flattened your hair sort of. I'm sorry we left that hairbrush behind."

"So am I."

Cressie stared at the drugstore owner and he looked away. "I'm going to run away if she tells me she sees a baby in my lap," she said.

"What," said Paul, "are you talking about?"

"The lady who ran the junk shop on Charles Street, the one who told us about Mrs. Blake. That's what Mrs. Blake saw in her daughter's lap."

"A baby?"

"Of course. She discovered that she was pregnant a few months later. Only she was married to a carpenter."

"Well, that sounds Biblical."

Cressie was for a moment arrested by the coincidence, but only for a moment.

"What if?" she said.

"Cressie." Paul spread his hands patiently on the red marble counter. "It's *im*possible."

"Nothing's impossible. Nothing that Nature has anything to do with. It happened to you once."

He turned to her and there was hurt in his eyes, more than a flash of it. Cressie had always thought that brown eyes were inexpressive because they did not change color, but she knew, since Paul, that the light could go out somewhere behind them. She wanted to tangle her hands in his hair, but she was stubborn.

"Well, it happened," she said.

"I was very careless. I've told you that. Finish your coffee and let's go."

"I'll run away to Kansas," Cressie muttered doggedly, "if she tells me that."

It was enough to make him laugh and put his arm around her.

Mrs. Blake lived on the residential side of the Sadagwa River. The road that crossed the bridge was being widened, and they had to wait in line while a white-gloved policeman synchronized traffic.

"*Stop* when I hold my hand up," he yelled at Paul, who had stopped. "Maybe if you cut your hair you could see something."

"They're Fascists," Cressie murmured in Paul's ear. "It's a police state if you're in a minority group. I never realized that."

"I can't hear you," Paul said. "Look for house numbers."

On the river side, houses were squeezed between road and water with only swatches of ground. On the land side, green, flat lawns stretched before houses painted red, white and corn-chowder yellow. They were heavily ornamented, with pillars and porticoes and crenellated towers.

After some distance, the houses became newer and closer together, set gable-end to the road, huddled to conserve ground. They had been built since the war, and all were painted white or light green. One alone stood out, by virtue of being on a slight rise and flying a regulation-size American flag.

Paul slowed down. "Oh damn," he muttered. "That'll be the one."

"She'll see through you," Cressie chortled, putting her hands on his shoulders. "She'll know you don't believe in the war."

They stopped and parked the motorcycle and took off their helmets.

"I could wait out here," Cressie said.

"Come on," he said. "We're here. You come, too."

They rang the bell and waited. Mrs. Blake came through the house door into the foyer. She did not unlock the screen door.

"Yes?" she said.

Behind Paul, Cressie could see little—just a small, stout woman in a housecoat.

"We called," Paul was saying. "We had an appointment for ten-thirty this morning. I think we're a little early."

"You didn't speak to me," the woman said evasively. "You must have spoken to my sister. I have a student coming at ten-thirty. She didn't know. I'll have to give you another day."

"But we've come all the way from Boston," Paul said. "We can't come back tomorrow."

She hesitated.

"All right. Come back at one." She turned and hurried through the door into the house.

"She probably won't answer the bell at one," Cressie whispered as they went down the steps. "I think she's a fake."

"Didn't you see that big bump on her forehead?"

"No. But then I couldn't see much. She was on the other side of the screen door. Do you think it's worth waiting?"

They had reached the curb. Paul stood with his arms spread wide, dangling the helmets, apologetically stubborn.

"We've come all this way."

Cressie knew that he was right and felt abashed at giving in to her own fear. "O.K.," she said. "It's so sunny. I wish we could go to the beach till then."

"We're not far from the coast," Paul said.

But in the end they went to a small park on the river, across a dead-end channel from the boatyard. Paul parked the bike and lay on top of it. Cressie sat near him on a bench with her face in the sun. She began to fidget when the sun got too hot and made Paul sit up while she dismantled the top of the pyramid of luggage to get at "Selected American Short Stories." It was not in the top of her Pan Am bag, and so Paul had to untie the rope, string, and electric wire that held the pyramid together, and let her wrestle the blue bag to the ground. She was unpacking it when an old lady came across the park toward them. Cressie had already noticed her, hovering on the other side of the street. She came directly toward them as if her aim was to come to them rather than the park. She addressed her remarks to Paul.

"My goodness, have you come a long way?"

Her accent was Middle European. She made delighted grandmotherly noises of amazement when Paul told her that they had come from Boston and were going to the Cape.

"A long way," she murmured, "a long way. You ride a long way."

She looked at Cressie for the first time. "Together?" she asked. Cressie nodded.

"Such a long way to go on the back of such a thing. I come often to this park. I live near, by the river, with my daughter. She is married to a Frenchman."

She stood, weight on her heels, hips tilted forward. The scarf about her head fluttered slightly, a bright swath of flowers and Paisley.

"Where do you come from?" Cressie asked.

"Poland." The woman smiled bashfully, proudly—a contradictory look like so many of Paul's. "I come after the First War," she went on. "I am very young, seventeen. I come to Ipswich to work in the factory. You know Ipswich?"

"Yes," Cressie said. "I love it. It's a pretty place."

"Pretty," she said uncomprehendingly. "Yes, I love it, too. I live there in a house with other Polish. I make ten dollars a week in the stocking factory and every week I send home five dollars to my mother in Poland. Then I marry a Polish man. Two years ago, he died. He was sick for a long time. It was his stomach. Ulcers."

Paul winced slightly. The woman's attention turned to him.

"A handsome boy," she said. And to Cressie, "You are very lucky."

Cressie smiled. Paul grinned, sitting up straight now.

"Did you hear that, Cress," he said when the woman had wandered away. "You're lucky."

"Uhm."

"That was odd," he said after a little thought. "Do you think it could have been Mrs. Blake come to check us out? To see if we were dangerous?"

"Mrs. Blake isn't foreign. And she didn't look like that. Not through the screen door, anyway."

"Not that she *is* Mrs. Blake. But maybe Mrs. Blake in another form."

"Oh, come on. She's not a witch."

"No. But maybe she can go with people astrally or something and see through their minds. Oh, I don't know." He lay down flat again and closed his eyes.

At one, Mrs. Blake let them in. She was welcoming and vague, an ordinary woman in a cotton housecoat—far more ordinary than the Polish woman. She led Paul, who was to go first, into her music room. Through the glass door, Cressie could see a huge piano covered with framed photographs. She thought of it as she sat under the cherrywood clock, amid the lace doilies and the copies of the *Reader's Digest*, as Mrs. Blake's crystal ball—as if the images she conjured up appeared in the glass of each of those framed photographs in turn.

Half an hour went by, clearly marked on the face of the cherry-wood clock. Cressie read several Unforgettable Characters and forgot them. The telephone rang. She dared not answer it, though it rang for a long time. Out of a sense of superstitious propriety, she went to sit in the hallway, where she could not hear anything said in the music room.

She was halfway through another article when three girls came chattering up to the front door. The one in the lead, with shingled blond hair, put her head against the screen and peered in.

"We have an appointment with Mrs. Blake," she said.

"Mrs. Blake has someone with her now," Cressie said. "And I'm supposed to be next."

This confused them. In dismay, they hurtled together crying, "Oh!" One of them—the smallest, with a round, frightened face—almost bolted down the steps.

"Come on, Noreen," said the blond one. "If we let you go now, you'll kick yourself for not staying."

The third girl, teased black hair pinned up in an outdated mass, got behind Noreen, and together, blond and black, they shoved her through the screen door. They stood awkwardly for a moment, and then all three collapsed on the chaise longue opposite the bench Cressie sat on. They whispered among themselves while Cressie went on reading.

"How long has someone been in there?"

"He's been in there for three-quarters of an hour," Cressie replied, surprised at her use of the masculine pronoun.

The girls registered dismay. Noreen put her hands over her mouth and bugged her eyes.

"A whole hour for everyone," the blond girl murmured.

"I guess so," Cressie said. "I haven't been."

They looked at her.

"Aren't you scared?" gasped Noreen.

"I don't think," Cressie said, "that they ever tell you terrible things. It's all about who you'll marry and so on."

They smiled. The one with the black hair had a sweet smile. "Do you live around here?" she asked.

Paul came out before Cressie could answer and beckoned to her. The girls stared at them.

"Go on in," Paul said.

"Paul, it's time for their appointment."

"She's waiting for *you*. Go on in."

Mrs. Blake rocked in a painted rocker with calico cushions. She never looked at the frames on the piano but stared straight at Cressie with eyes huge behind magnifying lenses. Though she addressed questions to her, she did not hear when Cressie answered, or paid no attention. Cressie wondered if this were a trance. Mrs. Blake told her to take cod-liver oil, for she would be having ear trouble in November, that she would be married within two years and to start saving money, and that she would get a letter from someone named George in Vietnam. She also talked about seeing members of Cressie's family and mentioned a summer house. But Cressie felt that it was superficial, that Mrs. Blake could not find as much to say to her as she had to Paul.

The girls were bunched together when she came out.

"What did she tell you?" they whispered.

"Nothing much," said Cressie.

She found Paul out with the motorcycle. He had his helmet on and was sitting backward on the seat. She could tell, so pensive was he, that Mrs. Blake had told him something good.

"Let's go," she said crossly. "She told you you'd be famous."

Paul nodded.

"A famous writer?"

He nodded again.

"What did she tell you?"

"To take cod-liver oil and save money."

"Cress," he said, "that can't be all of it."

"The whole thing was crummy—let's go. Anyway, she didn't see a baby sitting in my lap."

They had to stay on highways most of the way to the Cape. The noise and the heavy, vibrating feel of the helmet made Cressie sleepy and she drowsed except when passing trucks shuddered her awake. After crossing the Cape Cod Canal on a bridge that looked like a hunk of scrap metal, they stopped to eat fried clams.

"Are we going all the way to the ferry tonight?" Cressie asked.

"No, let's look for a place on the ocean. There's a beach near here on the map called Sands Beach."

"Are we going to sleep on it?"

"I hope not. It's pretty cold."

The fried clams, as usual, made Cressie feel sick before she'd finished eating them. Paul ate the rest of her share while she drank a root beer.

"I'm really glad about that," Cressie said. "About what Mrs. Blake didn't tell me."

"About the baby?"

"Yes. I wish she had told me I'd be famous."

It was near dusk when they started off again, and already chill on the back of the motorcycle. The neon along the highway outshone the sunset. Hot-dog stands and pizza palaces changed places with motels and souvenir shops in an endless reel. Cressie shut her eyes most of the time.

"There's an A. & W.," she yelled on opening them. "I want another root beer."

By dark they had reached the road to Sands Beach. It was cold now, even when they stopped for traffic lights, and Cressie gave up trying to hold on, and just leaned against Paul and thrust her hands in her pockets. On one side of the road were houses set high on green lawns, on the other more houses set in groves of pine, facing the sea. Cressie was reminded of the street in Mayville.

Then, on either side, the houses ended and the pines made a
dark screen as solid as boulders. Out of this a sudden light flashed
green and red and yellow. Paul braked so hard that Cressie hit
her chin on his shoulder.

They were at the mouth of a gravel driveway, and at the end of
it the source of the flashing light was visible—a group of white
cottages. A sign tacked to one of the pines identified them. "MRS.
BIRCH'S GUEST COTTAGES," it read.

"A mirage," breathed Cressie.

The cottages were on the ocean; its roar could be heard halfway
down the driveway. At the end it could be seen, stretched out
silver behind the cottages. The cottage with the flashing light was
covered with hand-painted signs: "COTTAGES FOR RENT BY WEEK OR
MONTH," "OCEAN FRONT, PRIVATE BEACH, KITCHEN FACILITIES," "STAY
WITH US A-WILE," "SPECIAL RATES FOR LONG RENTELS."

Cressie nudged Paul. "Did you see how they spelled 'rentals'?"

"Well, at least," Paul said, "they don't say cut your hair."

He handed Cressie his helmet and black leather jacket, and she
waited with them and the motorcycle under the trees. He stood
by the front steps where the light touched him—green, then red,
then yellow for a moment—and then he came back.

"Come with me, Cress. We look more respectable together."

The cottage had a screened-in front porch that acted like a
scrim between the steps and the lighted living room. Paul rang
the bell. There was shuffling inside and an old lady came onto
the porch. Behind her, in the doorway, stood a gaunt old man,
his shoulders hunched in an ineffectual posture of menace.

"Yes?" said the old lady without unlocking the screen door. She
had a lantern jaw and did not look frightened.

"Excuse me, Ma'am," Paul said. "Have you a cabin we could
rent just for tonight?"

The woman looked at them, giving Cressie an especially sharp,
vertical look.

"Your wife?" she said to Paul.

He nodded.

Mrs. Birch seemed to feel that his assertion had cleared her of
guilt rather than affirmed a truth, but she said that she had one
and unlocked the screen door. As they entered, the old man re-

treated. They never saw his face. He took up his stance in a darkened hallway off the living room.

Paul paid and signed the register while Cressie looked around the room. Sometimes she felt rather like a bodyguard, always being left to scan the surroundings while Paul paid and signed. There were signs all over the wall—the kind of signs bought in gift shops, lettered on varnished pieces of wood. They said things like "SOME PEOPLE PUT THEIR MOUTHS IN HIGH GEAR BEFORE THEIR MINDS ARE TURNING OVER." There were a lot about fishermen, that perennial joke of the gift shop. Then there were homemade signs, penned in Magic Marker on yellowing index cards. One said, "OUR GUESTS ARE OUR FAMILY, DROP US A LINE WHEN YOU'RE AWAY." Obviously, a lot of people had. Wherever the signs had left space, postcards were tacked—bright technicolor pictures of every region of the United States.

At last, Mrs. Birch accepted their traveller's check and handed over their key. She followed them to the porch and stared after them.

"It's the last one to the left," she called.

The cottage looked just like Mrs. Birch's, with the same screened porch. Inside, there were no poems on the wall but a wallpaper covered with seagulls.

"At least it doesn't smell like a motel," Cressie said.

Paul heaped their luggage in the middle of the braided rug. It looked, with its tails of rope and electric wire, like something the plumbers had left. They did not unpack but lay down together on the bed under the frosted-glass hurricane lamp.

"Well, it's a place," Paul said.

"It's nice," Cressie said, stretching out.

Paul put his hand on her head. "You know, I think I will end up in southern California," he said.

"Maybe you'll be a movie star."

"No. . . . I don't think so. I'll be writing, I guess. And working —enough to support my family. If I have one."

"Mrs. Blake didn't see a baby in your lap?"

He turned to look at her and laughed.

"No."

"He's going to look for you one day, that child," Cressie said, as if she had to say it, not really wanting to. "Did Mrs. Blake tell you that?"

He stood up.

"Let's go for a walk, Cress." His voice was flat and he did not look at her.

"All right," she said, half afraid.

The tide was coming in when they started down the beach. They walked very close together, and Cressie, who had a tendency to swerve to the right, kept bumping into Paul. He did not change his stride or seem to notice. They climbed over a breakwater. Ahead, the rocks rose in a curve, topped with scrub pine. The beach curved, too, but the sand became gravel and mud.

"Can you climb?" he said.

"Where do you want to go?"

"Up there." He pointed to a jutting nose of rock at the periphery of the trees.

"I guess I can."

The hillside was sand, softer and damper than the sand of the beach, and Cressie's sneakers filled with it. They sat just above the rock and looked over the water. A lighthouse at the end of another promontory flashed weakly against a pearly sky.

Paul lay in the sand, head thrown back so that his profile was defiant, self-sufficient.

"You're angry." Cressie sighed.

"Why did you say that?"

"It's true."

"That's not *why* you said it."

"I guess I don't understand. I want to know why you aren't curious about it."

"I don't think you know what it's like if you've never seen the person pregnant even. It's like a ghost—a living ghost."

Paul raised his head higher.

"And you're not curious at all? You don't want to see it?" Cressie said to him.

"She—well, she was like those girls at the seer's. An ordinary girl."

"Oh," Cressie said.

"If it were you, Cress—" He took a strand of her hair and ran it through his fingers.

"You'd never find me," Cressie said. "I'd run away to Kansas or Monterey. I haven't decided yet."

"I'd run after you."

"You'd never find me," she repeated.

"Cressie, if you were pregnant, you wouldn't go. You'd want me to stay with you."

"You're wrong. If Mrs. Blake had told me she saw a baby in my lap, I'd have run right out the back door. You'd never have seen me again."

Abruptly, he rolled over and put his arms around her.

"That makes everything very easy for me."

Cressie stiffened in his arms. "It doesn't really affect you, does it?" she said.

"Cress, some things you just have to put out of your mind. It does no good to go over them. *You* try to wallow in guilt. A thing happens. You do what you can and then it's over."

They were silent, lying rigid in the sand, for several minutes.

"Do you think I should have married her?" he said carefully.

"No!" Cressie exploded. "Not at all. I just think you should— No. I don't think you should anything. I just wonder why you aren't curious."

He did not respond, and she continued.

"If I had a child alive somewhere in this world I'd search and search for it because I wouldn't believe anyone else could really understand it."

He pulled her closer to him in silence.

"I'm sorry," Cressie said after a few minutes.

They stayed on the dune until the sky was completely black and the rays from the lighthouse clear. Then they wandered back.

They had left the porch light on, and there was a praying mantis clinging to the screen of the porch door.

"It's going to die out here," Paul said. "It's pretty cold."

"Do they live through the winter?"

"I don't think so."

Paul opened the screen door very carefully, and Cressie slipped through. He closed it gently behind them and stood looking at the praying mantis through the screen. It crouched, frail, with long, hairlike antennae, its minute claw feet gripping the wire.

Cressie went into the cottage and began to unpack her blue bag.

Through the cottage door, she could see Paul still staring at the praying mantis. She heard the screen door open and close, and Paul came in with his bandanna handkerchief held gingerly in his left hand.

"I'm bringing her in," he said.

"Where will you put her?"

"In the bathroom."

He let her go on the rim of the tub, after putting a towel over the toilet so that she could not fall in. He closed the door and put the bathmat along the crack so that she could not escape.

"Be careful when you go in," he said to Cressie. "It would be ironic to bring her in from the cold only to have her stepped on."

He sat on the bed.

"It was pretty cold out there," he said.

GEORGE BLAKE has had many of his short stories published in the literary quarterlies, and one of the stories appeared in *Best American Short Stories 1967*.

A Modern Development

MYERSON sat stiff and alert in the front seat between his son and his daughter-in-law, and in the back on his suitcase sprawled the blind mongrel bitch, and as the VW sped out over the Tappan Zee Bridge the smell of the river came into the car and the bitch arched her head toward the window. Last April Myerson had enjoyed immensely sitting beside his wife in the back. It was thrilling to look at the back of his son's dark head, his strong pink neck, the delicate ears of his daughter-in-law. Myerson had squeezed his wife's hand. That meant he was proud to be driven out to the suburbs to spend an afternoon in his son's new house. Imagine, Emma, only thirty-one and such a house. Jerry will be sixty-one before it's paid up, said his wife.

When I retire we'll live with you, he told his son. Of course, papa. Who's kidding who! Myerson laughed. You think mama and me could stand living upstate!

Myerson retired from the fresh produce section of the A&P after thirty years, but they remained in their flat in Brooklyn. But he was still joyfully proud that his son continued to ask him. If something happens to one of us, the other will come and live with you, his wife said. And what's going to happen? asked Myerson. Did they put me in oxygen last month for no reason, answered his wife.

The evening after the funeral they stood over him weaving swift

"A Modern Development"—George Blake, *Kansas Quarterly*, Copyright © 1968 by the University Press of Kansas.

words close around him, making, it seemed, two magical nets, one to carry him off, the other to lower forever where he would never be able to find his furniture, two old hats for deep sea fishing, his postcard collection, the odds and ends of his and his Emma's life together. Doctor Oldendorf from the flat below held his wrist. A house in the country, you should be pleased, Herman! The mongrel Myerson had always ignored he suddenly began to stroke, and she was allowed to come. The parakeets were handed encaged to Mrs. Oldendorf, whose husband detested them.

Now they were leaving the Parkway, and as they turned into the development the truth that he was powerless to leap from the car repeated itself and stood forth solid and real in the night like the hundreds of identical houses. Myerson got out, and the dog stayed close to his leg. I'll carry my suitcase, he said to his son. Of course, papa. The bitch was sniffing the dark which smelled of freshly cut grass. What's wrong, papa? Myerson looked about, skeptical. A temple's within walking? His son and daughter-in-law looked at each other. His son nodded. Good, said Myerson. Not to walk is bad, but to ride in a VW yet! I don't understand, papa. Myerson picked up his suitcase and strode up toward the door. From what I see in the driveways of your fine neighbors neither do they. A car is a car, said his son. You married a philosopher, eh, Ruthy? Tell him a gas oven's also a gas oven. Please, papa. Yes, said his daughter-in-law, let's go in so I can show you your room, and then I'll make coffee. Coffee, no, said Myerson. But tea, yes. Of course in a glass.

The room had not changed since last spring except for the orange-colored accordion door. You just slide it closed when you want to go to bed, said his daughter-in-law. Or privacy, said his son. Yes, or privacy, said his daughter-in-law, see, like this. And then you take off the spread, see it unzips, and the couch becomes a bed. In the morning you put back the pillows and spread and it's a couch again. You shower in here, said his son, standing inside the tin booth.

Myerson looked about, inspecting. He now clasped the blind bitch and sat down on the couch as though testing. His near-sighted eyes blinked at the great waves of light that flashed up from the linoleum floor. The dog hopped down and began to sniff. On the linoleum were blue cowboys and red Indians. Arrows were flying. Myerson desperately, suddenly, wished to express what he felt. But he said, In the city you get thirteen channels, here too? His daughter-in-law touched the rabbit ears. Here too. What do you think this is, papa, the country? his son laughed. Naturally the country, Myerson said. Where can you buy the New York Post, where can you buy cigars? I bet you got to ride five miles. Papa, his son said, this is Rockland County, the smallest county in New York State but the second fastest growing. Housing developments, shopping centers going up all over. Last week a new Korvettes!

Myerson went to the window and looked out into the dark. Future slums! he said. And besides, I don't think I'll like living upstate. Upstate! said his son. Why, papa, we're thirty minutes from Times Square. Speak for yourself, philosopher, Myerson said. He turned to his daughter-in-law. Please, Ruthy, maybe now a glass of tea? Then I'll go to bed. Following them up the short flight of stairs which led to the living room which opened onto the dining room which opened onto the kitchen he said, By the way, Tootsie sleeps downstairs by me, not in garage. Who said anything about Tootsie? his son asked.

After finishing his tea, he said goodnight quite formally and went down into his room. For a moment he stood about. Then he opened his suitcase and took out his nightshirt. The dog no longer sniffed but lay down in the corner, her back flush to the wall. So, Tootsie, what do you think of it? He patted her head and then went over to the sliding door. He slid it back and forth several times, as though practicing. You going to sleep out there or in here? Make up your mind, I'm closing the accordion. The dog padded over and lay down on the foot of the couch.

Myerson could not fall asleep. He sat up and said to the dog, I should've stayed in the city. Who'll I talk to, my God! He got up and walked across the cold floor to the window. Emma, he said. My God, Emma. He parted the drapes and peeked out into the night. A dog barked. For you at least there are other dogs. No, he said, patting the dog's head. They'll be young frisky dogs. Not old, not blind.

He lay down again. He closed his eyes, pressing the tips of two fingers over each lid. Maybe if I smoke a cigar I'll sleep. He could not find a match. He searched through his trousers and suitcoat. He took his shirts, ties, socks, and underwear out of the suitcase. I could go upstairs, he said. He slid open the door.

Who's he talking to? he heard his daughter-in-law say. To the dog, who else? After all, it's my old man's first night here. After all, a strange room, who gets to sleep?

Myerson went back and sat on the edge of the couch. He slid the unlit cigar neatly back into its wrapper. Then he rose and slid the accordion door. He lay in the close darkness. He thought of his son and daughter-in-law. If I had a grandson, he said, we could take walks together. He thought specifically of his daughter-in-law. So her breasts appear full and round from the outside of the dress. But the full and round one can't always do the nursing. Besides what they wear underneath today, who can tell? He pictured the breasts of his daughter-in-law. I'm not so old as all that, he said to himself. Gradually, irresistibly, he saw his wife's body the way it was young in the first years of their nighttimes. Oh, he said to it, oh, you were lovely, each part of you, Emma. Momentarily, with quick seriousness, he touched himself in that place to know the truth of his not being old.

Myerson woke very early. He immediately rose, showered and shaved, and sat very neat in a clean white shirt, polished shoes, by the window whispering to the dog. He thought he would never hear: first, the creak of bed springs? then, naked feet shuffling; at last, the true hello to the day: the flush of the toilet.

In the mornings his son would drive to the city where he worked as an accountant for a chemical firm, and Myerson dried the breakfast dishes for his daughter-in-law. He took a long time, polishing each glass and dish so that it shone. In the beginning, he went with his daughter-in-law shopping. But he could not agree with her about the selection of fresh vegetables, often taking out of her cart those she had chosen and substituting his choices, so that he was no longer asked to accompany her. Thus he took longer and longer to dry the dishes and glasses. It was either this or watch Captain Kangaroo or other such children's programs on TV. But is this all I can do? he asked himself. Simply polish so I can see my face in a dish?

Of course he took short walks, but the development was still in the sawing, banging process of building, only short sections of

roads were laid, vast puddles appeared erratically overnight even
when no rain fell . . . We're on a swamp here! Myerson told his
son one evening over chicken soup by way of making up after saying nasty words to his daughter-in-law: What kind of wife are you,
making chicken soup from a can! But his son was not impressed.
What d'you mean swamp, papa? All right, so we have a little
drainage problem, but wait till they get sewers in.

Winter came, and, as Myerson prophesied, mountains of snow
clogged the unpaved streets, and with spring, water invaded; his
toes made the discovery. What's going on! he yelled upstairs, wak-
ing them up. I should sleep in a boat maybe!

But at least the *development of the development,* as he called
it, was something to take an interest in. Thus, Myerson got lost.
For there seemed no end to the erection of houses. The woods
behind his son's house was felled in one day. Suddenly trees lay
with their roots waving crazily in the March wind. And so farther
and farther Myerson went each day, observing creation. One blond
and blue windy noon he did not appear for lunch. Or, as the
first few stars blinked down, for supper. Myerson stood looking up
surrounded by skeletons of, it seemed, a thousand future houses.
Don't worry, Tootsie. It's just a question of going back by the
way that we came.

It was almost time for the Late Show to start when the police
car deposited him in front of the house. From now on, his son
said, you stay on the street. From the kitchen where he was
scrambling an egg Myerson said, Am I a child to stay on the
street? Please, papa, his daughter-in-law called, come in, sit with
us, it's Paul Muni. Myerson appeared holding his glass of tea and
his plate of scrambled egg. For your information, he told them
both, I once sold Paul Muni carrots. Neither paid attention to him.
He sat down between them on the couch. Carrots, three bunches.
A real gentleman. You could tell. But short. On the screen, taller,
but in life much shorter. His son reached over and turned up the
volume. Myerson rocked back and forth. Let's get it straight, I'm
not staying just by the street!

He found the card pinned inside his coat the next afternoon.
His son's neat writing read: This gentleman is Herman Myerson.
Should you find him lost, please phone Jerry Myerson, his son.
El-6-7102, residence 1234 Forest Lane, Hickory Tree Development.

Ashamed, hurt, what could he do? So I'll leave it pinned. So my
son knows that I know, but we're supposed not to let on? What
can I do?

With a safetypin yet, like a baby, he thought. But Myerson did
not remove the card. He brooded miserably over it for days, at last
going so far as to write a card of his own: This is Jerry Myerson,
the foolish, arrogant son of Herman Myerson, who has shut his
father up behind a false door. He even stole up to the closet in the
hall, a straight pin held fast between forefinger and thumb, but
just as he was about to pin the card above the breast pocket of his
son's suit, he relented. Sitting on the edge of the couch, while figures from the Late-Late-Late Show cast shadows across the
Western scene at his feet, he tore the card to bits.

He took to writing long letters to faceless friends, some of whom
he knew were probably dead. A few answered, telling him of
grandchildren whom he had never seen and would, he knew,
never see. The third week in April a letter arrived at last not from
Mr. Oldendorf but his wife. Hardly a letter really, saying that her
husband had died three weeks ago. My sister Ellie is coming from
Denver to take me back with her, Mrs. Oldendorf wrote.
I don't think I can take the birds as I'm going by bus. What
should I do? You want them back? If I don't hear from you, I'll
know anything I decide is O.K. P.S. Your last letter upset Mr.
Oldendorf very much.

A hobby, papa, his son said, you need to develop a hobby. Golf
you mean maybe? Myerson said.

Even a man with nothing to do can look only so long at houses
being built. So Myerson began to walk farther. One afternoon in town . . . he had ventured that far . . . he stood in front
of a new supermarket. From lamp-poles in its parking lot colored
banners hung limp in the damp air. From somewhere strident
band music poured impatiently, waves of cars screeched into the
parking lot, disgorging, Myerson intuitively sensed, not a human
being above the age of forty. Where are my people? he thought.
Amidst the band music a voice boomed: Grand Opening! Grand
Opening! Caught up in the sea of celebrants, Myerson was swept
inside. It's like something out of Miami! Myerson gasped. Swaying, self-poised, surrounded by TV's, electric can openers, lamps,
freezers, stoves, toy bazookas, hair driers, electric carving knives,

all interspersed with chickens, waving celery stalks, mountains of potatoes . . . above this ocean of hard and soft goods and meats and produce hovered a golden platform on which . . . Myerson rubbed his eyes . . . three girls, in shimmering golden bangles, bounced and jerked like spastics. Cash registers chimed in time to the music and the golden girls. Dazed, Myerson clasped a trembling, hot, damp hand to his chest, suddenly wincing from a sharp, narrow pain. Holding his hand to his chest, he struggled toward one of the glass doors.

And then Myerson heard, *Shalom.*

A man of his time, bald, with a wrinkled throat rippling into a wrinkled face, stood before him holding in each hand, like bright green globes, two heads of lettuce.

Shalom, Myerson replied.

Some grand opening, eh? the stranger asked, taking in everything with a slow sweep of his sad eyes.

Some opening, Myerson agreed.

You're shopping?

Myerson shrugged, biting his lower lip as the pain stabbed again. Only looking. From what you got on, the white apron, you're maybe in produce here?

You don't look so good, the man replied evasively. Perhaps you should take off the coat?

Myerson let himself be helped. Wonderfully, the pain stopped. The man folded the coat and handed it to Myerson, saying, A nice piece of goods.

Myerson wondered, Why not? Is he younger than me? What it would mean! No more drying the dishes! No more Captain Kangaroo! Myerson extended his hand, Herman Myerson.

Samuel Fedder. You sound like from Brooklyn.

Is true. And you?

From Frisco, replied Fedder mirthlessly. I'm now with my daughter and son-in-law.

But you work here? Myerson asked pointedly.

Why else would I be uncrating this lettuce?

So, Myerson mused.

So?

What I mean is maybe they could use me too?

Fedder shook his head skeptically. Pardon me, no insult intended, you're over sixty-five?

Reluctantly, Myerson agreed. So? Aren't you?

Fedder nodded confidently. But my son-in-law, he's manager here.

No!

What's so wonderful?

Myerson took Fedder by the arm. May I speak frankly, Fedder? So, speak.

Thus, in Myerson's mind, it was arranged. Fedder would ask his son-in-law that day if he, Myerson, could be employed in the produce section. Myerson was to report tomorrow to find out.

You have influence with your son-in-law? Myerson asked in parting.

Fedder squinted one eye sagely. My son-in-law doesn't know from what I don't tell him. Believe me, Myerson, your troubles are over.

Rubbing his chest . . . it still smarted strangely . . . Myerson strode toward home. The sun came out, and he, Herman Myerson, who had given up going to Temple after seeing the young rabbi drive up in his yellow VW convertible one Saturday eight months ago, lowered his chin on his chest and prayed.

He told no one but Tootsie.

He spent a sleepless, tossing night. Shaving, his hand shook. In the shower he made the discovery. A short deep scratch on his chest. The pin from the card, of course! Sure enough, the safety pin on the inside lining of his coat was unclasped. About to destroy the card, he thought, No. I'll return today from getting the job and present the card to my son at supper: Is a man who works again lost? Take back your card and feel shame! He repinned the card, dressed, and with a wink that made his daughter-in-law gasp, left the house. About to leave the development, Myerson heard Tootsie barking. Go back, Tootsie! Foolish old dog, go home!

So? Why not? Shouldn't Tootsie also go back into the world? Thus Myerson arrived in the produce section holding his dog in his arms. Fedder was nowhere to be seen. Tootsie squirmed in his arms. Be quiet, be patient. Ah, Fedder, here you are!

Fedder glanced mirthlessly at the dog. So why do you carry your dog? Why not a leash?

Who cares about leash. What did he say?

At your age to walk around with a dog!

So I'll buy her a leash. What did he say, you son-in-law?

Fedder busied himself with bunches of radishes. Forgive me, Myerson, but business is business. You agree?

So? Myerson felt his heart slowing.

It's a question of social security plus the union . . . Please, Myerson, your dog shouldn't perhaps make on the lettuce?

It required all of Myerson's strength to restrain the squirming dog. You mean he said No?

Believe me, Myerson, consider my situation. I'm here three thousand miles from home in my son-in-law's spare room. So what can I do, Myerson, what can I do?

Myerson's heart sank. But Fedder! Tootsie leaped. Myerson's words were buried beneath an avalanche of, first lettuce, then carrots and potatoes, and lastly pineapple, for the dog's last leap carried her over the fruit counter. Both Fedder and Myerson plunged to retrieve the dog but were stopped, buffeted, and knocked down by the landslide of produce. Heedlessly, the blind dog careened toward Hard Goods.

Authority appeared wearing horn-rimmed glasses and six pencils clasped to its shirt: What's going on?

My son-in-law, explained Fedder, helping Myerson to his feet.

A hundred dollars' worth ruined! Authority screamed. Who wants squashed lettuce?

Myerson picked a leaf from his brow. My dog, it . . .

Authority unclipped a pencil, poising its point above his cuff. I'll send you the bill. Your name and address?

Fedder hung his head. Please, his dog . . .

You're working for me or for him? Authority snapped.

The culprit appeared at their feet among the radishes, raised her blind eyes, then arched out her left rear leg.

Out! Out! screamed Authority.

Interrupted in her toilet by Myerson's shaking hands, the dog howled. Cradling her, Myerson fled.

The bill! The bill! My son will get the bill! raced through Myerson's brain. Fedder's son-in-law, a smarty, he'll find me out! Already he's probably phoning!

The sun, a false summer sun, flashed in Myerson's feverish eyes. I got to sit down! I got to think! Still grasping the whining dog, Myerson looked about. But my god, not here on the curb!

Myerson came in time down a road in the clanging process of construction. Bulldozers, steam shovels growled. Beyond the rise of the grassy embankment, Myerson saw them: bleachers rising tier on tier into the sky. Scrambling laboriously through the tall grass, his heavy coat and the dog weighing him down, he puffed to the top. His chest abruptly smarted painfully. The pin, he thought. To take off a heavy coat and hold a squirming dog is not easy. The dog leaped. Surprisingly, it remained by his side, sniffing, attentive. Myerson folded his coat and, the dog trotting beside him, at last arrived to sit on the first step of the bleachers.

He heard them first. The capricious wind whipped their laughter to him from across the field. Led by a stocky woman blowing a whistle, the file of girls advanced to stand at last in a row before the targets. Behind them, an expanse of brick and glass, loomed the school. The dog cocked her head hearing the zing of the arrows. Myerson saw them through a haze. Myerson breathed hard.

You can't sit here, it said.

Myerson looked up. The stocky woman, her whistle bright on her chest, stood a few paces in front of him. So? Why not? Can't an old man rest?

She was standing over him now. You can't sit here and watch my girls.

Myerson lifted his eyes. So, why not? Just to rest, what's wrong?

She placed a sneakered foot on the bleacher and leaned close. I'm telling you you can't sit here and watch my girls. I know about you old men.

Myerson was so hurt and infuriated that he felt dizzy in his head. He almost slipped rising from the bleacher, and in a turmoil of anguish he regained his balance. He strode off very straight, but without knowing so, in the opposite direction. Something was going zing-g-g in his head. The dog trotted beside him looking up with her black, white-centered eyes.

He knew he must sit down immediately to stop the dizziness, but he knew if he sat still for even a moment the woman's meaning would become real to him. He glanced to either side of the road for a spot to rest. Oh, I know the stories they tell about old men, he said aloud.

The spring sun danced in his eyes. His breath came hard. Waiting for a time when no cars passed, he climbed the embankment, moved through the tall grass and lay down on his back. He looked up at white clouds. My God! What a thing to suggest! he muttered.

He could still hear the laughter of the girls, and when he presently sat up, breathing easier now, he saw through the tall grass the athletic field below. The girls were still poised in a straight line. He noticed immediately the girl nearest to him at the end of the line. She had red hair, the color of his wife's hair when she was young. She was a vain, perky girl with long legs. She tossed her red hair in the sunlight. When she hit the bull's-eye she danced and clapped her hands over her head.

The woman was blowing her whistle. The girls picked up their arrows and bows and strolled off in twos and threes toward the school. The girl with red hair was the last and she walked alone. She watched to be sure the teacher wasn't looking, then turned and aimed an arrow straight toward the sun. Myerson was amazed and oddly stirred at the brashness of the girl. He saw that the girl had a delicate, brave Slavic face like his wife's. The woman saw the girl shoot the arrow. She was yelling at her when the arrow stabbed into the earth. Now the girl was climbing the fence. Now she was jumping to the ground. Myerson, now on his knees, grabbed the arrow and extended it up to her. Now the girl was looking down through the grass. Now she was placing her hands in tight fists to her mouth, and uttering high squeals. She ran through the grass toward the fence.

What did I do, Emma? Myerson called. Emma, wait, wait!

The coat, but who cares? The thing is to get to the house!

The phone was still ringing as Myerson entered the house. Trembling now, he went into his son's room to answer it. I'm sorry to bother you, the voice said, but this is Mr. Waldren, Superintendent of New City Junior-Senior High School. You got the wrong number, Myerson said, you got the wrong number.

Myerson crouched on the couch behind the accordion door. He

held the dog on his lap. The phone rang again. He lost count of its ringing.

He heard the VW first, then his son bounding above rushing to answer the phone. Myerson grasped the dog so tightly she squealed and squirmed to the floor. He heard his son and daughter-in-law whisper excitedly; now they were coming down the short flight of steps toward his movable wall. Myerson stared at the wall which, it suddenly struck him, could open and close like walls in dreams, and would quite soon find a way to drive him mad.

Papa? You're in there, papa?

Myerson tiptoed to the wall. Pressing his lips against it, he whispered, So, where else? But do not disturb, do not disturb.

JONATHAN STRONG was born in 1944 and grew up in Winnetka, Illinois. He now lives in Somerville, Massachusetts, and is
at work on a novel. His stories have appeared in *Partisan Review,
Tri-Quarterly, Atlantic* and *Shenandoah,* and his first book, *Tike
and Five Stories,* was published in 1969. The story "Supper-
burger" was the third prize story in the 1967 O. Henry collection.

Patients

TIM was a thirteen-year-old fat boy, the youngest patient on the
ward. I knew him after I had been at the hospital several weeks
and had begun to get myself back in touch. We talked first in the
lounge on a rainy afternoon listening to a Donovan record.

"Jamie," said Tim, "that's your name, right?"

"Right," I said.

"You been here long?" His round face was red because it had
been hard for him to start talking to me.

"Three weeks," I said. "Don't you remember?"

"I been here so long I don't remember who were here when. I
been here eight months. Where you from?"

"Winnetka," I said.

"Is that your car, the turquoise-blue one?"

"Yep."

"You must be rich," he said.

"I wouldn't say so. Where you from?"

"Skokie." He had a bright voice that was starting to get lower
but was mostly high-pitched still. His teeth stuck out a little, but
he could have been handsome if he were not so fat. "I love rainy

days," he said. "I hate sunny days. I love it when it's all gray and soggy."

"Are you kidding?" I said.

"Nope," said Tim. "I really do."

Our ward was in the basement of the building. The lounge was built of gray concrete blocks, and the windows at the ceiling showed clouds and long grass that had not been clipped. There were about fifty of us day patients. A lot of guys were in for drugs, but there were all kinds—straight guys, suburban ladies with nerves, some far-out chicks, old ladies having shock treatments, two old men who played chess. I slowly made friends all around, but I mostly stayed with the guys my age with the same experiences.

I had sat with Tim once before at the O.T. table when he was drawing a bullfrog that turned out quite well. I had been working on a leather belt myself. We had not talked then, but now in the lounge we had. He sat back in his chair, and his T-shirt lifted up to show his round middle. We did not talk anymore for a while but listened to the Donovan record, with the rain in the background. Tim had brought the record in. The lounge had a Victrola donated by someone, but we had to bring our own records. The younger patients were usually the ones who brought records in, though sometimes we had to suffer through some lady's Dean Martin album.

"Hey, Jamie," said Tim, "you like this song?"

"Yep," I said. It was "Mad John's Escape," which I think is a cool song.

"I play the bass guitar, you know," said Tim.

"You do?"

"I couldn't get into a group yet, but I'm learning it."

"Great," I said.

"You play?"

"Some," I said. "Hey, how's the bullfrog?"

"Miss Hedrick wants me to enter it in the hospital art show." Miss Hedrick was the O.T. nurse and a cool chick.

"Great," I said.

"I love frogs," said Tim. "Except you know a funny thing? When I were little, I used to dread lily pads."

"What?"

He was sitting on the edge of his chair, and his friendly eyes were looking at me. "I don't understand it," he said. "I actually dreaded lily pads, I dreaded them."

"How come, do you suppose?"

"I don't know. When I were little, a wet lily pad blew onto my stomach and stuck when I were swimming up in Wisconsin. I couldn't get it off. I were really scared."

"How come you always say were instead of was?"

"I don't know," said Tim. "I just do."

Though he was seven years younger than me, I did feel like being his friend in a way. I found him a cool person. He was very bright for his age, not that he necessarily knew a lot, but he responded with a lot of feelings to things. I myself had been such a dead kid at his age. We went on talking most of the afternoon. I had nothing else to do, having got my work therapy out of the way that morning. We talked about his family and his lack of friends. He brought up his fatness, which I was going to ignore, but I should have known he would want to talk about it. He said Miss Hedrick told him he would look something like Donovan if he lost some weight.

I was a particular friend of Tim's for the rest of my time at the hospital. He said he did not have anyone he could talk to about his life except me and of course his doctor. Every day we sat and talked, particularly about the things he wanted to know about sex. He worried about getting excited seeing girls on the bus on his way to the hospital in the mornings. Once he went three stops beyond the hospital and had to take another bus back because he could not stand up without grossing-out the whole car, as he put it. He wanted to know all about my chick Diane, and every morning he asked me if I had slept with her last night.

I made several other close friends too, but I do not feel like writing about other guys who were into drugs. I talked with them about drugs the same as if we knew each other on the outside. I was trying to get away from all that. My friends and I had spent the winter in one apartment or another turning on. They were still doing it. My doctor and I agreed that while I was in the hospital I would not hang around with my friends outside anymore. I only saw them for an hour or so in the evenings on the way home, and they thought it was very mystical and mind-blowing to be in the hospital. I spent most of my time at home and with some old straight friends from high school. I did not mind the quiet evenings, because my days were busier, and I slept a lot. I soon got sort of attached to the hospital. It was an experience I was having by myself which my friends could not share.

One Monday I wanted to talk to a chick who had just been admitted to the ward, but she was withdrawing, sitting with her head between her knees, rocking a little back and forth. While I was sitting beside her on the green plastic couch in the lounge, I heard a crash in the dayroom. I got up and went in, and it was Tim throwing things. He had tipped over a bridge table and thrown a chair. The ladies at the sewing table were all scared but trying not to notice what he was doing. Mrs. Fisk, the head nurse, was standing facing Tim with her hands on her hips. I realized that though I had thought of him as my friend, I did not know him well enough to do anything at that point. I could not go up to him and try to calm him down because I was not his doctor and I did not know what was involved. That was the hard thing about making friends at the hospital.

They put him on restrictions for the rest of the week. He could not leave the dayroom to go to the gym or the grille or even the lounge, and the attendant had to go to lunch with him. The next day I tried to talk to him, but he did not want to talk. They had upped his dose of Thorazine, and that kept him pretty much subdued. He said he wanted to go to sleep, but it was against the rules to put your head down or close your eyes, and the nurses kept making him sit up.

Tim spent the week at the O.T. table painting. His first bullfrog was so good, he did more of them. He modified them till they were simple heart-shaped green things with one eye and feet. Then he started to do them in all colors. The last one he did was not even a frog but blobs of dark colors which he called "Frog at Night." While he was painting frogs, I wrote a poem about drowning which I hoped one of my friends outside could make into a song, and I submitted it to the hospital newspaper. The girl who had been withdrawing read it and said it was "a real trip."

The next week Tim was off restrictions, and we sat in the lounge again listening to records. I brought in the Cream and the Doors, and Tim brought Tim Buckley. He told me then what had caused his tantrum. He had gone with Lucille, a teeny-bopper who was really tough, into the closet where they stored the gym equipment, and she had got him excited and unzipped his fly, and they had made love sitting on a chair. Tim had told his doctor because he thought he would keep it secret, but his doctor told the entire staff. Tim was so mad when one of the nurses talked to him about it that he started throwing things. Of course his doctor had to tell Lucille's doctor and the staff, but Tim did not understand. Now he wanted to know more about sex. It had not been very good, he said. He felt all funny about it. I told him that for it to be good you had to care something for the girl and you had to do it more relaxedly, in your bed, not in some closet.

That week Tim became troublesome again. Though he was still on Thorazine, he burped very loudly all the time and made the ladies at the sewing table cringe. In our talks he got more dirty-minded and talked about bathroom things a lot. I tried not to laugh and told him I did not want to talk to him if he would not be serious. He showed me a picture he had drawn of himself looking like a meatball standing behind his doctor, who was throwing up into the toilet and saying, "Tim, what a stupid, disgusting patient you are, you make me vomit!" I told him he should show it to his doctor. He said he already had.

My work therapy was changed from the shop to the grille, and Tim used to meet me on my break and have a milk shake. Once I told him to have a Diet-Pepsi instead, but he said Diet-Pepsi made him vomit, and he let out a burp. Everyone in the grille, mostly patients, looked at him.

"Jamie, why am I such a stupid baby?" he said to me.

"You're not stupid," I said.

"I know. You might not believe it. I have a very high I.Q. When I were tested, they said my I.Q. were near genius level."

"I can believe it, Tim," I said.

"But I always act like such a baby. If I were only handsome like you."

"Cut out the milk shakes every day. Have a grapefruit juice if you don't like Diet-Pepsi."

"Oh, puke," said Tim. "You know what that is you're eating?" I was eating a strawberry-rhubarb pie with powdered sugar.

"I hate to think," I said.

"It's bloody snots with curdles." I just kept eating and ignored him.

"I told you I want to talk to you without all that," I said.

"I can't help it. It just comes out. Like puke." He burped.

"Come on, Tim," I said. He looked at me with his friendly eyes.

"Why do you like to talk to me?" he said.

"Because I can really talk to you. I can tell you things. It helps me too, you know."

"But you'll be going soon, and you have all your friends and sexy Diane and your car. I'll be still here for years."

"It won't be years, Tim."

"Nothing will get any better."

"How do you know? Have faith in the place."

"They said I were getting worse."

"Well, I don't know, Tim."

"Why should some people be handsome like you and some ugly and fat?"

"Why don't you just try eating a little less each day?"

"You told me before I should starve myself for a couple of days so my stomach shrinks, and then I wouldn't want as much."

"Well, then try that. Doesn't your doctor give you a diet?"

"I'm mad at him now."

"Tim, you know, being thin doesn't mean you solve your problems." I felt bad saying that to him. To him being thin was a kind of solution.

The following week he was doing well enough to have work therapy. They assigned him to the grille with me, but he kept sneaking brownies and shakes. After a few days he had enough of work. When he was fooling around with the soda jet, it sprayed out onto some customers, and the manager of the grille sent him back to the ward.

I was going to be discharged, and I had told Tim about it. We were working at the O.T. table. I told him as casually as I could, and I immediately suggested that maybe I could still see him, maybe I could pick him up some afternoon and go to a movie. He said they would not allow it because patients cannot see each other on the outside. I told him I would not be a patient anymore, but he was still sure it would not be allowed. Anyway, I felt better saying I would try to see him again. It was going to be a hard thing leaving the hospital after so many weeks, especially the patients I meant something to.

My own therapy had been going pretty well. I would still see my doctor once a week to keep me in line for a while. I planned to get a job and hopefully go back to college in the fall. I really felt I was through with drugs, at least acid and speed for sure. I am not going to get into that kind of thing again.

Tim painted a lot during my last week. He was on restrictions again and taking a lot of Thorazine. I decided to paint too, and I did a psychedelic painting of the bottom of the sea with creatures crawling around. It was an illustration of my poem. Tim drew in a little frog at the top, swimming.

Once I went into the bathroom to clean off my brush, and when I came back the paints on my palette had all been swirled around in a big mess and VOMIT was written across my painting. Tim was not around. I did not see him the rest of the day.

The next day I was in the lounge listening to somebody's Donovan album, *Sunshine Superman.* It was a beautiful day outside, but of course we could not go out. I was glad I was being discharged before the really good weather started. The chick who had been withdrawing had become a pal of mine. She was sitting with me on the green couch making a string of beads. Tim came in and sat down across from us.

"Jamie," he said. "I'm sorry I wrote VOMIT on your painting."

"That's OK."

"I just had to get mad at you, for going."

"That's what I figured."

"I don't have any friends anywhere," he said. He looked up at the windows. "I wish it were gray and soggy out. I hate it like this."

"I asked my doctor about us getting together for a movie or something on the outside," I said. "He said he'd have to talk to your doctor, but it might be all right."

"It doesn't matter," said Tim. "When I get discharged from here, I can see you whenever I like." We sat and listened to the record, and then Mandy, the chick, had to go, so Tim and I were alone. The side was over, and the needle lifted up and started at the beginning again.

"I lost three pounds," said Tim.

"Great."

"You know what this looks like?" He was eating a brownie.

"You don't have to tell me," I said.

"Don't you want to know?" he said, sitting on the edge of the chair.

"I know."

"What?" He was chuckling.

"You know. I'm not saying."

"Did you sleep with Diane last night?"

"Nope," I said.

"I wish I could meet her," said Tim.

"Maybe you will," I said. Suddenly I felt sad encouraging him. I did not know if I would come through. "Dreaded any lily pads lately?" I said.

"Nope. I really used to though."

"You wouldn't make a very good frog."

"I know. But I wish I were a frog."

"Hey, Tim, I've got a present for you." I pulled off the belt I was wearing, the one I made in O.T., and gave it to him. "I'll make you a bet that when you're my age you'll be wearing this buckled at the same notch I do. That's this one." I took out my knife and scratched a cross on the next-to-tightest notch.

"Thanks, Jamie," he said and leaned forward to hold the belt. He put it on, but it did not go around him at all. I had not thought he was that fat.

"Oh, boy," I said. "Well, that's incentive then."

He smiled. Then we said what was hard for us to say. He started. "I'll miss you, Jamie, I'll really miss you here."

"I'll miss you too, Tim," I said. I remember him as he was then: he knew I was going outside and that I would change. It was like leaving him there.

The day I left the hospital it was hard saying good-bye to everyone. I talked with Miss Hedrick for a while, and I wished I had got to know her better before. Our doctors still had not decided whether Tim and I could get together for a movie. My record as a responsible guy was a little fuzzy. Anyway, I could not know all that was involved. Tim was a sick guy.

I promised to write him a song on frogs, something about the

Frog-who-would-a-wooing-go or the Frog Prince. My poem about
drowning was printed in the hospital newspaper that week. I will
put it at the end of this story.

DE OOZY BED

Layin in de oozy bed
Minners swim about me head.
Swarm o waterbug at play
Swim above me all de day.

Now me sinkin in de ooze,
Close me eye an take me snooze.
Do no hear de lates news,
Do no want an do no choose,
Nuttin here fo me to lose
Sleepin down among de ooze.

All dem fish no matter whose,
Comes in greens and comes in blues.
Crabbies crawlin by in twos,
Lobster grabbin at me shoes,
Crawdad an de octopooze
All a-livin in de ooze.

Sink into de oozy slime,
No mo place an no mo time.
All de oozy people knows
Here de place to close de eye.

H. E. F. DONOHUE was born in Trenton, New Jersey, and lives now in New York City. He has written many articles and short stories for magazines and has published two books, *Conversations with Nelson Algren* and *The Higher Animals: A Romance*.

Joe College

"WHAT'LL it be, Mrs. G.?" Fred the grocer said. "Four fine pork chops? Soon it'll only be three, huh Mrs. G.?"

Nell Gahagan silently swore: Say no more.

"Only three," Fred said, "with Mike leaving, huh?"

I would like from you, Nell Gahagan silently said, if along with a better grade of meat you would give me a shut mouth, you wall-eyed Polack-Wop thief. Aloud she asked calmly, "How are the chops tonight, Fred?"

"Just fine. Extra lean," Fred the Hungarian said, adding cheerfully, "Mike leaves soon, doesn't he?"

"Yes," she said. "How's the beef?"

"He'll come back a famous man," Fred said, "and move you all up to Hiltonia."

"The *beef*?" she insisted, knowing now that she would get the whole thing from Fred again. She got it from everybody. Now he will list all the colleges.

"What'll it be?" Fred said. "Princeton or Columbia? I hear he got scholarships to all them places."

The whole thing. Now he will tell me Princeton is fine because it is only half an hour away. The bus, he will tell me, stops right outside the door. Or Columbia, he will tell me, an hour away by train. Or Rutgers. Or Penn. All so close. Close enough so I could still see something of my youngest son who is going away now, leaving me, like all the rest of them.

Happily Fred listed the colleges and their closeness to them, bragging about how Michael had worked for four years in the store weekends. "At least," Fred said, "he's lucky enough to get away to college. When's he leaving, Mrs. G.?"

"Tomorrow," she said, whipping her head away to look at the bread.

"Tomorrow?" he said. "To where?"

"To some place down in Virginia," she snapped, staring back at him. "Just give me the four chops, Fred."

"Well," he said, as he lifted the meat to the chopping block, "you and your Mister must be so proud."

Proud, she asked herself, walking from the store and up the slight hill past the small park to her thin high brick house, planning the rest of her life along with the evening supper, How can I be proud? There were eight of us once. Me and Stephen and the six children. Now there only will be me and Stephen and Grace. Kevin, first, dying on us so young. Holy Mary, Mother of God. The year before the depression. The same year the first one, Patrick, moved out. Then Eddie leaving. Quiet Eddie, rushing out in a rage. Both gone now. Both gone away somewhere in this crazy world war. And even Mary gone, too. God save us. The little librarian as female Marine. Even Grace wants to leave, and not even fifteen. But Michael is the last one, the last son. He was going to move me up to Hiltonia. Like all the rest of them. They'll move me all right. Right into the nuthouse up there on Sullivan's Way. But Michael is leaving us. The one who said he'd never leave. Tomorrow he is gone. Not yet eighteen, not old enough for this war. Not yet. But gone away already away from home and just as far as he can get. So how can I be proud?

"You guys," Grace told her brother, "you guys just kill me."

"Do you wash," Michael said, "or dry?"

"Even the old man won't talk about it," Grace said. "And when *he* won't talk about something, it's time to run for the hills."

"Run," he said, "after we do the dishes."

Grace narrowed her eyes at him. "You can't kid *me*, Mike Gahagan."

"Let's get the dishes done."

"I know why you're not going to Princeton and not going to Rutgers and not going to Penn."

"You wash," he said, "and I'll dry."

"All that talk about going down south for a scholarship *and* a sure job," she said. "Baloney."

"Or," he said, "you wash and I'll dry."

"You," she told him, "you are going to that place down there because *you* are running away. So just don't tell *me* to run, wise guy. I think you are very mean. You're going to let me fold up here and die. I'll end up behind a counter at Woolworth's."

"Or Grant's," he said. "Or Kresges."

"You're so funny," she said. "You're so smart. It's okay for you. You *like* school. You're a dirty grind. So you get your stinking old scholarships and run away. Now I'll be left here all alone."

"Take it easy," he said. "You can leave, too."

"Hooey."

"Start studying a little. You can go to college."

"Bushwah."

"Next year," he said, "when I go into the army, I'll send you part of my pay, okay?"

"What about Mom?" she said. "I can't leave her here alone with *him*. You should leave for college every day. He hasn't been this sober since the last election."

"He's not that much of a drunk."

"You keep on saying that," she said. "You really do keep on saying that. But he acts like a drunk so he might as well *be* a drunk, right? And if he isn't a drunk, then what is he?"

"I don't know."

"Why not, wise guy? He's been talking to you almost every night now for the last four years, playing your stupid chess games. Why *don't* you know everything about him?"

would have good thing for the Church you're not

not?"

"Oh cut it *out*," she said. "Everybody knows you're nuts about somebody else's girl."

He looked at her. Then he dropped the dish towel on the sink and walked toward the stairs that went up two flights to his attic room. He could hear her talking at him as he walked.

"Is that why," she was saying, not believing it, "is *that* why you're running away?"

When Michael came out the back door to say goodnight, his mother and father were sitting in the beach chairs near his mother's flower patch at the far end of their small back yard, and his father noticed Michael was all dressed up for his final visit around and about town. He noticed Michael was wearing his good suit. And, by Jesus, a tie. All he needs now, his father decided, to be a real college type, is a pipe. A briar pipe.

"Where's your pipe?" he asked Michael, hoping he would get no reply, hoping Michael Aloysius Gahagan finally was learning how to handle the razz.

Michael's mother spoke. "Pipe! What pipe! Stephen," she told her husband, "you yourself have always said—"

"Oh for crice sake," Stephen Gahagan said, sipping his beer looking at Michael, keeping a straight face, waiting for Michael's face to break, hoping it wouldn't. If only, he thought, if only I had taught him how to have a little more shrewdness, a little more—What's that word? Guile. That's it. Guile. He's got about as much guile as a hen has balls.

"Smoking," she said, "is supposed to be bad for you."

It's bad, he thought as he lighted one of his cigars, it's bad for a man not to have guile in this world. I should know.

Michael spoke. "He's just kidding, Mom. Some college guys smoke a lot of pipes."

"Oh," she said, turning to look down at her Four O'Clocks which already had closed themselves for the coming night.

Oh, Stephen Gahagan added silently. Oh *and* oh. There he goes again, telling everything he knows. I've tried to tell him not to do that. I have *tried*. I've told him what happens when a man tells all he knows. I told him all about that six months ago when he asked me about college. Dad, he said, what would you say if I said I didn't want to go to college?

"Well," she said, looking over at her high Hollyhocks, "I certainly hope you don't pick up bad things down there."

Dad, he said, what would you say, he said, if I said I wanted to stay here and become a tool-and-die man, to learn your trade? And me, with all of my guile, I said *What?*

"I won't, Mom," Michael said, leaning on the broken wooden fence to look out into the small park which lay below them like a large dark garden beside their house.

We were playing chess, a fine college game, when he asked me about that, about learning my trade, the trade I started learning when I was fourteen, forty years ago, four-oh, in nineteen and ought two, forty years ago when they took me out of the eighth grade to pick the bugs off potato plants so I walked the goddam five miles over to the machine-shop in Stonington near rich Watch Hill where the shop was built out over a pier and I could see the fancy folks on their big boats while I was trying to read my micrometer, to understand the lathe. That machine shop was in a perfect spot for any apprentice. That shop built out over the water was in a very fine place because whenever you made a mistake you could drop the spoiled metal right through the window and down into the sea and then look further on out at the rich and happy folks frolicking on their fancy boats before the foreman came nosing around.

"Well," she said, staring at her dying Blue Flags, "you don't have to go far away just to learn those things."

He has the chance to go to college, at least for a year, at least to become some kind of ninety-day-wonder, and he asks me, the week Corregidor fell, with France gone and China falling and India all ready to drop, he asks me what would I say if he wanted to stay here and learn my trade. My trade. My goddam trade. The trade everybody and his brother said I was a ninny to learn forty years ago when the likes of me could only work the railroads or the cotton mills or on somebody else's building laying brick after goddam brick. Well, for ten years everybody and his brother was right. Nobody wanted a machinist after Hoover got in. Now with this war on that's all they want. This is a war of tools not men. We're losing this war because we've got the men but no tool-and-die men. Maybe Michael-A is not as dumb as he looks. Maybe he

98 *H. E. F. Donohue*

knows this. Maybe that's why he wanted to hang around here and learn my trade. Must be the reason.

"This place," she said, "can teach you all you have to know."

So I gave it to him straight. Shocking him a little. Him that's so easily shocked. But it was the right thing to do. I have to teach him *some*thing. I said that if he was my apprentice I would not teach him all I know. When he said *Why,* looking shocked, I said because if you were my apprentice and I taught you everything I know then you might take my job away from me. That twisted his head.

"The good," she told Michael, "and the not so good."

That got him good. He stumbled around after that saying he could go to college near here or far away and which one did I want him to go to and I said I did not give a tinker's dam if he went to Timbuctu as long as he got the hell away to college. Holy Christ. Who can stand the truth? Not women. Women teach the kids and keep them kids. Even in long pants.

"Long pants," he said to his son. "I did not know you wore long pants, Bucko."

"Sure," Michael said, keeping his face straight.

"Madam," his father said, turning to her, "did you know your baby boy now wears long pants?"

"Aa-yah," she said, speaking from New England in New Jersey.

Her husband let it go, saying to Michael instead, "Where to tonight, Romeo?"

"I'm going to see Miss Gillespie."

"Never heard of her."

"My science teacher," Michael said. "Then I'm seeing Mervin."

His mother spoke. "Mervin the clown," she said. "He has a dirty mind."

"A what?" his father said. "A dirty mouth?"

"He has a fancy mouth," his mother said, "behind which hides a dirty mind."

"Then," Michael quickly said, "we're going to see Lucy, Mervin's girl."

"Mervin's girl," his father said, shaking his head, "or nice little Margie, Mark's girl," his father said. "Just when, Michael-A, are you going to get your own girl?"

"Lucy has a cousin, visiting."

"Watch it, Madam," his father told her. "You are about to lose your boy to some young girl."

"Oh," she said, brushing something away from her lap, "there'll be time enough for all that."

Michael roused himself. "Good night, Mom," he said, kissing her on the top of her head, then stepping back, looking down on her.

She was leaning back in her beach chair, her head tipped over a little to one side, as if she were about to fall asleep, looking at her hands held open in her lap, just before she dozed off. "Be back before midnight," she told her hands. "You're not all packed yet."

"Okay, Mom," he said. Then he turned to his father, who was leaning over in his beach chair, filling his glass from the pitcher of beer. "Good night, Dad." His father finished filling his glass, placing the pitcher carefully back down on the grass, then he leaned back too, also cocking his head, looking up at Michael.

For the short time it took to have his father look at him as he prepared to leave the garden and their lives, Michael thought his father was going to say something to him—a joke perhaps, or their family parting: Take care, safe home. But his father said nothing. His father's face seemed to change as he looked at Michael saying nothing, as if they were playing chess and Michael had made a move his father had not been expecting, not a dangerous move, not one that would end the game or even make his father rearrange his playing, but a move which had not been expected and so had to be understood. His father's face seemed to change as he looked at Michael saying nothing. Then, as in chess, when the move had been understood, his father slowly nodded his head once, knowing something now that Michael, the cause of his understanding, of his increased knowledge, did not understand, did not know.

When Michael reached the street at the end of the driveway, he pretended he could not hear his mother's voice as she called out something to him, continuing down the street past the small park, wondering why he had lied about Lucy's cousin. Mervin was the one interested in the cousin, and Lucy of course could not be interested in him. Thinking of Lucy, he came upon the dark windows of Fred's store where he had worked weekends and when he saw that the small dim nightlight was on, hanging down over the cash register in the back of the store, he remembered he would not see his father again because his father would already be at work in the morning when he awoke to catch his train. He had only said good night to him when it really was good-by. He stopped and put his hands up to the window next to eyes to peer through the dark store to wonder about going back up the hill to say good-by. Then he turned and went on his way to see Miss Gillespie.

"Christmas, I suppose," Miss Gillespie gaily said as she turned away from one of her high curtained windows in her immense living room. Actually, she always reminded herself, it was not *her* living room. It was her mother's. So was the whole huge house. Her mother's. Her mother who was still ensconced in the master bedroom upstairs, bed-ridden there for the last fifteen years. Nan Gillespie turned from the curtained windows, curtained with outer velvet and inner lace, to say to Michael Gahagan, "Christmas and Easter. I'll see all of you again on those proper Christian occasions."

The notion made her smile. A private smile, that certain man had once said. Her private and, that certain man had said, her unnecessarily hurt smile. Oh, she said to herself in high good humor as she regarded Michael Gahagan grimly balancing the Lennox coffee cup and saucer quite properly on his right knee with the Irish linen napkin impeccably laid over his left, oh, she said to herself, you foolish thirty-five-year-old girl, what on earth ever made you once tell Mike Gahagan about that certain man? A poetry-reading contest in Jersey City? Good God!

Indeed, Michael had won the reading for the high school, mooning the Sandburg song about Indian maidens among the Pawpaws. And indeed no one on the English staff could go with him to the state finals in Jersey City. So she, Nan Gillespie, his homeroom teacher and head of the Science Club, had volunteered to go. Interesting. And a wasted trip because he had come in third. The Camden boy had won reading songs from the Bible, but not ho-ho from the Song of Songs, and Second had gone to the Montclair girl mangling some of the Master's mushier sonnets. Michael had seemed so surprised by his loss that she had bought him late supper and they had dawdled over their coffee, so that the only train they could make to get back to town early the next morning

had taken more than two hours. Had it been merely to assuage
some of his deep disappointment during that interminable local
train ride that she had told him something of that certain man in
her pristine life? Of course he first had told her of his feeling for
Margie. His secret. His universally known secret. And she, Nan
Gillespie, B.A., M.S., almost a Ph.D., had blathered almost all
about that man and his sensitivity about her private smile. Nan
Gillespie, she told herself, you are a proper Catholic woman teaching in a fine public school and privately you are a professional
disgrace. And yet, she reminded herself, neither she nor Michael
had ever mentioned the subject again. They had become uncommunicative conspirators about the secret places of their secret
hearts. Why had she trusted him, the one trying to prove so much
of everything, to understand and to rectify all, trying to learn the
connection between war and peace, the law of reflecting mirrors,
the structure of the benzene ring and maidens among the Pawpaws? Do you not know, Michael Gahagan, that to understand
anything is impossible? Scholarship boy soon gone off to this hor-
rendous war, why did you choose that dinky southern school over
our great and good local universities?

"Michael," she said, "would you like more coffee?"

"No, thank you."

He was sitting stiffly upright smack in the middle of her huge
sofa, so she sat in the somber wing-chair, observing him happily.
Before he could become uneasy with her watching him, she said,
"I suppose you do have to go. All of you are going. Mark gone
already. And Don."

"And Seymour."

"And Seymour," she said. "When did Margie go?"

"I'm not sure," he said. "Maybe last week."

All right, she told him silently, we shall not talk about that.
"The whole gang, then," she said, "all gone."

"But not Mervin," Michael said.

"No," she said, "not Mervin. And of all of you, Mervin is the
one who should most go."

"He says that with this war on you should either be fighting
or in a factory and he doesn't think he makes much of a fighter."
He paused, adding, "I'm seeing him tonight, at Lucy's."

She nodded. "Lucy. Mervin's girl."

"He says that with this war on nobody can have a girl because all of us guys are going to get killed."

"Oh?"

"But, you know, he's always clowning around a lot."

"Strange Lucy," she said. "And strange Michael as well."

"Pardon me?"

"Michael," she said, "are you sure you should be doing this—going to that college down there? They have no one in chemistry, you know. And no one in physics or math. And you had once shown an interest in those things. An interest and a capability."

He looked into his coffee cup.

"I'm a science teacher," she said, "and the world needs all the scientists it can get."

He put his cup on the coffee table and folded his napkin.

"We can arrange it," she said. "You can still go to a university near here."

He stood and said, "I told Mervin I'd meet him."

She sat still, looking at him, knowing her talk was over and done. "Very well," she said. "But if there is anything I can do for you, will you let me know?"

He nodded, walking slowly toward her chair. "I just wanted to thank you," he said.

"Of course, Michael."

"I just wanted to thank you for—for—"

"Yes," she said.

"Well," he said, "for being such a good teacher."

She could feel her smile, her private smile, take charge of her face.

"And," he said, standing near her chair, "for being my friend. I've never had a friend like you."

It took time. It took time for her to realize she had removed her hurt and private smile from her face. It took her time to realize she was looking up at him. And it took time for her to understand, as she looked into his face, that he was coming down toward her, slowly and sure, as she sat quite still and sure as he slowly leaned toward her face, to touch her, to brush his slight soft cool kiss on her soft warm cheek. It took time enough so that she did not move immediately when she realized he was moving away from her toward the door, instantly, instantly. It took time to feel he had left the room, the house, had closed the door as he went through it and out onto her front walk and down the street.

When finally she did move, she walked to the nearest high window and looked outside. He would be, of course, she knew, now out of her sight. Yet she stood gazing for a time through the large window out into the night. Then she carefully drew the velvet draperies, the velvet she dearly loved, over the fine clean delicate lace before she moved through the large living room and up the grand stairs to the master bedroom where she would begin to read ancient English poetry to her mother until her mother felt safe enough to fall carefully and privately asleep, after which, with her mother safe on the shores of sleep, she could begin to wonder why she had not cleared away their coffee cups, hers and Michael's, and why she had not turned off the lights, and why she had not yet locked the large front door.

"Have you read Veblen yet?" Mervin snapped. "Have you read Nietzsche? Freud?"

Michael looked down at the ground.

"Stop looking at my shoes," Mervin said.

Still looking down, Michael shook his head.

"You are looking at my shoes," Mervin said, "just because they curl up in front."

"I am not looking at your shoes," Michael said, "I'm looking at the ground."

"Any guy," Mervin said, "who would lie about my nutty girl, would lie about looking at my curled-up shoes."

Michael stepped into the street to look for the bus, his bus or the one which would be Mervin's.

"What went on back there?" Mervin said, sounding serious for the first time in his life. "What went on with you and Lucy while I was outside counting the stars with her sexy cousin?"

"Nothing," Michael said, seeing neither bus.

"Read Veblen," Mervin snapped. "Read Nietzsche. And Freud. Then you'll know why you lie so much, why you lie about Lucy, who does not care about *any* guy and now she says she's going to miss *you*."

Michael looked down at the ground, at Mervin's curled-up shoes.

"*Now,*" Mervin said, "are you looking at my shoes?"

"Yes," Michael said. Mervin was also looking down at his shoes.

"Well," Mervin said, "that's something. And I suppose you think my shoes curl up because I'm always walking in the rain?"

"That's what you keep telling me."

"Well, you are wrong, r-u-n-g! My shoes curl up because my toes do, too. Understand me," Mervin added, "I do walk in the rain. That way I do not bump into boring people while walking backwards. But the good white anglo-saxon God in heaven gave me curled-up toes so that if I *am* trapped by some boring type, which may be almost anybody, I can, while listening to their deadly talk, rock-rock-rock myself to beddy-by sleep, right?"

"Right," Michael said, still looking at Mervin's shoes.

"You betcha. But the rocking is not the hard part of falling asleep on your feet. The hard part is keeping the eyes stark staring wide open while you rock yourself to sleep. The tricky part with the eyes open is *not* to get a bright look in them or else the person boring you to death will think you are very interested. Got that?"

"Right," Michael said, noticing that Mervin was beginning to rock back and forth on his curled-up shoes.

Mervin pushed back the bit of light hair that kept falling over his left eye. It fell back down again. Mervin made a sound with his mouth. "I don't know why I'm telling you this," he said, "because it has already started."

Michael did not ask.

"Started," Mervin said again. "Commenced. Begun. You haven't even left town yet and already you're a Joe College."

Michael would not ask.

"A Joe College," Mervin said, opening his blue eyes quite wide, "is a lady killer see, who lies to his friends and then goes far away from home. That way nobody knows he's a lying lady killer Joe College type."

Michael glanced down the road for the bus.

"But," Mervin said, "but-but, the old goat said, I bet you've always been the Joe College type, always lying. Aren't you the guy who didn't know anything about girls? And tonight Lucy tells me she is going to miss you. Lucy! The girl who would not mind missing the Second Coming of Christ."

Michael gave him a hard look.

"Okay, okay, Joe Catholic," Mervin said. "No more blasphemy. But you even lied about Margie, about not caring about her. Wouldn't even go say good-by when she left for Columbia. Things like that. And you haven't read Veblen yet. I *told* you to read Veblen and you said you would and you haven't, right?"

Michael shook his head.

"See," Mervin said, turning to the nearest telephone pole, hands outstretched. "He hasn't read Veblen yet," he told the pole. "He hasn't read Nietzsche and he's still worried about his soul. Catholics get away with philosophical murder. Maybe that's why he doesn't have to read Freud. Not after Lucy. Not after to-night."

Michael sat down on the curb of the empty road while Mervin went on talking to the pole, rocking up closer to it, reading aloud the small metal sign nailed to the pole above his head.

"A new pole," Mervin told Michael, "with its own new number. What's your number, Joe College? You're so ready to fight all the fascists you don't even know what you're fighting for. Or against. You're dumb. I don't know why I talk to you. All you read is American history and that guy Hemingway. That big bird. That earnest hummingbird. Why do I talk to you? You don't know anything. I am not going to talk to you. I am stopping all talk to you. I have stopped."

He sat on the curb next to Michael, pulled out a green stem from a weed nearby and put it in the corner of his mouth.

"Murder," Mervin said. "A philosophical crime. Aren't you the guy who was going to work in the factory with his father? We were all going to work in the same plant, right? That way at least I could get you to read real people, like Veblen or Nietzsche. Or Freud. Maybe even a little Plato."

"I've read Plato," Michael said. "At least part of The Republic."

"At least," Mervin said, ignoring him, speaking around the weed in his mouth, "at least I could still talk to you about books, if you were still around. I don't mind talking to you even if you don't know anything, because there's nobody else around. I don't mind talking to you even if you always do try to hog the whole con-versation."

"I know one thing," Michael said. They both stood. Mervin's bus was coming.

"All you know," Mervin said, throwing away the weed, brushing his pants, "is that you're going to Virginia to hear the mocking-bird a-singing in the lilac bush."

"You," Michael said, "should get out of this town."

"Just remember, in the dark all cats are gray."

"Now what does *that* mean?" Michael said. The bus was slowing to a stop, wheezing.

"Oh-oh!" Mervin said, throwing up his arms again. "Have pity on those poor Virginia virgins!"

"Leave this town."

"Listen, Joe College," Mervin said, "somebody's got to stay." Then he was stepping up into the bus, already speaking to the bus-driver before the doors closed so that Michael could hear him barking at the driver as the bus began to pull away: "You read Veblen yet? Nietzsche? Freud?"

It was almost one o'clock when Michael faced his home and for a moment he was filled with the old fear that something terrible had happened because almost every light in the house was on. But no one was downstairs and no light was coming from under Grace's door on the second floor. At the other end of the hall he found his father in bed fast asleep with his glasses still on his sagging face, his mouth half hung open under the bright reading light, the small digest magazine standing on his chest like a little paper pup tent before the high belly hill. He sleeps the way he eats, Michael thought, and the way he walks and talks, the way he tries to read everything—always hungry. He's hungry right now, for sleep. The bully drunk, everybody says. The every night shouting drinking drunk who gets up every morning at six to work as a master precision machinist. Confusing.

He listened. Someone was moving about up in his attic room. Leaving his factory father to his magazine dreams, Michael slowly climbed the attic stairs knowing who was up there and knowing what she was doing. It was his mother, packing his clothes.

She would not look at him and she did not complain about his being late. "You don't have enough socks," she said. "I'll get some more downstairs."

As soon as she had gone he undressed down to his underwear and got into bed. Maybe that will make her go. She's finished up here. All the packing, except for the extra socks, was done. The one large old suitcase was full and ready to be closed. She had been polishing his second pair of shoes when he came in. Sharper than the serpent's tooth, he knew, is the ungrateful son. But he wanted to be alone. He wanted to be alone to think about things. To think about Lucy and what she had done.

Mervin, as usual, was right. He did not know much about girls. He knew that Margie was pure and perfect. He knew Lucy was supposed to be quite wild. So when Mervin said he was going to take her pretty cousin out to count the stars, Michael figured that was the signal for him to go home because he knew Lucy could not be interested in being alone with him. As he had headed for her front door Lucy had called out, "*Where* do you think *you're* going, you rusty old pot."

Lucy talked that way a lot but it was only the second time she had ever talked to him at all. Lucy, with her long light hair gently falling on her shoulders, with her soft grey sweater sleeves pushed up over her smooth elbows, one string of beads moving over her breasts when she moved, with her plaid skirt almost swinging open down one side above her long bare legs, her heels so high and ankles so thin they seemed ready to break, Lucy, who could look like an evil saint one day and the next day look like a cheerful bum, she had spoken straight at him only once before after he had won the big speech contest talking about how to solve all the problems of the world by paying attention to "The Future of Youth!" and everybody had congratulated him leaving him alone in front of his locker feeling pretty good when Lucy had walked by without stopping and said, "You don't know *any*thing about *any*thing, Gaggle-head."

She had not spoken to him again, not until tonight. Not even when they had passed each other alone late one day in the long hall outside the gym where she had come from swimming and he had come after his track shower feeling cleanly strong. Not even in New York on the Science Club trip when he had found her sitting next to him alone in the last row of the Planetarium, under the darkened dome of soft music and moving lights. He knew it was not her fault. What could he ever say back? So when she had razzed him earlier that night he had to think about it standing at her door deciding she was only telling him the truth. So he had

nodded once at her and she had made fun of him, nodding
back so hard her beautiful hair had bounced. Then she had
said, "Oh, come on back in here."

As usual, he had done as he was told. He sat with her on the
sofa as she told him to, even though he could not answer her
questions.

—Mervin says, she had said, Mervin says you're going far away
to a Protestant college to become a Catholic priest. Is that true?
That Mervin.

—Why are you shaking your head? she had said. It sounds
crazy to me. Are you crazy?
Why did I nod?

—Good, she had said. So am I. Ah, she had said, at least you can
smile. What else can you do? What else besides just sitting there
shrugging? Can you put your arms around me? No, not *that* way.
I'll show you. I turn around like this, see? And I sort of lie down.
My God! Mervin was right. You don't know anything, do you?
Why did I shake my head?

—In that case, she had said, her wide blue eyes calm and cool,
I'll show you some things. To remember when you are far away
with those Virginia girls. You do this with the hands. Now come
down here as you bring my head up and I'll show you what to do
with your mouth.

Michael lay back in bed remembering. He remembered that
kissing her had been different, the way she finally showed him
how to kiss. He remembered she had made fun again, asking why
he had to go so far away to become a priest. He remembered
hardly hearing her, wanting to kiss her again, and doing it, kissing
her, and remembering as he kissed her how she had moved his
hand up under her sweater until he knew that was all she was
wearing there. He remembered touching her there, remembering
that touch as he now knew he would never remember anything
else no matter how long he lived.

"I've got the socks," his mother said, puffing up the stairs. "My!"
she said. "Those stairs." Going over to the suitcase, not looking
at him as he sat up in bed, she said, "Now, do we have everything?"

The thing to do, he told himself, is to remember only certain
things.

"I sewed name labels on each thing," she said, tucking the socks into the corners of the suitcase, "so you'll always know what's yours."

Remember, he told himself, only the good things. He thought of Lucy. Well then, he told himself, remember only the real things.

"And those laundry cases," his mother said, "they hardly cost anything. I'll send you one later with your heavier things," she said, pressing the lapels of his jacket between the palms of her hands. "All you have to do is mail me your used clothes," she said, "and I can have them back to you, washed and pressed, within a week."

She sat down at the foot of the bed to get her breath back from the stairs and from her speech, still not looking at him, before she went on to talk of other things. Why, he wondered, do I hardly hear her? I should be listening to these things, remembering.

She was saying something about how his father was not going to work that morning, about how his father was going to drive him to the train. For the first time in God knows when his father was going to be late for work. He tried to remember that. She was saying something about how Grace had saved to buy his going-away gift, a fancy fountain-pen. He must remember that. She was saying something about how proud Fred was that he was getting away to college, if only for a year. Everyone was so proud of him, she was saying, particularly his father. As he tried to remember that, he heard the sense and tone of what she was saying change, knowing now why he was hardly hearing her, hardly remembering, knowing he had sensed what was coming, what she was saying now as her words changed in sense and tone.

For now she was saying something about his going so far away. "Oh," she was saying, not yet looking at him, twisting her hands in her lap, "oh, I promised myself I wouldn't do this. I swore I wouldn't act like an old fool."

And now he knew he would remember everything because he knew once again that knowing what was coming would not stop it from happening.

"Both of them," she was saying, shaking her head, "both your brothers gone away in this war. And your sister, Mary, too. Isn't that enough?"

And Kevin, he told himself, Kevin, my dead brother, the apple of her eye. Will she mention him?

"It isn't just for me," she was saying. "Not just for me do I want you some place close. Grace needs someone. She needs a brother. She talks to you. And your father. He needs somebody, too."

Soon, now he knew, she would turn to look at him as she spoke. And what she says is true.

"Oh," she was saying, as if surprised by her fight against the coming tears, "your father would not say so. Not even to me. Not in years have I heard him mention anything he needs. But he is going to feel alone. It's not just the chess. It's not just because by playing chess with you and talking about everything he has been drinking less. I can always handle his drinking. It is the talking with you that has made him feel less alone. The talking. The talking."

She, too, he told himself, she too knows what is coming. And she knows that knowing will not help, even if what she says is true.

"He must talk to someone," she was saying, the tears beginning to come, "and he must talk to someone, don't you see, to somebody besides me. To another man in his family. He has to talk to one of his children, to one of his sons. He has to be able to say whatever he wants to say and with you gone so far who can he talk to that way?"

He had not known the tears were going to come. And neither did you, he told her silently. You seem surprised by the tears. Has she, have they all, got me?

"Please," she was saying, looking at him finally, the streaks on her cheeks glistening, her head slowly bowing down to rest on the bed, talking into the covers, her words muffled as if coming from underground, "please stay somewhere near. If only for the year." She raised her head angrily and, looking away again, wiped at her eyes with the palms of her hands before searching for and finding a handkerchief in her apron pocket. "Then," she was saying, blowing her nose, "this war can have you. Maybe," she was saying, "it'll be over then, over and done. Will you," she was saying, staring at the wall, "will you please stay nearby? Will you please, Michael, my son?"

Yes, he had to decide, yes, he had to confess, lying back down

again on his bed with his hands behind his head, yes, they've
got me. All of them. His mother had him and so did his sister,
Grace, and even Kevin had him, the brother taken by early death.
Taken or blest? And Miss Gillespie's reliance had him, her world
of science had him in her large curtained room, and his mother's
surprised tears had him and Grace's hurt, too, and Miss Gillespie's
eyes and Mervin's curled-up toes in his curled-up shoes, they all
had him, and he knew from his remembered touch of Lucy how
much Lucy knew she had him, too. And going to college had
him, he knew, and the war the world called number Two, and the
whole small world in God's universe and all the angels in Heaven
and Hell and in Limbo. All, everybody, had him, but one. And because of that one, he, Michael-A, Romeo, Bucko, could say to his
mother in answer to her plea what he had to say as he knew he
would, as she seemed to know he would. So, in a quiet voice, a
voice sounding older and better than his own, a voice he could
remember as he would remember her quiet acceptance of what he
would say, her calm response to the one word he would reply
quietly and low, he answered her question with a calm and kind
and sure, "No."

They got to the station fifteen minutes ahead of the train and
Michael's father stayed with the car while she went down to the
platform with him. After the train had come in and moved out
south, they drove for a while before she turned to her husband
and said, "Drop me off at Fred's will you, Stephen?"

"All right, Nell," he said.

They drove for a while and then she asked him, "What would
you like for supper?"

He thought for a moment. "Breast of guinea hen," he said,
"under glass."

"Go on," she said, looking at him.

"Or," he said, watching the road, "small squid with large
snails."

She shuddered.

"With a college man in the family," he said, "we have to start
eating fancy."

"The hell we do," she said.

"Such language," he said. "Have you been drinking?"

They were in front of Fred's store. She sat, thinking. Then she said, "Would you like to go to a movie tonight?"

"I don't know. What's playing?"

"I'll find out from Grace," she said, "and we'll let you know at supper."

"All right, Nell."

She got out of the car, closed the door, and looked at him through the window before she said, "Drive carefully."

He nodded slowly. Then he drove away to work as she watched him go. She walked into Fred's store.

Fred's face brightened when he saw her. "What'll it be, Mrs. G.?" he said. "Some nice neat sole? Or fresh ground hamburger meat? Or trim flank steak, maybe?"

"We'll see, Fred," she said quietly. "We'll just take our time and see."

"Fine," Fred said, beaming. "That's just fine with me."

JAMES SALTER was born in New York City in 1926. He has had three novels published, the best known of which is *A Sport and a Pastime*.

Am Strande von Tanger

BARCELONA at dawn. The hotels are dark. All the great avenues are pointing to the sea.

The city is empty. Nico is asleep. She is bound by twisted sheets, by her long hair, by a naked arm which falls from beneath her pillow. She lies still, she does not even breathe.

In a cage outlined beneath a square of silk that is indigo blue and black, her bird sleeps, Kalil. The cage is in an empty fireplace which has been scrubbed clean. There are flowers beside it and a bowl of fruit. Kalil is asleep, his head beneath the softness of a wing.

Malcolm is asleep. His steel-rimmed glasses which he does not need—there is no prescription in them—lie open on the table. He sleeps on his back and his nose rides the dream world like a keel. This nose, his mother's nose or at least a replica of his mother's, is like a theatrical device, a strange decoration that has been pasted on his face. It is the first thing one notices about him. It is the first thing one likes. The nose in a sense is a mark of commitment to life. It is a large nose which cannot be hidden. In addition, his teeth are bad.

At the very top of the four stone spires which Gaudi left unfinished the light has just begun to bring forth gold inscriptions too pale yet to read. There is no sun. There is only a white silence.

"Am Strande von Tanger"—James Salter, *The Paris Review*, This work first appeared in issue no. 44 (Fall 1968) of *The Paris Review*.

Sunday morning. The early mornings of Spain. A mist covers all of the hills which surround the city. The stores are closed.

Nico has come out on the terrace after her bath. The towel is wrapped around her, water still glistens on her skin.

"It's cloudy," she says. "It's not a good day for the sea."

Malcolm looks up.

"It may clear," he says.

Morning. Villa-Lobos is playing on the phonograph. The cage is on a stool in the doorway. Malcolm lies in a canvas chair eating an orange. He is in love with the city. He has a deep attachment to it based in part on a story by Paul Morand and also on an incident which occurred in Barcelona years before: one evening in the twilight Antonio Gaudi, mysterious, fragile, even saintlike, the city's great architect, was hit by a streetcar as he walked to church. He was very old, white beard, white hair, dressed in the simplest of clothes. No one recognized him. He lay in the street without even a cab to drive him to the hospital. Finally he was taken to the charity ward. He died the day Malcolm was born.

The apartment is on Avenida General Mitre and her tailor, as Nico calls him, is near Gaudi's cathedral at the other end of town. It's a working class neighborhood, there's a faint smell of garbage. The site is surrounded by walls. There are quatrefoils printed in the sidewalk. Soaring above everything, the spires. *Sanctus, sanctus*, they cry. They are hollow. The cathedral was never completed. Its doors lead both ways into open air. Malcolm has walked, in the calm Barcelona evening, around this empty monument many times. He has stuffed peseta notes, virtually worthless, into the slot marked: donations to continue the work. It seems on the other side they are simply falling to the ground or, he listens closely, a priest wearing glasses locks them in a wooden box.

Malcolm believes in Malraux and Max Weber: art is the real history of nations. In the details of his person there is evidence of a process not fully complete. It is the making of a man into a true instrument. He is preparing for the arrival of that great artist he one day expects to be, an artist in the truly modern sense which is to say without accomplishments but with the conviction of genius. An artist freed from the demands of craft, an artist of concepts, generosity, his work is the creation of the legend of himself. So long as he is provided with even a single follower he can believe in the sanctity of this design.

He is happy here. He likes the wide, tree-cool avenues, the restaurants, the long evenings. He is deep in the currents of a slow, connubial life.

Nico comes onto the terrace wearing a wheat-colored sweater.

"Would you like a coffee?" she says. "Do you want me to go down for one?"

He thinks for a moment.

"Yes," he says.

"How do you like it?"

"*Solo*," he says.

"Black."

She likes to do this. The building has a small elevator which rises slowly. When it arrives she steps in and closes the doors carefully behind her. Then, just as slowly, she descends, floor after floor, as if they were decades. She thinks about Malcolm. She thinks about her father and his second wife. She is probably more intelligent than Malcolm, she decides. She is certainly stronger-willed. He, however, is better-looking in a strange way. She has a wide, senseless mouth. He is generous. She knows she is a little dry. She passes the second floor. She looks at herself in the mirror. Of course, one doesn't discover these things right away. It's like a play, it unfolds slowly, scene by scene, the reality of another person changes. Anyway, pure intelligence is not that important. It's an abstract quality. It does not include that cruel, intuitive knowledge of how the new life, a life her father would never understand, should be lived. Malcolm has that.

At ten thirty, the phone rings. She answers and talks in German, lying on the couch. After it is finished Malcolm calls to her,

"Who was that?"

"Do you want to go to the beach?"

"Yes."

"Inge is coming in about an hour," Nico says.

He has heard about her and is curious. Besides, she has a car.

The morning, obedient to his desires, has begun to change. There is some early traffic on the avenue beneath. The sun breaks through for a moment, disappears, breaks through again. Far off, beyond his thoughts, the four potent spires are passing between shadow and glory. In intervals of sunlight the letters on high reveal themselves: *Hosanna.*

Smiling, at noon, Inge arrives. She is in a camel skirt and a blouse with the top buttons undone. She's a bit heavy for the skirt which is very short. Nico introduces them.

"Why didn't you call last night?" Inge asks.

"We were going to call but it got so late. We didn't have dinner till eleven," Nico explains. "I was sure you'd be out."

No. She was waiting at home all night for her boyfriend to call, Inge says. She is fanning herself with a postcard from Madrid. Nico has gone into the bedroom.

"They're such bastards," Inge says. Her voice is raised to carry. "He was supposed to call at eight. He didn't call me until ten. He didn't have time to talk. He was going to call back in a little while. Well, he never called. I finally fell asleep."

Nico puts on a pale grey skirt with many small pleats and a lemon pullover. She looks at the back of herself in the mirror. Her arms are bare. Inge is talking from the front room.

"They don't know how to behave, that's the trouble. They don't have any idea. They go to the Polo Club, that's the only thing they know."

She begins to talk to Malcolm.

"When you go to bed with someone it should be nice afterwards, you should treat each other decently. Not here. They have no respect for a woman."

She has green eyes and white, even teeth. He is thinking of what it would be like to have such a mouth. Her father is supposed to be a surgeon. In Hamburg. Nico says it isn't true.

"They are children here," Inge says. "In Germany, now, you have a little respect. A man doesn't treat you like that, he knows what to do."

"Nico," he calls.

She comes in brushing her hair.

"I am frightening him," Inge explains. "Do you know what I finally did? I called at five in the morning. I said, why didn't you call? I don't know, he said—I could tell he was asleep—what time is it? Five o'clock, I said. Are you angry with me? A little, he said. Good, because I am angry with you. Bang, I hung up."

Nico is closing the doors to the terrace and bringing the cage inside.

"It's warm," Malcolm says, "leave him there. He needs the sunlight."

She looks in at the bird.

"I don't think he's well," she says.

"He's all right."

"The other one died last week," she explains to Inge. "Suddenly. He wasn't even sick."

She closes one door and leaves the other open. The bird sits in the now brilliant sunshine, feathered, serene.

"I don't think they can live alone," she says.

"He's fine," Malcolm assures her. "Look at him."

The sun makes his colors very bright. He sits on the uppermost perch. His eyes have perfect, round lids. He blinks.

The elevator is still at their floor. Inge enters first. Malcolm pulls the narrow doors to. It's like shutting a small cabinet. Faces close together they start down. Malcolm is looking at Inge. She has her own thoughts.

They stop for another coffee at the little bar downstairs. He holds the door open for them to go in. No one is there—a single man reading the newspaper.

"I think I'm going to call him again," Inge says.

"Ask him why he woke you up at five in the morning," Malcolm says.

She laughs.

"Yes," she says. "That's marvelous. That's what I'm going to do."

The telephone is at the far end of the marble counter. Nico is talking to him and he cannot hear.

"Aren't you interested?" he asks.

"No," she says.

Inge's car is a blue Volkswagen, the blue of certain air-mail envelopes. One fender is dented in.

"You haven't seen my car," she says. "What do you think? Did I get a good bargain? I don't know anything about cars. This is my first. I bought it from someone I know, a painter, but it was in an accident. The motor is scorched.

"I know how to drive," she says. "It's better if someone sits next to me, though. Can you drive?"

"Of course," he says.

He gets behind the wheel and starts the engine. Nico is sitting in the back.

"How does it feel to you?" Inge says.

"I'll tell you in a minute."

Although it's only a year old, the car has a certain shabbiness. The material on the ceiling is faded. Even the steering wheel seems abused. After they have driven a few blocks, Malcolm says,

"It seems all right."

"Yes?"

"The brakes are a little weak."

"They are?"

"I think they need new linings."

"I just had it greased," she says.

Malcolm looks at her. She is quite serious.

"Turn left here," she says.

She directs him through the city. There is a little traffic now but he seldom stops. Many intersections in Barcelona are widened out in the shape of an octagon. There are only a few red lights. They drive through vast neighborhoods of old apartments, past factories, the first vacant fields at the edge of town. Inge turns in her seat to look back to Nico.

"I'm sick of this place," she says. "I want to go to Rome."

They are passing the airport. The road to the sea is crowded. All the scattered traffic of the city has funneled onto it, buses, trucks, innumerable small cars.

"They don't even know how to drive," Inge says. "What are they doing? Can't you pass?

"Oh, come on," she says. She reaches across him to blow the horn.

"No use doing that," Malcolm says.

Inge blows it again.

"They can't move."

"Oh, they make me furious," she cries.

Two children in the car ahead have turned around. Their faces are pale and reflective in the small rear window.

"Have you been to Sitges?" Inge says.

"Cadaques."

"Ah," she says. "Yes. Beautiful. There you have to know some-one with a villa."

The sun is white. The land lies beneath it the color of straw. The road runs parallel to the coast past cheap bathing beaches, camp grounds, houses, hotels. Between the road and the sea is the railroad with small tunnels built beneath it for bathers to reach the water. After a while this begins to disappear. They drive along almost deserted stretches.

"In Sitges," Inge says, "are all the blonde girls of Europe. Swe-den, Germany, Holland. You'll see."

Ah, the hunter's nose. It deflects just slightly, imperceptibly, in her direction.

"The brown eyes of the Spaniards are irresistible to them," she says.

She reaches across him to blow the horn.

"Look at them! Look at them crawling along!

"They come here full of hopes," Inge says. "They save their money, they buy little bathing suits you could put in a spoon, and what happens? They get loved for one night, perhaps, that's all. The Spanish don't know how to treat women."

Nico is silent in the back. On her face is the calm expression which means she is bored.

"They know nothing," Inge says.

Sitges is a little town with damp hotels, the green shutters, the dying grass of a beach resort. There are cars parked every-where. The streets are lined with them. Finally they find a place two blocks from the sea.

"Be sure it's locked," Inge says.

"Nobody's going to steal it."

"Now you don't think it's so nice," she says.

They walk along the pavement the surface of which seems to have buckled in the heat. All around are the flat, undecorated façades of houses built too close together. Despite the cars, the town is strangely vacant. It's two o'clock. Everyone is at lunch.

Malcolm has a pair of shorts made from rough cotton, the blue glazed cotton of the Tauregs. They have a little belt, slim as a finger, which goes only half way around. He feels powerful as he puts them on. He has a runner's body, a body without flaws, the body of a martyr in a Flemish painting. One can see vessels laid like cord beneath the surface of his limbs. The cabins have a concrete back wall and hemp underfoot. His clothes hang shapeless from a peg. He steps into the corridor. The women are still undressing, he does not know behind which door. There is a small mirror hung from a nail. He smooths his hair and waits. Outside is the sun.

The sea begins with a sloping course of pebbles sharp as nails. Malcolm goes in first. Nico follows without a word. The water is cool. He feels it climb his legs, touch the edge of his suit and then with a swell, he tries to leap high enough, embrace him. He dives. He comes up smiling. The taste of salt is on his lips. Nico has dived, too. She emerges close by, softly, and draws her wetted hair behind her with one hand. She stands with her eyes half-closed, not knowing exactly where she is. He slips an arm around her waist. She smiles. She possesses a certain, sure instinct of when she is most beautiful. For a moment they are in serene dependence. He lifts her in his arms and carries her, helped by the sea, towards the deep. Her head rests on his shoulder. Inge lies on the beach in her bikini reading *Stern*.

"What's wrong with Inge?" he says.

"Everything."

"No, doesn't she want to come in?"

"She's having her period," Nico says.

They lie down beside her on separate towels. She is, Malcolm notices, very brown. Nico can never get that way no matter how long she stays outside. It is almost a kind of stubbornness as if he, himself, were offering her the sun and she would not accept.

She got this tan in a single day, Inge tells them. A single day! It seems unbelievable. She looks at her arms and legs as if confirming it. Yes, it's true. Naked on the rocks at Cadaques. She looks down at her stomach and in doing so induces it to reveal several plump, girlish rolls.

"You're getting fat," Nico says.

Inge laughs. Two Spanish youths are strolling past along the sea.

"They are my savings," she says.

They seem like that, like belts, like part of some costume she is wearing. When she lies back, they are gone. Her limbs are clean.

Her stomach, like the rest of her, is covered with a faint, golden down.

She is talking to the sky. If she goes to America, she recites, is it worthwhile to bring her car? After all, she got it at a very good price, she could probably sell it if she didn't want to keep it and make some money.

"America is full of Volkswagens," Malcolm says.

"Yes?"

"It's filled with German cars, everyone has one."

"They must like them," she decides. "The Mercedes is a good car."

"Greatly admired," Malcolm says.

"That's the car I would like. I would like a couple of them. When I have money, that will be my hobby," she says. "I'd like to live in Tangier."

"Quite a beach there."

"Yes? I will be black as an Arab."

"Better wear your suit," Malcolm says.

Inge smiles.

Nico seems asleep. They lie there silent, their feet pointed to the sun. The strength of it has gone. There are only passing moments of warmth when the wind dies all the way and the sun is flat upon them, weak but flooding. An hour of melancholy is approaching, the hour when everything is ended.

At six o'clock Nico sits up. She is cold.

"Come," Inge says, "we'll go for a walk up the beach."

She insists on it. The sun has not set. She becomes very playful.

"Come," she says, "it's the good section, all the big villas are there. We'll walk along and make the old men happy."

"I don't want to make anyone happy," Nico says, hugging her arms.

"It isn't so easy," Inge assures her.

Nico goes along sullenly. She is holding her elbows. The wind is from the shore. There are little waves now which seem to break in silence. The sound they make is soft, as if forgotten. Nico is wearing a grey tank-suit with an open back, and while Inge plays before the houses of the rich, she looks at the sand.

Inge goes into the sea. Come, she says, it's warm. She is laughing and happy, her gaiety is stronger than the hour, stronger than the cold. Malcolm walks slowly in behind her. The water *is* warm. It seems purer as well. And it is empty, as far in each direction as one can see. They are bathing in it alone. The waves swell and lift them gently. The water runs over them, laving the soul.

At the entrance to the cabins the young Spanish boys stand around waiting for a glimpse if the shower door is opened too soon. They wear blue woolen trunks. Also black. Their feet appear to have very long toes. There is only one shower and in it a single, whitened tap. The water is cold. Inge goes first. Her suit appears, one small piece and then the other, draped over the top of the door. Malcolm waits. He can hear the soft slap and passage of her hands, the sudden shattering of the water on concrete when she moves aside. The boys at the door exalt him. He glances out. They are talking in low voices. They reach out to tease each other, to make an appearance of play.

The streets of Sitges have changed. An hour has struck which announces evening, and everywhere there are strolling crowds. It's difficult to stay together. Malcolm has an arm around each of them. They drift to his touch like horses. Inge smiles. People will think the three of them do it together, she says.

They stop at a cafe. It isn't a good one, Inge complains.

"It's the best," Nico says simply. It is one of her qualities that she can tell at a glance, wherever she goes, which is the right place, the right restaurant, hotel.

"No," Inge insists.

Nico seems not to care. They wander on separated now, and Malcolm whispers,

"What is she looking for?"

"Don't you know?" Nico says.

"You see these boys?" Inge says. They are seated in another place, a bar. All around them, tanned limbs, hair faded from the long, baking afternoons, young men sit with the sweet stare of indolence.

"They have no money," she says. "None of them could take you to dinner. Not one of them. They have nothing.

"This is Spain," she says.

Nico chooses the place for dinner. She has become a different person during the day. The presence of this friend, this girl she casually shared a life with during the days they both were struggling to find themselves in the city, before she knew anybody or even the names of streets, when she was so sick that they wrote out a cable to her father together—they had no telephone—this sudden revelation of Inge seems to have deprived the past of decency. All at once she is pierced by a certainty that Malcolm feels contempt for her. Her confidence, without which she is nothing, has gone. The tablecloth seems white and dazzling. It seems to be illuminating the three of them with remorseless light. The knives and forks are laid out as if for surgery. The plates lie cold. She is not hungry but she doesn't dare refuse to eat. Inge is talking about her boyfriend.

"He is terrible," she says, "he is heartless. But I understand him. I know what he wants.

"Anyway a woman can't hope to be everything to a man. It isn't natural. A man needs a number of women."

"You're crazy," Nico says.

"It's true."

The statement is all that was needed to demoralize her. Malcolm is inspecting the strap of his watch. It seems to Nico he is permitting all this. He is stupid, she thinks. This girl is from a low background and he finds that interesting. She thinks because they go to bed with her they will marry her. Of course not. Never. Nothing, Nico thinks, could be farther from the truth, though even as she thinks she knows she may be wrong.

They go to Chez Swann for a coffee. Nico does not sit with them. She is tired, she says. She curls up on one of the couches and goes to sleep. She is exhausted. The evening has become quite cool.

A voice awakens her, music, a marvelous voice amid occasional phrases of the guitar. Nico hears it in her sleep and sits up. Malcolm and Inge are talking. The song is like something long-awaited, something they have been searching for. She reaches over and touches his arm.

"Listen," she says.

"What?"

"Listen," she says, "it's Maria Pradera."

"Maria Pradera?"

"The words are beautiful," Nico says.

Simple phrases. She repeats them, as if they were litany. Mysterious repetitions: dark-haired mother . . . dark-haired child. The eloquence of the poor, worn smooth and pure as a stone.

Malcolm listens patiently but he hears nothing. She can see it: he has changed, he has been poisoned while she slept with stories of a hideous Spain fed bit by bit until now they are drifting through his veins, a Spain devised by a woman who knows she can never be more than part of what a man needs. Inge is calm. She believes in herself, Nico thinks. She believes in her right to exist, to command.

The road is dark. They have opened the roof to the night, a night so dense with stars that they seem to be pouring into the car. Nico, in the back, feels abandoned. Inge is talking. She reaches over to blow the horn at cars which are going too slow. Malcolm allows it. There are private rooms in Barcelona where, with her lover, Inge spent winter afternoons before a warm, crackling fire. There are houses where they made love on blankets of fur. Of course, he was nice then. She had visions of the Polo Club, of dinner parties in the best houses.

The streets of the city are almost deserted. It is nearly midnight, Sunday midnight. The day in the sun has wearied them, the sea has drained them of strength. They drive to General Mitre and say goodnight through the windows of the car. The elevator rises very slowly. They are hung with silence. They look at the floor like gamblers who have lost.

The apartment is dark. Nico turns on a light and then vanishes. Malcolm washes his hands. He dries them. The rooms seem very still. He begins to walk through them slowly and finds her, as if she had fallen, on her knees in the doorway to the terrace. The bird is dead.

Malcolm looks at the cage. Kalil has fallen to the floor.

"Give him a little brandy on the corner of a handkerchief," he says.

She has opened the cage door.

"He's dead," she says.

"Let me see."

He is stiff. The small feet are curled and dry as twigs. He seems lighter somehow. The breath has left his feathers. A heart no bigger than an orange seed has ceased to beat. The cage sits empty

in the cold doorway. There seems nothing to say. Malcolm closes
the door.

Later, in bed, he listens to her sobs. He tries to comfort her
but he cannot. Her back is turned to him. She will not answer.

She has small breasts and large nipples. Also, as she herself says,
a rather large behind. Her father has three secretaries. Hamburg
is close to the sea.

BERNARD MALAMUD was born in Brooklyn and attended City College and Columbia University. He has taught at Oregon State University and Harvard and is now teaching at Bennington College. He has published four novels and two collections of short stories. For *The Magic Barrel* he received a National Book Award, and for *The Fixer*, a National Book Award and the Pulitzer Prize. His latest novel, *Pictures of Fidelman*, was published in 1969.

My Son the Murderer

HE wakes to a feeling his father is in the hallway, listening. Listening to what? Listening to him sleep and dream. To him get up and fumble for his pants. To him not going to the kitchen to eat. Staring with shut eyes in the mirror. Sitting an hour on the toilet. Flipping the pages of a book he can't read. To his rage, anguish, loneliness. The father stands in the hall. The son hears him listen.

My son the stranger, he tells me nothing.

I open the door and see my father in the hall.

Why are you standing there, why don't you go to work?

I took my vacation in the winter instead of the summer like I usually do.

What the hell for if you spend it in this dark smelly hallway watching my every move. Guessing what you don't see. Why are you spying on me?

My father goes to his room and after a while comes out in the hallway again, listening.

I hear him sometimes in his room but he don't talk to me and I don't know what's what. It's a terrible feeling for a father. Maybe someday he'll write me a nice letter, My dear father. . . .

My dear son Harry, open up your door.

My son the prisoner.

My wife leaves in the morning to be with my married daughter who is having her fourth child. The mother cooks and cleans for her and takes care of the children. My daughter is having a bad pregnancy, with high blood pressure, and is in bed most of the time. My wife is gone all day. She knows something is wrong with Harry. Since he graduated college last summer he is nervous, alone, in his own thoughts. If you talk to him, half the time he yells. He reads the papers, smokes, stays in his room. Once in a while he goes for a walk.

How was the walk, Harry?

A walk.

My wife told him to go look for work and a few times he went, but when he got some kind of offer he didn't take the job.

It's not that I don't want to work. It's that I feel bad.

Why do you feel bad?

I feel what I feel. I feel what is.

Is it your health, sonny? Maybe you ought to go to a doctor?

Don't call me by that name. It's not my health. Whatever it is I don't want to talk about it. The work wasn't the kind I want.

So take something temporary in the meantime, she said.

He starts to yell. Everything is temporary. Why should I add more to what is already temporary? My guts feel temporary. The world is temporary. On top of that I don't want temporary work. I want the opposite of temporary, but where do you look for it? Where do you find it?

My father temporarily listens in the kitchen.

My temporary son.

She said I'd feel better if I work. I deny it. I'm twenty-two, since last December, a college graduate and you know where you can stick that. At night I watch the news broadcasts. I watch the war from day to day. It's a large war on a small screen. I sometimes lean over and touch the war with the flat of my hand. I'm waiting for my hand to die.

My son with the dead hand.

I expect to be drafted any day but it doesn't bother me so much anymore. I won't go. I'll go to Canada or somewhere, though the idea is a burden to me.

The way he is frightens my wife and she is glad to go off to my daughter's house in the morning to take care of the three children. I'm left alone, but he don't talk to me.

You ought to call up Harry and talk to him, my wife says to my daughter.

I will sometimes, but don't forget there's nine years' difference between our ages. I think he thinks of me as another mother around and one is enough. I used to like him, but it's hard to deal with a person who won't reciprocate.

She's got high blood pressure. I think she's afraid to call.

I took two weeks off from work. I'm a clerk at the stamps window in the Post Office. I told the superintendent I wasn't feeling so good, which is no lie, and he said I should take sick leave, but I said I wasn't that sick. I told my friend Moe Berk I was staying out because Harry had me worried.

I know what you mean, Leo. I got my own worries and anxieties about my kids. If you have two girls growing up you got hostages to fortune. Still in all, we got to live. Will you come to poker Friday night? Don't deprive yourself of a good form of relaxation.

I'll see how I feel by then, how it's coming. I can't promise.

Try to come. These things all pass away. If it looks better to you, come on over. Even if it don't look so good, come on over anyway because it might relieve the tension and worry that you're under. It's not good for your heart at your age if you carry that much worry around.

This is the worst kind of worry. If I worry about myself I know what the worry is. What I mean, there's no mystery. I can say to myself, Leo, you're a fool, stop worrying over nothing—over what, a few bucks? Over my health that always stood up pretty good although I've had my ups and downs? Over that I'm now close to sixty and not getting any younger? Everybody that don't die by age fifty-nine gets to be sixty. You can't beat time if it's crawling after you. But if the worry is about somebody else, that's the worst kind. That's the real worry because if he won't tell you, you can't get inside the other person and find out why. You don't know where's the switch to turn off. All you can do is worry more.

So I wait in the hallway.

Harry, don't worry about the war.

Don't tell me what to worry about.

Harry, your father loves you. When you were a little boy, every night when I came home you used to run to me. I picked you up and lifted you to the ceiling. You liked to touch it with your small hand.

I don't want to hear about that anymore. It's the very thing I don't want to hear about. I don't want to hear about when I was a child.

Harry, we live like strangers. All I'm saying is I remember better days. I remember when we weren't afraid to show we loved each other.

He says nothing.

Let me cook you an egg.

I don't want an egg. It's the last thing in the world I want.

So what do you want?

He put his coat on. He pulled his hat off the clothes tree and went downstairs into the street. Harry walked along Ocean Parkway in his long coat and creased brown hat. He knew his father was following him and it filled him with rage.

He didn't turn around. He walked at a fast pace up the broad avenue. In the old days there was a bridle path at the side of the walk where the concrete bicycle path was now. And there were fewer trees now, their black branches cutting the sunless sky. At the corner of Avenue X, just about where you begin to smell Coney Island, he crossed over and began to walk home. He pretended not to see his father cross over, although he was still infuriated. The father crossed over and followed his son home. When he got to the house he figured Harry was already upstairs. He was in his room with the door shut. Whatever he did in his room he was already doing.

Leo took out his key and opened the mailbox. There were three letters. He looked to see if one of them was, by any chance, from his son to him. My dear father, let me explain myself. The reason I act as I do is. . . . But there was no such letter. One of the letters was from the Post Office Clerks Benevolent Society, which he put in his coat pocket. The other two letters were for his son. One was from the draft board. He brought it up to his son's room, knocked on the door and waited.

He waited for a while.

To the boy's grunt he said, There is a draft board letter for you.

He turned the knob and entered the room. Harry was lying on the bed with his eyes shut.

You can leave it on the table.

Why don't you open it? Do you want me to open it for you?

No, I don't want you to open it. Leave it on the table. I know what's in it.

What's in it?

That's my business.

The father left it on the table.

The other letter to his son he took into the kitchen, shut the door and boiled up some water in a kettle. He thought he would read it quickly and then seal it carefully with a little paste so that none leaked over the edge of the flap, then go downstairs and put it back in the mailbox. His wife would take it out with her key when she returned from their daughter's house and bring it up to Harry.

The father read the letter. It was a short letter from a girl. The girl said Harry had borrowed two of her books more than six months ago and since she valued them highly she would like him to send them back to her. Could he do that as soon as possible so that she wouldn't have to write again?

As Leo was reading the girl's letter Harry came into the kitchen and when he saw the surprised and guilty look on his father's face, he tore the letter out of his hands.

I ought to kill you the way you spy on me.

Leo turned away, looking out of the small kitchen window into the dark apartment-house courtyard. His face was a mottled red, his eyes dull, and he felt sick.

Harry read the letter at a glance and tore it up. He then tore up the envelope marked personal.

If you do this again don't be surprised if I kill you. I'm sick of you spying on me.

Harry left the house.

Leo went into his room and looked around. He looked in the dresser drawers and found nothing unusual. On the desk by the window was a paper Harry had written on. It said: Dear Edith, why don't you go fuck yourself? If you write another such letter I'll murder you.

The father got his hat and coat and left the house. He ran for a while, running then walking, until he saw Harry on the other side of the street. He followed him a half block behind.

He followed Harry to Coney Island Avenue and was in time to see him board a trolleybus going toward the Island. Leo had to wait for the next bus. He thought of taking a taxi and following the bus, but no taxi came by. The next bus came by fifteen minutes later and he took it all the way to the Island. It was February and Coney Island was cold and deserted. There were few cars on Surf Avenue and few people on the streets. It looked like snow. Leo walked on the boardwalk, amid snow flurries, looking for his son. The grey sunless beaches were empty. The hot-dog stands, shooting galleries, and bathhouses were shuttered up. The gun-metal ocean, moving like melted lead, looked freezing. There was a wind off the water and it worked its way into his clothes so that he shivered as he walked. The wind white-capped the leaden waves and the slow surf broke on the deserted beaches with a quiet roar.

He walked in the blow almost to Sea Gate, searching for his son, and then walked back. On his way toward Brighton he saw a man on the beach standing in the foaming surf. Leo went down the boardwalk stairs and onto the ribbed-sand beach. The man on the shore was Harry standing in water up to his ankles.

Leo ran to his son. Harry, it was my mistake, excuse me. I'm sorry I opened your letter.

Harry did not turn. He stayed in the water, his eyes on the leaden waves.

Harry, I'm frightened. Tell me what's the matter. My son, have mercy on me.

It's not my kind of world, Harry thought. It fills me with terror. He said nothing.

A blast of wind lifted his father's hat off his head and carried it away over the beach. It looked as if it were going to land in the surf but then the wind blew it toward the boardwalk, rolling like a wheel along the ground. Leo chased after his hat. He chased it one way, then another, then toward the water. The wind blew the hat against his legs and he caught it. He pulled the freezing hat down tight on his head until it bent his ears. By now he was crying. Breathless, he wiped his eyes with icy fingers and returned to his son at the edge of the water.

He is a lonely man. This is the type he is, Leo thought. He will always be lonely.

My son who became a lonely man.

Harry, what can I say to you? All I can say to you is who says life is easy? Since when? It wasn't for me and it isn't for you. It's life, what more can I say? But if a person don't want to live what can he do if he's dead? If he doesn't want to live maybe he deserves to die.

Come home, Harry, he said. It's cold here. You'll catch a cold with your feet in the water.

Harry stood motionless and after a while his father left. As he was leaving, the wind plucked his hat off his head and sent it rolling along the sand.

My father stands in the hallway. I catch him reading my letter. He follows me at a distance in the street. We meet at the edge of the water. He is running after his hat.

My son stands with his feet in the ocean.

PATRICIA BROWNING GRIFFITH was born in Fort Worth, Texas, and grew up in the northeast corner of the state near the Red River. She came to New York City after college, and now she and her husband live in Washington, D.C. She has just completed work on her first novel.

Nights at O'Rear's

CRUMMY, dirty, ugly O'Rear's; mecca, umbilicus, polestar of our universe. Who cared about its gritty-edged coffee cups, greasy french fries, gristly chili. O'Rear's sold setups to anyone old enough to sit upright, and kept the jukebox bawling loud enough to hear from the highway as you drove by. There, boisterous, smug, indifferent, suffering, we gathered around the small white building like an automotive crap game, conducting our social lives within the confines of our Detroit armor—though a lot of them bore a sign in the back window, "Made in Texas by Texans."

O'Rear's Round-Up Drive-in was a square box like the drive-in in every town in the country, flat-topped and glass-fronted, tacked with pictures of faded sandwiches and voluptuous ice-cream sodas that never quite came true, with a luminous multicolored jukebox, its windowed head working continuously conveying, impaling, spinning discs which exploded into Ruth Brown or Nat Cole or Tommy Edwards or Hank Thompson or Lefty Frizzell. O'Rear's was not even so ambitious an undertaking as to entice us with neon, but relied instead on a wooden sign with the red "O" in "O'Rear's" painted to resemble a lasso. But then it didn't need neon to attract us.

There was little to do in that town; the movie was about all.

The skating rink closed for the hot months, the rodeo lasted only a week, the Saturday night drag races had been closed by the sheriff, and the Baptists wouldn't allow dancing—so we drove. We drove and drove and drove for hours always within a radius of fifteen miles, up one of the two main streets, down the other, dragging from the city limit sign to the cemetery road, turn here, then there, like a child's pony ride, the same circle, the same path, day after day, night after night, sweating and sticking against the plastic seat covers, strewing the roads with beer cans, gunning our motors, squealing our tires, popping our mufflers, a primitive mating rite with horsepower trappings. Religiously we stopped at O'Rear's, where cars swarmed on Friday, Saturday, and Sunday nights as if it were a Billy Graham crusade. Finally if we had a date we'd park on lovers' lane, a road between the railroad tracks and the cemetery. If we didn't have a date we'd circle the main street again, drive down lovers' lane to see who was there, and go home, hopes building toward the next night.

In that town people actually stayed in cars so much it was possible to know a person all summer without ever having seen him from the chest down. Men cared for their cars as women cared for their children. They were discussed, cleaned, decorated, and primed; they were readily identifiable. Chrome was very big. Also it was important that the back of the car be weighted so that it was lower than the front. We looked like a whole town of bootleggers. Flashy seat covers were in great demand. Backseat radio speakers were absolutely necessary. It was essential to drive fast with the window down and your arm resting on the door but still provide music for the people in the back seat since everyone, every night listened to Randy's Record Shop in Gallatin, Tennessee. As cars pulled up to O'Rear's chances were twenty to one the program turned off in each car would be Randy's with someone like Chuck Berry "Maybelline"-ing it along.

Our leading, swashbuckling driver was Max Corley, whose '51 Fordomatic traveled with outside sun visor, spotlight, twin sideview mirrors, fender skirts, continental tire rack, ripple bar wheeldiscs, imitation leopard-skin seat covers, a backseat speaker on each side, a nude-decorated steering nob, and a beer opener chained to the back of the ashtray. Max Corley foraged the countryside in his green chromey car, a Western Genghis Khan in ducktail and a Stetson, backed by Bobby Jack Owens and the Riley boys, Floyd and Warren, who were probably as unsavory to some eyes as the Asian hordes might have been. Max had actually enjoyed a brief popularity among the average Christian-type children in grade school but by high school most people tried to stay out of his way, knowing it was Harry-hang-the-flag for any kid who crossed him. We simply called him a bully, accepting that as the exhaustive truth, for that was how we saw things—unvarnished but oversimplified with everyone explained by our one-word character labels—friendly, ugly, stuck-up, sweet, cute, pious, and so on. There was no doubt, however, that Max Corley possessed a certain dark, solemn charm which could be summoned forth for his purposes, so that any nice-looking new girl was liable to find herself in the back seat of his green and chrome car before anyone else got her name straight. A lot of women found his glum, sideburns type attractive. In fact it was remarked on several occasions that the service he received at O'Rear's was exceptionally good.

O'Rear's had two carhops—Mildred Temple, a tall, flat-faced girl with dull brown hair and acne, and Dorothy Lester, a good professional carhop. Short, stocky, blondined, sturdy as a tractor, she strode from car to car, balancing trays as if her hands were a foot square, waiting on four cars in the time it took Mildred to handle one. She had a sharp, crude tongue and the ability to create that happy rapport that sometimes exists between men and waitresses.

Mildred, on the other hand, was slow at writing her orders, slow at delivering them, and between cars she'd rest on the Dell Dairy Ice Cream bench beside the screen door fanning herself with her red cowboy hat which, with black slacks and white blouses, made up the uniform of the O'Rear's waitresses. Early in the afternoon when business was slack, Mildred would sit on the bench writing letters on her stationery box, gazing across the highway now and then where two orange gas pumps and an oak tree in the pasture beside them looked like mere toys below the immense steel-gray backdrop of Texas sky.

"My dearest darling," or, "My darling sweetheart," she'd begin the letters and fill pink page after pink page with her small handwriting. She wrote always with a snapshot before her, taken from her billfold, fat with pictures of elderly relatives singly or in groups, standing on the porch of a farmhouse, in front of a barn, or beside a car. But the recipients of the long pink letters were two gaunt-faced servicemen posed in twenty-five-cent photo booths. One picture was inscribed in the corner—"Love ya, Freddy."

They were both fiances, she'd explained. Around her neck she wore a large white enamel locket with a rose on it, which contained other pictures of the fiances. Freddy had been cut from a group snapshot and was so tiny about all you could see was the outline of a face under a soldier's cap worn low on the forehead. The other fiance was a large, disembodied face with the chin cropped off. She couldn't decide which one to marry, but she worried more about Freddy, she said, since he was clear to Europe.

Despite the fiances, on Saturdays Mildred would be in the early movie sitting on the back row with strange boys who wore T-shirts with a pocket on the chest and worked on road construction crews. They were always just passing through town, and hung out in the Post Office Cafe, where Mildred met them. In deference to her fiances, however, she would claim they were cousins or just friends or went to her church.

A couple of years before O'Rear's opened Mildred had made a brief excursion into high school. It was hard to understand why she came to school in the first place since she spent every period reading confession magazines hidden inside her notebook. As far as anyone noticed, the only time she paid attention was the day the males and females were separated and shown a film on venereal diseases, and the day we read "O my luve is like a red, red rose," and Max Corley caught her copying it into a letter.

The population of our school was divided into cliques of town girls and cliques of country girls while the boys mingled democratically. But Mildred belonged to another group, a few really poor girls who sometimes wore dirty clothes and needed baths and had hair-pulling fights after school. These girls spent lots of time in the rest room putting on makeup and sneaking puffs off cigarettes and were blamed for the four-letter words scrawled on the rest room walls in lipstick and pencil which the rest of us read so avidly.

After three or four months Mildred dropped out of school and until O'Rear's opened we'd only see her now and then on Saturdays snuggled on the back row of the movie. She had always been a pleasant girl, with a big gummy smile, and Max Corley and his friends had always teased her so that it was easy enough to resume at O'Rear's.

"Who you writin', Mildred?" Max called as she sat on the bench one afternoon. She closed her stationery box quickly, revealing the word "love" drawn over and over again on the top of it and decorated with flowers at the top of the "l" and the end of the "e."

"I bet she's writin' her boyfriend in California," Bobby Jack said from his seat beside Max. Mildred approached the car self-consciously as if her size had come upon her only the night before. Bobby Jack was tall and skinny with two yellowed teeth, which we attributed to his having drunk West Texas water for the first eleven years of his life. "That perfumed paper you writin' on, Mildred?" he asked.

Mildred pulled her order pad out of her side pocket. "No it ain't," she said gruffly.

"Who you writin', Mildred?" Max demanded.

Mildred lifted her well-plucked eyebrows and turned away, shielding her eyes from the sun with her hand as she did. Her nails were large but short and painted purple-red. "My fi-an-ce." She said the words importantly.

"Your fi-an-ce!" they mocked.

Bobby Jack lounged with his arm resting across the back of the imitation leopard-skin seats. "Who you in love with today, Mildred? The one with the big nose or the one with the pimple face?" he asked.

Floyd and Warren in the back seat laughed, slapping the knees of their Levis with their freckled hands.

Mildred ignored them and pulled out her white dime-store sunglasses. She had used the same purple-red nail polish to paint red stripes around the white rims.

"How do you know when you're in love, Mildred?" Max asked her thoughtfully. He seemed to be staring at her thin lips where lipstick had caked like tiny red scabs along the edges.

"Does your heart pound when you're in love?" Bobby Jack took up the game.

"Do your knees knock?" Max asked solemnly.

"Do you have hot and cold flashes?" Floyd Riley asked.

Mildred wiped the lenses with the tail of her white blouse and held them against the sun for inspection. Bobby Jack leaned toward her and spoke with conviction. "I'll bet it's just an itch where you can't scratch," he said. Mildred adjusted the sunglasses and tried to fluff her short permanented hair back over her ears while they laughed.

"Didn't I see you parked down on lovers' lane, Mildred?" they'd ask. Or, "Who was that you were smooching in the movie Saturday, Mildred?" "Do you really believe in LOVE, Mildred?"

Now and then she'd smile broadly at their ridiculous questions as she's smiling in our class picture taken early in the year while she was there. She stands the tallest of all the girls, her black patent shoulder-strap purse hung around her neck and encircling one arm like part of a soldier's gear, a kooky look in her eyes caught unflatteringly half-closed by the camera. The rest of us look shockingly young and deceptively innocent and it's a great surprise since my mind's eye remembers us as simply shorter adults, like the pictures in *Beautiful Stories from Shakespeare*.

The spring Mildred began working at O'Rear's Sonny Morris, owner of the Grand movie theater, opened a radio station outside of town. It was the type of station that broadcast the local Baptist minister on Sunday mornings and filled every afternoon with a musical request program. *We have a card here from Shirley W. says, "Please play 'I'd Walk a Mile' for Jimmy and Diane, Ronnie and Sue, Larry and Wilma Jean, and that good looking Sophomore M. L." Also a card from . . .*

Saturday morning was the local talent show featuring church ladies' trios and men's quartets, and infantile voices interspersed with the dull, heavy shuffling of tap shoes. Sonny Morris scouted all the rural communities in the area to fill up those three Saturday morning hours. There were four of us girls who used to harmonize now and then at church socials when people were desperate for entertainment or wanted the main attraction to seem better than it was. So one Saturday morning we drove to the station set in what had recently been a calf lot, and straining toward the microphone sang "Moonlight Bay" with echoing parts. Sonny

Morris read off a commercial for a local hardware store and then introduced the Lord's Lights trio from the Pine Grove Baptist Mission. Sonny Morris liked his better groups to have names, so the Lord's Lights had been created right there in front of the Dr. Pepper machine. They sang "In the Garden" and "Were You There?" in close harmony. Mildred was a Lord's Light. She and another brunette slumped stiffly on either side of a short, fat redhaired soprano who bobbed her head as she sang.

After a cornet solo Mildred came back to the microphone. We expected another hymn and you couldn't tell by the introduction since the pianist began all the songs with the last four bars and an opening chord so that even "King Sized Papa" sounded like a hymn. She stood with her fists doubled at her sides staring at the clock in the back of the room. She was dressed up for the Saturday movie in a limp green sweater and a black skirt, a gold ankle bracelet, and a string of brown wooden beads. In her attempt at theatrical makeup, round patches of rouge sat on either cheek and black lines winged from either side of her eyes. She took a deep breath and closed her eyes.

"It was beside the Pontchartrain . . . beside the Pontchartrain," she began to sing. The first notes nearly knocked us out of our folding chairs. We'd never heard anyone sing so loudly. Her voice was so strong and intense with a husky quality, it stunned us. She gripped each note with her nasal alto, wringing it dry before she slid to the next. Now and then her body would sway and her eyes close again as she made a long note a sort of country tremolo. The song was a queer, minor melody that groaned out the story, rhymed in hillbilly unsubtlety, of love, betrayal, and death on the shores of that gloomy lake. The Mildred before us, looking like a pimple-faced Olive Oyl, seemed to drift away and reappear in a world of Spanish moss, veiled by the misty fog of the lake, suffering over love as we had only dreamed it could be suffered. All our backseat automobile romancing shrank to dull insignificance. We drank in each strange, loud note, even though slightly embarrassed to see in Mildred an experience of love we had only dreamed of. That evening she became the star.

"Can I have your autograph?" Bobby Jack said as she set eight bundled hamburgers on their tray.

"Heard you knocked 'em dead today, Mildred," Max said. "Heard they had to call the sheriff to calm the fans."

Mildred smiled trying to hide her pleasure by fishing in her side pocket for money. "I'm gonna sing next week, too," she said proudly. Max cocked his head sideways and watched her slide their change across the metal tray, counting aloud as she did.

"I believe Mildred'll be a *star!*"

"A star!" Bobby Jack shrieked. He shouted into the back seat as if Floyd and Warren hadn't heard. "Mildred's gonna be a *star!*" He hopped out of the car, bounded to another, and shouted, "Mildred's gonna be a *star!*"

That week everyone teased Mildred about being a star. It was the chic thing to do. That's the way an idea was, very clever for about a week and then suddenly one night, as if by magic decree, it wasn't and only real clods trying too hard would say it again.

It was hot that week. The temperature passed a hundred every day. Housewives, husbands, old people in cars with "See You in Church Sunday" stickers drove to O'Rear's and sat fanning themselves and wishing for a breeze. Mildred and Dorothy abandoned their hats and wore pink snoods that made sacks for their hair in back and tied on top of their heads. Mildred's hair was shorter than the net so the snood drooped down in back like a damp fish net.

Every night Max and his friends discussed Mildred's career with her.

"You do your do-re-mi's today, Mildred?" Max would ask.

"I been thinkin' you oughta get a lot of sexy costumes," Bobby Jack said one night and they all broke up with laughter.

Mildred would blush and smile at Max, flattered by his attention and never certain whether it was total teasing or not.

"You better be thinkin' about takin' your fiances along with you when you hit the big time," Bobby Jack advised her one night. He reared back pulling change for the jukebox from the front pocket of his tight Levis. Mildred picked up her big white locket which left a greenish "V" on her neck and ran it back and forth absent-mindedly on the chain as she waited. "You gotta be sure those fiances have class," he said.

Mildred rarely paid attention to Bobby Jack's comments, but she listened to Max.

"You gotta take care of yourself, Mildred," Max said. "You oughta have a scarf around your throat." It was scathingly hot but he insisted Bobby Jack wrap a handkerchief around her neck. For the rest of the evening they called her Tonto.

On Friday night before her performance Max told her to give it everything she had. "You never know who might be listening," he said soberly.

"That's right, Mildred. Roy Acuff might be listening in person," Bobby Jack said.

"Ernest Tubb might be listening," Floyd said.

"Minnie Pearl might be listening," Bobby Jack added and they began laughing.

Max had taken Warren Riley's rabbit's foot away from him and given it to Mildred for good luck. "It's been in my family since the days of Davy Crockett," Max said, "but I want you to have it."

Everybody at O'Rear's had taken up the game and was wishing her good luck and saying how Hollywood or the Grand Ole Opry would be the next stop. Mildred would smile gratefully. "Don't forget to suck a lemon in the morning soon as you get up," Bobby Jack called before they roared away.

The next morning Sonny Morris saved Mildred's song till near the end of the program and presented her as returning due to popular demand. There was the sound of a chair scraping then a few seconds later Mildred at the microphone. "I'd like to dedicate this song to all my good friends at O'Rear's and especially to Max Corley for encouraging my career," she said. Then she launched into "Are Ya Half as Good a Girl, As Your Mother Thinks You Are" while all over town people were gasping and thumping their radios in disbelief. It was the most exciting thing to happen in weeks. Max would be furious, outraged! There was no telling what he might do. Poor Mildred, we said to one another and giggled.

The movie was always jammed on Saturday nights and especially that Saturday since it was the coolest place in town. But as soon as the last feature was over there was a race to O'Rear's to see what Max was going to do.

"You sang real good," people called to Mildred when they drove up and in the next breath they'd ask if Max had been there yet.

She'd shake her head disgustedly. She'd been teased about the dedication all afternoon though she insisted that she meant nothing by dedicating that song to Max. They were just friends, she said, and she wished people wouldn't always be making things outa nothing.

Earlier Max had been zooming around town like a tornado before he crossed the river to Oklahoma and Johnny's Roadside "21" Club and Restaurant. Johnny's specialized in fried catfish and hot hush puppies and featured on Saturday night a hillbilly band with the kind of dancing that was accompanied by a lot of stomping and frequent fistfights.

It was nearly midnight before Max came roaring up with the Riley boys, his twin Hollywood tail pipes thundering behind, and Bobby Jack tailing him in his father's blue pickup. They circled a couple of times, long enough to stir up a cloud of dust that floated into everyone's root beers and then screeched to a halt with a spray of gravel. They were all wearing Western hats and smoking cigars and passing around a bottle of whiskey wrapped in a paper sack. Bobby Jack left his pickup and lumbered over to lean on the door of Max's car next to Warren. From the jukebox Ray Charles was shouting, *"Hallelujah I just love her so . . ."* Bobby Jack ducked his head between his arms to kick a rock under the car and swayed his bottom to the music.

Mildred was across the drive-in, her pencil poised above her order pad when Max drove up. "Here he comes," someone called to her. She dropped her order pad and bumped her head on a side-view mirror picking it up. When Max flashed his lights for service Mildred was on her way to another car. She walked on as if expecting Dorothy to wait on Max. Then Floyd Riley stuck his head out the back window and yelled, "Sooey!"

Mildred stopped.

"Sooey," Floyd bellowed again.

She pushed back her bangs that were sticking to her shiny forehead. Then walking unevenly over the gravel as if her feet hurt, carrying a tray half full of paper cups and bottles, she went to Max's car.

"Hi, Max," she said shyly trying to push a stray lock of hair under the snood. Max stuck a cigar in the side of his mouth and tilted his head back to stare at her from under his Western hat. In the heat her thick black mascara had drooped from the top of her eyelashes and formed a black crescent under each eye.

"We wrote a song for you, Mildred, you wanna hear it?" Warren asked. He, Floyd, and Bobby Jack began singing to the tune of "Tennessee Border" . . . *"Her eyes are red, her teeth are yellow . . . , her head is like a watermelon . . ."* At that point laughter broke up the singing. "There's more," Floyd said but started laughing again.

Max motioned to Mildred with a crook of his finger as if he had a secret to tell. When she took a hesitant step nearer the car Max reached out the window and with one hand shoved the tray, scattering bottles and cups to the ground. Mildred jumped back pulling at her wet blouse where icy root beer had spilled. She looked up at Max as if expecting some reasonable explanation, but he'd turned his back to her and was lighting the cigar. She picked up the bottles, her face scarlet, then hobbled back to the front counter, shoved the tray inside, and hurried to the side of the building where she entered the door marked with a crudely drawn sign "Cowgirls."

After a word from Max, Bobby Jack jumped into his truck, slamming the door three times before it closed with the tinny wallop of a pickup door. Max revved his engine and they pulled up to either side of the door Mildred had entered. They left no more than a car's length between them and the building.

"If you've got the money, honey, I've got the ti-i-i-me . . ." Lefty Frizzell sang through the hot night as they waited.

When Mildred opened the door Warren was ready with the spotlight. It flashed against the coarse white-painted concrete blocks of the building and circled a moment before he caught her squarely in the center of light. She held up one hand to shield her eyes, holding the other arm to her side as if she were trying to retract within herself like one of those cheap Japanese fans. She had tried to rinse the root beer from her white blouse, which now hung damply outside her black slacks. The stray hair was tucked back inside the snood and the mascara scrubbed from below her eyes. After a moment she started toward the front, down the narrow sidewalk that ran alongside the building. Quickly Max pulled forward, his front wheels on the sidewalk, his front bumper touching the building, blocking her path. She was no more than six feet from the car and in the spotlight she looked surprised as if she'd not realized what they intended.

On the other side of O'Rear's a few people left their cars and wandered over to watch, leaning against other cars and chatting with the people inside.

"Run through the middle, Mildred," someone shouted. She stood still a minute then cautiously as though measuring her possibilities began walking between the cars. Slowly, alongside her Max and Bobby Jack backed until they formed a "V" in front of her.

"Come on, Mildred," a voice called, "leap over the car," and there was laughter.

Max still had the cigar clamped in the side of his mouth and he'd pulled his Western hat low on his forehead so that his eyes were nearly hidden. He was steering the car with one hand and Warren was holding the spotlight on her.

Mildred walked back to the sidewalk and bit her lip. She looked as if she might burst into tears but she put her hands on her hips and tried to look tough. "Okay, Max," she said nodding her flat face at him and trying to sound threatening. She turned abruptly and started limping vigorously toward the back of the building. Since the curb was higher toward the back of the building Bobby Jack had to back once and pick up speed to climb the curb then slam on his brakes to keep from hitting the building. This time the pickup was no more than a yard from her.

"You're slow as Christmas, Mildred," Bobby Jack said to her leaning both arms out the window and shaking his head. Mildred turned back toward the front.

Dorothy carrying three stacked trays came around the building and stopped to appraise the situation. "You on vacation, Mildred?" she called. She looked from Bobby Jack to Max. "Why don't you pick on somebody who ain't working, Max," she said. Floyd gave her the finger and she stomped away.

Mildred removed a tissue from her pocket and stuffed it in the heel of her right shoe. She pushed her foot down a couple of times, testing it for comfort then leaned against the side of the building and folded her arms as if prepared to wait it out. About that time, bald Mr. O'Rear with a white cloth tucked into his pants for an apron leaned around the corner and said that if Max didn't cut out that spotlight and foolishness he was gonna call the sheriff. They were interfering with his business. Furthermore if Mildred didn't get back to work she could in the future collect her check from another establishment.

Max backed so that Warren could switch the spotlight to Mr. O'Rear as he spoke and everybody laughed until Mr. O'Rear retreated inside, muttering to himself. Mildred looked helplessly toward Mr. O'Rear as he spoke. She seemed about to call out to him when she saw Max had taken his eyes off her to laugh at Mr. O'Rear. She stood very still weighing her chance to escape against the danger of angering Max further. Then she put one hand against the building as if to bolster herself. Slowly she began edging along the sidewalk in front of Max, tiptoeing, her eyes focused on his head.

"Max!" Bobby Jack shouted from behind her.

Max seemed instantaneously aware of his negligence. He stomped on the gas before turning to see her half across in front of him. She pressed herself against the wall as if she were facing a knife thrower. The green car moved steadily toward her.

"Run, Mildred," someone yelled impatiently, for Max looked far enough away for her to get by, but she seemed unable to move.

Max's mood of confidence seemed to change. He gripped the wheel and leaned forward as if he might will her to move. Only her hand jerked up to clutch her locket.

When he hit the sidewalk and didn't stop, her mouth opened in a silent panic and she finally started to turn and retreat. Max hit the brakes but it was all too late. She screamed a long, low chilling scream, the car slammed her against the side of the building. The bumper hit her below the knees and she seemed to fold up, and only then did the scream stop. For a moment it was quiet enough to hear a car passing on the highway and far off a dog barking hoarsely. The spotlight shone on a Big Daddy Burger sign on the side window.

"Jesus Christ!" Dorothy cried out from beside a nearby car. Then the jukebox which had been between records blared and people moved. Mr. O'Rear stalked out, cursed at Max, and hurried back inside to phone for the sheriff and the ambulance from the funeral home. For a minute Max sat stunned, bent over the steer-

ing wheel. Finally he removed his hat and smoothed his ducktails
and with his arm wiped the sweat from his forehead. Warren
rubbed his head where he'd hit the windshield.

"*I found my thrill, on blueberry hill . . .*" Fats' genial voice was
singing. Before the record ended, the ambulance could be heard
over the jukebox. There was considerable discussion as to who
would ride with her the thirty miles to the hospital. When they
put her on the stretcher she cried out, her voice, deep and loud,
her mouth an open rectangle, "Ah-ah-ah . . ."

The next week there was a new carhop, a bosomy girl with a
harelip called Sissy. She was terrified of Max, having been told a
hundred different stories about how he'd run down the last waitress, though the sheriff after talking to a few bystanders ruled it
an accident.

We never again saw Mildred Temple around town or in the
movie or at O'Rear's. Mr. O'Rear said she would be in the hospital for quite a while and Dorothy and a few others chipped in to
send an arrangement of gladiolas and signed the card from "Your
friends at O'Rear's." Months later someone claimed to have seen
her working as a carhop in another town. (In our area there's always a big demand for an experienced waitress.) We talked about
organizing a caravan and going over there and kidding around
with her but we never did. That was actually out of our orbit and
we always seemed to have plenty to do right there at O'Rear's.

TOM COLE was born in Paterson, New Jersey, in 1933. *An End to Chivalry*, his first book, won the Rosenthal Award of the National Institute of Arts and Letters in 1966. He divides his time among writing, translating and film work, and is an Associate Professor of Literature at M.I.T. Two earlier stories, "Familiar Usage in Leningrad" and "On the Edge of Arcadia," were O. Henry prize winners in 1962 and 1966, respectively.

Saint John of the Hershey Kisses: 1964

THREE Negro children were playing at the sidewalk's edge. From his second-story window, John, a white man, watched. One of them he knew—it was little Donald who wouldn't tell him his last name, or anything else, but who was always nearby, always *nigh*. He had named him Donald Bane; Donald, the bane of his existence, a witness to the fundamental, probably incurable evil of the human heart (with wide innocent smile), a useful reminder that politics was, in all likelihood, useless. "Donald Bane!" he shouted, at least once a day, "get out of my sight! You are the bane of my existence." Donald loved this and told all white volunteers that his name was Bane. Once, a nice lady from Brattle Street (fifteen minutes away by VW), standing bravely near a cockroach, said, "Oh, how do you *do*, Donald? And is this Mrs. Bane?" *This*—the large Negro woman with orange-rinsed hair near whom Donald was standing—was Eleanor Rose Carroll, whose fantasies dwelt upon flamboyant explosions in the oil systems of absentee landlords. They all had a good laugh about that. One didn't have many good laughs with Mrs. Rose Carroll, and so John began to call her Mrs. Bane, until, at a general campaign meeting while he struggled to preside, she suddenly flayed him for his condescension, his fatuousness: ". . . this boy still thinks he can fob us off with nicknames. Well I have news for *him!* We-are-in-a-re-vo-lu-tion . . ."

At the edge of the sidewalk, Donald Bane and the second little boy shouted nose to nose while the third boy slipped around behind, and crouched. Abruptly the second boy was folded backward over the body of the third and landed in the gutter, howling.

John wanted to leap from the second-story window—the high-hurdler in him being, after all, antecedent to the minister, who was in turn antecedent to the worker for the disadvantaged—for he wanted to grab Donald Bane's shoulders and shake that boy's meanness out of his tight little head; he wanted to rub Donald's face in the blood that was sure to appear on the skin of boy number two, sprawled on his gutter-bed of broken glass. But then John had to ask himself: did he *want* boy number two to be cut just so that he, Honest John, could read the lesson for today to Donald Bane? Wasn't there a darker wish for the blood to be little Donald's, so that the brash starling within that boy would be tamed and out would come instead some well-tuned suburban bird, a robin? Now John saw himself as if from a great distance or through the eyes of the derelicts who sat beneath his window (and the next window, and the next): a tall white man in seersucker shaking the life out of a Negro child. Was it for this that he had made his decision? Was it for this that his own children were "deprived" of the autumn already haunting the New England countryside a half-hour away? Was it thus that black and white together would overcome?

John was depressed. He sat by the window listening to the shriek of boy number two and the morning murmurs of the unemployed. He sniffed cheap wine and urine as the sun warmed the steps below him, and he felt on all sides a weight of the thick inattentive city to which he simply could not accustom himself. But he took comfort in studying the poster hanging beneath his window with the Candidate's face—round, brown, calm—foreshortened from this angle, and the words also foreshortened, bordering the chin like a mottled collar.

MASON BARNES FOR CONGRESS
JOBS   HOUSING
SCHOOLS

Boy number two's cuts were evidently slight, and forgiven, for now all three boys raced up the staircase, laughing, and burst into the office, Donald ahead with his incandescent smile, the others hanging back, suddenly shy.

"Good morning," John said.

"Hey, man, what's my name?"

"Donald Bane."

The laughter pealed from Donald's face, slightly tinged with hysteria; the others joined.

"He *always* call me that!"

"He always *calls* me that," emended John.

"Yeah."

"Well," John looked at his watch with a flourish—8.05 A.M.—"I'm glad to welcome the day's first volunteers."

"Where am I?" Donald asked.

"Always nigh," answered John, and Donald's entourage again charged after him to the edge of frenzy.

"See?" Donald pointed out. "He *always* give that answer."

"He always *gives*—oh, skip it," said John.

He was charmed, and a bit uneasy, to see the way this dark little boy pounced upon his own verbal foibles. "Nigh" was a word left over from his first ministry in a village thirty miles west among white clapboards and apple orchards. During the mid-1950s the flight from the city had brought to the Unitarian Church a new circle of young couples—agnostic, quick-witted, almost all (now) divorced. His role among these people had been to mock his own secularity by playing the genteel canon out of late Victorian fiction, full of nighs and nays. The word slipped out only occasionally now; but Donald's antennae were so quick. He overheard John use it in charming one of the Cambridge ladies (one hour's charm equaled $500 in the campaign till), and now it was one of their games.

"Where am I?"

"Always nigh."

"Hey, give us some Kisses, man!"

Donald was already rummaging in the bottom drawer of a bat-
tered desk, where the Hershey Kisses were kept. The chocolates
had achieved a fame in the neighborhood because they were left
unlocked. It was John's way; he was convinced that he was right.
When they were all given out by the campaign staff or stolen by
the children who wandered through the open office door, John
bought a new bagful. It was regarded as another sign of his sup-
posedly unlimited wealth, and he was despised for it. He knew
that. He also knew—only the Candidate and he knew among the
crowd here—how hopelessly he was in debt.

"Donald, put those Kisses back. What are they for?"

"Eatin'."

"You listen to me, now. I've told you this ten times before, and
I'm going to tell you every time you go near that drawer. I'm a
patient man. Understand?"

Malice and boredom fought for possession of Donald's eyes. He
clutched the chocolates and it was clear that he would give them
back only if they were pried out of his hands. Other workers
scolded him, especially the black ones, but he could always get
past John. It was another of their games.

"Those candies are for workers. You give out some stickers,
hand out some pamphlets when Mr. Mason Barnes speaks to the
people, and then you can take some chocolates. All right?"

Donald said nothing.

"All right, then. Put the chocolates back."

Nothing.

"Put them back, Donald Bane."

The boy exploded. "*I gonna work!* I *told* you! Shit."

"When? When are you going to work for us, Donald?"

"Soon."

"Promise?"

"Promise."

"All right, I'll charge them to your account. How many have
you got there?"

"Five."

He had eight.

In a diary John made a stroke with a ballpoint pen that was
dry, on a long-lapsed page.

"Get out of my sight until you're ready to work. You know what you are."

The others bolted, but Donald held his ground.

"Well?"

"Say it, man."

"The bane of my existence," intoned John, suddenly sick unto death of all his games. But Donald retreated with laughter, dissatisfied with John's performance and therefore rising into a bright insolence that trailed after him as he descended the stairwell.

Outside, beneath the window, he handed out Kisses to his friends, threw one to skip across the concrete, gave a few to the men on the stoop, who looked up toward the campaign office in sour derision.

Alone in the office, John surveyed the unfinished pamphlets, undistributed folders, blank mimeograph sheets with coffee cup rings, sign-out boards that no one used, personnel chain of command with most of the spaces blank, his own name in the top slot and others filled with pseudonyms as obvious as Vladimir Horowitz and Emily Dickinson. The Barnes campaign was staffed chiefly by white radicals, some too young to vote, almost all outside the district anyway, none much enamored of order (or himself). Then there was Eleanor Rose Carroll. But there was also Mrs. Graves. And the Candidate, of course. And himself, Honest John. Earlier this morning, walking downtown, he had met a tennis partner of summers past, who carried a briefcase and waved briskly, saying, "Oh hi, Jawn. Still working for that Communist coon?"

The boy with the fiercely ruffled hair—a Soc. Rel. concentrator at Harvard—stared at John in disgust, as he did every day by 5.00. "John, how can you still play that Cold War liberal tune? Look at the street in front of your eyes, look at the fifteen-year-old whores, look ten feet from your goddamned sanctimonious nose . . ."

"Let's split, Ronnie," said the high school girl with long brown hair, a peacemaker by nature whose every second word was brotherhood and third was love, who annoyed John even more than her fiery *guru* did.

"Honest John, do me a favor. Banish Stalin and Russia from

your vocabulary. Okay? Show me a little participatory democracy
five minutes in any direction from this office and I promise I'll sit
up with you nights and worry about life in the Urals. Okay? But
until then, for Christ's sake——"

"Let's split, Ronnie."

They did, and went off to fight the good fight, unquestionably
the best harvesters of voter registrations on John's staff. They
worked in tandem—a vaudeville act of virtue called Ronnie and
Sally—unafraid of rebuffs, doing what the economics consultant
from M.I.T. called "noodgying people into consciousness." A few
times a day they checked into the office to spill instant coffee on
John's fund-raising sheets, and to bait him on his quaint politics.
Today the Peace Corps had come up and he had ventured to say
that they were doing good work in some areas, whereupon Ronnie
flew into a rage, said he was worse than Wallace—"At least you
know where reactionaries stand"—and doubtless would have
reached one of his more satisfying crescendoes if the Candidate
had not appeared at the door, dark, urbane, too heavy in the
jowls for a man of twenty-eight, by his very manner a banisher
of quibbles, leading Sally to insist on splitting.

The two smiled gaily as they passed the Candidate, who said
with a stage Russian accent, "Go with God. Raise the peoples
from their torpor." Then he ambled toward John's corner, shed-
ding good nature amid the chaos. The sweat marks under the
arms of his short-sleeved shirt were spreading; his voice was per-
ceptibly hoarser than it was last week.

He put his hand heavily on John's shoulder.

"How's Saint John?"

"How are you, Mase? They didn't call me Saint John today.
Just a Boy Scout. They compared me to somebody on the far
right—Hitler, if I remember—distinctly in his favor."

"'The best lack all conviction,'" intoned the Candidate,
"'while the worst are full of passionate intensity.'"

"You know I don't believe that, Mase."

"I know you don't. I know you claim you don't. But maybe it's
true."

John did not answer. Now, with Mason, he must try to think,
for the first time this day, but his head was addled with slogans,
raised voices, deficits.

Volunteer ladies tapped on the old typewriters. Two college

boys argued about which ward Dover Street was in (they'd lost the district map). A third cursed the mimeograph machine, which had jammed in the heat of battle. A poet was repeating slogan-words to himself: "alienation-anguish-hopelessness-silence . . ." Donald Bane was diligently teaching some new recruits how to steal chocolates.

"I like to come here," the Candidate said, "to hear all about me the incompetence of the New Left."

"I'm competent," announced Wilfred, en route to repairing the mimeo machine (having already solved the Dover Street ward problem, having disengaged Donald from a clump of Hershey Kisses).

"Yes, Wilfred," said the Candidate. "But you're not human."

Wilfred puffed a pipe all day to comfort people with the illusion that he had a vice. He was thin and quiet, had a doctorate in mathematics at age twenty-three, organized, wrote, analyzed, persuaded, swept floors, calmed bigots at street rallies, disappeared occasionally to earn his living, and never raised his voice. He had become a radical just before puberty upon first examining class relationship in Omaha, Nebraska, and had seen nothing since to change his mind.

Passing John, he announced, "That girl you hired for press releases is illiterate. I put her in charge of the paste-mixing crew for the poster orgy."

"Did you insult her?"

"No, we talked about the beauty of doing simple things with your hands. That means somebody has to get out a release on Vietnam. Should you do it, or I?"

John smiled. "Well, Wilfred, I'd do a slower job on it. But, as compensation, it would be sloppier."

"I'll take care of it. You and Mase have some rallies coming up." Wilfred's voice was already muffled, through the entrails of the mimeograph machine; his pipe and brown pullover rested on a chair. He was the only man on the staff who had a graduate degree but no button-down shirts.

John and Mason strolled together into a corner cubicle where he kept a desk relatively free of debris. There they tried to talk through the main lines of this campaign, into which Mason had been drafted and John drifted.

"Want a coffee, Mase?"

"There are certain things about the Negro Movement I don't quite fathom," said Mason for an answer. "As, for example, why am I at this moment the only Negro in this office?"

"It's a quiet time of day. Rose Carroll and Mrs. Graves will be in after 5.00. We have some new students giving out buttons. I've also been talking to——"

"Yes, yes, Reverend. Very comforting."

They stood at the window looking out upon one of those back lots that everywhere dotted the neighborhood. On an ash heap interlarded with bottles, sodden cardboard, bashed pails, boots, and cans lay a refrigerator on its side, its mouth gaping open. There was a single ailanthus tree still in leaf. Beyond the lot the backs and chimneys of red row houses retreated toward a horizon of brick, pierced abruptly by 55 stories of steel-and-glass sailing into the sunlight—the new insurance tower.

John spoke. "This view always makes me think of a medieval town. The houses huddled in the foreground; the spire hanging over them. It's seven, eight centuries and the towers still go up for the same reason. It's a question of how we organize for the death of all those bodies."

"Don't philosophize, John."

John tried to keep the panic from his eyes, where he knew it was too legible: What else am I good for?

"You're not being paid for that."

"Paid!"

"I'm worried about your life, John. I mean it. You're neither here nor there. You gave up the suburbs but you cling to your debts. Give them up, man! Fall all the way through, you'll feel a lot better. Let the men in blue come attach your wife and kids, your pipe collection. Hear? What more can they do? You'll feel new-washed, like a babe. You'll be free."

"I can't be free until I've——"

"Oh, that's wrong!"

"You didn't hear what I wanted to say."

"Wrong, wrong. Debt is a luxury. It's the most expensive thing this society sells. You can't afford it. Neither can the people in this district. Comes the revolution, first thing we do is have a big bonfire of all the debts. You'll see. People like you will jump in and char their fingers trying to save their installment schedules like they were their babies. But Wilfred and I will beat them back with clubs. One fat black and one lean white, fools for freedom. Right, Wilfred?"

The typewriter paused. Wilfred's lips let out the monosyllable which was his acknowledgment of the world's tendency to chatter.

In the streetlight, John was smiling. He had his station wagon full of life again—viz, Ronnie and Sally and Wilfred, pails of paste, brushes, squeegees, stacks of posters, extensible aluminum ladder, flashlights—the prospect of loping about the night city pasting the Candidate's face to blank walls.

They had been up to their elbows in pails of paste, kneading out the lumps, even Wilfred gossiping, and when enough gear and volunteers had been gathered in the office, John had instructed them to divide up, three or four to a car—"If there is one square foot of brick, one slat of fence in this district without Mason's picture on it by tomorrow morning, well, some heads are gonna roll around here. You better believe it!" (Mirth from the regulars, who always liked John in the role of briefing officer.) "Don't let the cops see you. If they're cruising, let them cruise right on by, then complete your mission. What they don't actually see go up they're too lazy to take down. Any questions? All right, good luck and . . . good hunting!"

Chairs scraped, staple guns and brushes were snatched from the arsenal, and away went youth to tilt at politics, but Ronnie and Sally and Wilfred stayed near.

"What are you waiting for?"

"We want to be on your team," said Sally, batting her eyelashes.

"But I'm a Cold War Liberal."

"Yeah, but you're tall," Ronnie said and actually laughed.

"We need you to put the truth high for all people to see. Then you can wither away, like the state. Come"—this was Wilfred, of course—"we'll help you fulfill your historical role."

John held the car door for them to clamber in among the pails and ladder. They seemed so young and slight—all three—causing this streetlit smile to ease his face.

("I don't suppose anybody wants to go apple-picking?" he would say on October Saturdays, and his children would cheer, piling into the station wagon. They were an itinerant team, welcomed by the farmers; they carried their own ladder, and they would be paid in baskets of McIntoshes or jugs of cider. Afterward, he would talk with those intelligent, narrow-minded men, challenge their scorn for the rest of the world as he never could from the pulpit, and his wife Rosemary talked to their wives and his children played in their trees sometimes until the twilight was pierced with frost, and they would drive home, subdued, with burning foreheads, rolling down the windows to sniff at woodsmoke from the dusk.)

"Hey!" A small shadow shouted its way into the streetlight, casting its own shadow behind. "Ho Jo! Ho Jo, the man-man. It's me!"

John turned eagerly. "Donald Bane! A sight for sore eyes."

"Yeah."

"Donald. You're just in time. I don't suppose you want to go out putting up posters with us? Just for an hour . . ."

"Shit," said Donald, and merged with his shadow, down the street.

The ladder was extended to its full beneath John. The exposed flank of this rooming house was too good to resist, standing five stories high on a hill. He had the whole city beneath him, even a corner of the harbor where aircraft carriers sat shrouded, and it gave him great satisfaction to be placing a good man's face so high and huge where thousands would have to see him in daytime, even if only one in ten cast a vote for him—at best, one in ten. John had raised the money for these Gargantuan posters from one of the Cambridge ladies and now, teetering on a rung above the edge of the city, he was brushing out the bubbles on Mason's face, which seemed enormous enough to swallow him calmly up. He and Mason had first met on a Peace March which John, as parson *engagé*, was leading; it was so pleasant to lead peace marches when he had a house in the country to return to— just another weekend outing and all the nicest people there, the graduate school wives, the guitar twangers, the Negroes with earnest elocution. Much had happened since. "Hey down there, is it on straight?"

Cheers floated up. Sally's face itself floated up the ladder. "Oh, hey, John, it *really* looks great," and she took the brush and squeegee from him, while John stepped after, carrying the pail. Working together in the rubble, they collapsed the ladder, stranding Mason above in his panel of seriousness, and carried everything back to the Pontiac. Wilfred said that by random sampling he reckoned their labors to be earning 3.7 votes per minute, so that if they continued now for 2700 minutes they would have their ten per cent of the vote. Rustling the district maps, they settled into the Pontiac and slammed the last door shut just as a patrol car came out of a shadow near the demolition equipment, with its blue light pulsing, and pulled up alongside.

"All finished, boys and girls?" asked one of the policemen, agreeably.

"Yes, sir," said John.

"Okay. Now, here's what you do. Get out your ladder. Go up there again. And take it down."

In the office, later, a girl with a black braid and a Sarah Lawrence sweatshirt was indignant under the lightbulb. "We just finished putting up a poster and two drunks came by, I mean they were far gone, and they start laughing this falsetto, sadistic laughter. I was sort of scared, you know, but I got sort of mad too, you know, what right do they have to laugh at us any more than we do at them? But they weren't laughing at us. Better if they had. They started saying, 'That fat bastard! Oh my, who gonna give a diddly vote to that fat bastard?' I mean, how can they talk about Mason like that? He's one of their own. It's for them he's running. Oh God, I'm sorry, but it gets me down."

Wilfred studied the bowl of his pipe. "What do you mean, exactly, 'one of their own'?"

"Well . . ."

But John turned away from the prospect of a painful interrogation to tend to a mote at the corner of his field of vision. Donald Bane was sitting alone on the floor by his desk. Ominously, he was not riffling through the chocolates.

"Donald," John said. "How about some Hershey Kisses? Donald. Donald Bane!"

"Don't call me that." The boy's face was clamped in a bitter pout.

"What should I call you?"

"Call him Donald X," Ronnie offered, ruffling at the boy's hair, but Donald shied off the hand with a wild jittery twist of his head.

John looked about the room. Saying nothing, he eased Ronnie away and came back to bend over Donald, who shrank away from him.

"A change of policy," John announced. "Campaign non-worker formerly called Donald Bane henceforth to be known as Donald Nigh. Is that acceptable?"

The wannest smile imaginable escaped from Donald. "Yeah. Call me that."

"Donald Nigh. What are you doing out so late?"

"It ain't late."

"It's after 9.30."

"We got locked out."

"Who's 'we'?"

"Jenny and Ann and me."

"You can't find your mother and father?"

"Yeah, father."

"Okay, then, what about your mother?"

Donald shrugged his shoulders irritably.

"Don't you know anybody else in the building? Why did you come here?"

The boy put on his Donald Bane mask again. "I figured you had all them chocolates."

"Yes, but you're not eating them, are you?"

"No, I ain't eatin' them, am I?"

"Did you have any supper?"

No reaction.

"Did your sisters have any supper?"

Donald shrugged.

"Well, look . . ." John reached into his pocket.

"Wilfred," he called. "Something's come up. Take my car and

finish up the postering, will you? Leave it in front here and give me the keys tomorrow. Can you drive?"

"No," said Wilfred, already herding Ronnie, Sally and two others into the street.

"Let's go," said John to Donald.

Donald led him through streets that were either silent, or broken by noises that were too harsh. Things were meager; or they were garish. Where there was light, it seemed bare. They did not speak.

The house was a four-story bow-front brick on a block of four-story bow-front bricks, fine structures that had acquired a flayed look. The staircase smelled, but did not reek; it was painted the color that Mason called end-of-the-road-green, and flaking; it was lit, but poorly. Jenny and Ann—one small, the other more so—sat silently together. Donald surprised John by offering introductions. "This is my sisters. This is Honest John. He works around with fat Mason."

While John considered his next move, and idly held the two girls' hands, Donald said in a voice quite sullen, as if challenging him to think otherwise, "She always leave us supper. On the table."

John tried the doorknob, tried his various house and office keys, tried his shoulder against the door, and made enough rumpus to bring a man down from one of the rooms on the landing above. He was squat and bald, wearing a red flannel shirt and rolled-up fatigue trousers, a Negro, and he eyed John without a word. John told his story, feeling vaguely guilty—he was too white, his voice to appeasing, he had been, after all, trying to break down a door —and the neighbor asked Donald, "You got a police lock, kid?"

Donald started to answer, then stopped. The neighbor glared not at Donald, but at John, who felt out of his depth.

"You got it, or not?"

Donald reluctantly shook his head, and without a word the squat man climbed up to his own room and back down again. He worked with a bent paper clip and a playing card, slipped the lock and pushed the door open, but did not look in. The children dashed into their room. "Thank you," John said to the neighbor, or rather to his broad, ascending back. The man answered, "Sure," without turning, without malice, without pleasure.

Inside, there was the aura of roaches, and of the struggle against roaches.

The lights were shaded, the linoleum cracked, the table clean, the beds crowded, and the electric wiring that came from the two-burner hot plate was a disaster.

On the table was a soup bowl with some cold rice and another with what looked to be a soybean mixture. There was a plate of biscuits and a small pitcher. "What's in the pitcher?" John asked.

"Syrup," the girls answered in unison, and giggled.

John watched as they washed their hands, and he asked Donald whether everything would be all right now.

"Yeah, it's okay, man. I'll feed 'em."

But Jenny, or Ann, burst into a howl when John said his brisk goodbye. She came to the door, leaned against his leg, and continued to howl.

"Shit," said Donald. He tugged at his miniature sister, and for each tug she raised the volume, whooping like a naval battle-horn.

"You better stay, Ho Jo. She don't ever stop, once she start. Now the other one"—and Donald patted her head, gingerly— "she's real good. She's a cool, calm kid. But this one, she's the bane of my existence."

Donald, the accuser, pointed his finger at the howling mouth, which bit at it with startling speed while John burst into laughter, for the first time that day (although he had, once, smiled).

The company of four sat to dinner. The howler had to bear the name of Ann Bane, the quiet sister was Jenny Nigh, Donald was simply Donald, and John remained Honest John or "man," and it was as a man that he portioned out the rice and soybeans, broke the biscuits equally and passed them around. Donald assumed a casualness, but the little girls' great eyes never left John's face. He said he was afraid they would put the rice into their ears instead of their mouths, a joke which seemed indefinitely renewable until Ann Bane proceeded to do just that. John told them a story about a weather balloon—how much of the world it gets to see—and even Donald's attention was held for a time, although he did not, as he never had in John's presence, open his eyes all the way. The story grew by question and answer, and as John's voice poured out he saw a mockery of himself: Minister of the Seersucker Sect out on just another "home visit"; but this visit was so different from the only other one he had paid during his month in the city, in Mrs. Graves's parlor, all starched curtains and courtesy, where the politically conscious Negro ladies of the district sat on the edges of their chairs and wore hats that seemed made of the same stiff curtains and courtesy; no, this home visit was, well, touching of course, but also somehow more valid, more *real*, be-cause—of course, just because it was non-political, because it was a miniature, didn't pretend to change anything or anybody, just a heartstring-tugging little genre scene (The Soybean Eaters), and as John's voice droned on, he had a memory of a decade ago when the America he visited played behind picture windows its hypocrite routine of the Happy Land, until behind his smile he hungered for anything rough, anything tragic, hiding in his li-brary to read about Auschwitz, Nagasaki, anything to help him feel that the darkness he cherished inside himself wasn't totally outmoded, and yet now when he had his wish, when anyone could see that this was a land smitten with plague, he wanted to turn his eyes away and to look instead for those signs of decency and random kindness (pint-sized Donald tending his half-pint sisters) which would make him feel that Things Are Not So Bad, after all . . .

The girls were beating their forks on the plastic tabletop and laughing at him. The point was that they had cleaned their plates, and now it was time for dessert. Dessert was syrup and biscuits, but John had already given them the biscuits—in fact, they had used them to clean their plates. How could they have biscuits and syrup for dessert if the man had already given out the biscuits? This idea was turned over and over. John asked why they hadn't told him ahead of time, and he got laughter for his answer. He proposed that they have syrup without biscuits; he would have some, too: more laughter. "Ho Jo," wailed Donald, "you just no good at dessert!"

John laughed, two syllables' worth. "I guess I'm not much good at anything."

"No," Donald said, perfectly straight, "you good at some things. You just no damn' good at dessert."

"We gotta eat our syrup *with* something." Ann Bane spoke slowly, to make sure that John understood, as the policeman had an hour before.

"Eat it with your spoon," said John.

Then Jenny Nigh's voice was heard, a whisper. "No," she said. "She mean, we gotta eat our syrup with some food."

"I'll look in the fridge," John offered, chagrined, moving toward a box that wore a great coil on top, like a harridan at the hairdresser's, and there he found a pound of lard, a pot with brown remnants of carrots, perhaps beans, certainly grease, and a bottle with not much milk. When John held the milk out, questioningly, Donald said, "Give it to them," while the boy himself took a cup to the sink, ran the hot tap for a moment, tested it with his finger, filled the cup and came back to the table. John realized that he had never before in his life seen anyone drink warm water straight from the tap.

In such light as the TV could cast from its corner, Rosemary sat, wearing her pale unadorned robe and pale unillusioned look. She was watching a map of the continental United States, upon which bolts of toy lightning flashed, toy rain fell here and there in rhythmic segments, winds puffed out their cheeks near the Great Lakes, but over New England there was a smiling round sun. A man in business suit pointed at the toy phenomena and murmured; the sound was turned down because the children were sleeping. The apartment was, as Rosemary liked to say, cheap but small.

"Where the hell have you been?"

"We had to work late, putting up posters all over the district. The powers-that-be aren't very fond of us, so we have to go around at night."

"Yes?"

"Yes."

"Does sticking paper on walls make 'fuller use of your capacities as a human being'?"

"Why must you keep such a tight score?"

"You want to destroy yourself, John. It's perfectly obvious."

"No, I don't think I want to destroy myself. I just like to suffer."

"Did it ever cross your mind that perhaps *we* don't like to suffer —the children and I?"

"Well, yes. It has crossed my mind."

"What are you going to do about it?"

"I saw Teddy Whorf this morning. Remember him? He asked me if I liked working for a Communist coon."

"John! Don't you dare impute to me the opinions of an empty-headed tennis-clubbing arrested adolescent! Teddy Whorf! You *know* what's on his mind. You're a traitor to your class. That's all. There's us and there's them, and if you go over he figures that you've got some crazy kind of deal going, like Alcibiades. And you know that's not what I think of Mason. He's a fine man, in his own way. But you were fine, too, in your way . . . You were the most promising human being around. Everybody thought so. Even I thought so."

"Yes. That's still the accepted view among ladies with pretty houses."

"The children send you their regards. They particularly urged me to deliver that message."

"How are they?"

"Terrible. In my opinion, they're terrible."

"Oh."

"How you expect them to survive while you indulge your whim for mortification is beyond me."

"What happened in school today?"

"Oh, no. You think you can wander in at midnight and have me conveniently stoke up the fires of your guilt. If you want fresh stories of atrocities in the fourth grade, come home in time and ask them yourself."

"It's only been a couple of weeks——" he began.

"I went down to your so-called office this afternoon. I was feeling miserable and I wanted to apologize for our fight last night. God knows the people in the streets around there are in trouble, I can almost see how you feel. But you weren't in the office, you know. You and Mason were out somewhere crying in the wilderness and all I saw were these swarms of True Believers, mostly unwashed Jewish girls, running off mimeographs and wallowing in their own virtue and gushing about Negro goodness. It was revolting! Occupational therapy should be done in private."

"It's not like that."

"I was *there!*"

"You see what you want to see."

"For heaven's sake! Why do you have to give up your pulpit just to play altar-boy to Mason? Why does Mason have more right to a pulpit than you?"

"Because what I had to say made no real difference."

"That's not true."

"I gave my best sermons on Adlai Stevenson."

"Oh, John!"

"You know, I'm not sure I could be a minister any more. I seem to have lost my mind. Or at least misplaced it."

"I've observed that."

"Things have glazed. I can't tell Tillich from Pascal. I don't see any reason why I ought to."

"What you want is to be rid of *things*. You want to be shorn of responsibilities, of ideas, of us, of everything."

"I don't know," he said, reflectively.

"Then why didn't you just *do* it? Why did you have to drag the children here to choke on carbon monoxide while you work up your courage?"

"I didn't agree with you. I said I didn't know."

"I know! I know. What you want is martyrdom. I ought to pack the kids into the Pontiac right now and go back. You can let us know when your delicious expiations are over. We'll see if there's still room for you."

"You can't do that."

"Don't try me too often, John."

"The Pontiac isn't here."

"Oh, God! You gave it away."

"I did."

"To a Negro mother of nine, blinded in a laundry accident?"

"No, to a white Ph.D. Want to hear what happened?"

"No."

On and on they went, their argument being a midnight ritual which they could not do without. They had to reach a certain point, when she would say, "Well, you can come home tomorrow night or not, it makes no difference to me," while he sat silently. That moment having received its due, they were allowed once

more into the same bed. From the corner, light from within a
hearth-shaped frame played over their faces, pallid, pulsating and
blue, a light that issued not from flames but from faces murmur-
ing away in curious mimicry of their own, for there in another
ritual of midnight a good-looking, clean-cut fella was interviewing
an intelligent, lively gal.

Mason had a stubborn core of resistance to the idea of his
own campaign. To excite people with visionary gestures was unfair, he insisted; it was just another way of having the victims
turn on. What was fair was to boycott the schools, one by one,
to run a rent strike on one block, to build with your own hands
a children's playground. Yet visionary energies seemed to collect around him. His own eloquence and bursts of militancy had
drafted him, and not the Committee itself, which he blamed.
"Politics is a game of false promises." He had always hated it.
He believed in neighborhoods, not in wards, and as a result people who thought instinctively in wards, in blocs, despised his type,
and that infuriated him. Then he would play that game, too,
with attacks of fanatical energy, raising the lost from the very
gutters to follow him, and as a result he would distrust himself:
"Where am I taking them?"

He particularly disliked being photographed in the pose of a
savior.

"Come on, now," Wilfred said. "No soul-searching. Just raise
your arm."

"This shot just doesn't *feel* like me!"

John said, "We're not taking pictures of you as Mason. We
need you as the Candidate."

"That's well said, Honest John. Come, come, be the Candidate. Put on the robes."

As Mason the Candidate, he raised his arm, condemning rubble. As Mason, he said, "The quick lean whites hound the lazy
brown buck."

Wilfred snapped the picture.

There was a deep-South, bucolic air to the time and place: the
sleepy morning heat, the disused park, men dark and white sitting
apart on the crumbling benches. Mason's arm was raised against
a doorway and an alleyway of pint bottles, beer cans, shoes, plas-

tics, rags, bones. He was angry at John for forcing him into this "one-man-against-dreck" role, but the anger, as caught, developed, cropped, and printed by Wilfred, would not easily be glossed over in the city that autumn.

After the click of the camera, the man inside the image turned away, like a knight walking softly out of his armor.

"Mason doesn't like this," John said. "But with time and money, we could carve the sense of him into every conscience within miles."

"Yes," said Wilfred. "That way, he'd be carved into about ten consciences."

John held the telephone to his left ear, awaiting what was sure to be the refusal from the friend of a friend on the New York *Sunday Times Magazine* to grant his demand (or plea) that this campaign be given national coverage ("But this is a unique political event . . . the peace movement, the civil rights movement, the grass-roots city revival people behind a man who can speak for all of them . . . no, the local papers aren't too sympathetic, because we're threatening the . . ."). By his right ear, a girl in a neat jumper and sweater waited: she was leaving college to commit herself to work meaningfully for the Movement, and John was to tell her, as soon as the telephone call was through, how she could help, "in specific terms." But John was listening somehow between the telephone and the commitment-girl to a different sound: the noon migration of the school kids, in the street below. There was something he admired in that screeching infantry which daily moved through the land. The telephone voice began to buzz into his ear; John said, "But this is a unique political event——" The girl in the jumper stirred, restless to begin her commitment. Donald appeared, with three other foot soldiers. He pushed John's elbow, hard, with both hands, laughing.

"Hello, Donald," John said, smiling briefly with his hand over the telephone mouthpiece.

"Hey, man. What's my name?"

"We see it as a merging point for the movements of hope, a campaign where anger and protest can be——"

"What's my name!" This was a shout. The commitment-girl

put out her hand to calm him, but Donald told her to go fuck herself.

"Just a moment," John said into the phone, and took a long look at the boy, who seemed through his slit eyes to be seething on the edge of hysteria.

"Donald Bane?"

Donald wailed with laughter, whipping his followers up with him. "See? He *always* call me that!"

"Not always," John said, but Donald's laughter rang, false; it was put on. Faces in the office studied him, with mixed effect.

"If you could send someone up here for a day or two," John was saying. "It's awfully difficult to catch a sense of it by telephone."

"Where am I?" asked Donald.

He pushed the telephone away from John's face. "I said, 'Where am I?'"

John paused. "I'll be right with you, Donald. Why don't you and your friends give out some buttons, down below, until I'm finished here? Sorry," he resumed into the phone, but held a box of round lapel pins bearing Mason's picture for the boys to draw from.

"God *damn!*" cried Donald and yanked open the Hershey Kisses drawer, excavating two huge handfuls, but, as he wheeled toward his friends, Mason loomed above him.

"Got the *Times Mag* here," John mouthed to the Candidate. "Want to talk to them?"

Mason's attention, however, was on Donald's hands. "Little man," he said, "didn't you hear what the big man said about the buttons?"

The Candidate's presence and voice invaded Donald's eyes, which grew solemn, illegible.

Mason said, "Don't you like politics? Don't you want people to see my ample angry face?"

The commitment-girl contributed, "We're all going to work together. That's the best thing we can do for each other."

In a telephonic pause, John smiled. "You're good at some things, Donald. But you're no damn' good at politics."

Gentle Mrs. Graves, who had arrived to work during her lunch hour, said, "You can't just take what you want in this world, dear. You got to *give* somethin' in return."

"Yes, he *would* write it himself," John assured the telephone, waving down Mason's mimed horror. "We have some first-rate action pictures, in the streets . . ."

Communications at this point suffered a break. Chocolates pelted into John's face and the commitment-girl's. With one wild swing, Donald knocked the telephone from its perch to plummet to the floor, pulling John after, and with another he swept as many stacks of paper from the desk as he could, and raced out in soprano leaps, dodging Mason's ponderous attempt at a tackle.

The four boys screamed in triumph down the street, while John stuttered into the telephone, his cheek near the floor, and Mason bent to help him, laughing condolingly at John's absurd, red, sudden rage.

A surprising number of ladies arrived by taxi. They gave the supermarket the atmosphere of a theater where continuous improvisation was in session, from which they then emerged carrying bright sacks stuffed with their prizes, with chuck roasts and greens and bread.

It was late afternoon; deep in the Negro district. Some faces listened to Mason, or at least watched him, from windows across the way. The ladies hurried by, pushing their market baskets or hailing their cabs. A few men in work clothes stood to listen, and also some very old people, who seemed perplexed, but there were more of the young, schoolboys and schoolgirls, alert, at least during the momentary pause in their promenade, some of them already part-time workers for Mason, all too young to vote.

Mason spoke into the hand-mike, his back to the vast red letters —CHUCK. Ronnie tended the public address system within the car. John stood by, supervising his pamphlet crew. Traffic moved and held, moved and held again, according to its own lava-flow laws.

"There is work to be done in these streets. You know it, I know it. These streets are full of men who aren't working—*who can't find work!* Downtown they say we don't work around here because we don't want to. Hear? *Because we don't want to.* As if any man would rather rot than respect himself . . ."

(The bland smile fell from John's mouth; he felt the serious-ness of a voice he believed, and there was great comfort in that.)

"The city won't do anything about these houses? About the rats, the plumbing, the firetraps. They won't enforce the regula-tions? Then we don't pay the rent. We're going to have some rent strikes!"

(Mild cheers from across the street.)

"That money that doesn't go into the pockets of landlords we're going to pay to our own unemployed, to fix these houses. We're going to have an army out in these streets, working *for themselves* for a change. We're going to clear out these garbage lots and make a place for our children to play. We're going to work with *pride*. If the city doesn't like how we're using the rent money and they start evicting, then we go to live in the churches. People like Rev-erend John over here——"

(John shifted on his feet and nodded.)

"—are ready to take us in, they're *for* us. If the churches get full, then we'll make a tent city downtown in the Common. The Com-mon of this town belongs to the people, and you are the people. Don't you forget that!"

(A cheer or two; prayer-meeting affirmation.)

"This avenue right here heads straight downtown. The fat cats need it to go to work, and they need it to go home to their old ladies. Well, we're going to sit down right in the middle of it, until things change around here. And things *are* going to change around here! *We are going to change them.* You, and I, and that man next door you never talk to. That world of enemies outside your doorstep is going to be a world of friends, working for each other. That's why I'm here, talking to you. That's why I want to be in Congress, representing you."

(A quick look askance to John, who knew Mason didn't want to be in Congress at all; he wanted to work with poor kids in the daytime, and, at night, to read.)

"We need schools here, we need playing fields, libraries, street-lights, and where is the money going that ought to pay for them? I'll tell you where—it goes to pay the people who make the bombs to drop in Vietnam. Well, we've got to change that, too. That's where the peace movement and the Negro movement come to-gether. And I'm not talking only about us, either. I mean all the

people on the bottom, who are not getting a decent life in this
rich country. We must make common cause . . ."

There was a thin, insistent applause when Mason finished.

"Well, let's strike the tent and move on," he said.

John held the car door open for him. "You know, Mase, every
time I hear you talk about some of these——"

"They've got their hearing aids turned off, Honest John. You're
the only one who listens. You *are* going to vote for me, aren't
you?"

The Candidate lowered his bulk wearily into the back seat, and
John followed after.

"They'll go straight Democratic, or they won't register at all. I
feel it in my bones."

"Our bones tell us different, Mase."

"Your bones. Your bones haven't been clanking around here
long enough. I can't trust your bones."

"Tell us again, Mrs. Rose Carroll."

"Oh, children. That day will come."

"And what will happen on that day, Mrs. Rose Carroll?"

The Committee consultants were gathering, and the fund rais-
ers, the leading student workers, some of the diffident Negro ladies
—those few whose husbands allowed them to attend night meetings in this area—and an occasional dark straggler who would back
out and mumble, "Oh, very sorry, very sorry," upon not finding
what must have seemed from street level to be vivid public festivi-
ties. The office was bursting with heat and noise, even before the
rows of folding chairs were filled. The Candidate's face on one of
the large placards was partially obscured by smoke; beneath it he
and John were reviewing the agenda for the night, while Mrs.
Rose Carroll tapped off some of her excess energy by regaling the
students with their weekly *bedtime* story. It was always a variation
of the same story: The Great Oil Explosion, or The Day the Absentee Landlord Got It. Some of the statelier volunteers, geo-
graphically and economically not so remote from Mr. Absentee
Landlord as they might be, had been known to laugh rather wanly
at certain of Mrs. Rose Carroll's details.

"I see those hedges, I see those maples and flowering magnolias,
and then coming on up through them all I see nature's most beau-

tiful sight of all—*Vavoom!*—that big balloon of orange cloud, all streaked and veined in black. Those hedges look like a row of whiskers, those magnolias are flecks . . . Oh, children, there isn't anything can measure up to a good oil explosion. But it's not only the cloud has the glory, children, it is the things, the *items* that fly on up with it. I can just sit for hours and watch them head skywards. I see those pretty gold cuff links. I see a nice piece of paunch, fat and white like fish-belly. I see a Lincoln Continental, whole and *in*tact, headin' right into orbit. And I do think I see a half a bikini, with girl included, my, my, they must have been sitting by the pool when the disaster struck . . ."

Mason's smile was indulgent, his voice hoarse: "Is that a non-violent reverie, Mrs. Rose Carroll?"

"It is only a reverie, Mr. Barnes. Only a reverie."

"Nevertheless. I wonder whether it's good for the children's overheated fancies."

"Local determination, Mr. Barnes. Let's let the children decide."

Ronnie said, "Tell us the worst, Mrs. Rose Carroll."

Out of her immense hauteur, Eleanor Rose Carroll studied the frenzy of his curled head, the ink on his brow. She herself was so formidably neat and self-contained, using her jocundity of figure and face as a Trojan horse from which would unexpectedly burst forth the shock waves of her righteousness and her absolutes. In day-to-day achievement of civil rights, she was perhaps the most powerful worker in the city, rivaled only by Mason and one or two others.

"The worst, young soldier? You want to hear the worst? Well, I don't perceive you are ready for the worst, but I do distinguish another pale *item* flying from that cloud. Let's get it in focus now. It's definitely bigger than a cuff link and smaller than a paunch. Why, it appears to be a detachable part of the old gentleman's body, it's white and curved. But don't tremble, children. It's only a nose. But why *does* it have that strange curve to it, can anyone volunteer to tell me, why *does* it bear that resemblance to a comma——?"

"That's not necessary, Mrs. Rose Carroll," said John, quite sharply. "Let's get on into the meeting."

"Not necessary? Well, you are the number one boss-man of the meetin'. That is a fact. If you say it's not necessary, then it's not necessary. Now, if we cease talking about what's necessary and turn our attention to what is *true* . . ."

John quivered. "It is not necessary, and it is not true. Now we've argued about this before, Eleanor——"

"Don't you call me Eleanor! Who gave you the right to call me Eleanor? Now every week you find some way to toy around with my dignity. Last week you were trying to get away with calling me Mrs. Bang, or whatever, but we put a quick end to *that*, didn't we! This is no kindergarten! You can't get around me with pet names and first names. We're no lifelong friends. You wouldn't hear *me* calling *you* Jacky-boy in front of all these people!"

"I'm sorry, Mrs. Rose Carroll. Let's stick to the point. I have the figures on . . . ethnic origins of the property holders in this district. I think we should clear this up. There simply is not the statistical support for your prejudice."

"Yes, figures, yes, statistics, that's your line, but you don't *know* the first thing about life around here, do you! You don't *know* who puts the squeeze on us day by day, you don't *know* anything! I mean, what *are* you? You're just a white schoolboy, it's not your fault. I mean you're still wet behind the ears——"

Mason faced her. "Calm down, Mrs. Rose Carroll. We need your anger for better things. We can't afford to waste it on petty bigotry."

"Bigotry, now! You think I'm down on the Reverend here because he's white! Well, you've got me all wrong, Mr. Barnes. I'm no bigot. Fact is, I don't even discriminate between you two at all. Neither one of you knows the people down here. You're just the same, with your Ivy League talk, I hear you whispering in those corners. Well, whispering isn't going to do any good now, we've got to get out there and shout. It's getting *late!* You think you can get to the people by singing your tune twice a day into your little microphone, why that's no better than *him* givin' out chocolates to a bunch of useless kids. Now Mrs. Graves and I and a lot of other people are going door by door to meet the people of this district for you, and what do you do? You sit up here looking at pretty pieces of paper with a bunch of white people you let run this campaign! Now this is *our* fight! This is a Negro re-vo-lu-tion . . ."

Wilfred dissected the charged air with the utter everyday tranquility of his voice. "True, Mrs. C., but there are stages to every such movement, when——"

"Oh, I don't mean you, Wilfred dear. You're different. You can call me Eleanor any time." (She held this audience in such storms of guilt that every hint of her smile was pure halcyon.) "No, that's what I mean, I don't put Wilfred down because he's white. He's out with me, and with Mrs. Graves, hour after hour, ringing doorbells. He's going inch by inch, he's *laboring* in these vineyards, and he is getting in touch with the people. They know him, but they don't know you two up there at the head table looking so high and mighty. I don't care if one of you is skinny and white, and the other is round and black, you're birds of a feather! Neither one of you is willing to get out and get your hands dirty around the ordinary people."

John, strangling a shout, said, "That's absolutely unfair! Mason Barnes is giving up his life to live here, to work——"

"Stow it, John," Mason cautioned, *sotto voce*. "You're saying exactly the wrong thing."

"Giving up his life!" Eleanor Rose Carroll fairly bellowed. "You hear? You hear? Mr. Archangel Barnes is throwin' over all his celestial advantages to descend and actually *live* among us diddy-boppers. Halleloo! Well, what about all the folks on this block and the next block, don't have any advantages to give up? Who's going to speak for them? I mean, both of you can leave here any time you want, get yourselves nice fat desk jobs in the U.N. or something, but there's some of us born and brought up right here who are going to stay and fight this thing to the end. Well, I say we should have some authority, we should be granted some *dignity!*"

Mrs. Graves, who had been calculating her moment, put a gentle hand on her friend's arm. "Leave them alone now, Ellie. They're tryin' their best."

And indeed Mason and John stood slightly wilted, while Mrs. Rose Carroll settled back with her forearms massively folded but still seemed to steam and hiss somewhat, in slow subsidence.

"Ladies and gentlemen," John said, quietly and firmly, "we want to thank you again for coming out in such faithful numbers to back this campaign. Tonight's meeting has been given its baptismal fire, as usual, by Mrs. Eleanor Rose Carroll, whom many of you know as one of the stoutest workers on our staff. All I can say

is, thank God she's not against us. It's bad enough as it is. I think
some of her anger is justified, but I want to say on behalf of the
campaign leadership that we have made every effort to encourage
Negro participation on every level, and it is not always so easy as
one might——"

"You want more *indigenous* volunteers?" asked Mrs. Rose
Carroll.

"Not only volunteers. We have some small paying jobs. Typing,
driving . . ."

"Well, now that's what I mean. There's no communication here.
Why didn't you ask me? What are you, ashamed?"

"Could you, Mrs. Rose Carroll?"

"I'll do the enlisting, Reverend John. You just make sure they
got jobs to do before you start handing smiles around."

"Thank you. I will. Now to move on into the agenda, if we
may, with the question of . . ."

John let himself in with the stealth of midnight, prepared to
undergo condemnation by flickering light, but there was no light
in the apartment at all. Over the face of the TV set, a sheet of
notebook paper hung, attached from the top with scotch tape.

Dear John (I'm afraid this *is* a "Dear John"):

This is something you have to work out for yourself. We have become irrelevant to you now and so we're going back out to the country
to enjoy our irrelevance under stars instead of fumes. All the school arrangements are made. They're delighted to have the kids back. These
are exceptionally good kids, but that's the whole point, isn't it? After a
while, if nothing happens, we'll have to work out a separation agree-
ment. I'm willing, for a month or so, to sponge off my sister. In a
grudging way, I admire what you're trying to do, and if you had once
intimated to me after the Big Decision that you still loved me or even
liked me I probably would have seen you through it. As it is, I blame
you for carbon monoxide and you blame me for capitalism and it's all
really too tedious. I still feel so much need to live and to feel, but half
of life is gone.

Love,
Rosemary

In the morning, early, John looked into the mirror. There he still saw his ingenuous and hopeful eyes, even before he began to shave.

Ronnie at the office door: "Honest John! Christ! Where have you been?"

John had been arguing for an hour with the political editor of the paper which that morning had branded Mason's campaign as irresponsible and his campaign workers as "dupes-of-if-not-them-selves-international-Communist-conspirators," and he began to explain this to Ronnie, who blurted at him, "Mason's finking out!"

"What do you mean, finking out?"

"Finking out. Like, he's not showing up at the Monroe Street rally."

The Monroe Street Housing Project was new, and there was nothing to be seen from its concrete center in any direction but itself and sky. Tall shells containing small shells containing people in their own shells, was Mason's description. It would be a testing ground for his new community politics, and there, starting at 5.00, was to be a key rally. Mason's picture was everywhere, circulars had been pushed under every door in the vast warren, the loud-speaker car had been cruising and blaring all afternoon, everybody available had been canvassing personally so that there could be a piazza-like excitement in those vacuous spaces during the after-work hour, and now, with twenty minutes to go, Ronnie keened, Mason had gone into hiding and wouldn't even answer his phone!

"He can't let people down like this! We've all been killing ourselves for him. Sally's over there crying her eyes out."

Past Ronnie's shoulders John saw the typewriters, the mimeo machine, the desks and charts and files, and he felt the deadness of all this material, unless it be quickened with a human voice. At the same time he knew that he had been expecting Mason's silence, and repressing that expectation because it was *unthinkable*.

John, with his notebook out and already planning possible apologies, asked whether this had come suddenly. There were three other speaking engagements scheduled in the earlier afternoon, but Ronnie said Mason had met them all. He himself had heard two of them.

"How was he?"

"Well, you know, the same. He really laid it on the line. But he didn't look edgy, the way he has the last few days. He had this definite look, like you know when somebody decides it's all going to be fine because he can always commit suicide?"

"Yes, I guess I do know."

"No, you don't know, Honest John. You're too damned straight!"

"This is no time for our personal quibble, young man."

"Okay, okay. But what are we going to do? There must be a few hundred out waiting for him already. They're pretty hopped up— you know, nobody ever speaks to people over there right in the project."

"Yes, that's the point. Why hasn't anybody gone over to his place to talk to him? Why do you all have to wait for me?"

"We've been over there in platoons. His wife says from the window that he's had it and can't get up, but he'll start in again tomorrow morning."

John mused. "Maybe that is best. There's still almost two months to go."

"John, there's not going to *be* any tomorrow morning if he finks out on a thing like this. Use your head! Who's going to be out in the streets whipping people out for him if they think he might let them down any time? This is a fragile business, this relationship between leader and worker . . ."

"Don't lecture me on relationships!"

They had a glum silence, until Ronnie pleaded, contritely, "Go over there, will you? You're the only one who can get to him in a personal way."

"Can you stall people off, with music or something?"

"What speech was Mase going to give?"

"On creating community."

"Well, you wrote that one, didn't you, Ho Jo? Couldn't you give it if we're stuck?"

"We wrote it together. I'll either bring him back alive or try to give it myself. Wilfred knows the essence of it. Have him and Mrs. Rose Carroll improvise something if I'm not back in time. We'll salvage what we can."

Mason's apartment was on a hill in a half-demolished neighborhood where he had been doing community work. Inside there were books and records, and a few handsome objects, and it had been broken into several times; one rang the bell in a dark entrance way and then retreated into the street to be recognized from above.

John rang, and stood back to wait. He resolved to be as firm as he could. His only office of the moment was to remove Mason, who contained a needed voice, from this private shelter and out into a public space. Nothing else counted.

But it was Mason's wife, of course, who came to the window. Her eyes grew wide with alarm.

"Oh, John, hi. We thought you would be over at the rally."

"I was downtown, actually." John waved vaguely at the distance. "Did you see the *Ledger* yet?"

"I've kept it away from him so far. This is no day . . ."

"He's feeling pretty low, I guess."

"Oh, John, he's had it. Honestly. He's not a machine, you know."

"I know. I know."

"But he'll be relieved to know you're here. He thought you were sending over all those emissaries because you were so disgusted with him yourself."

"How could I be disgusted with Mason?"

"He hasn't had a quiet minute to himself in the last month. *You* know. He's been on the stump seven times since noon yesterday. There's a moment when an organism just gives out."

"I know."

"You know, he's got to keep going for forty or fifty more days, and a rest till tomorrow would put him right back in shape. He'd really be revived."

"I know."

"There really ought to be some regular scheduled rests. That's your job, John. If you want to get the best out of him."

"I really should, Grace. I'll see to it."

"Mase says you can give this talk better than he can, anyway. He says the basic ideas are yours, and you actually have more experience as a speaker than he does."

"That's very flattering, but I'm just an errand boy. He is the one

people want to hear. He is the Candidate, and he is a Negro,
which we can't——"

"You sound just like Mrs. Rose Carroll!"

"Well, she has a point. These people don't want to hear me."

"I like to hear you talk. I'm Negro."

"Come on, Gracey. Anyway, you're just another Ivy League
type. Those people down in the Project need to hear a voice that's
close to the bone. They need to see a man they can identify
with . . ."

"John, listen to me. Please don't force him to go out now. For
all our sakes. He doesn't even know you're here yet, he's lying in
bed."

"I'm sorry. You'd better tell him."

"Why can't he rest until tomorrow? He needs to recoup!"

"I know it sounds officious, but timing means a lot here. There
are moments you can't have back if you once miss them, and this
rally is one we just can't pass over. The kids who have set this up
need to be reinforced by what Mason can do. In all honesty, he
owes them this one. You can guess, the relationship between
leader and followers is a fragile—well, a subtle business. If he lets
them down——"

"Don't make him feel guilty, John! He's been giving everything
he can. He's not *made* for this!"

"See if you can get him to the window," John insisted. "We'll
arrange a retreat for both of you next week. A few days up in New
Hampshire."

For a moment longer she stared down at him. Then she withdrew and John turned to look back over the fractured lot. Three
Negro children, who had been watching the conversation, began
to play, rather pensively, in the rusted chassis of a Chevrolet.
When John turned, to find Mason's window still blank, they stared
again, until he turned toward them, whereupon they pretended
to be busy, and so on, until two of them began to laugh. John
began to laugh, too, and they waved to each other, the boys very
tentatively. The temptation to yield to Mason's weariness (or
worse than weariness) grew stronger. He wanted to call up to the
window: "No, forget about it. Let's all just be nice to each other."
But he remained silent, and watched the boys as they ripped out
the upholstery of their Chevrolet carcass.

It was Grace who came back to the window.

All right, she said in a flat tone, she had passed John's views on to Mason, and he would be out at Monroe Street in fifteen minutes. But he did not feel up to talking through the window just yet.

John offered to wait and drive him out there, so that he could relax just that much more.

She accused him of not even trusting Mason to be as good as his word. In the same curiously flat tone, she said, "You got what you wanted, John. Now go along."

"It's not what *I* wanted, Grace!"

But she was gone from the window before he could persuade her of any such distinctions.

At the Monroe Street Project, the tumult he heard was mostly in his head, for Ronnie's "few hundred" eagerly awaiting the Candidate had multiplied now that the hour had come into fifty or so idlers, more women than men. But of course when the loudspeaker began to boom, faces might appear all up and down the vertiginous brick pueblos with their row on row of half-open windows. The only white faces anywhere were clustered near a huge poster of Mason.

"Yes, he'll be here all right," said John. He tried to keep the self-congratulation out of his voice.

"Oh, hey, John, that's really——" said Sally, shining with relief.

"Man, when the chips are down," said one of the Negro students.

Mrs. Rose Carroll, making her announcement, typically, in the manner of a flagship hanging out signals: "That is a task well done, Reverend John, and I hope you gave him what for! We must not any of us allow personal weakness to jeopardize the cause we have chosen to serve."

"Now, it's unfair to call it personal weakness, Mrs. Rose Carroll."

"What would you call it?"

Wilfred took him by the arm, saying they had to improvise some kind of action until Mason came, or else lose his audience. "It's my opinion," he went on in his usual cool manner, "that we should have called this whole thing off."

"But——"

"A rally's only a rally. Sound and fury. Mase is a sensitive guy, and I hate to think of him getting embittered this early in the game."

They had strolled a few steps away from the others.

Wilfred mildly proceeded. "He needs a lot of encouragement, you know. You did put it on the basis of how much you liked his speeches lately?"

"Well, not really," John faltered. "No, I have to admit I didn't think of that tack, under the pressure . . ."

"So you harped on his obligation." The cool tone was raised a fraction. "You were a minister, John. At least you could understand something about people."

"I thought it was important for the campaign," John said.

Wilfred shrugged. His eyes, which had looked on the most outrageous corruptions with equanimity, now fixed on John with an icy and undisguised contempt.

When Mason arrived, to the dot of his promise, seeming to be held together with paper clips, John introduced him through the public address system, and then left as soon as "Thank you for those kind words, Reverend John," faded into the substance of the talk.

He emerged from that improbable enclave into a street of good old-fashioned squalor. Behind him he heard the first round of uncertain, stubborn applause. He walked on through a glaze of last afternoon light and then through the shadow several blocks long cast by the steel insurance tower over all these houses with their cracked stoops and occasional sunflowers, until he arrived, stepping stiffly as if in shock, at a familiar street.

In front of the office (which he realized with another shock he had left unlocked and untended; the typewriters and machines were probably stolen, the records looted), he saw a flare of activity on the hood of his car.

Donald Bane and some friends were having a party there. It consisted of eating chocolates, as far as John cared to find out, or of throwing them in bright silvered arcs to people passing by.

When John walked up, Donald dropped from the hood to meet him.

"Hey, man," he said.

"Donald, I have to go someplace. Would you mind? . . ."

Donald screeched at his friends. "Git off the man's car!"

They did. They were wearing Mason Barnes buttons, as was Donald.

"Hey, man," he said, more softly, close by the window of John's car. He held up one cupped hand to show a mixture—two or three Hershey Kisses, two or three Mason Barnes buttons—and his eyes were open wide as if to make an announcement.

John turned the ignition and in frozen silence waited for Donald to free the car window with his other hand.

Then he drove off.

But where to? John slowed down after the first impulse of flight, began to see these streets again with their somber twilight coming on, began to reason with himself. And something in Donald's stance now came back, a repeated and fading flash of a small dark boy holding out one hand . . .

And John made a U-turn.

He had to drive half a block past the office to find Donald standing by a dusty tree, with hands hanging along his sides. The Pontiac stopped, and John mustered through the window his old enthusiasm.

"Hey, Donald! Were those buttons you were giving out just now? That's great!"

Donald stared at him across a gulf, his eyes hooded again. "Shit," he said.

JOHN UPDIKE was born in Shillington, Pennsylvania, in 1932. The author of five novels and numerous short stories, poems and essays, he lives in Ipswich, Massachusetts, with his wife and four children. This is the fifth of his stories to receive an O. Henry Award.

Bech Takes Pot Luck

THOUGH Henry Bech's few persistent admirers among the critics praised his "highly individual and refractory romanticism," his "stubborn refusal to mount, in this era of artistic coup d'état and herd movement, any bandwagon but that of his own quixotic, excessively tender, strangely anti-Semitic Semitic sensibility," the author nevertheless had a sneaking fondness for the fashionable. Each August, he deserted his shabby large apartment at Ninety-ninth and Riverside and rented a cottage on a Massachusetts island whose coves and sandy lanes were crammed with other writers, television producers, museum directors, under-secretaries of State, old *New Masses* editors possessively squatting on seaside acreage bought for a song in the Depression, movie stars whose forties films were now enjoying a Camp revival, and hordes of those handsome, entertaining, professionless prosperous who fill the chinks between celebrities. It innocently delighted Bech, a child of the lower middle class, to see these luxurious people padding in bare feet along the dirty sidewalks of the island's one town, or fighting for overpriced groceries in the tiny general store of an up-island hamlet. It gratified him to recognize some literary idol of his youth, shrunken and frail, being tumbled about by the surf; or to be himself recognized by some faunlike bikinied girl who had been assigned "Travel Light" at the Brearley School, or by a cozy Westchester matron, still plausible in her scoop-back one-piece, who amiably confused Bech's controversial chef-d'œuvre "The Chosen" with a contemporary best-seller of the same title. Though often thus accosted, Bech had never before been intercepted by a car. The little scarlet Porsche, the long blond hair of its driver flapping, cut in front of Bech's old Ford as he was driving to the beach, and forced him to brake within inches of two mailboxes painted with flowers and lettered, respectively, "Sea Shanty" and "Avec du Sel." The boy—it was a boy's long blond hair—hopped out and raced back to Bech's window, extending a soft hand that, as Bech docilely shook it, trembled like a bird's breast. The boy's plump face seemed falsified by the uncut mane; it engulfed his ears and gave his mouth, perhaps because it was unmistakably male, an assertive quarrelsome look. His eyebrows were sun-bleached to invisibility; his pallid blue eyes were all wonder and love.

"Mr. Bech, hey. I couldn't believe it was you."

"Suppose it hadn't been me. How would you explain forcing me into this ditch?"

"I bet you don't remember who I am."

"Let me guess. You're not Sabu, and you're not Freddie Bartholomew."

"Wendell Morrison, Mr. Bech. English 1020 at Columbia, 1963." For one spring term Bech, who belonged to the last writing generation that thought teaching a corruption, had been persuaded to oversee—it amounted to little more than that—the remarkably uninhibited conversations and to read the distressingly untidy manuscripts of fifteen undergraduates. Languid and clever, these young people had lacked not only patriotism and faith but even the coarse morality competitiveness imposes. Living off fathers they despised, systematically attracted to the outrageous, they seemed ripe for Fascism. Their politics burlesqued the liberal beliefs dear to Bech; their literary tastes ran to chaotic second-raters like Miller and Tolkien and away from those saints of formalism—Eliot, Valéry, Joyce—whose humble suppliant Bech had been. Bech even found fault with them physically: though the girls were taller and better endowed than the girls of his youth, with neater teeth and clearer skins, there was something doughy

about their beauty; the starved, conflicted girls of Bech's generation had had distinctly better legs. He slowly remembered Wendell. The boy always sat on Bech's left, a fair-haired young Wasp
from Stamford, crewcut, a Connecticut Yankee, more grave and
respectful than the others, indeed so courteous Bech wondered if
some kind of irony were intended. He appeared to adore Bech;
and Bech's weakness for Wasps was well known. "You wrote in
lower case," Bech said. "An orgy with some girls in a house full of
expensive furniture. Glints of pink flesh in a chandelier. Somebody
defecated on a polar-bear rug."

"That's right. What a great memory."

"Only for fantasies."

"You gave it an A, you said it really shook you up. That meant
a hell of a lot to me. I couldn't tell you then, I was playing it cool,
that was my hangup, but I can tell you now, Mr. Bech, it was real
encouragement, it's really kept me going. You were great."

As the loosening of the boy's vocabulary indicated a prolonged
conversation, the woman beside Bech shifted restlessly. Wendell's
clear blue eyes observed the movement, and obligated Bech to
perform introductions. "Norma, this is Wendell Morris. Miss
Norma Latchett."

"Morrison," the boy said, and reached in past Bech's nose to
shake Norma's hand. "He's beautiful, isn't he, Ma'am?"

She answered dryly, "He'll do." Her thin brown hand rested in
Wendell's white plump one as if stranded. It was a sticky day.

"Let's *go*," a child exclaimed from the back seat, in that dreadful
squeezed voice that precedes a tantrum. Helplessly Bech's hands
tightened on the steering wheel, and the hairs on the back of his
neck stiffened. After two weeks, he was still unacclimated to the
pressures of surrogate paternity. The child grunted, stuffed with
fury; Bech's stomach sympathetically clenched.

"Hush," the child's mother said, slow-voiced, soothing. "Uncle
Harry's talking to an old student of his. They haven't seen each
other for years."

Wendell bent low to peer into the back seat, and Bech was
obliged to continue introductions. "This is Norma's sister, Mrs.
Beatrice Cook, and her children—Ann, Judy, Donald."

Wendell nodded four times in greeting. His furry plump hand

clung tenaciously to the sill of Bech's window. "Quite a scene," he said.

Bech told him, "We're trying to get to the beach before it clouds over." Every instant, the sky grew less transparent. Often the island was foggy while the mainland, according to the radio, blissfully baked.

"Where's everybody staying?" The boy's assumption that they were all living together irritated Bech, since it was correct.

"We've rented a shoe," Bech said, "from an old lady who's moved up to a cigar box."

Wendell's eyes lingered on the three children crammed, along with sand pails and an inflated air mattress, into the back seat beside their mother. He asked them, "Uncle Harry's quite a card, huh, kids?"

Bech imagined he had hurt Wendell's feelings. In rapid atonement he explained, "We're in a cottage rented from Andy Spofford, who used to be in war movies—before your time, he played sidekicks that got killed—and lives mostly in Corsica now. Blue mailbox, third dirt road past the Up-Island Boutique, take every left turning except the last, when you go right, not *hard* right. Mrs. Cook is up from Ossining visiting for the week." Bech restrained himself from telling Wendell that she was going through a divorce and cried every evening and lived on pills. Bea was an unspectacular middle-sized woman two years younger than Norma; she wore dull clothes that seemed designed to set off her sister's edgy beauty.

Wendell understood Bech's apologetic burst as an invitation, and removed his hand from the door. "Hey, I know this is an imposition, but I'd love to have you just glance at the stuff I'm doing now. I'm out of that lower-case bag. In fact I'm into something pretty classical. I've seen the movie of 'Ulysses' twice."

"And you've let your hair grow. You're out of the barbershop bag."

Wendell spoke past Bech's ear to the children. "You kids like to Sunfish?"

"Yes!" Ann and Judy chorused; they were twins.

"What's Sunfish?" Donald asked.

Going to the beach had been the children's only entertainment. Their mother was drugged and dazed, Norma detested physical

activity before dark, and Bech was frightened of the water. Even
the ferry ride over to the island felt precarious to him. He never
sailed, and rarely swam in water higher than his hips. From his
apartment on Riverside Drive, he looked across to New Jersey
as if the Hudson were a wide flat black street.

"Let's do it tomorrow," Wendell said. "I'll come for them
around one, if that's O.K., Ma'am."

Bea, flustered to find herself addressed—for Bech and Norma
had almost enforced invisibility upon her, staging their fights and
reconciliations as if she were not in the cottage—answered in her
melodious grief-slowed voice, "That would be lovely of you, if you
really want to bother. Is there any danger?"

"None. I have life jackets. I used to be a camp councillor."

"That must have been when you shot your polar bear," Bech
said, and pointedly restarted the motor.

They arrived at the beach just as the sun went behind one of
those irregular expanding clouds whose edges hold blue sky at bay
for hours. The children, jubilant at freedom and the prospect of
Sunfishing, plunged into the surf. Norma, as if unwrapping a
fragile gift in faintly poor taste, removed her beach robe, revealing
a mauve bikini, and, inserting plastic eyecups in her sockets, arranged herself in the center of a purple towel the size of a double
bed. Bea, disconsolate in a loose brown suit that did not do her
figure justice, sat down on the sand with a book—one of Bech's,
curiously. Though her sister had been his mistress for two and a
half years, she had just got around to doing her homework. Embarrassed, fearful that the book, so near his actual presence,
would somehow detonate, Bech moved off a few strides and stood,
bare-chested, gazing at his splendid enemy the sea, an oblivious
hemisphere whose glitter of whitecaps sullenly persisted without
the sun. Shortly, a timid adolescent voice, the voice he had been
waiting for, rustled at his shoulder. "I beg your pardon, sir, but by
any chance are you . . . ?"

Wendell found Bech's diffident directions no obstacle and came
for the children promptly at one the next day. The expedition
was so successful Beatrice prolonged her visit another week. Wendell took the children clamming and miniature-golfing; he took
them to an Indian burial ground, to an abandoned windmill, to

grand beaches fenced with No Trespassing signs. The boy had
that Wasp knowingness, that facility with things: he knew how
to insert a clam knife, how to snorkle (just to put on the mask
made Bech gasp for breath), how to bluff and charm his way onto
private beaches (Bech believed everything he read), how to excite
children with a few broken shell bits that remotely might be remnants of ceremonially heaped conch shells. He was connected to
the land in a way Bech could only envy. Though so young, he had
been everywhere—Italy, Scandinavia, Mexico, Alaska—whereas
Bech, except for Caribbean holidays and a State Department-
sponsored excursion to some Communist countries, had hardly
been anywhere. He lived twenty blocks north of where he had
been born, and couldn't sleep for nervousness the night before he
and Norma and his rickety Ford risked the journey up the sea-
board to the ferry slip. The continent-spanning motorcyclists of
"Travel Light" had been daydreams based upon his Cincinnati
sister's complaints about her older son, a college dropout. Wendell, a mere twenty-three, shamed Bech with his Yankee ingenuity,
his native woodcraft—the dozen and one tricks of a beach picnic,
for instance; the oven of scooped sand, the corn salted in seawater,
the fire of scavenged driftwood. It all seemed adventurous to Bech,
as did the boy's removal, in the amber summer twilight, of his
bathing suit to body-surf. Wendell was a pudgy yet complete
Adonis stiff-armed in the waves, his buttocks pearly, his genitals
distinctly visible when he stood in the wave troughs. The new
generation was immersed in the world that Bech's, like a foolish
old bridegroom full of whiskey and dogma, had tried to mount
and master. Bech was shy of things, and possessed few, not even
a wife; Wendell's room, above a garage on the summer property
of some friends of his parents, held everything from canned
anchovies and a Bible to pornographic photographs and a gram
of LSD.

Ever since Bech had met her, Norma had wanted to take LSD.
It was one of her complaints against him that he had never got
her any. He, who knew that all her complaints were in truth that
he would not marry her, told her she was too old. She was thirty-
six; he was forty-one, and, though flirting with the senility that
comes early to American authors, still absurdly wary of anything
that might damage his brain. When, on their cottage porch, Wen-

dell let slip the fact that he possessed some LSD, Bech recognized Norma's sudden new mood. Her nose sharpened, her wide mouth rapidly fluctuated between a heart-melting grin and a severe down-drawn look almost of anger. It was the mood in which, two Christmases ago, she had come up to him at a party, ostensibly to argue about "The Chosen," in fact to conjure him into taking her to dinner. She began to converse exclusively with Wendell.

"Where did you get it?" she asked. "Why haven't you used it?"

"Oh," he said, "I knew a turned-on chemistry major. I've had it for a year now. You just don't take it, you know, before bedtime like Ovaltine. There has to be somebody to take the trip with. It can be very bad business"—he had his solemn whispering voice, behind his boyish naïve one—"to go on a trip alone."

"You've been," Bech said politely.

"I've been." His shadowy tone matched the moment of day. The westward sky was plunging toward rose; the sailboats were taking the final tack toward harbor. Inside the cottage, the children, happy and loud after an expedition with Wendell to the lobster hatchery, were eating supper. Beatrice went in to give them dessert, and to get herself a sweater.

Norma's fine lean legs twitched, recrossing, as she turned to Wendell with her rapacious grin. Before she could speak, Bech asked a question that would restore to himself the center of attention. "And is this what you write about now? In the classic manner of 'Ulysses' movies?"

Under the embarrassment of having to instruct his instructor, Wendell's voice dropped another notch. "It's not really writable. Writing makes distinctions, and this breaks them down. For example, I remember once looking out my window at Columbia. Someone had left a green towel on the gravel roof. From sunbathing, I suppose. I thought, Mmm, pretty green towel, nice shade of green, *beau*tiful shade of green—and suddenly the color at*tacked* me!"

Norma asked, "How attacked you? It grew teeth? Grew bigger? What?" She was having difficulty, Bech felt, keeping herself out of Wendell's lap. The boy's innocent eyes, browless as a Teddy bear's, flicked a question toward Bech.

"Tell her," Bech told him. "She's curious."

"I'm *hor*ribly curious," Norma exclaimed. "I'm *so* tired of being myself. Liquor doesn't do anything for me anymore, sex, *any-thing*."

Wendell glanced again toward Bech, worried. "It—attacked me. It tried to become me."

"Was it wonderful? Or terrible?"

"It was borderline. You must understand, Norma, it's not a playful experience. It takes everything you have." His tone of voice had become the unnaturally, perhaps ironically, respectful one he had used in English 1020.

"It'll even take," Bech told her, "your Saks charge-a-plate."

Bea appeared in the doorway, dim behind the screen. "As long as I'm on my feet, does anybody want another drink?"

"Oh, *Bea*," Norma said, leaping up, "stop being a martyr. It's my turn to cook, let me help you." To Bech, before going in, she said, "*Please* arrange my trip with Wendell. He thinks I'm a nuisance, but he *adores* you. Tell him how good I'll be."

Her departure left the men silent. Sheets of mackerel shards were sliding down the sky toward a magenta sunset; Bech felt himself being sucked into a situation where nothing, neither tact nor reason nor the morality he had learned from his father and Flaubert, afforded leverage. Wendell at last asked, "How stable is she?"

"Very un-."

"Any history of psychological disturbance?"

"Nothing but the usual psychiatry. Quit analysis after four months. Does her work apparently quite well—layout and design for an advertising agency. Likes to show her temper off but underneath has a good hard eye on the main chance."

"I'd really need to spend some time alone with her. It's very important that people on a trip together be congenial. They last at least twelve hours. Without rapport, it's a nightmare." The boy was so solemn, so blind to the outrageousness of what he was proposing, that Bech laughed. As if rebuking Bech with his greater seriousness, Wendell whispered in the dusk, "The people you've taken a trip with become the most important people in your life."

"Well," Bech said, "I want to wish you and Norma all the luck in the world. When should we send out announcements?"

Wendell said, "I feel you disapprove. I feel your fright."

Bech was speechless. Didn't he know what a mistress was? No

sense of private property in this generation. The early Christians; Brook Farm.

Wendell went on carefully, considerately, "Let me propose this. Has she ever smoked pot?"

"Not with me around. I'm an old-fashioned father figure. A mixture of Abraham and Fagin."

"Why don't she and I, Mr. Bech, smoke some marijuana together as a dry run? That way she can satisfy her female curiosity and I can see if we could stand a trip together. As I size her up, she's much too practical-minded to be an acidhead; she just wants to make the sixties scene, and maybe to bug you."

The boy was so hopeful, so reasonable, that Bech could not help treating him as a student, with all of a student's purchased prerogatives, a student's ruthless power to intrude and demand. Young American minds. The space race with Russia. Bech heard himself yielding. "O.K. But you're not taking her over into that sorcerer's-apprentice cubbyhole of yours."

Wendell puzzled; he seemed in the half light a blameless furry creature delicately nosing his way through the inscrutable maze of the other man's prejudices. At last he said, "I think I see your worry. You're wrong. There is absolutely no chance of sex. All these things of course are sexual depressants. It's a medical fact."

Bech laughed again. "Don't you dare sexually depress Norma. It's all she and I have anymore." But in making this combination of joke and confession, he had absolved the boy of the maze and admitted him more deeply into his life than he had intended—all because, Bech suspected, at bottom he was afraid of being out-of-date. They agreed that Wendell would bring back some marijuana and they would give him supper. "You'll have to take pot luck," Bech told him.

Norma was not pleased by his arrangements. "How ridiculous of you," she said, "not to trust me alone with that child. You're so immature and proprietorial. You don't own me. I'm a free agent, by your preference."

"I wanted to save you embarrassment," he told her. "I've read the kid's stories; you don't know what goes on in his mind."

"No, after keeping you company for three years I've forgotten what goes on in any normal man's mind."

"Then you admit he *is* a normal man. *Not* a child. O.K. You stay out of that bastard's atelier, or whatever he thinks it is. A pad."

"My, aren't *you* the fierce young lover? I wonder how I survived thirty-three years out from under your wing."

"You're so self-destructive, I wonder too. And by the way it's not been three years we've been keeping company, it's two and a half."

"You've been counting the minutes. Is my time about up?"

"Norma, *why* do you want to cop out with all these drugs? It's so insulting to the world, to me."

"I want to have an ex*peri*ence. I've never had a *ba*by, the only wedding ring I've ever worn is the one you loan me when we go to St. Croix in the winter, I've never been to Pakistan, I'm *never* going to get to Antarctica."

"I'll buy you a freezer."

"That *is* your solution, isn't it?—buy another box. You go from box to box, each one snugger than the last. Well I for one *don't* think your marvellous life-style, your heady mixture of art for art's sake and Depression funk, entirely covers the case. My life is closing in and I hate it and I thought this way I could open it up a little. Just a *little*. Just a teeny *crack*, a splinter of sunshine."

"He's coming back, he's coming back. Your fix is on the way."

"How can I *possibly* get high with you and Bea sitting there watching with long faces? It's too grotesque. It's too limiting. My kid sister. My kindly protector. I might as well call my mother— she can fly up from West Orange with the smelling salts."

Bech was grateful to her, for letting her anger, her anguish, recede from the high point reached with the wail that she had never had a baby. He promised, "We'll take it with you."

"Who will? You and Bea?" Norma laughed scornfully. "You two nannies. You're the two most careful people I've ever met."

"We'd *love* to smoke pot. Wouldn't we, Bea? Come on, take a holiday. Break yourself of Nembutal."

Beatrice, who had been cooking lamb chops and setting the table for four while Bech and her sister were obstructively gesturing in the passageway between the kitchen and the dining area, stopped and considered. "Rodney would have a fit."

"Rodney's divorcing you," Bech told her. "Think for yourself."

"It makes it *too* ridiculous," Norma protested. "It takes *all* the adventure out of it."

Bech asked sharply, "Don't you love us?"

"Well," Bea was saying. "On one condition. The children must be asleep. I don't want them to see me do anything wild."

It was Wendell's ingenious idea to have the children sleep on the porch, away from what noise and fumes there might be. He had brought from his magical cache of supplies two sleeping bags, one a double, for the twins. He settled three children under the stars, pointing out the constellations and the area of the sky where they might, according to this week's newspapers, see shooting stars. "And when you grow tired of that," Wendell said, "close your eyes and listen for an owl."

"Are there owls?" one twin asked.

"Oh, sure."

"On this island?" asked the other.

"One or two. Every island has to have an owl, otherwise the mice would multiply and multiply and there would be no grass, just mice."

"Will it get us?" Donald was the youngest, five.

"You're no mouse," Wendell whispered. "You're a man."

Bech, eavesdropping, felt a pang, and envied the new Americans their easy intermingling with children. How terrible it seemed for him, a Jew, not to have children, to lack a father's dignity. The four adults ate a sober and unconversational meal. Wendell asked Bech what he was writing now, and Bech said nothing, he was proofreading his old books, and finding lots of typos. No wonder the critics had misunderstood him. Norma had changed into a shimmering housecoat, a peacock-colored silk kimono Bech had bought her last Christmas—their second anniversary. He wondered if she had kept on her underclothes, and finally glimpsed, as she bent frowning over her overcooked lamb chop, the reassuring pale edge of a bra. During coffee, he cleared his throat. "Well, kids. Should the séance begin?"

Wendell arranged four chairs in a rectangle, and produced a pipe. It was an ordinary pipe, the kind that authors, in the corny days when Bech's image of the literary life had been formed, used to grip on dust-jacket photographs. Norma took the best chair, the wicker armchair, and impatiently smoked a cigarette while Beatrice cleared away the dishes and checked on the children. They were asleep beneath the stars. Donald had moved his sleeping bag against the girls' and lay with his thumb in his mouth and the other hand on Judy's hair. Beatrice and Bech sat down, and Wendell spoke to them as if they were children, showing them the magic substance, which looked like a residue of pencil shavings in a dirty tobacco pouch, instructing them how to suck in air and smoke simultaneously, how to "swallow" the smoke and hold it down, so the precious narcotic permeated the lungs and stomach and veins and brain. The thoroughness of these instructions aroused in Bech the conviction that something was going to go wrong. He found Wendell as an instructor pompous. In a fury of puffing and expressive inhaling, the boy got the pipe going, and offered first drag to Norma. She had never smoked a pipe, and suffered a convulsion of coughing. Wendell leaned forward and greedily inhaled from midair the smoke she had wasted. He had become, seen sidewise, with his floppy blond hair, a baby lion above a bone; his hungry quick movements were padded with a sinister silence. "Hurry," he hoarsely urged Norma, "don't waste it. It's all I have left from my last trip to Mexico. We may not have enough for four."

She tried again—Bech felt her as tense, rebellious, all too aware that, with the pipe between her teeth, she became a sharp-nosed crone—and coughed again, and complained, "I'm not *getting* any."

Wendell whirled, barefoot, and, stabbing with the pipestem, said, "Mr. Bech."

The smoke was sweet and circular and soft, softer than Bech could have imagined, ballooning in his mouth and throat and chest like a benevolent thunderhead, like one of those valentines from his childhood that unfolded into a three-dimensional tissue-paper fan. "More," Wendell commanded, thrusting the pipe at him again, ravenously sniffing into himself the shreds of smoke that escaped Bech's sucking. This time there was a faint burning —a ghost of tobacco's unkind rasp. Bech felt himself as a domed chamber, with vaults and upward recesses, welcoming the cloud; he shut his eyes. The color of the sensation was yellow mixed with blue yet in no way green. The base of his throat satisfyingly burned.

While his attention was turned inward, Beatrice was given the pipe. Smoke leaked from her compressed lips; it seemed intensely poignant to Bech that even in depravity she was wearing no lipstick. "Give it to *me*," Norma insisted, greedily reaching. Wendell snatched the pipe against his chest and, with the ardor of a trapped man breathing through a tube, inhaled marijuana. The air began to smell sweetish, flowery, and gentle. Norma jumped from her chair and, kimono shimmering, roughly seized the pipe, so that precious sparks flew. Wendell pushed her back into her chair and, like a mother feeding a baby, insinuated the pipestem between her lips. "Gently, gently," he crooned, "take it in, feel it press against the roof of your mouth, blossoming inside you, hold it fast, fast." His s's were extremely sibilant.

"What's all this hypnosis?" Bech asked. He disliked the deft way Wendell handled Norma. The boy swooped to him and forced the pipe into his mouth. "Deeper, deeper, that's it, good . . . good . . ."

"It burns," Bech protested.

"It's supposed to," Wendell said. "That's beautiful. You're really getting it."

"Suppose I get sick."

"People never get sick on it, it's a medical fact."

Bech turned to Beatrice and said, "We've raised a generation of amateur doctors."

She had the pipe; handing it back to Wendell, she smiled and pronounced, "Yummy."

Norma kicked her legs and said savagely, "Nothing's *hap*pening. It's not *do*ing anything to me."

"It will, it will," Wendell insisted. He sat down in the fourth chair and passed the pipe. Fine sweat beaded his plump round face.

"Did you ever notice," Bech asked him, "what nifty legs Norma has? She's old enough to be your biological mother, but condescend to take a gander at her gams. We were the Sinewy Generation."

"What's this generation bag you're in?" Wendell asked him, still rather respectfully English 1020. "Everybody's people."

"*Our* biological mother," Beatrice unexpectedly announced, "thought actually *I* had the better figure. She used to call Norma nobby."

"I *won't* sit here being discussed like a piece of meat," Norma said. Grudgingly she passed the pipe to Bech.

As Bech smoked, Wendell crooned, "Yes, deeper, let it fill you. He really has it. My master, my guru."

"Guru you," Bech said, passing the pipe to Beatrice and speaking with a rolling slowness, sonorous as an idol's voice. "All you flower types are incipient Fascists." The *a*'s and *s*'s had taken on a private richness in his mouth. "Fascists *manqués*," he said.

Wendell rejected the pipe Beatrice offered him. "Give it back to our teacher. We need his wisdom. We need the fruit of his suffering."

"*Manqué* see, *manqué* do," Bech went on, puffing and inhaling. What a woman must feel like in coitus. More, more.

"*Mon maître*," Wendell sighed, leaning forward, breathless, awed, loving.

"Suffering," Norma sneered. "The day Henry Bech lets himself suffer is a day I'm dying to see. He's the safest man in America, since they retired Tom Dewey. Oh, this is horrible. You're all being so silly and here I sit perfectly sober. I hate it. I hate *all* of you, absolutely."

"Do you hear music?" Bech asked, passing the pipe directly across to Wendell.

"Look at the windows, everybody people," Beatrice said. "They're coming into the room."

"*Stop* pretending," Norma told her. "You *always* played up to Mother. I'd rather be nobby Norma than bland Bea."

"She's beautiful," Wendell said, to Norma, of Beatrice. "But so are you. The Lord Krishna bestows blessings with a lavish hand."

Norma turned to him and grinned. Her tropism to the phony like a flower's to the sun. Wide warm mouth wherein memories of pleasure become poisonous words.

Carefully Bech asked the other man, "Why does your face resemble the underside of a colander in which wet lettuce is heaped?" The image seemed both elegant and precise, cruel yet just. But the thought of lettuce troubled his digestion. Grass. All men. Things grow in circles. Stop the circles.

"I sweat easily," Wendell confessed freely. The easy shamelessness purchased for an ingrate generation by decades of poverty and war.

"And write badly," Bech said.

Wendell was unabashed. He said, "You haven't seen my new stuff. It's really terrifically controlled. I'm letting the things dominate the emotions instead of vice versa. Don't you think, since the 'Wake,' emotions have about had it in prose?"

"Talk to *me*," Norma said. "He's absolutely self-obsessed."

Wendell told her simply, "He's my god."

Beatrice was asking, "Whose turn is it? Isn't anybody else worried about the windows?" Wendell gave her the pipe. She smoked and said, "It tastes like dregs."

When she offered the pipe to Bech, he gingerly waved it away. He felt that the summit of his apotheosis had slipped by, replaced by a widespread sliding. His perceptions were clear, he felt them all trying to get through to him, Norma seeking love, Wendell praise, Beatrice a few more days of free vacation; but these arrows of demand were directed at an object in metamorphosis. Bech's chest was sloping upward, trying to lift his head into steadiness, as when, thirty years ago, carsick on the long subway ride to his Brooklyn uncles, he would fix his eyes in a death grip on his own reflection in the shuddering black glass. The funny wool Buster Brown cap his mother made him wear, his pale small face, old for his age. The ultimate deliverance of the final stomach-wrenching stop. In the lower edge of his vision Norma leaped up and grabbed the pipe from Beatrice. Something fell. Sparks. Both women scrambled on the floor. Norma arose in her shimmering kimono and majestically complained, "It's out. It's all gone. Damn you, greedy Bea!"

"Back to Mexico," Bech called. His own voice came from afar, through blankets of a gathering expectancy, the expanding motionlessness of nausea. But he did not know for a certainty that he was going to be sick until Norma's voice, a few feet away in the sliding obfuscation, as sharp and small as something seen in reversed binoculars, announced, "Henry, you're absolutely yellow!"

In the bathroom mirror he saw that she was right. The blood had drained from his long face, leaving like a scum the tallow of his summer tan, and a mauve blotch of sunburn on his melancholy nose. Face he had glimpsed from a thousand pits, in barbershops and barrooms, in subways and airplane windows above the Black Sea, before shaving and after lovemaking, it witlessly smiled, the eyes very tired. Bech kneeled and submitted to the dark ecstasy of being eclipsed, his brain shouldered into nothingness by the violence of the inversion whereby his stomach emptied itself, repeatedly, until a satisfying pain scraped tears from his eyes, and he was empty.

Beatrice sat alone in the living room by the dead fireplace. Bech asked her, "Where is everybody?"

She said, unmoving, uncomplaining, "They went outside and about two minutes ago I heard his car motor start."

Bech, shaken but sane, said, "Another medical fact exploded."

Beatrice looked at him questioningly. Flirting her head, Bech thought, like Norma. Sisters. A stick refracted in water. Our biological mother.

He explained, "A, the little bastard tells me it won't make me sick, and B, he solemnly swears it's a sexual depressant."

"You don't think—they went back to his room?"

"Sure. Don't you?"

Beatrice nodded. "That's how she is. That's how she's always been."

Bech looked around him, and saw that the familiar objects—the jar of dried bayberry; the loose shell collections, sandy and ill-smelling; the damp stack of books on the sofa—still wore one final, gossamer thickness of the mystery in which marijuana had clothed them. He asked Bea, "How are you feeling? Do the windows still worry you?"

"I've been sitting here watching them," she said. "I keep thinking they're going to tip and fall into the room, but I guess they won't really."

"They might," Bech told her. "Don't sell your intuitions short."

"Please, could you sit down beside me and watch them with me? I know it's silly, but it would be a help."

He obeyed, moving Norma's wicker chair close to Bea, and observed that indeed the window frames, painted white in unpainted plank walls, did have the potentiality of animation, and a disturbing pressingness. Their center of gravity seemed to shift from one corner to the other. He discovered he had taken Bea's hand—limp, cool, less bony than Norma's—into his. She gradually turned her head, and he turned his face away, embarrassed that the scent of vomit would be still on his breath. "Let's go outside on the porch," he suggested.

The stars overhead were close and ripe. What was that sentence from "Ulysses"? Bloom and Stephen emerging from the house to urinate, suddenly looking up—*The heaventree of stars hung with humid nightblue fruit.* Bech felt a sadness, a terror, that he had not written it. Not ever. A child whimpered and rustled in its sleep. Beatrice was wearing a loose pale dress luminous in the air of the dark porch. The night was moist, alive; lights along the horizon pulsed. The bell buoy clanged on a noiseless swell. She sat in a chair against the shingled wall and he took a chair facing her, his back to the sea. She asked, "Do you feel betrayed?"

He tried to think, scanned the scattered stars of his decaying brain for the answer. "Somewhat. But I've had it coming to me. I've been getting on her nerves deliberately."

"Like me and Rodney."

He didn't answer, not comprehending and marvelling instead how, when the woman crossed and recrossed her legs, it could have been Norma, a gentler, younger Norma.

She clarified, "I forced the divorce."

The child who had whimpered now cried aloud; it was little Donald, pronouncing hollowly, "The owl!"

Beatrice, struggling for control against her body's slowness, rose and went to the child, kneeled and woke him. "No owl," she said. "Just Mommy." With that ancient strange strength of mothers she pulled him from the sleeping bag and carried him back in her arms to her chair. "No owl," she repeated, rocking gently, "just Mommy and Uncle Harry and the bell buoy."

"You smell funny," the child told her.

"Like what funny?"

"Like sort of candy."

"Donald," Bech said, "we'd never eat any candy without telling you. We'd never be so mean."

There was no answer; he was asleep again.

"I admire you," Beatrice said at last, the lulling rocking motion still in her voice, "for being yourself."

"I've tried being other people," Bech said, fending, "but nobody was convinced."

"I love your book," she went on. "I didn't know how to tell you, but I always rather sneered at you, I thought of you as part of Norma's phony crowd, but your writing, it's terribly tender. There's something in you that you keep safe from all of us."

As always when his writing was discussed to his face, a precarious trembling entered Bech's chest. A case of crystal when heavy footsteps pass. He had the usual wild itch to run, to disclaim, to shut his eyes in ecstasy. More, more. He protested, "Why didn't anybody at least knock on the door when I was dying in the bathroom? I haven't whoopsed like that since college."

"I wanted to, but I couldn't move. Norma said it was just your way of always being the center of attention."

"That bitch. Did she really run off with that little prep-school woolly bear?"

Beatrice said, with an emphatic intonation dimly, thrillingly familiar, "You *are* jealous. You *do* love her."

Bech said, "I just don't like creative-writing students pushing me out of my bed. I make a good Phoenician Sailor but I'm a poor Fisher King."

There was no answer; he sensed she was crying. Desperately changing the subject, he waved toward a distant light, whirling, swollen by the mist. "That whole headland," he said, "is owned by an ex-member of the Communist Party, and he spends all his time putting up No Trespassing signs."

"You're nice," Beatrice sobbed, the child at rest in her arms.

A motor approached down the muffling sandy road. Headlights raked the porch rail, and doubled footsteps crashed through the cottage. Norma and Wendell emerged onto the porch, Wendell carrying a messy thickness of typewriter paper. "Well," Bech said, "that didn't take long. We thought you'd be gone for the night. Or is it dawn?"

"Oh, Henry," Norma said, "you think *every*thing is sex. We went back to Wendell's place to flush his LSD down the toilet, he felt so guilty when you got sick."

"Never again for me, Mr. Bech. I'm out of that subconscious bag. Hey, I brought along a section of my thing, it's not exactly a novel, you don't have to read it now if you don't want to."

"I couldn't," Bech said. "Not if it makes distinctions."

Norma felt the changed atmosphere and accused her sister, "Have you been boring Henry with what an awful person I am?

How could the two of you *ima*gine I'd misbe*have* with this *boy* under your noses? Surely I'm subtler than *that*."

Bech said, "We thought you might be high on pot."

Norma triumphantly complained, "I never got *any*thing. And I'm *po*sitive the rest of you faked it." But, when Wendell had been sent home and the children had been tucked into their bunks, she fell asleep with such a tranced soundness that Bech, insomniac, sneaked from her side and safely slept with Beatrice. He found her lying awake waiting for him. By fall the word went out on the literary circuit that Bech had shifted mistresses again.

DAVID GRINSTEAD grew up in Barrington, Illinois, and graduated from Yale in 1961. After a four-year period with the Marine Corps, he wrote for a newspaper, a television news show and a wire service. He is now traveling in Europe where he plans to continue writing.

A Day in Operations

IT IS A compressed Vietnamese morning, hot, bright and steamy. I feel the weight of air and sunlight. Flies buzz solidly. Odors have earthy textures. Everything in the shade dots and smells. Everything in the sunlight bakes and shimmers. The surrounding jungle resembles impervious, shiny, hot green vinyl.

I am sitting here in a musty dark office tent in battalion headquarters and I am watching Major Burgoyne. Major Burgoyne sits at a green, iron-bound fiberboard field desk on the other side of the tent. He says, "That patrol ought to be back by *now*," and he cranks a battery-powered EE-8 field phone on his desk. He is trying to reach Mark Lion, the battalion switchboard.

Major Burgoyne is brown and wrinkled, his face a leathery mask. His gray hair is close-cropped; he has cultivated the appearance of a man of action, and his gray eyes have a chameleon ability to display active moods, darting and flashing. But his eyes in repose, or unguarded as they are now, are watery, dull pouches.

The major stands and cranks the phone faster. The operator has not answered. There could be a dozen reasons: a faulty wire-splice; a pinhole in the insulation; or perhaps the switchboard

"A Day in Operations"—David Grinstead, *The Literary Review*, Copyright © 1968 by Fairleigh Dickinson University. Reprinted from *The Literary Review* (Autumn 1968, Volume 12, Number 1), published by Fairleigh Dickinson University, Rutherford, New Jersey.

drop lever has gone down and the operator is tired and has not noticed it; or perhaps the wire has been cut by a vehicle.

The major mutters, "Goddam operator's sacked out. Lazy!" He cranks and puffs. "Mark Lion? Mark Lion?" There is no response. "Mark Lion—dammit! Who's on this line? Who's *ON* this *LINE?*" He is leaning across his desk, huddling over his phone. With his right hand, he clamps the handset against his ear; with his right elbow, he steadies the canvas phone case on his desk top. He cranks with his left hand. "Mark Lion? *MARK LION?*" He cranks frantically, and his shoulders and back pick up the rhythm. He is wrapped around the phone, shaking. "Is *ANYONE* on this *LINE?*" His voice has become a quaver. The edges of his lips work around his front teeth. He squints painfully. His face crumples and he seems on the verge of tears. Then he self-consciously forms his eyes into inscrutable slits. He straightens, puts the handset on his desk, and shakes the phone case. He frowns and purses his lips.

I continue working at my desk: that is, I look busy. I doodle deceptive straight lines on a lined pad. I have a field manual on ordnance trajectories open before me. He does not know I am charting the parabola of his destruction.

Now he has noticed that the phone is loose. He shakes it again. Last month he ran wire through the phone case buckles and through the iron fittings on his desk, lashing the phone down so that he could crank it easily. He forgot he had done this. Early this morning I loosened the lashings. Now he has made his ridiculous appearance. The disintegration has started. Sweat runs from him; his hands fall limply from the phone, and he flops back into his chair. He has lost this skirmish. He consolidates. Standing, he puts on his cap and says, "I'm going to breakfast, Corporal." He walks out of the tent, stooping. It is 0725. The work day has just begun.

Major Burgoyne is the battalion operations officer. I am a clerk in operations section. I am a corporal, twenty-two years old. I was drafted out of college last year. I was majoring in philosophy, and I think I accepted the draft philosophically. When my draft notice came, I shrugged and said, "Well, they can do it." I have tried to maintain this attitude. I have tried to avoid committing myself to any abstract rules or theoretical judgments during this experience, hoping instead to form these more rationally later.

In the States, our training base had its adjacent base town. It seemed every bar in town had retired master-sergeant bartenders who served us watered beer while telling us their war experiences ("You kids don't know what it's like"). When this happened, I just said, "Well, they can do it." And if police arrested us in bars and whorehouses and laid fines on us, I just said, "Well, they can do it." The town was segregated, formed of neat houses with American flags in front; its stores sold expensive, shoddy merchandise. When the base ran compulsory fund drives for good-neighbor relations with the town, I just said, "Well, they can do it." Finally when our division was alerted for Viet Nam, some of the towns-people handed us Bibles and prayed for us to kill Communists, and other townspeople, merchants, lobbied to keep the division on base. About both actions I just said, "Well, they can do it."

Of course, I could not remain completely detached in Viet Nam. I was in Charlie Company, one of the rifle companies in this battalion. I was a squad leader and was promoted quickly. All my friends are in Charlie Company. I permit the generalization that collective fear breeds collective friendship. In some ways, it was a small relief to go into combat with Charlie Company. For the first time since I was drafted, there were no veterans of previous wars talking about their wars and telling us what we were fighting for. I know what we fought for in Charlie Company. We fought for our asses—or, if you will, for our existence. We were too close to the Viet Cong to fight for anything else. Charlie Company was too close to the Viet Cong for anyone to deliver abstractions to us. We were committed to concretenesses.

Several weeks ago I was hurt and went to the division hospital. While I was in the hospital, someone in Battalion Personnel looked at my file and saw that I had three years of college, so I was assigned to Battalion Headquarters. The personnel officer told me I'd had my war and assigned me to S-3, operations section, as a clerk. I reported to Major Burgoyne in the operations tent. He sat behind his desk and looked at me. Smiling, he said, "How fast did you make corporal, son?"

"Ten months, sir."

He leaned back in his chair, looked at the tent roof. "Ahhh—

I made it that fast in World War Two. About your age. I went into an operations office then, too. I was commissioned in Korea." He faced me. "Field commission." He sat up. "Well, if you want to stay in, this is the place. You can be operations NCO. We need experienced people. I use my experience every day. You will too. Helps you to analyze nervous reports, sort among all the confusion." He looked steadily at me. "That's what courage is, you know —you remember. Rising above all that confusion."

He rose and gestured to his map-board, an acetate-covered map mounted on plywood, resting on an easel. On the acetate, blue rectangles showed friendly forces, red rectangles showed enemy. "That is your eyesight," he said. "That's the big picture. As you can see . . ." he pointed at neatly spaced grease pencil lines on the acetate, ". . . we use, we *rely* on our phase lines and patrol routes. With everyone chasing these guerrillas we have to keep from running into one another. We have our own area to operate and patrol in, and we have to stay in it, and faithfully stick to our phase lines and routes. This is the best way to control the fighting."

He walked from behind his desk and waved at an array of green radios in one tent corner. "Those are our voices and ears. Communication is control. We filter all information through the phone and radios, and through my experience . . ." again, he looked at me, ". . . and through your experience, son. We put it all in order." He smiled. "Especially in jungle warfare we can't afford to miss seeing the forest for the trees." He laughed, then stopped and frowned. "We control all the fighting here in S-3, Corporal. It's a serious job." Then he gestured to my desk and I started work.

That was not the first time I saw Major Burgoyne. I first saw Major Burgoyne the day I was hurt. All the night before, my squad had been on a routine patrol. It had rained all night, and we were chilled and mud-caked from six hours of crawling through a palm grove looking for two local-force snipers. We and the locals had patrolled around each other so often that we continually outguessed each other, each failing to trap the other, sharing the same rotten weather and tense darkness. Sometimes I felt we knew the VC better than we knew Americans outside of Charlie Company. The VC got more sack time than we did, and when they were chipper they shot wildly trying to make us thrash around or charge them. Anyway, we didn't catch them that night.

At dawn, I brought my squad back to Charlie Company's muddy tent camp. The rain stopped and immediately it was steaming hot. At Charlie Company there was barely enough water to refill canteens, so we couldn't wash in our helmets. We stripped and scraped the caked mud from between our toes and legs, and we cleaned our weapons and smoked our first cigarettes in ten hours. It was already too hot to eat, and most of us were still too nervous to be hungry.

Everyone in my squad was developing immersion foot. Two men had festering jungle sores, and another had clap aggravated from crawling. Another worried about his pregnant wife, and another worried about his sluttish wife, and all of us thought about death in a bleak way ("What, and miss all *this*?"). At twenty-two, I was the oldest, and I half-coaxed, half-kidded the others into cleaning themselves and their weapons. We were sitting together in the brown mud, staring at our mud-streaked toes and wiggling them in the hot sunlight, thinking about a mail delivery and more water, when word came down that Charlie Company was moving out.

So we dressed and moved out with a common mood of "My God, what'll it be *next*?" We willed to survive each patrol and operation as it came up. None of us had any fond eternal hopes, just a low-key persistent drive to make it through the next five minutes, and the next, and the next, and the next.

Charlie Company plodded down a sucking, red, clay-mud road toward a breathless, hot green valley. The sun beat down on us and sweat ran down our noses and spines, salt-caking our dirt-stiff clothes. Heavy mud clung to our feet and ankles. To our right and left, several hundred meters away, other troops from other companies marched through low green brush toward the same valley. From behind us and overhead, our artillery rounds made sounds like ripping canvas, and impacted far ahead, exploding orange and gray on the green valley walls.

In Charlie Company we cooperated and moved smoothly. As the clay road turned and entered the valley, without spoken command the company deployed on either side of the road and continued forward. Since my squad had been up all night, my platoon leader put us in reserve, at the rear of the platoon. I was moving my squad off the road when all of Charlie Company came under fire. I took my squad forward a few meters to a deep gully, and we stooped under its earth bank.

Ahead of us, irregular small arms fire rattled and knocked. The fire came from some thorny hedgerows two hundred meters forward on both sides of the road. The hedgerows surrounded a brown thatched-roof hamlet. Beyond the hamlet lay a wide expanse of rice paddy, filling the valley floor.

Other reserve people, from other platoons in Charlie Company, moved into the gully. More troops were lying and crawling ahead of us, taking cover from the hamlet's fire. Occasionally rifle rounds slapped the top of the bank, showering us with dirt. We had clogged noses, cotton-mouth, itchy skin and smelly clothes. Flies and gnats swarmed around us.

My platoon leader and company commander were forward, looking at the hedgerows. They ran, crouching, to the gully, and dived over the bank. Following shots whacked overhead and thudded into the bank. The two were talking about ways to clear the hedgerows when Major Burgoyne appeared.

The major walked up the road from behind us. A few meters behind him chugged his radio jeep. The major said something about always walking around with troops, that it looked bad to ride. Then a machine gun in the hamlet sent dirt-kicking rounds tracking along the road after the jeep, and the jeep lurched forward and swerved heavily off the road into the sheltering gully. The driver sat clenching his wheel, fish-pale, eyes and mouth wide open, trembling. Machine gun rounds hammered the bank, more dirt fell on us, everyone crowded against the bank, and I watched Major Burgoyne and my company commander.

The major smiled, first, then yelled above the noise, "My God, we haven't had an operation in a week. You should be hot to go! You letting one machine gun hold you up?"

My company commander tried to answer him. In the States, most of us smiled or laughed in ranks when he talked—he was a homely, solid, inarticulate ex-tackle. When he spoke to the major he laboriously laid out homely, solid thoughts.

"There is, uh, resistance, like, you can see that machine gun is firing from the hedgerows, the wrong place, like, I think maybe there is more than the gun *inside* the hamlet, see? . . . and maybe we oughta ziggy around and, from the side, hit 'em, like over that way." He pointed, then opened one palm and looked at it and hit it with a meaty fist. "Envelopment," he said.

Major Burgoyne was standing up straight, in the lee of the earth bank. His eyes flashed and he said, "Look—what are you talking about? You're holding up the whole battalion. You are supposed to be on the paddy dike on the other side of the hamlet by now. That's Phase Line Zulu. The other companies are already there."

"Well, uh, it's—they're not *defending* the hedgerows right. They're *nibbling* like they want to sucker us into the hamlet, maybe, maybe zap us from the valley. Hills, I mean. So I don't think we should go straight from here to the hamlet. No frontal."

"Look, Captain—Artillery has the valley sealed off. The operation order calls for companies advancing on parallel axes. The other companies are ahead of you and all you have in your way is one dinky little hamlet, probably with old farmers, local forces— and I have to have a whole battalion waiting on you. You had the road to come up on."

"Major, if I was going to sucker-trap some company I'd hope like hell they diddy-bop up a road through hedgerows in a hamlet. And that paddy dike is out in the open."

The major stood at rigid attention and said, "The paddy dike is clear. Other companies are already on the paddy dike. Follow the order. Get through that hamlet to the dike. That is your phase line and I want you there by 1500 and the colonel wants you there by 1500." The major stared around at us in the gully, turned back to the company commander, and said, "Get these people moving."

My company commander led well enough by being himself. Beefy and earnest, he had a genuine charisma. Because he had charisma, I felt his exasperation. He kept his face impassive. He waved at my platoon leader, and said, "Frontal—you get to the left of the road." Then he turned and waved to another platoon leader. My platoon leader whistled at his other squad leaders and pointed at the hedgerows. Then he turned toward me and raised his eyebrows. I shrugged. Ahead, other troops rose and moved toward the hedgerows. Then all of us climbed out of the gully and moved forward, tired, slack-kneed and breathless, leaving the major with his radio jeep back in the gully.

The major and the captain were both right, in theory. The paddy dike was clear and the valley had been sealed off by artillery fire; the fire had driven Viet Cong into the hamlet. The hedge-rows were a sucker trap. Rural lads from somewhere were deployed in fire teams and squads among hedges and haystacks and hog wallows. They had Sudayev assault rifles, Degtyarev light machine guns, string-fuzed Chinese grenades, and dozens of punji stakes.

In the hamlet, I was moving my squad toward a haystack, all of us trying to look and listen everywhere at once. My right sock had fallen and bunched under my arch and my right heel was chafing. I was watching my leading rifleman and thinking mostly about my right sock when I realized I could not move my left foot. Looking down, I saw a barb-tipped metal rod sticking through the caked mud at the instep of my left boot, straight up from the ground through my foot. No one in my squad was killed that day.

I do not like my headquarters job. I do not like being a clerk. The staff people seem small, vain and uncooperative. The clerks from other sections talk of patriotic hardships, and we are surrounded by neutral and ironic luxuries: water, daily mail and electric lights.

Last night, I had taken a shower, guiltily, and read my mail, guiltily, and I was writing a letter under a light bulb in the operations tent. Patrol operations were going on. Field generators hummed, flies buzzed, and officers murmured around a table. From the corner of the tent, a squawk box speaker began crackling. Hogfat, the battalion tactical radio net, relayed a patrol's transmission. It was a two-squad patrol led by a lieutenant, the first platoon leader of Charlie Company.

"Hogfat Three, Hogfat Three, this is Hogfat Charlie One Actual, over?"

The major was in the tent. He took the radio handset and answered, "Hogfat Charlie One Actual, this is Hogfat Three Actual, over?"

"Hogfat Three Actual, this is Hogfat Charlie One Actual. We are in vicinity Checkpoint Lima. We are off route. I say again, we are off route. Assigned route has Victor Charlie activity. I say again, route full of Victor Charlie. We are surrounded. I say again, we are surrounded. Do you understand, over?"

When I heard the radio I froze and stared at my desk top. I had this feeling I sometimes had on patrols, when I knew everything was about to turn to worms and I could do nothing about it so I would sit motionless and wait for targets. I waited at my desk.

The major told Charlie One to wait, handed the handset to the radioman, and walked over to his map. He uncovered the map and studied it, looking for Checkpoint Lima. I visualized the lieutenant and his two squads, sweat-slick, wide-eyed, breathing softly, listening, waiting. The major ran his finger over the acetate.

"My God," he said. "If they're off by Lima, that puts them in Sand Hog's area." Sand Hog was the adjacent battalion. The major pursed his lips. "Careless! Sloppy! This is the *third* goddam patrol that's strayed out of our area." He stared at the squawk box and at the handset the radioman held out. He turned to the battalion mortar platoon commander and asked if mortars could reach the patrol. The mortar platoon commander shook his head. The artillery officer said:

"Artillery can reach that patrol, Major. We can just tell Sand Hog we want to shoot."

The major shook his head. "Negative. It'll make us look bad. We were in their area just last week. And if we use artillery we won't be the only ones who'll know about this. Division will know. That'll make the colonel look bad."

The major looked at the tent roof and at the bare, glaring light-bulbs strung along the beam. The generators coughed and hummed. The major took the handset.

"Hogfat Charlie One, Hogfat Charlie One, this is Hogfat Three Actual, over?"

"This is Hogfat Charlie One Actual, over?"

"Hogfat Charlie One Actual, there is no support available. I say again, there is no support available. Utilize your organic weapons. I say again, utilize your organic weapons. Execute your mission. I say again, execute your mission. Do you understand, over?"

"This is Hogfat Charlie One Actual. Interrogative. Did you say there was no support available, over?"

"Hogfat Charlie One, this is Hogfat Three Actual. That is correct, over?"

"This is Hogfat Charlie One Actual. Interrogative your last. You said there was no goddam support. Is that what you said, over?"

"Hogfat Charlie One, this is Hogfat Three Actual. Refrain from profanity on the net. I say again, do not use profanity on the net. Execute your mission. Good luck. This is Hogfat Three Actual, out."

And the squawk box was silent and the generators and flies continued making their minor noises. But there was no rumble of artillery in the night air, and there was no sound of aircraft anywhere overhead and the two squads by Checkpoint Lima could hear the silence too. They must have realized supporting fires were not committed elsewhere, and I could feel them thinking: Liar, Liar; Liar; Liar; Liar.

I did not sleep last night. Insomnia has bothered me since I came to headquarters. I just lay in the dark and strained, listening for fire fight noises. Finally, I dressed and went to the operations tent. The major had gone to bed. A duty officer sat by the radios. I waited for information on the patrol. I devised an operation plan. If I abstracted anything from guerrilla warfare, it is that subtle actions alone can cause a stupid enemy to destroy himself. I loosened Major Burgoyne's phone.

At 0530 the sun rose and birds started chattering. At 0615, heat and rotten jungle smells began flowing and roiling through the air. At 0700 the major came into the tent. At 0715 he had his skirmish with the phone. At 0725 he left for breakfast. Charlie Company called at 0730 with a report. I took the call. The patrol returned to Charlie Company this morning, dead and wounded on ponchos; had met and evaded North Vietnamese troops; various other details. The major was at breakfast when the phone call came. When he returned he did not ask about the patrol. He sat down and closed his eyes.

Now he sits at his desk, nodding. The battalion commander, a lieutenant colonel, enters the tent. I rise.

"What's the word on Charlie Company's patrol?"

"They just called in, sir," I say. "They had seven killed, thirteen wounded, estimate thirty enemy casualties, all friendly casualties back. Enemy were North Vietnamese with mortars and recoilless rifles. No enemy weapons brought back. The patrol . . ."

The major rises and breaks in. "The patrol really ran into a buzz saw. Yessir, it was pretty rough but they gave as good as they got. Estimate that's an NVA battalion, since their mortars and recoilless rifles are usually in *their* battalion headquarters. Or it might be a special weapons company." The major walks to his map. He draws boxed red X's on the acetate. "We know now," he begins portentously, "that they are in some strength here, here and here." He frowns. He juts his jaw and draws a sturdy blue arrow, bigger than any of the red boxes. The blue arrow points menacingly at the red boxes. He shows confidence, and says, "Now, all we have to do is sweep along this way . . ." he taps a hachure-marked valley behind the red boxes, ". . . and we can scoop 'em up just like coal in a bin!" He stands erect, beaming, triumphant.

The battalion commander stands looking at the map. Major Burgoyne waits, then resumes. "This valley . . ." the major indicates the dark line of hachures, ". . . has pretty steep sides. The North Vietnamese are pretty heavily-armed, so they ought to have a tough time trying to get up those sides."

The battalion commander waves his hand impatiently. "You know these maps are inaccurate. That's a French map, isn't it?"

"Yessir."

"Well, I'll reserve decision on *that* operation until intelligence gives me some good maps and a little bit more on that North Vietnamese battalion, or *whatever* it might be." The battalion commander frowns, thinks and asks, "This patrol . . . wasn't their mission simply to check the trail and call back if they ran into something big?"

"Yessir, it sure was, but somehow the patrol leader got them off their route, and when they ran into the North Vietnamese they were in a bad location for supporting fires."

"Who briefed them?"

The major pauses, then answers, "I briefed the company commander, sir. The lieutenant was there." The major raises his eyes to the tent roof. "I *told* the company commander to go over the details with his patrol leader after I laid down the guidelines . . ." His voice dies with a pious sigh, and his eyes watch it disappear through the canvas.

The battalion commander coughs. He stares at the major a moment, then walks out of the tent.

Major Burgoyne wheels on me; his eyebrows and mouth are wrenched and snarled. "Who in hell are you to be briefing the colonel, Corporal?"

"Sir, he asked me, and the information had just . . ."

"Why did you give him those *figures*? How do you know they are right?"

"The company commander called . . ."

"Seven killed! Thirteen wounded! That's pretty damn *high* for a two-squad patrol, Corporal . . . you should know that by now! You've been in this office awhile!"

"The company commander personally made the call, sir."

"Why in hell did you take those figures on the *phone*? You *know* casualty figures are classified!"

"The captain shackled those figures, sir. He put them in the shackle code."

The major snorts. He faces about, walks to his chair, collapses in it, and looks at the tent roof. "Damn!" he sighs. He works his lips. He says slowly, "Thirteen wounded . . . *that* sounds like a lot." He brightens. "Probably some of the kids scratched themselves on the elephant grass. Wanted an easy morning at sick call." He sits up, and reaches across his desk for the phone. He cranks tentatively. He pulls both hands back and stares at the phone. He narrows his eyes and squints at the phone.

"You want the operator, sir?" I ask.

He nods, still looking at the phone.

I lean out of the tent and whistle. From the mail tent behind this one, a PFC, bespectacled and smooth-cheeked, sticks out his head.

"PFC, go down to the switchboard and tell the operator to ring us."

The PFC blinks. "I can't. We're sorting now and I . . ."

I feel myself flushing, swelling. I yell, "Get DOWN there or I'll break your goddam NECK you little JERK!" He scampers out of his tent, down to the switchboard. Our phone rings. The major picks it up and barks at the operator for not answering earlier. He connects with Charlie Company's commander.

"What the hell kind of show are you running down there?" he begins. The phone buzzes. "I *know*," the major says, I *know* they got into a fire fight. What were they *doing* there, anyway?"

The phone buzzes at length.

"Discretionary order! *I* don't care if they were *five* meters off their route! They were still off their route!"

The phone buzzes.

"You hold your tongue, Captain! Loose talk about supporting arms . . ."

The phone buzzes loudly, interrupting the major.

"All right, where's your lieutenant? You *know* he's supposed to be here for debrief!" The major listens to the buzz, explodes, "I don't *care* if he's at the aid station! He's not *here!*"

A measured, even buzz.

"That's *all*, Captain!" The major slams the handset on his desk. "*Another* goddam example of the tail wagging the dog!"

Then he faces me. He leans forward, and says, "In Big Two and Korea, dammitall, we didn't pussyfoot around with all these patrols!" He stands and looks over my head at the canvas. "We'd just put a force in the field, and *they'd* put a force in the field, and by God, we'd slug it out and the best outfit would win!" There is a pause. Flies buzz and heat and odors solidify in the tent. He looks at me. He is looking into my eyes, and his eyes recede, unfocus. He looks away.

I volunteer to go to the aid station to check on casualties. He authorizes. I leave. I walk out of the tent along a neatly raked path lined with office tents laid in shimmering rows. In the tents, clerks and officers fold, shuffle, and file. I will ask Personnel to put me back in Charlie Company, later, after my details here are finished. I am tired. This is enough for today.

Stopping at my tent for cigarettes, I see a tarantula on my cot. I scoop the tarantula into my canteen cup and stab it with my pencil. I can put the dead tarantula in his field desk tonight; utilizing a tarantula will be like crossing a phase line. I take cigarettes to the aid station, to my friends.

NANCY WILLARD is from Ann Arbor, Michigan, and is currently teaching in the English Department at Vassar. "Theo's Girl" is part of a collection, *An American Childhood*. Her published works include *The Lively Anatomy of God* and *Skin of Grace*, a collection of poems.

Theo's Girl

SHE woke up suddenly, with the feeling she had overslept an exam. Someone was throwing stones at her window. She peered at the luminous dials of the clock; the hands said four. If I can get outside without turning on the lights, she thought, I won't wake anybody up.

But there was her mother, standing at the foot of the stairs.

"It's a mighty funny time to be going out with him," she observed. "Did you sleep in those clothes?"

"I just lay down in them. I didn't want to miss him."

"Sit down and eat. I got oatmeal made and everything. You want to ask Theo to come in?"

She couldn't get up earlier than her mother, try as she might. There was always that oatmeal waiting for you, no matter how quiet you were.

"I don't have time. He'll be late."

Her mother made a motion as if to throw it all in the sink, and Erica repented.

"Save it for me," she said. "Save it till we get back."

Theo was in the truck, drumming his fingers on the side view mirror, and she squeezed in beside him. The back, empty now, with its double doors clearly visible, resembled a sepulchre.

"Theo's Girl"—Nancy Willard, *The Massachusetts Review*, Copyright © 1969 by The Massachusetts Review, Inc.

"Did you wake your mother?"

"Nope. She's still in bed."

"She didn't think it was funny? Like we were eloping?"

"No. She knows I wouldn't do a thing like that."

It sounded hollow, it hung in the air like a defeat. She should have been capable of it. As they drove out of the city and turned onto the superhighway, Theo stretched in his seat and leaned forward, resting his elbows on the wheel.

"Well, this is another job I'm going to lose. I've been late the last three times. It takes an hour to get to Detroit, another hour to bring the bagels back, and there's a line of people outside Sol's store by eight."

"You overslept."

"Clock didn't go off. The cat slept on the plunger."

They rumbled along quietly; she was falling asleep.

"Hey, wake up. Did I tell you about my new job?"

"Another job?"

"Yeah. At the undertaker's. There's a German family in town, wants me to make a death mask of the uncle."

"Aren't you studying for your exams at all?"

He gave a grand wave of his hand.

"I got all my sculpture projects in. All I have is French."

She leaned her head against the window, trying to keep awake. For days she had imagined the two of them, rolling softly, secretly, into the morning, and here she was, hardly able to realize it. The broad backs of the Ford factories glittered past, the river and the island flashed at them once and disappeared. When she opened her eyes, the heat of the city laid its weight on her, and the bakers were already running back and forth, red-faced, stuffing the last bags of bagels into the back of the truck.

"You goon! Some company you were!" laughed Theo.

But it was the trip home she loved best anyway, she decided, when the bagels filled the whole cab with a smell of onions and fresh dough. Theo reached behind and feeling the top of the bags, helped himself to a bagel, broke it, and handed her half. In silence they watched the sky lighten and the trees grow friendly again as the dark lumps of leaves opened to lacy green. The truck turned into her street; no one was stirring.

"I'll pick you up later if you want to come with me."

"Where?"

"To the undertaker's."

She lingered outside, one foot propped in the open door.

"If you want me to, I will. My Aunt Minnie's supposed to come today."

"She's still working to get you baptized, huh?"

"No."

"You know, if you let her do that to you, we're through."

"I know," said Erica.

"Well, what for, then?"

She had half a mind not to tell him, but she was no good at keeping secrets.

"She's taking us to Hannah's. Now can't you guess?"

"Say it."

"A wedding dress. Hannah's making it."

"Jesus!" He shook his head and smiled broadly. "You really mean it, don't you?"

She nodded seriously.

"I'll wear my *Croix de guerre* that I won in France."

"You've never been to France," said Erica.

Theo pulled a look of broad astonishment.

"Would I lie to you?"

"Mother says you've never been there or won any cross."

"My blue heron," said Theo, reaching over to stroke the hair which swung over her face when she put her head down. "If I can just get you out of here before you start listening to your mother."

Her mother was waiting in the doorway, holding her pink wrapper closed, watching them with that wistful smile she got sometimes.

"I kept it warm for you."

There were moments when Erica wanted to kiss her mother, like just then, but she would have felt funny doing it. Neither of them was very demonstrative. They went into the kitchen, and Erica got herself a dish and skimmed the crust off the oatmeal. Her mother beamed.

"You used to do that when you were a little girl."

She walked around the kitchen talking while her mother handed her things: orange juice, prunes, toast, always enough for a battalion. It was a mutual nervous mannerism, her mother handing her things, Erica taking them, putting them down here and there, talking while her mother beamed.

Far overhead, a cracked voice burst into "What a Friend We Have in Jesus."

"I forgot to tell you—Minnie came in last night," said her mother.

Every weekend she came, ostensibly to get her new Ford fixed. There seemed to be no Ford repairman in Detroit. On Sundays she drove back to attend church. When the semester ended, she would move into the spare third floor room for long periods altogether.

"She's taking us to Hannah's. But she's got to study."

"Study?"

"They're doing the new math in the fourth grade, and she says it's difficult. You got to learn it to teach it. She's got a new electric organ, she says. And a scalp vibrator."

Instead of a husband, said Theo somewhere in the back of her mind, and she shuddered. But Minnie had had husbands enough. Four. Two insurance men, a floor walker, and—the first one—an engineer. Erica could not imagine what it felt like to have run through so many. A different life with each one—did they fall away like so many winters? But when you repent of your sins, all that is changed and forgiven, said Minnie. Changed and forgiven. You are a new person in Christ. A new person.

And the husbands, thought Erica. Had they been baptized away, the hurts and losses drowned somewhere forever?

"I ate almost all the oatmeal," she said. "I'm sorry."

"Never mind. I can make some more."

Thump, thump. She picked up her orange juice and wandered into the living room. Her father peered up from the floor where he lay on his back, slowly raising his legs and letting them down again. Usually he was up before any of them. Once, on a dark winter morning, she had thought it was a burglar.

"We had a good time, Daddy."

"Eh?" His legs paused in mid-air, and he lifted his head. His grey hair snapped with electricity from the rug.

"I said, we had fun."

"Where were you?"

"Theo took me to pick up the bagels."

"To pick up what?" He had probably never seen a bagel, let alone eaten one. "He still got that old car of his?"

"No," said Erica. "It quit running. He abandoned it."

"Lord," said her father. He lowered his head and closed his eyes. Then he opened them again suddenly, as if something had bitten him.

"Minnie driving you to Hannah's?"

"Yes."

They never spoke much. It wasn't just the gap of generations, though; she didn't know what it was. Now that he was retired she felt she ought to speak to him more, but she didn't know what to say. All he could remember about Theo was that he had a broken car. Sometimes he asked if Theo had gotten the left headlight fixed yet, so it didn't shine into second story windows when he drove at night.

The voice upstairs gave way to a chorus. Erica heard hymns jogging closer, as from a wayward procession; then they clicked into silence. She went into the dining room and Minnie looked up brightly. Her hair, newly tinted auburn, had an odd shiny look, as if it were cased in plastic.

"If I can just hear a good sermon," she observed, "it makes my day. It's such a blessing to me, this program. I'll be ready to go as soon as I find my teeth. I always throw them out, in the night. It's my bridge, with the two front ones on it."

And then, as she pierced her grapefruit into sections with the wrong end of her spoon: "Why do old people look so bad without them? I look at my kids in school; they lose them and they look cute."

In their identical pink wrappers, her mother and Minnie really did look like sisters, though Minnie was thinner and better preserved. Except she always *looks* preserved, thought Erica, and she felt herself getting depressed, as if some blight had touched her. She let her mother bring her a cup of coffee and tried to be cheerful.

"How old is Hannah now?" she asked.

Her mother considered.

"She must be in her eighties. Imagine, living all alone on that farm, with nothing but sewing to support herself!"

"She has a brother, though," remarked Minnie.

"Divorced."

"No, that was the other brother," Minnie corrected her. "Jonathan went into a bakery and made real good. And when he started, he drove the wagon for twenty dollars a month."

"She's got a half-sister who lives in town."

"She must have married well."

"No, she didn't. She taught piano all her life. I got a letter from her husband after she died, so I wouldn't send any more Christmas cards."

There was a long silence, during which they all avoided looking at one another. Then Minnie said slyly, humming under her breath,

"Is this your wedding dress Hannah is making?"

Erica had her mouth open to speak, but her mother got there first.

"It's just some white sewing. It could be a very nice graduation dress."

"I thought you told me it was satin."

"Lots of dresses are made out of satin these days."

"*White* satin?"

"Someday I could get married," said Erica in a small voice.

"*If* she decides to get married," added her mother. "There's lots of other things she could do. Paint, for example."

"You have to be terribly careful when you marry. They say you never know anyone till you're married to them," said Minnie. "Oh, I turned down some good ones, all right."

"Remember Irving Tubbs? I'd say you'd have made it best with him."

"Too late now," shrugged Minnie, without bitterness.

But already Erica had that sinking feeling again. They always seemed to be picking on her—not directly, of course, but in conversations she felt were performed for her benefit. My blue heron, I'm not your father, Theo would say. You don't want a father, you want a husband.

She thought of his little room over the laundromat; she had painted mermaids in the shower for him and had lettered his favorite epigram on a sign which he kept over his desk: ENERGY IS ETERNAL DELIGHT.

Sometimes they would lie down on the bed together and listen

to the flute player in the coffeeshop next door one floor down,
he wholly relaxed, she with one foot on the floor. For running.

That's how it is with you, he'd say angrily. Always one foot on
the floor. Who do you think is going to come in, anyway? Your
mother?

Did you lock the door, she'd whisper, agonized.

I locked the door, yes. Maybe your mother can go through
locked doors?

"Immersion," Minnie was saying. "What have you got to lose?
If the Bible says that you shall be saved through water and the
spirit, why take the risk?"

"I'd feel a little odd about it," her mother answered. "If it's so
good, why don't the Presbyterians have it?"

Minnie shook her head. "Billy Graham preaches it. I'd arrange
for a very private service."

"And you wouldn't tell anybody?"

"Not a soul."

Suddenly Erica felt ill. Why don't you say it, she thought angrily; he's an atheist, a black atheist. It never bothered her until
they talked about immersion, and then only in a sort of superstitious way because she felt she might be missing out on something
—a heavenly reward she wasn't sure she deserved but might, by
some fluke, get anyhow. It was that feeling of something left undone that bothered her most. Prudence—the seventh deadly virtue, Theo called it, and sometimes she felt that Theo was more
religious than all of them put together. But art is not a religion,
said Minnie. All the painting and sculpture in the world won't gain
you the kingdom.

Erica had, somewhere, a paper napkin on which he had written,
"Someday I will show you all the kingdoms of *my* world." They
were sitting in the German restaurant downtown, which was always so full at noon that they could hardly hear one another.

What kingdoms? she asked him then.

My blue heron, he said. My little Eurydike.

And a few days later he took her to see his city, which he was
starting to build on the empty lot behind the laundromat.

It was a city to be made entirely of junk, he told her. Already
she could see it rising into shape as they walked between the walls
made of washing machines, fire hydrants, clocks, mirrors, and fend-

ers, between the towers made of wagons and marbles, bicycles and animal skulls, wired and cemented together, all the paraphernalia of human life.

And it shall be fifty cubits long to the east, Theo intoned, and fifty cubits to the west. And there shall be an hundred furnaces beneath the foundations, and an hundred mirrors to catch the sun. And over the flagpole, a garbage can.

Where did you get the parking meter?

I took it from my room, said Theo. Didn't you see it in my room? I used to time my eggs by it when I had a hotplate.

He sat down on a large bed, painted silver. He had stuck paper flowers in the springs. Around it the walls glittered with bedpans, coffee pots and false teeth.

I have a hundred and five sets of false teeth, he declared solemnly. And a medallion of William Blake. You've got to learn how much is worth saving in this world.

Later they were crossing the alley behind Woolworth's on the way home from the nine o'clock show, and they both saw it: a pair of legs sticking out of a trash can.

Jesus! Somebody's fallen in!

The feet were hollow, the legs straight. Pushing aside broken boxes and excelsior, they set them upright.

Too bad it's only the bottom half, said Theo. Who'd throw out a thing like that?

Are you going to keep it? asked Erica.

Put it in the city, he answered. Grow beans on it, or roses. All my life I had to look at saints and flamingoes in my mother's garden. Nobody ever had a pair of legs like these. You take his feet.

As they emerged from the alley, a black car pulled up across the street.

Just keep walking, said Theo. And follow me.

He was humming happily to himself. He turned the corner with easy nonchalance and broke into a gallop. Erica, holding the feet, felt herself pelting after him.

You want to rest? he said at last.

They had stopped in front of the drugstore; a balding man in a pharmacist's white jacket was rolling up the awnings. The neon lights in the window winked out, leaving them in the blue mercu-

rial haze of the street lamps. The streets were empty. They set
the legs down on the pavement and seated themselves on the
curb. In spite of the warm air of summer almost here, Erica felt
a great weariness flood her like a chill. Theo reached over to stroke
the hair that swung over her face when she lowered her head.

Will you come and live in my city?

They arrived at Hannah's early in the afternoon. Hannah, on
hearing the car, had come out to meet them and was standing by
the pump in her long blue print dress. Behind her the house, low-
slung and weathered nearly black, crouched in the shadow of
several freshly painted barns. She seemed to have been born ancient; Erica could not remember a time when her thin hair, tucked
under the green eyeshade, was not already white.

"Afternoon," said Hannah, shyly.

As they stepped up to her, she kissed them one by one, a dry
musty kiss on the cheek. The pin cushion she wore at her lapel
pricked Erica's face.

Hannah led the way through the kitchen. The low ceiling made
Erica want to stoop. There was a wooden sink, deeply stained, and
an enamel bucket with a chipped rim beside it. On a pedestal near
the front door, a large Christmas cactus trailed its branches in
all directions.

"A hundred years old," said Hannah proudly, "and it bloomed
this year. I called the paper about it, but Mrs. Schultz had already
called them about *her* cactus, and they wasn't interested in two
of 'em."

"But you aren't a hundred years old," exclaimed Erica.

"It come with the house, I think. Oh, I could have had a
sign out in front about the house, but Jonathan was never much
on publicity."

They went into the living room for the fittings. Boxes of cards
and buttons spilled over the wicker sofa onto a piano which served
as a shelf for photographs and birthday cards and was by this
time nearly inaccessible; the keyboard looked permanently shut.
On the sewing machine, with its faint traces of elegant scrolls,
a cat lifted its head and blinked at them, then stretched itself
back to sleep again.

For some reason the signs of faith were less depressing here
than they might have been at home, thought Erica, forgiving

Hannah the ceramic plaque, JESUS NEVER FAILS and the sign lettered in silver paint, GOD GRANT ME THE SERENITY TO ACCEPT THINGS I CANNOT CHANGE. On the walls, the sepia faces of an earlier generation looked out from absurd gilt frames. They were always stiff, her father told her, because the pictures were time exposures and you had to wear a clamp on your neck inside the collar that kept you from moving.

Suddenly she saw it, hanging on a coat rack shining out over the faded coats brought in for mending and the shapeless dresses of old women.

"You want to try on the white sewing first?" asked Hannah, noticing her gaze. "It's just basted."

Her mother started to hum.

"I got some stuff for you to do, when you're done with that," she said. And Erica saw her studying the pictures on the wall, pausing before a confirmation certificate, lettered in German, showing in faded tints the parables and deeds of Christ. Stuck on the frame was a tiny star-shaped pin, from which several bars fell in ladder-fashion: five years, ten years, fifteen years.

"You never miss a day of church, do you, Hannah?" said her mother. "I'll bet nobody's got a record like you do."

"Raise your arms," said Hannah, and Erica felt the sudden cool weight of satin falling over her body. "Only one man had a better record than mine; he got the twenty-five year bar, but the last year they had to bring him in on a stretcher."

She stood with her arms out while Hannah pinned and clucked to herself. Her hands were warm and light, almost like mice walking on her flesh, thought Erica. Minnie cleared a place for herself on the sofa and stretched out, running her eye over the dresses on the coat rack.

"That's a handsome black one," she said. "Who's that for?"

"Me," said Hannah, "to be buried in. Thought I might as well get some wear out of it."

"Remember how Grandma had a dress she kept in her drawer to be buried in? White wool, it was."

"Fits pretty good," said Hannah. "Now, try on this overslip."

She shook it over Erica's head—light, vaporous stuff, embroidered with flowers. Fullskirted like a child's dress. Theo hated full skirts. Minnie bent forward to examine it.

"Imagine," she said, "a machine to put in all those flowers."

"How does it fit around the arms?"

Erica nodded.

"Good. 'Course it'll take a little time—"

"No hurry," snapped her mother.

"—since I lost my ripper. I told Mrs. Mahoney to pick me up one somewhere."

"Mahoney?" mused Minnie. "Not Jack Mahoney?"

"He's dead now, just tipped over quick," said Hannah.

"Seems like all the people I went with are dead now," said Minnie softly.

Erica edged herself carefully out of the white dress, trying not to prick herself with pins. Her mother had already put on a lace one. Hannah and Minnie eyed her critically.

"Lace," observed Hannah. "Looks like you're going to a wedding."

"No wedding," said her mother. "Make it an inch shorter, don't you think, in the front? I haven't got a bosom like this—"

She pulled the front out like a tent.

"'Course, skirts is shorter now," said Hannah reluctantly. "Even the choir wears 'em shorter. Course a thing goes across the front so it don't show their knees. I could put some darts in the front."

"The lace is torn, too; do you mend lace?"

"Lace isn't good except for weddings," said Hannah, shaking her head.

He wouldn't like the dress, thought Erica. She scowled at it, hanging on the coat rack. He wouldn't like it because her mother had picked the design, not for his marriage but for marriage in general. Somehow the dress looked like her mother. She did not know why.

Late in the afternoon, Theo appeared at her house, dressed in a black suit with a bag of tools at his side.

"You coming with me to the undertaker's?"

She had not told her mother about this job. They took her bicycle, she sitting on the seat, he pumping in front, his haunches striking her in the stomach as they pitched uphill, past the park.

"I can get off, if you want to walk."

"No, you're light enough."

When they arrived at the funeral parlor, they were both damp with effort. They reached for the knocker, but a man in a moth-grey suit had already opened the door. Over his shoulder, Erica saw the rooms, with their high ceilings and French doors, opening into infinity, multiplying like a house of mirrors. She remembered this house from her grandmother's funeral two years before; the parlors where the dead awaited visitors and the carpets that flowed from one room to another, gathering up all human sounds. Was it in this large room they had laid her out and Erica had cried, not for grief but because her mother was crying?

The man led them over to a small group of people huddled together on a sofa at the other end of the room: two men and two women, all middle-aged with pointed sallow faces. The women had covered their heads with black lace mantillas.

"This is the young student."

They rose and looked at him rather severely, then turned to Erica.

"My wife," said Theo. "She assists me."

The women removed their gloves and extended their hands to her. Then the taller of the two men inquired in an accent so pronounced that Erica wondered if it were real, "You have done this before? You know—"

"Of course," said Theo. "I have studied the trade in Germany."

"Well, then!"

They all looked immensely relieved. With a polite nod, the undertaker indicated that they might sit down and motioned Theo to follow him.

The body had been laid out, fully dressed, on a table and wheeled into a private room, empty save for a sink at one end. For a moment Erica caught her breath, but Theo gave her a look, and she said nothing. The undertaker lingered a bit.

"Won't take you very long, I suppose."

"No, not very long. You will excuse me—I prefer to do this work alone."

Blushing deeply, the other man muttered a little and bowed into the doorway.

"His face has already been shaved."

Pause.

"The family will be down in—say—half an hour?"

Theo nodded and waved him away. The door slammed, and his composure dropped like scales from her eyes.

"Open the tool case quick," he said. "Twenty minutes. Get out the plaster of paris. Can you mix plaster of paris?"

"I think so."

She rummaged through the little bag, pulled out a chisel and a towel, then a tin bowl and the bag of plaster, carefully averting her eyes from the body. Thinking only of what she must do with her hands, she carried everything to the sink, filled the bowl, turned on the water and began to stir.

"Stir faster," cried Theo.

"You never really were in Germany, were you?"

"Christ, no. Give me the plaster—quick, before it dries."

Now she stepped forward and watched, fascinated, breathing very lightly to avoid the real or imagined smell of formaldehyde in the room. Theo had spread the towel over the body, tucking it in at the collar like a napkin. The face looked much like those she had seen upstairs; about thirty, she thought, maybe older. It neither grieved nor frightened her, this thing. Theo loaded his trowel and spread plaster over the chin and nose, then lathered it over the eyes and stood up straight.

"Now we wait for it to dry." He was looking cheerful again. "Who knows, maybe he'll come out looking like William Blake."

It was at that moment a kind of chill touched her.

"Where do you think he is—really?"

"Right here, all there is of him." Theo was washing his hands at the sink. "Your aunt been working on you again? Listen"— he looked very fierce—"if you let her baptize you, it's all over between us. Christ, you're not marrying me, you're marrying your mother!"

"They can hear you upstairs," she hissed.

"Listen," he said, in a gentler voice, pointing to the body. "*This* isn't anything to be afraid of. I've got to get you out of that house of old women."

"I think it's dry."

He tested the mask with his finger.

"Not yet. We'll wait a few more minutes."

They slid down on the floor, leaning against the wall in ominous silence. Presently Theo got up, bent over the body and took the edges of the mask in both hands.

"A little cool, but it's dry enough."

He tugged, carefully at first, then more roughly.

"Give me a hand," he said urgently.

She stumbled to her feet and, suddenly nauseous, swallowed hard and touched the rough plaster edge over the ear.

"Push your fingers under it. You need leverage. Pull!"

"It's stuck!" she cried in terror. "Why is it stuck?"

"I think," said Theo, in an odd voice, "that I forgot to grease the face."

He had climbed up on the table by this time and was straddling the dead man's chest, clawing furiously at the mask.

"Chip it! Get the chisel! We'll chip it away!"

There was a muffled cry behind them, and turning, Erica saw that someone had opened the door. In the doorway stood the bereaved, their sallow faces livid with rage.

The tallest man made a leap for Theo but missed. Theo was already on the ground, and he plunged like a wild horse through the door. Erica followed him, running as if the dead man himself were after them.

They sat, shaking, in a cranny of rubber tires, at one end of Theo's city. The sun beat down on them, the hundred mirrors turned on their hooks and wires, and the springs, sleds, motors, rowboats, saws, clocks, flowerpots, and bedpans of humanity twirled past them. They sat in the shadow of a hundred furnaces.

"Best thing to do," said Theo at last, "is to forget the whole thing. A death mask, for Christ's sake!"

"If we were married and you died first, would you want to be buried?" she asked timidly, and realized, as she said it, that she was really asking something else.

"Ashes to ashes and dust to dust. No coffin for me. I want to go back to the earth."

A loneliness foamed up in her mouth when he said that. She had always assumed she would lie down with the rest of the family in one of the plots her father had bought years ago. Enough for the generations, he said. It wasn't a thing to take lightly. For when the trumpet sounded and everyone stood up in their graves, it was important, said her mother, to be among people you knew.

But by this time, lots of bodies must have scattered to dust.

The Lord knows his own, said her mother stoutly.

Erica saw them all very clearly, standing up in the graves and rubbing their eyes as after a long sleep, Hannah in the black dress she'd made for her funeral, her mother in the lace, Minnie, singing along with the heavenly host because she alone knew the words to the hymns, and herself in the white dress which would be her best dress forever.

"I took my French this morning," said Theo.

"You didn't tell me. How was it?"

"Awful. I flunked. I'm ready to pull out of this place." He touched her hair lightly. "And I want to take you with me. You got to trust me more, Erica. I'm not like your dad, but I'm all right."

"What are you going to do now?"

He shrugged.

"Go to some city, I guess. You can always find people in a city." Suddenly restless, he jerked himself up. "It's hot here. You want to rent a boat and go to the island for a swim?"

"I have to go home and get my suit."

"Jesus! Whoever swims near the island? Go in your underwear."

"A nice day," said the old man, sitting on a kitchen stool in front of the canoe shed. He looked past the open door toward the river, as if expecting someone to appear there. "Don't know why there aren't more folks out on the water."

The three of them went inside. Erica had yet to see a canoe in the canoe shed. Instead, it was full of nickelodeons, scrolled and flowered to resemble circus wagons, with the works decorously exposed. Behind little windows, the captive performers slept: drumsticks and cymbals, gears and piano rolls, perforated for the syntax of dead voices.

"Sign the book," said the old man, slipping behind a counter and handing Theo a pen. "You get number twenty-five. That really plays, Miss."

Erica was staring at the silver anatomy of a violin, spread open and joined to hundreds of tiny threads and wheels, as if awaiting a surgeon. She had not noticed it the last time. On the glass was a neatly typed label: JUDGED THE EIGHTH GREATEST INVENTION IN THE WORLD. CHICAGO WORLD'S FAIR. 1933.

"It sounds just like a real violin. Listen."

The old man took a nickel from his pocket and dropped it into the back of the machine. From deep inside she heard a sputter and a whirr. Theo bent closer to look; then all at once they heard a nervous spidery response, ping! ping! Wheels spun, silver pistons scraped the strings. The whole effect was oddly touching, as if they were watching a fading performer's come-back from senility. When its shrill and complicated heart fell silent, they all three burst into applause.

"You don't know that tune, I bet," said the old man, pleased and shy. "Go out that door to the docks and take the first boat on the end. The paddles are inside."

The island looked small, the way places always looked to Erica when she had known them as a child and then revisited them as an adult. Rocks scratched against the bottom of the boat, and she climbed out, bunching her skirt in her arm. Theo lifted the prow and together they pulled the boat over the thin strip of beach toward the trees.

"Come on," said Theo. "I'm going in."

He vanished into a bush. Erica waded along the edge of the water. The white skeleton of a crayfish surfaced as she dug her toes into the sand.

"Are you going swimming in your dress?"

She could not look at him.

"Somebody might come." But she knew there was nobody here but themselves.

"Good Christ," shouted the bush. "Since when is your own flesh a thing to be ashamed of?"

And when the voice spoke again, it was softer and more winning.

"Here I am."

Drawn by its strangeness, she turned. There he stood, very white and thin-legged, and oddly exotic in his nakedness, like a unicorn.

"Well, I'm going into the water."

He plunged forward with studied casualness, but his whole body grimaced when the water touched his waist. Then he stopped and carefully splashed his ribs and arms, humming quietly to himself. In the sunlight, his back was as round and white as a loaf of dough. Dazzled by the brightness of things, gazing about him at the mainland some distance away, he seemed to have sprung from the dark flesh of the water itself. Suddenly a whistle bleated so close to them that Erica started.

"Are you coming in?"

He was looking at her, over his shoulder, which prickled into gooseflesh as she watched him.

The whistle hooted again, louder this time, and they both turned in alarm. A steamer, covered with tiers and tiers of children, was chugging toward them, under the green banner of the Huron Park Day Line. As the whole side of the boat broke into shouting and waving, she opened her mouth to speak, but Theo was already lumbering toward the woods, the water weighing him down like a heavy garment.

"Jesus!"

Now it was passing them, slowly and steadily, but she could see the children jumping up and down, and she could hear the way they called her, *Hey lady, hey lady!* not because they knew her but because they did not know her. She shaded her eyes and waved, like one who has been working and glances up to see something amazing, a unicorn in the bush, a caravan of pilgrims on the road, a shipload of souls, rollicking and rolling into the new world.

JAMES ALAN MCPHERSON is from Savannah, Georgia. He graduated from Morris Brown College in Atlanta and then earned a degree at Harvard Law School. He attended the Writer's Workshop at the University of Iowa and is at present a Lecturer in Literature at the University of California at Santa Cruz. The story "Of Cabbages and Kings" is from a collection of short stories, *Hue and Cry*, published in 1969.

Of Cabbages and Kings

CLAUDE SHEATS had been in the Brotherhood all his life, and then he had tried to get out. Some of his people and most of his friends were still in the Brotherhood and were still very good members, but Claude was no longer a good member because he had tried to get out after over twenty years. To get away from the Brotherhood and all his friends who were still active in it, he moved to Washington Square and took to reading about being militant. But, living there, he developed a craving for whiteness the way a nicely broke-in virgin craves sex. In spite of this, he maintained a steady black girl, whom he saw at least twice a month to keep up appearances, and once he took both of us with him when he visited his uncle in Harlem who was still in the Brotherhood.

"She's a nice girl, Claude," his uncle's wife had told him that night, because the girl, besides being attractive, had some very positive ideas about the Brotherhood. Her name was Marie, she worked as a secretary in my office, and it was on her suggestion that I had moved in with Claude Sheats.

"I'm glad to see you don't waste your time on hippies," the uncle had said. "All our young men are selling out these days."

The uncle was the kind of fellow who had played his cards right. He was much older than his wife, and I had the impression that night that he must have given her time to experience enough and to become bored enough before he overwhelmed her with his success. He wore glasses and combed his hair back and had that oily composure that made me think of a waiter waiting to be tipped. He was very proud of his English, I observed, and how he always ended his words with just the right sound. He must have felt superior to people who didn't. He must have felt superior to Claude because he was still with the Brotherhood and Claude had tried to get out.

Claude did not like him and always seemed to feel guilty whenever we visited his uncle's house. "Don't mention any of my girls to him," he told me after our first visit.

"Why would I do that?" I said.

"He'll try to psych you into telling him."

"Why should he suspect you? He never comes over to the apartment."

"He just likes to know what I'm doing. I don't want him to know about my girls."

"I won't say anything," I promised.

He was almost twenty-three and had no steady girls except Marie. He was well built so that he had no trouble in the Village area. It was like going to the market for him. During my first days in the apartment the process had seemed like a game. And once, when he was going out, I said: "Bring back two."

Half an hour later he came back with two girls. He got their drinks, and then he called me into his room to meet them.

"This is Doris," he said, pointing to the smaller one, "and I forgot your name," he said to the big blonde.

"Jane," she said.

"This is Howard," he told her.

"Hi," I said. Neither one of them smiled. The big blonde in white pants sat on the big bed, and the little one sat on a chair near the window. He had given them his worst bourbon.

"Excuse me a minute," Claude said to the girls. "I want to talk to Howard for a minute." He put on a record before we went outside into the hall between our rooms. He was always extremely polite and gentle, and he was very soft-spoken in spite of his size.

"Listen," he said to me outside, "you can have the blonde."

"What can I do with that amazon?"

"I don't care. Just get her out of the room."

"She's dirty," I said.

"So you can give her a bath."

"It wouldn't help much."

"Well, just take her out and talk to her," he told me. "Remember, you asked for her."

We went back in. "Where you from?" I said to the amazon.

"Brighton."

"What school?"

"No. I just got here."

"From where?"

"Brighton!"

"Where's that?" I said.

"England," she said. Claude Sheats looked at me.

"How did you find Washington Square so fast?"

"I got friends."

She was very superior about it all and showed the same slight irritation of a professional theater critic waiting for a late performance to begin. The little one sat on the chair, her legs crossed, staring at the ceiling. Her white pants were dirty too. Both girls looked as though they would have been relieved if we had taken off our clothes and danced for them around the room and across the bed, and made hungry sounds in our throats with our mouths slightly opened.

I said that I had to go out to the drugstore and would be back very soon; but once outside, I walked a whole hour in one direction, and then I walked back. I passed them a block away from our apartment. They were walking fast and did not slow down or speak when I passed them.

Claude Sheats was drinking heavily when I came into the apartment.

"What the hell are you trying to pull?" he said.

"I couldn't find a drugstore open."

He got up from the living room table and walked toward me.

"You should have asked me," he said. "I got more than enough."

"I wanted some mouthwash too," I said.

He fumed a while longer, and then told me how I had ruined his evening because the amazon would not leave the room to wait for me and the little one would not do anything with the amazon around. He suddenly thought of going down and bringing them back, and he went out for a while. But he came back without them, saying that they had been picked up again.

"When a man looks out for you, you got to look out for him," he warned me.

"I'm sorry."

"A hell of a lot of good *that* does. And that's the last time I look our for *you*, baby," he said. "From now on it's *me* all the way."

"Thanks," I said.

"If she was too much for you I could of taken the amazon."

"It didn't matter that much," I said.

"You could of had Doris if you couldn't handle the amazon."

"They were both too much," I told him.

But Claude Sheats did not answer. He just looked at me.

After two months of living with him I concluded that Claude hated whites as much as he loved them. And he hated himself with the very same passion. He hated the country and his place in it, and he loved the country and his place in it. He loved the Brotherhood and all that being in it had taught him, and he still believed in what he had been taught, even after he had left it and did not have to believe in anything.

"This Man is going *down*, Howard," he would announce with conviction.

"Why?" I would ask.

"Because it's the Black Man's time to rule again. They had five thousand years, now we get five thousand years."

"What if I don't *want* to rule?" I asked. "What happens if I don't want to take over?"

He looked at me with pity in his face. "You go down with the rest of the country."

"I guess I wouldn't mind much anyway," I said. "It would be a hell of a place with nobody to hate."

But I could never get him to smile about it the way I tried to smile about it. He was always serious. And once, when I questioned the mysticism in the teachings of the Brotherhood, Claude almost attacked me. "Another man might kill you for saying that," he had said. "Another man might not let you get away with saying something like that." He was quite deadly, and he stood over me with an air of patient superiority. And because he could afford to be generous and forgiving, being one of the saved, he sat down at the table with me under the single light bulb and began to teach me. He told me the stories about how it was in the beginning before the whites took over, and about all the little secret significances of black, and about the subtle infiltration of white superiority into everyday objects.

"You've never seen me eat white bread or white sugar, have you?"

"No," I said. He used brown bread and brown sugar.

"Or use bleached flour or white rice?"

"No."

"You know why, don't you?" he waited expectantly.

"No," I finally said. "I don't know why."

He was visibly shocked, so much so that he dropped that line of instruction and began to draw on a pad before him on the living room table. He moved his big shoulders over the yellow pad to conceal his drawings and looked across the table at me. "Now I'm going to tell you something that white men have paid thousands of dollars to learn," he said. "Men have been killed for telling this, but I'm telling you for nothing. I'm warning you not to repeat it because if the whites find out, you know, you could be killed too."

"You know me," I said. "I wouldn't repeat any secrets."

He gave me a long, thoughtful look.

I gave him back a long, eager, honest look.

Then he leaned across the table, and whispered: "Kennedy isn't buried in this country. He was the only President who never had his coffin opened during the funeral. The body was in state all that time, and they never opened the coffin once. You know why?"

"No."

"Because he's not *in it!* They buried an empty coffin. Kennedy was a Thirty-third Degree Mason. His body is in Jerusalem right now."

"How do you know?" I asked.

"If I told you, it would put your life in danger."

"Did his family know about it?"

"No. His lodge kept it secret."

"No one knew?"

"I'm telling you, *no!*"

"Then how did you find out?"

He sighed, more from tolerance than from boredom with my inability to comprehend the mysticism of pure reality in its most unadulterated form. Of course I could not believe him, and we argued about it, back and forth; but to cap all my uncertainties he drew the thirty-three-degree circle, showed me the secret signs that men had died to learn, and spoke about the time when our black ancestors chased an evil genius out of their kingdom and across a desert and onto an island somewhere in the sea; from which, hundreds of years later, this same evil genius sent forth a perfected breed of white-skinned and evil creatures who, through trickery, managed to enslave for five thousand years the onetime Black Masters of the world. He further explained the significance of the East and why all the saved must go there once during their lifetime, and possibly be buried there, as Kennedy had been.

It was dark and late at night, and the glaring bulb cast his great shadow into the corners so that there was the sense of some outraged spirit, fuming in the halls and dark places of our closets, waiting to extract some terrible and justifiable revenge from him for disclosing to me, an unbeliever, the closest-kept of secrets. But I was aware of them only for an instant, and then I did not believe him again.

The most convincing thing about it all was that he was very intelligent and had an orderly, well-regimented life-style, and yet *he* had no trouble with believing. He believed in the certainty of statistical surveys, which was his work; the nutritional value of wheat germ sprinkled on eggs; the sensuality of gin; and the dangers inherent in smoking. He was stylish in that he did not believe in God, but he was extremely moral and warm and kind; and I wanted sometimes to embrace him for his kindness and bigness and gentle manners. He lived his life so carefully that no matter what he said, I could not help believing him sometimes. But I did not want to, because I knew that once I started I could not stop; and then there would be no purpose to my own beliefs and no real conviction or direction in my own efforts to achieve when always, in the back of my regular thoughts, there would be a sense of futility and a fear of the unknown all about me. So, for the sake of necessity, I chose not to believe him.

He felt that the country was doomed and that the safe thing to do was to make enough money as soon as possible and escape to the Far East. He forecast summer riots in certain Northern cities and warned me, religiously, to avoid all implicating ties with whites so that I might have a chance to be saved when that time came. And I asked him about *his* ties, and the girls, and how it was never a movie date with coffee afterward but always his room and the cover-all blanket of Motown sounds late into the night.

"A man has different reasons for doing certain things," he had said.

He never seemed to be comfortable with any of the girls. He never seemed to be in control. And after my third month in the apartment I had concluded that he used his virility as a tool and forged, for however long it lasted, a little area of superiority which could never, it seemed, extend itself beyond the certain confines of his room, no matter how late into the night the records played. I could see him fighting to extend the area, as if an increase in the number of girls he saw could compensate for what he had lost in duration. He saw many girls: curious students, unexpected bus-stop pickups and assorted other one-nighters. And his rationalizations allowed him to believe that each one was an actual conquest, a physical affirmation of a psychological victory over all he hated and loved and hated in the little world of his room.

But then he seemed to have no happiness, even in this. Even here I sensed some intimations of defeat. After each girl, Claude would almost immediately come out of his room, as if there were no need for aftertalk; as if, after it was over, he felt a brooding, silent emptiness that quickly intensified into nervousness and instantaneous shyness and embarrassment, so that the cold which sets in after that kind of emotional drain came in very sharp against his skin, and he could not bear to have her there

244 *James Alan McPherson*

any longer. And when the girl had gone, he would come into my room to talk. These were the times when he was most like a little boy; and these were the times when he really began to trust me.

"That bitch called me everything but the son of God," he would chuckle. And I would put aside my papers brought home from the office, smile at him, and listen.

He would always eat or drink afterward, and in those early days I was glad for his companionship and the return of his trust, and sometimes we drank and talked until dawn. During these times he would tell me more subtleties about the Man and would repredict the fall of the country. Once he warned me, in a fatherly way, about reading life from books before experiencing it; and another night he advised me on how to schedule girls so that one could run them without being run in return. These were usually good times of good-natured arguments and predictions; but as we drank more often he tended to grow excited and quick-tempered, especially after he had just entertained. Sometimes he would seethe with hate, and every drink he took gave life to increasingly bitter condemnations of the present system and our place in it. There were actually flying saucers, he told me once, piloted by things from other places in the universe, which would eventually destroy the country for what it had done to the black man. He had run into his room on that occasion, and had brought out a book by a man who maintained that the government was deliberately withholding from the public overwhelming evidence of flying saucers and strange creatures from other galaxies that walked among us every day. Claude emphasized the fact that the writer was a Ph.D. who must know what he was talking about, and insisted that the politicians withheld the information because they knew that their time was almost up and if they made it public, the black man would know that he had outside friends who would help him take over the world again. Nothing I said could make him reconsider the slightest bit of his information.

"What are we going to use for weapons when we take over?" I asked him once.

"We've got atomic bombs stockpiled and waiting for the day."

"How can you believe that crap?"

He did not answer, but said instead: "You are the living example of what the Man has done to my people."

"I just try to think things out for myself," I said.

"You can't think. The handkerchief over your head is too big."

I smiled.

"I know," he continued. "I know all there is to know about whites because I've been studying them all my life."

I smiled some more.

"I ought to know," he said slowly. "I have supernatural powers."

"I'm tired," I told him. "I want to go to sleep now."

Claude started to leave the room, then he turned. "Listen," he said at the door. He pointed his finger at me to emphasize the gravity of his pronouncement. "I predict that within the next week something is going to happen to this country that will hurt it even more than Kennedy's assassination."

"Good-night," I said as he closed the door.

He opened it again. "Remember that I predicted it when it happens," he said. For the first time I noticed that he had been deadly serious all along.

Two days later several astronauts burned to death in Florida. He raced into my room hot with the news.

"Do you believe in me *now?*" he said. "Just two days and look what happened."

I tried to explain, as much to myself as to him, that in any week of the year something unfortunate was bound to occur. But he insisted that this was only part of a divine plan to bring the country to its knees. He said that he intended to send a letter off right away to Jeane Dixon in D.C. to let her know that she was not alone because he also had the same power. Then he thought that he had better not because the FBI knew that he had been active in the Brotherhood before he got out.

At first it was good fun believing that someone important cared enough to watch us. And sometimes when the telephone was dead a long time before the dial tone sounded, I would knock on his door and together we would run through our telephone conversations for that day to see if either of us had said anything implicating or suspect, just in case they were listening. This feeling of persecution brought us closer together, and soon the instruction

sessions began to go on almost every night. At this point I could
not help believing him a little. And he began to trust me again,
like a tolerable little brother, and even confided that the summer
riots would break out simultaneously in Harlem and Watts during
the second week in August. For some reason, something very difficult to put into words, I spent three hot August nights on the
streets of Harlem, waiting for the riot to start.

In the seventh month of our living together, he began to intro-
duce me to his girls again when they came in. Most of them came
only once, but all of them received the same mechanical treatment. He discriminated only with liquor, the quality of which
improved with the attractiveness or reluctance of the girl: gin
for slow starters, bourbon for momentary strangers, and the
scotch he reserved for those he hoped would come again. There
was first the trek into his room, his own trip out for the ice and
glasses while classical music was played within; then after a while
the classical piece would be replaced by several Motowns. Finally,
there was her trip to the bathroom, his calling a cab in the hall,
and the sound of both their feet on the stairs as he walked her
down to the cab. Then he would come to my room in his red
bathrobe, glass in hand, for the aftertalk.

Then in the ninth month the trouble started. It would be very
easy to pick out one incident, one day, one area of misunderstand-
ing in that month and say: "That was where it began." It would
be easy, but not accurate. It might have been one instance or a
combination of many. It might have been the girl who came into
the living room when I was going over the proposed blueprints
for a new settlement house, and who lingered too long outside his
room in conversation because her father was a builder somewhere. Or it might have been nothing at all. But after that time
he warned me about being too friendly with his company.

Another night, when I was leaving the bathroom in my shorts,
he came out of his room with a girl who smiled. "Hi," she said to
me.

I nodded hello as I ducked back into the bathroom.

When he had walked her down to the door he came to my room
and knocked. He did not have a drink. "Why didn't you speak
to my company?" he demanded.

"I was in my shorts."

"She felt bad about it. She asked what the hell was wrong with you. What could I tell her—'He got problems'?"

"I'm sorry," I said. "But I didn't want to stop in my shorts."

"I see through you, Howard," he said. "You're just jealous of me and try to insult my girls to get to me."

"Why should I be jealous of you?"

"Because I'm a man and you're not."

"What makes a man anyway?" I said. "Your fried eggs and wheat germ? Why should I be jealous of you *or* what you bring in?"

"Some people don't need a reason. You're a black devil and you'll get yours. I predict that you'll get yours."

"Look," I told him, "I'm sorry about the girl. Tell her I'm sorry when you see her again."

"You treated her so bad she probably won't come back."

I said nothing more, and he stood there silently for a long time before he turned to leave the room. But at the door he turned again, and said: "I see through you, Howard. You're a black devil."

It should have ended there, and it might have with anyone else. I took great pains to speak to his girls after that, even though he tried to get them into the room as quickly as possible. But a week later he accused me of walking about in his room after he had gone out some two weeks before.

"I swear I wasn't in your room," I protested.

"I saw your shadow on the blinds from across the street at the bus stop," he insisted.

"I've *never* been in your room when you weren't there," I told him.

"I *saw* you!"

We went into his room, and I tried to explain how, even if he could see the window from the bus stop, the big lamp next to the window prevented any shadow from being cast on the blinds. But he was convinced in his mind that at every opportunity I plundered his closets and drawers. He had no respect for simple logic in these matters, no sense of the absurdity of his accusations, and the affair finally ended with my confessing that I might have done it without actually knowing, and if I had, I would not do it again.

But what had been a gesture for peace on my part became a

vindication for him, proof that I *was* a black devil, capable of lying and lying until he confronted me with the inescapable truth of the situation. And so he persisted in creating situations from which, if he insisted on a point long enough and with enough self-righteousness, he could draw my inevitable confession.

And I confessed eagerly, goaded on by the necessity of maintaining peace. I confessed to mixing white sugar crystals in with his own brown crystals so that he could use it and violate the teachings of the Brotherhood; I confessed to cleaning the bathroom all the time merely because I wanted to make him feel guilty for not having ever cleaned it. I confessed to telling the faithful Marie, who brought a surprise dinner over for him, that he was working late at his office in order to implicate him with the girls who worked there. I confessed to leaving my papers about the house so that his company could ask about them and develop an interest in me. And I pleaded guilty to a record of other little infamies, which multiplied into countless others, and again subdivided into hundreds of little subtleties until my every movement was a threat to him. If I had a girlfriend to dinner, we should eat in my room instead of at the table because he had to use the bathroom a lot, and he was embarrassed to be seen going to the bathroom.

If I protested, he would fly into a tantrum and shake his big finger at me vigorously. And so I retreated, step by step, into my room, from which I emerged only to go to the bathroom or kitchen or out of the house. I tried to stay out on nights when he had company. But he had company so often that I could not always help being in my room after he had walked her to the door. Then he would knock on my door for his talk. He might offer me a drink, and if I refused, he would go to his room for a while and then come back. He would pace about for a while, like a big little boy who wants to ask for money over his allowance. At these times my mind would move feverishly over all our contacts for as far back as I could make it reach, searching and attempting to pull out that one incident which would surely be the point of his attack. But it was never any use.

"Howard, I got something on my chest, and I might as well get it off."

"What is it?" I asked from my bed.

"You been acting strange lately. Haven't been talking to me. If you got something on your chest, get it off now."

"I have nothing on my chest," I said.

"Then why don't you talk?"

I did not answer.

"You hardly speak to me in the kitchen. If you have something against me, tell me now."

"I have nothing against you."

"Why don't you talk, then?" He looked directly at me. "If a man doesn't talk, you think *something's* wrong!"

"I've been nervous lately, that's all. I got problems, and I don't want to talk."

"Everybody's got problems. That's no reason for going around making a man feel guilty."

"For God's sake, I don't want to talk."

"I know what's wrong with you. Your conscience is bothering you. You're so evil that your conscience is giving you trouble. You got everybody fooled but *me*. I know you're a black devil."

"I'm a black devil," I said. "Now will you let me sleep?"

He went to the door. "You dish it out, but you can't take it," he said. "That's *your* trouble."

"I'm a black devil," I said.

I lay there, after he left, hating myself but thankful that he hadn't called me into his room for the fatherly talk as he had done another time. That was the worst. He had come to the door and said: "Come out of there, I want to talk to you." He had walked ahead of me into his room and had sat down in his big leather chair next to the lamp with his legs spread wide and his big hands in his lap. He had said: "Don't be afraid. I'm not going to hurt you. Sit down. I'm not going to argue. What are you so nervous about? Have a drink," in his kindest, most fatherly way, and that had been the worst of all. That was the time he had told me to eat in my room. Now I could hear him pacing about in the hall, and I knew that it was not over for the night. I began to pray that I could sleep before he came. I did not care what he did as long as I did not have to face him. I resolved to confess to anything he accused me of if it would make him leave sooner. I was about to go out into the hall for my confession when the door was kicked open and he charged into the room.

"You black son of a bitch!" he said. "I ought to *kill* you." He stood over the bed in the dark room and shook his big fist over me. And I lay there hating the overpowering cowardice in me, which kept my body still and my eyes closed, and hoping that he would kill all of it when his heavy fist landed.

"First you insult a man's company, then you ignore him. I been *good* to you. I let you live here, I let you eat my uncle's food, and I taught you things. But you're a ungrateful m-f. I ought to *kill* you right now!"

And I still lay there, as he went on, not hearing him, with nothing in me but a loud throbbing which pulsed through the length of my body and made the sheets move with its pounding. I lay there secure and safe in cowardice for as long as I looked up at him with my eyes big and my body twitching and my mind screaming out to him that it was all right, and I thanked him, because now I truly believed in the new five thousand years of Black Rule.

It is night again. I am in bed again, and I can hear the new blond girl closing the bathroom door. I know that in a minute he will come out in his red robe and call a cab. His muffled voice through my closed door will seem very tired, but just as kind and patient to the dispatcher as it is to everyone, and as it was to me in those old times. I am afraid, because when they came up the stairs earlier they caught me working at the living room table with my back to them. I had not expected him back so soon; but then I should have known that he would not go out. I had turned around in the chair, and she smiled and said hello, and I said "Hi" before he hurried her into the room. I *did* speak, and I know that she heard. But I also know that I must have done something wrong; if not to her, then to him earlier today or yesterday or last week, because he glared at me before following her into the room, and he almost paused to say something when he came out to get the glasses and ice. I wish that I could remember just what it was. But it does not matter. I *am* guilty, and he knows it.

Now that he knows about me I am afraid. I could move away from the apartment and hide my guilt from him, but I know that he would find me. The brainwashed part of my mind tells me to call the police while he is still busy with her, but what could I charge him with when I know that he is only trying to help me?

I could move the big ragged yellow chair in front of the door, but that would not stop him, and it might make him impatient with me. Even if I pretended to be asleep and ignored him, it would not help when he comes. He has not bothered to knock for weeks.

In the black shadows over my bed and in the corners I can sense the outraged spirits who help him when they hover about his arms as he gestures, with his lessons, above my bed. I am determined now to lie here and take it. It is the price I must pay for all the black secrets I have learned, and all the evil I have learned about myself. I *am* jealous of him, of his learning, of his girls. I am not the same handkerchief-head I was nine months ago. I have Marie to thank for that, and Claude, and the spirits. They know about me, and perhaps it is they who make him do it and he cannot help himself. I believe in the spirits now, just as I believe most of the time that I am a black devil.

They are going down to the cab now.

I will not ever blame him for it. He is helping me. But I blame the girls. I blame them for not staying on afterward, and for letting all the good nice happy love talk cut off automatically after it is over. *I* need to have them there, after it is over. And he needs it; he needs it much more and much longer than they could ever need what he does for them. He should be able to teach them, as he has taught me. And he should have their appreciation, as he has mine. I blame them. I blame them for letting him try and try and never get just a little of the love there is left in the world.

I can hear him coming back from the cab.

JOYCE CAROL OATES is the author of many short stories and several novels, the latest of which, *Them*, was published last fall. Her recent works also include a collection of poems, *Anonymous Sins and Other Poems*, and a book of critical essays to be published this spring. She first appeared in the O. Henry collection in 1963 and again in 1964, 1965, 1967, 1968, 1969 and 1970. Her story "In the Region of Ice" won first prize in 1967.

Unmailed, Unwritten Letters

Dear Mother and Father,

The weather is lovely here. It rained yesterday. Today the sky is blue. The trees are changing colors, it is October 20, I have got to buy some new clothes sometime soon, we've changed dentists, doctors, everything is lovely here and I hope the same with you. Greg is working hard as usual. The doctor we took Father to see, that time he hurt his back visiting here, has died and so we must change doctors. Dentists also. I want to change dentists because I can't stand to go back to the same dentist anymore. He is too much of a fixed point, a reference point. It is such a chore, changing doctors and dentists.

Why are you so far away in the Southwest? Is there something about the Southwest that lures old people? Do they see images there, shapes in the desert? Holy shapes? Why are you not closer to me, or farther away? In an emergency it would take hours or days for you to get to me. I think of the two of you in the Southwest, I see the highways going off into space and wonder at your courage, so late in life, to take on space. Father had all he could

do to manage that big house of yours, and the lawn. Even with
workers to help him it was terrifying, all that space, because he
owned it. Maybe that was why it terrified him, because he owned
it. Out in the Southwest I assume that no one owns anything.
Do people even live there? Some people live there, I know. But
I think of the Southwest as an optical illusion, sunshine and sand
and a mountainous (mountainous?) horizon, with highways perfectly divided by their white center lines, leading off to Mars or the
moon, unhurried. And there are animals, the designs of animals,
mashed into the highways! The shape of a dog, a dog's pelty
shadow, mashed into the hot, hot road—in mid-flight, so to speak,
mid-leap, run over again and again by big trucks and retired
people seeing America. That vastness would terrify me. I think of
you and I think of protoplasm being drawn off into space, out
there, out in the West, with no human limits to keep if safe.

Dear Marsha Katz,

    Thank you for the flowers, white flowers, but why that deli-
cate hint of death, all that fragrance wasted on someone like myself who is certain to go on living? Why are you pursuing me?
Why in secrecy? (I see all the letters you write to your father,
don't forget; and you never mention me in them.) Even if your
father were my lover, which is not true and cannot be verified,
why should you pursue me? Why did you sign the card with the
flowers *Trixie*? I don't know anyone named Trixie! How could I
know anyone named Trixie? It is a dog's name, a high school
cheerleader's name, an aunt's name . . . why do you play these
games, why do you pursue me?
    Only ten years old, and too young for evil thoughts—do you
look in your precocious heart and see only grit, the remains of
things, a crippled shadow of a child? Do you see in all this the
defeat of your Daughterliness? Do you understand that a Daughter, like a Mistress, must be feminine or all is lost, must keep up
the struggle with the demonic touch of matter-of-fact irony that
loses us all our men . . . ? I think you have lost, yes. A ten-year-
old cannot compete with a thirty-year-old. Send me all the flowers
you want. I pick them apart one by one, getting bits of petals

under my fingernails, I throw them out before my husband gets
home.

Nor did I eat that box of candies you sent. Signed "Uncle
Bumble"!

Are you beginning to feel terror at having lost? Your father
and I are not lovers, we hardly see each other any more, since last
Wednesday and today is Monday, still you've lost because I gather
he plans on continuing the divorce proceedings, long distance,
and what exactly can a child do about that . . . ? I see all the
letters you write him. No secrets. Your Cape Cod sequence was
especially charming. I like what you did with that kitten, the kitten that is found dead on the beach! Ah, you clever little girl,
even with your I.Q. of uncharted heights, you couldn't quite conceal from your father and me your attempt to make him think 1)
the kitten suggests a little girl, namely you 2) its death suggests
your pending, possible death, if Father does not return. Ah, how
we laughed over that! . . . Well, no, we didn't laugh, he did not
laugh, perhaps he did not even understand the trick you were
playing . . . your father can be a careless, abrupt man, but things
stick in his mind, you know that and so you write of a little white
kitten, alive one day and dead the next, so you send me flowers
for a funeral parlor, you keep me in your thoughts constantly so
that I can feel a tug all the way here in Detroit, all the way from
Boston, and I hate it, I hate that invisible pulling, tugging, that
witch's touch of yours. . . .

Dear Greg,

We met about this time years ago. It makes me dizzy, it frightens me, to think of that meeting. Did so much happen, and yet
nothing? Miscarriages, three or four, one loses count, and eight
or nine sweet bumbling years—why do I use the word *bumbling*,
it isn't a word I would ever use—and yet there is nothing there, if
I go to your closet and open the door your clothes tell me as much
as you do. You are a good man. A faithful husband. A subdued
and excellent husband. The way you handled my parents alone
would show how good you are, how excellent. . . . My friend X,
the one with the daughter said to be a genius and the wife no one

has ever seen, X couldn't handle my parents, couldn't put up with my father's talk about principles, the Principles of an Orderly Universe, which he sincerely believes in though he is an intelligent man. . . . X couldn't handle anything, anyone. He loses patience. He is vulgar. He watches himself swerve out of control but can't stop. Once, returning to his car, we found a ticket on the windshield. He snatched it and tore it up, very angry, and then when he saw my surprise he thought to make a joke of it—pretending to be tearing it with his teeth, a joke. And he is weak, angry men are weak. He lets me close doors on him. His face seems to crack, with sorrow, but he lets me walk away, why is he so careless and weak . . . ?

But I am thinking of us, our first meeting. An overheated apartment, graduate school . . . a girl in dark stockings, myself, frightened and eager, trying to be charming in a voice that didn't carry, a man in a baggy sweater, gentle, intelligent, a little perplexed, the two of us gravitating together, fearful of love and fearful of not loving, of not being loved. . . . So we met. The evening falls away, years fall away. I count only three miscarriages, really. The fourth a sentimental miscalculation.

My darling,

I am out somewhere, I see a telephone booth on a corner, the air is windy and too balmy for October. I won't go in the phone booth. Crushed papers, a beer bottle, a close violent stench. . . . I walk past it, not thinking of you. I am out of the house so that you can't call me and so that I need not think of you. Do you talk to your wife every night, still? Does she weep into your ear? How many nights have you lain together, you and that woman now halfway across the country, in Boston, weeping into a telephone? Have you forgotten all those nights?

Last night I dreamt about you mashed into a highway. More than dead. I had to wake Greg up, I couldn't stop trembling, I wanted to tell him of the waste, the waste of joy and love, your being mashed soundlessly into a road and pounded into a shape no one would recognize as yours. . . . Your face was gone. What will happen to me when your face is gone from this world?

I parked the car down here so that I could go shopping at Saks but I've been walking, I'm almost lost. The streets are dirty. A tin can lies on the sidewalk, near a vacant lot. Campbell's Tomato Soup. I am dressed in the suit you like, though it is a little baggy on me, it would be a surprise for someone driving past to see a lady in such a suit bend to pick up a tin can. . . . I pick the can up. The edge is jagged and rusty. No insects inside. Why would insects be inside, why bother with an empty can? Idly I press the edge of the lid against my wrist, it isn't sharp, it makes only a fine white line on my skin, not sharp enough to penetrate the skin.

Dear Greg,

I hear you walking downstairs. You are going outside, out into the back yard. I am tempted, heart pounding, to run to the window and spy on you. But everything is tepid, the universe is dense with molecules, I can't get up. My legs won't move. You said last night, "The Mayor told me to shut up in front of Arthur Grant. He told me to shut up." You were amused and hurt at the same time, while I was furious, wishing you were . . . were someone else, someone who wouldn't be amused and hurt, a good man, a subdued man, but someone else who would tell that bastard to go to hell. I am a wife, jealous for her husband.

Three years you've spent working for the Mayor, His Honor, dodging reporters downtown. Luncheons, sudden trips, press conferences, conferences with committees from angry parts of Detroit, all of Detroit angry, white and black, bustling, ominous. Three years. Now he tells you to shut up. All the lies you told for him, not knowing how to lie with dignity, he tells you to shut up, my body suffers as if on the brink of some terrible final expulsion of our love, some blood-smear of a baby. When a marriage ends who is left to understand it? No witnesses. No young girl in black stockings, no young man, all those witnesses gone, grown up, moved on, lost.

Too many people know you now, your private life is dwindling. You are dragged back again and again to hearings, commission meetings, secret meetings, desperate meetings, television interviews, interviews with kids from college newspapers. Everyone has a right to know everything! *What Detroit Has Done to Combat Slums. What Detroit Has Done to Prevent Riots* updated to *What Detroit Has Done to Prevent a Recurrence of the 1967 Riot.* You people are rewriting history as fast as history happens. I love you, I suffer for you, I lie here in a paralysis of love, sorrow, density, idleness, lost in my love for you, my shame for having betrayed you. . . . Why should slums be combatted? Once I wept to see photographs of kids playing in garbage heaps, now I weep at crazy sudden visions of my lover's body become only a body, I have no tears left for anyone else, for anything else. Driving in the city I have a sudden vision of my lover dragged along by a stranger's car, his body somehow caught up under the bumper or the fender of a car and dragged along, bleeding wildly in the street. . . .

My dear husband, betraying you was the most serious act of my life. Far more serious than marrying you. I knew my lover better when he finally became my lover than I knew you when you became my husband. I know him better, now, than I know you. You and I have lived together for eight years. Smooth coins, coins worn smooth by constant handling. . . . I am a woman trapped in love, in the terror of love. Paralysis of love. Like a great tortoise, trapped in a heavy death-like shell, a mask of the body pressing the body down to earth. . . . I went for a week without seeing him, an experiment. The experiment failed. No husband can keep his wife's love. So you walk out in the back yard, admiring the leaves, the sky, the flagstone terrace, you are a man whom betrayal would destroy and yet your wife betrayed you, deliberately.

To the Editor:

Anonymously and shyly I want to ask—why are white men so weak, so feeble? The other day I left a friend at his hotel and walked quickly, alone, to my car, and the eyes of black men around me moved onto me with a strange hot perception, seeing everything. They knew, seeing me, what I was. Tension rose through the cracks in the sidewalk. Where are white men who are strong, who see women in this way? The molecules in the air of Detroit are humming. I wish I could take a knife and cut out an important piece of my body, my insides, and hold it up . . . on a street corner, an offering. Then will they let me alone? The black men jostle one another on street corners, out of work and not wanting work, content to stare at me, knowing everything in me, not surprised. My lover, a white man, remains back in the hotel, his head in his hands because I have walked out, but he won't run after me, he won't follow me. *They* follow me. One of them bumped into me, pretending it was an accident. I want to cut up my body, I can't live in this body.

Next door to us a boy is out in his driveway, sitting down, playing a drum. Beating on a drum. Is he crazy? A white boy of about sixteen pounding on a drum. He wants to bring the city down with that drum and I don't blame him. I understand that vicious throbbing.

Dear Marsha Katz,

Thank you for the baby clothes. Keep sending me things, test your imagination. I feel that you are drowning. I sense a tightness in your chest, your throat. Are your eyes leaden with defeat, you ten-year-old wonder? How many lives do children relive at the moment of death?

Dear Mother and Father,

The temperature today is   . Yesterday at this time,   . Greg has been very busy as usual with   ,   ,   . This weekend we must see the   's, whom you have met. How is the weather there? How is your vacation? Thank you for the postcard from   . I had not thought lawns would be green there.

. . . The Mayor will ask all his aides for resignations, signed. Some he will accept and others reject. A kingly man, plump and divorced. Why can't I tell you about my husband's job, about my life, about anything real? Scandals fall on the head of my husband's boss, reading the paper is torture, yet my husband comes home and talks seriously about the future, about improvements, as if no chaos is waiting. No picketing ADC mothers, no stampede to buy guns, no strangled black babies found in public parks. In the midst of this my husband is clean and untouched, innocent, good. He has dedicated his life to helping others. I love him but cannot stop betraying him, again and again, having reclaimed my life as my own to throw away, to destroy, to lose. My life is my own. I keep on living.

My darling,

It is one-thirty and if you don't call by two, maybe you won't call, I know that you have a seminar from two to four, maybe you won't call today and everything will end. My heart pounds bitterly, in fear, in anticipation? Your daughter sent me some baby clothes, postmarked Boston, I understand her hatred, but one thing: how much did you tell your wife about me? About my wanting children? You told her you no longer loved her and couldn't live with her, that you loved another woman who could not marry you, but . . . did you tell her this other woman had no children? And what else?

I will get my revenge on you.

I walk through the house in a dream, in a daze. I am sinking slowly through the floor of this expensive house, a married woman in a body grown light as a shell, empty as a shell. My body has no other life in it, only its own. What you discharge in me is not life but despair. I can remember my body having life, holding it. It seemed a trick, a feat that couldn't possibly work: like trying to retain liquid up a reed, turning the reed upside down. The doctor said, "Babies are no trouble. Nothing." But the liquid ran out. All liquid runs out of me. That first week, meeting with you at the Statler, everything ran out of me like blood. I alarmed you, you with your nervous sense of fate, your fear of getting cancer, of having a nervous breakdown, I caused you to say stammering *But what if you get pregnant?* I am not pregnant but I feel a strange tingling of life, a tickling, life at a distance, as if the spirit of your daughter is somehow in me, lodged in me. She sucks at my insides with her pinched jealous lips, wanting blood. My body seeks to discharge her, magically.

My dear husband,

I wanted to test being alone. I went downtown to the library, the old library. I walked past the hotel where he and I have met, my lover and I, but we were not meeting today and I was alone, testing myself as a woman alone, a human being alone. The library was filled with old men. Over seventy, dressed in black, with white shirts. Black and white: a reading room of old men, dressed in black and white.

I sat alone at a table. Some of the old men glanced at me. In a dream I began to leaf through a magazine, thinking *Now I am leafing through a magazine; this is expected*. Why can't I be transformed to something else—to a mask, a shell, a statue? I glance around shyly, trying to gauge the nature of the story I am in. Is it tragic or only sad? The actors in this play all seem to be wearing masks, even I am wearing a mask, I am never naked. My nakedness, with my lover, is a kind of mask—something he sees, something I can't quite believe in. Women who are loved are in perpetual motion, dancing. We dance and men follow to the brink of madness and death, but what of us, the dancers?—when the dancing ends we stand back upon our heels, back upon our heels, dazed and hurt. Beneath the golden cloth on our thighs is flesh and flesh hurts. Men are not interested in the body, which feels pain, but in the rhythm of the body as it goes about its dance, the body of a woman who cannot stop dancing.

A confession. In Ann Arbor last April, at the symposium, I fell in love with a man. The visiting professor from Boston University —a man with black-rimmed glasses, Jewish, dark-eyed, dark-haired, nervous and arrogant and restless. Drumming his fingers. Smoking too much. (And you, my husband, were sane enough to give up smoking five years ago.) A student stood up in the first row and shouted out something and it was he, my lover, the man who would become my lover, who stood up in turn and shouted something back . . . it all happened so fast, astounding everyone, even the kid who reported for the campus newspaper didn't catch the exchange. How many men could handle a situation like that, being wilder and more profane than a heckler? . . . He was in the group at the party afterward, your friend Bryan's house. All of you talked at once, excited and angry over the outcome of the symposium, nervous at the sense of agitation in the air, the danger, and he and I wandered to the hostess's table, where food was set out. We made pigs of ourselves, eating. He picked out the shrimp and I demurely picked out tiny flakes of dough with miniature asparagus in them. Didn't you notice us? Didn't you notice this dark-browed man with the glasses that kept slipping down his nose, with the untidy black hair? We talked. We ate. I could see in his bony knuckles a hunger that would never be satisfied. And I, though I think I am starving slowly to death now, I leapt upon the food as if it were a way of getting at him, of drawing him into me. We talked. We wandered around the house. He looked out a window, drawing a curtain aside, at the early spring snowfall, falling gently outside, and he said that he didn't know why he had come to this part of the country, he was frightened of travelling, of strangers. He said that he was very tired. He seduced me with the slump of his shoulders. And when he turned back to me we entered another stage of the evening, having grown nervous and brittle with each other, the two of us, suddenly conscious of being together. My eyes grew hot and searing. I said carelessly that he must come over to Detroit sometime, we could have lunch, and he said at once, "I'd like that very much . . ." and then paused. Silence.

Later, in the hotel, in the cheap room he rented, he confessed to me that seeing my face had been an experience for him—did he believe in love at first sight, after all? something so childish? It had been some kind of love, anyway. We talked about our lives, about his wife, about my husband, and then he swung onto another subject, talking about his daughter for forty-five minutes. . . . A genius, a ten-year-old prodigy. I am brought low, astounded. I want to cry out to him, *But what about me! Don't stop thinking about me!* At the age of six his daughter was writing poems, tidy little poems, like Blake's. *Like Blake's? Yes.* At the age of eight she was publishing those poems.

No, I don't want to marry him. I'm not going to marry him. What we do to each other is too violent, I don't want it brought into marriage and domesticated, nor do I want him to see me at unflattering times of the day . . . getting up at three in the morning to be sick, a habit of mine. He drinks too much. He reads about the connection between smoking and death, and turns the page of the newspaper quickly. Superstitious, stubborn. In April he had a sore throat, that was why he spoke so hoarsely on the program . . . but a month later he was no better: "I'm afraid of doctors," he said. This is a brilliant man, the father of a brilliant child? We meet nowhere, at an unimaginative point X, in a hotel room, in the anonymous drafts of air from blowers that never stop blowing, the two of us yearning to be one, in this foreign dimension where anything is possible. Only later, hurrying to my car, do I feel resentment and fury at him . . . why doesn't he buy me anything, why doesn't he get a room for us, something permanent? And hatred for him rises in me in long shuddering surges, overwhelming me. I don't want to marry him. Let me admit the worst —anxious not to fall in love with him, I think of not loving him at the very moment he enters me, I think of him already boarding a plane and disappearing from my life, with relief, I think with pity of human beings and this sickness of theirs, this desire for unity. Why this desire for unity, why? We walk out afterward, into the sunshine or into the smog. Obviously we are lovers. Once I saw O'Leary, from the Highway Commission, he nodded and said a brisk hello to me, ignored my friend, obviously we are lovers, anyone could tell. We walked out in the daylight, looking for you. That day, feverish and aching, we were going to tell you everything. He was going to tell his wife everything. But nothing happened . . . we ended up in a cocktail lounge, we calmed down. The air conditioning calmed us. On the street we passed a Negro holding out pamphlets to other Negroes but drawing them back when whites passed. I saw the headline—*Muslim Killed in Miami Beach by Fascist Police.* A well-dressed Negro woman turned down a pamphlet with a toothy amused smile—none of that junk for her! My lover didn't even notice.

Because he is not my husband I don't worry about him. I worry about my own husband, whom I own. I don't own this man. I am thirty and he is forty-one, to him I am young, what a laugh, I don't worry about his coughing, his drinking (sometimes over the telephone I can hear ice cubes tinkling in a glass—he drinks to get the courage to call me), his loss of weight, his professional standing. He didn't return to his job in Boston, but stayed on here. A strange move. The department at Michigan considered it a coup to get him, this disintegrating, arrogant man, they were willing to pay him well, a man who has already made enemies there. No, I don't worry about him.

On a television program he was moody and verbose, moody and silent by turns. Smokes too much. Someone asked him about the effect of something on something—Vietnam on the presidential election, I think—and he missed subtleties, he sounded distant, vague. Has lost passion for the truth. He has lost his passion for politics, discovering in himself a passion for me. It isn't my fault. On the street he doesn't notice things, he smiles slowly at me, complimenting me, someone brushes against him and he doesn't notice, what am I doing to this man? Lying in his arms I am inspired to hurt him. I say that we will have to give this up, these meetings; too much risk, shame. What about my husband, what about his wife? (A deliberate insult—I know he doesn't love his wife.) I can see at once that I've hurt him, his face shows everything, and as soon as this registers in both of us I am stunned with the injustice of what I've done to him, I must erase it, cancel it out, undo it, I caress his body in desperation. . . . Again and again. A pattern. What do I know about caressing the bodies of men? I've known only two men in my life. My husband and his successor. I have never wanted to love anyone, the strain and risk are too great, yet I have fallen in love for the second time in my life and this time the sensation is terrifying, bitter, violent. It ends the first cycle, supplants all that love, erases all that affection—destroys everything. I stand back dazed, flat on my heels, the dance being over. I will not move on into another marriage. I will die slowly in this marriage rather than come to life in another.

Dear Mrs. Katz,

I received your letter of October 25 and I can only say
I don't know how to begin this letter except to tell you
Your letter is here on my desk. I've read it over again and again all morning. Is it true, yes, that I have made the acquaintance of a man who is evidently your husband, though he has not spoken of you. We met through mutual friends in Ann Arbor and De-

troit. Your informant at the University is obviously trying to upset you, for her own reasons. I assume it is a woman—who else would write you such a letter? I know nothing of your personal affairs. Your husband and I have only met a few times, socially. What do you want from me?

And your daughter, tell your daughter to let me alone!

Thank you both for thinking of me. I wish I could be equal to your hatred. But the other day an old associate of my husband's, a bitch of a man, ran into me in the Fisher lobby and said, "What's happened to you—you look terrible! You've lost weight!" He pinched the waist of my dress, drawing it out to show how it hung loose on me, he kept marvelling over how thin I am, not releasing me. A balding, pink-faced son of a bitch, who has made himself rich by being on the board of supervisors for a county north of here, stuffing himself at the trough. I know all about him. A sub-politician, never elected. But I trust the eyes of these sub-men, their hot keen perception. Nothing escapes them. "One month ago," he said, "you were a beautiful woman." Nothing in my life has hurt me as much as that remark, *One month ago you were a beautiful woman. . . .*

Were you ever beautiful? He says not. So he used you, he used you up. That isn't my fault. You say in your letter—thank you for typing it, by the way—that I could never understand your husband, his background of mental instability, his weaknesses, his penchant (your word) for blaming other people for his own faults. Why tell me this? He isn't going to be my husband. I have a husband. Why should I betray my husband for yours, your nervous guilty hypochrondriac husband? The first evening we met, believe it or not, he told me about his *hurts*—people who've hurt him deeply! "The higher you go in a career the more people take after you, wanting to bring you down," he told me. And listen: "The worst hurt of my life was when my first book came out, and an old professor of mine, a man I had idolized at Columbia, reviewed it. He began by saying *Bombarded as we are by prophecies in the guise of serious historical research . . .* and my heart was broken." We were at a party but apart from the other people, we ate, he drank, we played a game with each other that made my pulse leap, and certainly my pulse leaped to hear a man, a stranger, speak of his heart being broken—where I come from men don't talk like that! I told him a *hurt* of my own, which I've never told anyone before: "The first time my mother saw my husband, she took me aside and said *Can't you tell him to stand up straighter?* and my heart was broken. . . ."

And so, with those words, I had already committed adultery, betraying my husband to a stranger.

Does he call you every night? I am jealous of those telephone calls. What if he changes his mind and returns to you, what then? When he went to the Chicago convention I'm sure he telephoned you constantly (he telephoned me only three times, the bastard) and joked to you about his fear of going out into the street. "Jesus, what if somebody smashes in my head, there goes my next book!" he said over the phone, but he wasn't kidding me. I began to cry, imagining him beaten up, bloody, far away from me. Why does he joke like that? Does he joke like that with you?

Dear Mother and Father,

My husband Greg is busy with   . Doing well. Not fired. Pressure on, pressure off. Played golf with   . I went to a new doctor yesterday, a woman. I had made an appointment to go to a man but lost my courage, didn't show up. Better a woman. She examined me, she looked at me critically and said, "Why are you trying to starve yourself?" *To keep myself from feeling love, from feeling lust, from feeling anything at all.* I told her I didn't know I was starving myself. I had no appetite. Food sickened me . . . how could I eat? She gave me a vitamin shot that burned me, like fire. Things good for you burn like fire, shot up into you, no escape. You would not like my lover, you would take me aside and say *Jews are very brilliant and talented, yes, but. . . .*

I am surviving at half-tempo. A crippled waltz tempo. It is only my faith in the flimsiness of love that keeps me going—I know this will end. I've been waiting for it to end since April, having faith. Love can't last. Even lust can't last. I loved my husband and now I do not love him, we never sleep together, that's through. Since he isn't likely to tell you that, I will. He would never even think about it.

Lloyd Burt came to see my husband the other day, downtown.

Eleven in the morning and already drunk. His kid had been stopped in Grosse Pointe, speeding. The girl with him knocked out on pills. *He* had no pills on him, luckily. Do you remember Lloyd? Do you remember any of us? I am your daughter. Do you regret having had a daughter? I do not regret having no children, not now. Children, more children, children upon children, protoplasm upon protoplasm. . . . Once I thought I couldn't bear to live without having children, now I can't bear to live at all, I must be the wife of a man I can't have, I don't even want children from him, I sit here in my room with my head and body aching with a lust that has become metaphysical and skeptical and bitter, living on month after month, cells dividing and heating endlessly. I don't regret having no children. I don't thank you for having me. No gratitude in me, nothing. No, I feel no gratitude. I can't feel gratitude.

My dear husband,

I want to tell you everything. I am in a motel room, I've just taken a bath. How can I keep a straight face telling you this? Sat in the bath tub for an hour, not awake, not asleep, the water was very hot. . . .

I seem to want to tell you something else, about Sally Rodgers. I am light-headed, don't be impatient. I met Sally at the airport this afternoon, she was going to New York, and she saw me with a man, a stranger to her, the man who is the topic of this letter, the crucial reason for this letter. . . . Sally came right up to me and started talking, exclaiming about her bad fortune, her car had been stolen last week! then when she and a friend took her boat out of the yacht club and docked it at a restaurant on the Detroit River, she forgot to take the keys out and someone stole her boat! twenty-thousand dollars' worth of boat, a parting gift from her ex-husband, pirated away downriver. She wore silver eyelids, silver stockings, attracting attention not from men but from small children, who stared. My friend, my lover, did not approve of her— her clanking jewelry made his eye twitch.

I am twenty miles from Detroit. In Detroit the multiplication of things is too brutal, I think it broke me down. Weak, thin, self-

ish, a wreck, I have become oblivious to the deaths of other people (Robert Kennedy was murdered since I became this man's
mistress, but I had no time to think of him—I put the thought of
his death aside, to think of later. No time now.) Leaving him and
walking in Detroit, downtown, on those days we met to make love,
I began to understand what love is. Holding a man between my
thighs, my knees, in my arms, one single man out of all this multiplication of men, this confusion, this din of human beings. So it
is we choose someone. Someone chooses us. I admit that if he did
not love me so much I couldn't love him. It would pass. But a
woman has no choice, let a man love her and she must love him,
if the man is strong enough. I stopped loving you, I am a crimi-
nal. . . . I see myself sinking again and again beneath his body,
those heavy shoulders with tufts of dark hair on them, again and
again pressing my mouth against his, wanting something from
him, betraying you, giving myself up to that throbbing that arises
out of my heartbeat and builds to madness and then subsides
again, slowly, to become my ordinary heartbeat again, the heart-
beat of an ordinary body from which divinity has fled.

Flesh with an insatiable soul. . . .

You would hear in a few weeks, through your innumerable far-
flung cronies, that my lover's daughter almost died of aspirin poi-
son, a ten-year-old girl with an I.Q. of about 200. But she didn't
die. She took aspirin because her father was leaving her, divorcing
her mother. The only gratitude I can feel is for her not having
died. . . . My lover, whom you hardly know (he's the man of
whom you said that evening "He certainly can talk!") telephoned
me to give me this news, weeping over the phone. A man weeping.
A man weeping turns a woman's heart to stone. I told him I would
drive out at once, I'd take him to the airport. He had to catch the
first plane home and would be on stand-by, at the airport. So I
drove to Ann Arbor to get him. I felt that we were already married and that passion had raced through us and left us, years ago,
as soon as I saw him lumbering to the car, a man who has lost
weight in the last few months but who carries himself a little clum-
sily, out of absent-mindedness. He wore a dark suit, rumpled. His
necktie pulled away from his throat. A father distraught over his
daughter belongs to mythology. . . .

Like married people, like conspirators, like characters in a diffi-

cult scene hurrying their lines, uncertain of the meaning of lines.
. . . "It's very thoughtful of you to do this," he said, and I said,
"What else can I do for you? Make telephone calls? Anything?"
Should I go along with you? So I drive him to the airport. I let
him out at the curb, he hesitates, not wanting to go without me,
he says, "But aren't you coming in . . . ?" and I see fear in his
face, I tell him yes, yes, but I must park the car. This man, so
abrupt and insulting in his profession, a master of whining rhetoric, stares at me in bewilderment as if he cannot remember why
I have brought him here to let him out at the United Airlines
terminal, why I am eager to drive away. "I can't park here," I tell
him sanely, "I'll get a ticket." He respects all minor law; he nods
and backs away. It takes me ten minutes to find a parking place.
All this time I am sweating in the late October heat, thinking that
his daughter is going to win after all, has already won. Shouldn't
I just drive home and leave him, put an end to it? A bottle of
aspirin was all it took. The tears I might almost shed are not tears
of shame or regret but tears of anger—that child has taken my
lover from me. That child! I don't cry, I don't allow myself to cry,
I drive all the way through a parking lot without finding a place
and say to the girl at the booth, who puts her hand out expecting
a dime, "But I couldn't find a place! I've driven right through!
This isn't fair!" Seeing my hysteria she relents, opens the gate,
lets me through. *Once a beautiful woman,* she is thinking. I try
another parking lot.

Inside the terminal a moment of panic—what if he has already
left? Then he hurries to me. I take his arm. He squeezes my hand.
Both of us very nervous, agitated. "They told me I can probably
make the two-fifteen, can you wait with me?" he says. His face,
now so pale, is a handsome man's face gone out of control; a pity
to look upon it. In a rush I feel my old love for him, hopeless. I
begin to cry. Silently, almost without tears. A girl in a very short
skirt passes us with a smile—lovers, at their age! "You're not to
blame," he says, very nervous, "she's just a child and didn't know
what she was doing—please don't blame yourself! It's my fault—"
But a child tried to commit suicide, shouldn't someone cry? I am
to blame. She is hurting me across the country. I have tried to
expel her from life and she, the baby, the embryo, stirs with a
will of her own and chooses death calmly. . . . "But she's going

to recover," I say to him for the twentieth time, "isn't she? You're sure of that?" He reassures me. We walk.

The airport is a small city. Outside the plate glass airplanes rise and sink without effort. Great sucking vacuums of power, enormous wings, windows brilliant with sunlight. We look on un-amazed. To us these airplanes are unspectacular. We walk around the little city, walking fast and then slowing down, wandering, holding hands. It is during one of those strange lucky moments that lovers have—he lighting a cigarette—that Sally comes up to us. We are not holding hands at that moment. She talks, bright with attention for my friend, she herself being divorced and not equipped to live without a man, he smiles nervously, ignoring her, watching people hurry by with their luggage. She leaves. We glance at each other, understanding each other. Nothing to say. *My darling!* . . .

Time does not move quickly. I am sweating again, I hope he won't notice, he is staring at me in that way . . . that way that frightens me. I am not equal to your love, I want to tell him. Not equal, not strong enough. I am ashamed. Better for us to say goodbye. A child's corpse between us? A few hundred miles away, in Boston, are a woman and a child I have wronged, quite inten-tionally; aren't these people real? But he stares at me, the maga-zine covers on a newsstand blur and wink, I feel that everything is becoming a dream and I must get out of here, must escape from him, before it is too late. . . . "I should leave," I tell him. He seems not to hear. He is sick. Not sick, frightened. He shows too much. He takes my hand, caresses it, pleading in silence. A terrible sensation of desire rises in me, surprising me. I don't want to feel desire for him! I don't want to feel it for anyone, I don't want to feel anything at all! I don't want to be drawn to an act of love, or even to think about it, I want freedom, I want the smooth sterility of coins worn out from friendly handling rubbing to-gether, I want to say goodbye to love at the age of thirty, not being strong enough for it. A woman in the act of love feels no joy but only terror, a parody of labor, giving birth. Torture. Heart-beat racing at 160, 180 beats a minute, where is joy in this, what is this deception, this joke, isn't the body itself a joke?

He leads me somewhere, along a corridor. Doesn't know where he is going. People head toward us, with suitcases. A soldier on leave from Vietnam, we don't notice, a Negro woman weeping over another soldier, obviously her son, my lover does not see. A man brushes against me and with exaggerated fear I jump to my lover's side . . . but the man keeps on walking, it is nothing. My lover strokes my damp hand. "You won't . . . you're not thinking of. . . . What are you thinking of?" he whispers. Everything is open in him, everything. He is not ashamed of the words he says, of his fear, his pleading. No irony in him, this ironic man. And I can hear myself saying that we must put an end to this, it's driving us both crazy and there is no future, nothing ahead of us, but I don't say these words or anything like them. We walk along. I am stunned. I feel a heavy, ugly desire for him, for his body. I want him as I've wanted him many times before, when our lives seemed simpler, when we were both deluded about what we were doing . . . both of us thought, in the beginning, that no one would care if we fell in love . . . not my husband, not his family. I don't know why. Now I want to say goodbye to him but nothing comes out, nothing. I am still crying a little. It is not a weapon of mine—it is an admission of defeat. I am not a woman who cries well. Crying is a confession of failure, a giving in. I tell him no, I am not thinking of anything, only of him. I love him. I am not thinking of anything else.

We find ourselves by Gate 10. What meaning has Gate 10 to us? People are lingering by it, obviously a plane has just taken off, a stewardess is shuffling papers together, everything is normal. I sense normality and am drawn to it. We wander on. We come to a doorway, a door held open by a large block of wood. Where does that lead to? A stairway. The stairway is evidently not open. We can see that it leads up to another level, a kind of runway, and though it is not open he takes my hand and leads me to the stairs. In a delirium I follow him, why not? The airport is so crowded that we are alone and anonymous. He kicks the block of wood away, wisely. We are alone. On this stairway—which smells of disinfectant and yet is not very clean—my lover embraces me eagerly, wildly, he kisses me, kisses my damp cheeks, rubs his face against mine. I half-fall, half-sit on the stairs. He begins to groan, or to weep. He presses his face against me, against my breasts, my body. It is like wartime—a battle is going on outside, in the corridor. Hundreds of people! A world of people jostling one another! Here,

in a dim stairway, clutching each other, we are oblivious to their
deaths. But I want to be good! What have I wanted in my life,
except to be good? To lead a simple, good, intelligent life? He
kisses my knees, my thighs, my stomach. I embrace him against
me. Everything has gone wild, I am seared with the desire to be
unfaithful to a husband who no longer exists, nothing else matters
except this act of unfaithfulness, I feel that I am a character in a
story, a plot, who has not understood until now exactly what is
going to happen to her. Selfish, eager, we come together and do
not breathe, we are good friends and anxious to help each other,
I am particularly anxious to help him, my soul is sweated out of
me in those two or three minutes that we cling together, in love.
Then, moving from me, so quickly exhausted, he puts his hands
to his face and seems to weep, without tears, while I feel my eyelids closing slowly upon the mangled length of my body. . . .

This is a confession but part of it is blacked out. Minutes pass
in silence, mysteriously. It is those few minutes that pass after we
make love that are most mysterious to me, uncanny. And then we
cling to each other again, like people too weak to stand by ourselves; we are sick in our limbs but warm with affection, very good
friends, the kind of friends who tell each other only good news.
He helps me to my feet. We laugh. Laughter weakens me, he has
to hold me, I put my arms firmly around his neck and we kiss, I
am ready to give up all my life for him, just to hold him like this.
My body is all flesh. There is nothing empty about us, only a close
space, what appears to be a stairway in some public place. . . .
He draws my hair back from my face, he stares at me. It is obvious
that he loves me.

When we return to the public corridor no one had missed us.
It is strangely late, after three. This is a surprise, I am really surprised, but my lover is more businesslike and simply asks at the
desk—the next plane? to Boston? what chance of his getting on?
His skin is almost ruddy, with pleasure. I can see what pleasure
does to a man. But now I must say goodbye, I must leave. He
holds my hand. I linger. We talk seriously and quietly in the middle of the great crowded floor about his plans—he will stay in
Boston as long as he must, until things are settled; he will see his
lawyer; he will talk it over, *talk it over*, with his wife and his daughter, he will not leave until they understand why he has to leave.

. . . I want to cry out at him, *Should you come back?* but I can't say anything. Everything in me is a curving to submission, in spite of what you, my husband, have always thought.

Finally . . . he boards a plane at four. I watch him leave. He looks back at me, I wave, the plane taxis out the runway and rises . . . no accident, no violent ending. There is nothing violent about us, everything is natural and gentle. Walking along the long corridor I bump into someone, a woman my own age. I am suddenly dizzy. She says, "Are you all right?" I turn away, ashamed. I am on fire! My body is on fire! I feel his semen stirring in my loins, that rush of heat that always makes me pause, staring into the sky or at a wall, at something blank to mirror the blankness in my mind . . . stunned I feel myself so heavily a body, so lethargic with the aftermath of passion. How did I hope to turn myself into a statue, into the constancy of a soul? No hope. The throbbing in my loins has not yet resolved itself into the throbbing of my heart. A woman does not forget so quickly, nothing lets her forget. I am transparent with heat. I walk on, feeling my heart pound weakly, feeling the moisture between my legs, wondering if I will ever get home. My vision seems blotched. The air—air-conditioning—is humming, unreal. It is not alien to me but a part of my own confusion, a long expulsion of my own breath. What do I look like, making love? Is my face distorted, am I ugly? Does he see me? Does he judge? Or does he see nothing but beauty, transported in love as I am, helpless?

I can't find the car. Which parking lot? The sun is burning. A man watches me, studies me. I walk fast to show that I know what I'm doing. And if the car is missing, stolen . . . ? I search through my purse, noting how the lining is soiled, ripped. Fifty thousand dollars in the bank and no children and I can't get around to buying a new purse, everything is soiled, ripped, worn-out . . . the keys are missing . . . only wadded tissue, a sweetish smell, liquid stiffening on the tissue . . . everything hypnotizes me. . . . I find the keys, my vision swims. I will never get home.

My knees are trembling. There is an ocean of cars here at Metropolitan Airport. Families stride happily to cars, get in, drive away. I wander around, staring. I must find my husband's car in order to get home. . . . I check in my purse again, panicked. No, I haven't lost the keys. I take the keys out of my purse to look at

them. The key to the ignition, to the trunk, to the front door of
the house. All there. I look around slyly and see, or think I see,
a man watching me. He moves behind a car. He is walking away.
My body still throbs from the love of another man, I can't concentrate on a stranger, I lose interest and forget what I am afraid
of. . . .

The heat gets worse. Thirty, forty, forty-five minutes pass. . . .
I have given up looking for the car. . . . I am not lost, I am still
heading home in my imagination, but I have given up looking for
the car. I turn terror into logic. I ascend the stairway to the wire-
guarded overpass that leads back to the terminal, walking sensibly,
and keep on walking until I come to one of the airport motels.
A small city, this motel, the bizarre made domestic. I ask them for
a room. A single. Why not? Before I can go home I must bathe, I
must get the odor of this man out of me, I must clean myself. I
take a room, I close the door to the room behind me, alone, I go
to the bathroom and run a tubful of water. . . .

And if he doesn't call me from Boston then all is finished, at an
end. What good luck, to be free again and alone, the way I am
alone in this marvelous empty motel room! the way I am alone in
this bathtub, cleansing myself of him, of every cell of him!

My darling,
You have made me so happy. . . .

How I Contemplated the World from the Detroit House of Correction and Began My Life Over Again

NOTES for an essay for an English class at Baldwin Country Day School; poking around in debris; disgust and curiosity; a revelation of the meaning of life; a happy ending. . . .

I. EVENTS

1. The girl (myself) is walking through Branden's, that excellent store. Suburb of a large famous city that is a symbol for large famous American cities. The event sneaks up on the girl, who believes she is herding it along with a small fixed smile, a girl of fifteen, innocently experienced. She dawdles in a certain style by a counter of costume jewelry. Rings, earrings, necklaces. Prices from $5 to $50, all within reach. All ugly. She eases over to the glove counter, where everything is ugly too. In her close-fitted coat with its black fur collar she contemplates the luxury of Branden's, which she has known for many years: its many mild pale lights, easy on the eye and the soul, its elaborate tinkly decorations, its women shoppers with their excellent shoes and coats and hairdos, all dawdling gracefully, in no hurry.

Who was ever in a hurry here?

2. The girl seated at home. A small library, paneled walls of

oak. Someone is talking to me. An earnest husky female voice
drives itself against my ears, nervous, frightened, groping around
my heart, saying, "If you wanted gloves why didn't you say so?
Why didn't you ask for them?" That store, Branden's, is owned
by Raymond Forrest who lives on DuMaurier Drive. We live on
Sioux Drive. Raymond Forrest. A handsome man? An ugly man?
A man of fifty or sixty, with gray hair, or a man of forty with earnest courteous eyes, a good golf game, who is Raymond Forrest,
this man who is my salvation? Father has been talking to him.
Father is not his physician; Dr. Berg is his physician. Father and
Dr. Berg refer patients to each other. There is a connection.
Mother plays bridge with. . . . On Mondays and Wednesdays our
maid Billie works at. . . . The strings draw together in a cat's
cradle, making a net to save you when you fall. . . .

3. *Harriet Arnold's.* A small shop, better than Branden's.
Mother in her black coat, I in my close-fitted blue coat. Shopping.
Now look at this, isn't this cute, do you want this, why don't you
want this, try this on, take this with you to the fitting room, take
this also, what's wrong with you, what can I do for you, why are
you so strange . . . ? "I wanted to steal but not to buy," I don't
tell her. The girl droops along in her coat and gloves and leather
boots, her eyes scan the horizon which is pastel pink and decorated
like Branden's, tasteful walls and modern ceilings with graceful
glimmering lights.

4. Weeks later, the girl at a bus-stop. Two o'clock in the afternoon, a Tuesday, obviously she has walked out of school.

5. The girl stepping down from a bus. Afternoon, weather
changing to colder. Detroit. Pavement and closed-up stores; grill-
work over the windows of a pawnshop. What is a pawnshop, exactly?

II. CHARACTERS

1. The girl stands five feet five inches tall. An ordinary height.
Baldwin Country Day School draws them up to that height. She

dreams along the corridors and presses her face against the Ther-
moplex Glass. No frost or steam can ever form on that glass. A
smudge of grease from her forehead . . . could she be boiled down
to grease? She wears her hair loose and long and straight in suburban teenage style, 1968. Eyes smudged with pencil, dark brown.
Brown hair. Vague green eyes. A pretty girl? An ugly girl? She
sings to herself under her breath, idling in the corridor, thinking
of her many secrets (the thirty dollars she once took from the
purse of a friend's mother, just for fun, the basement window
she smashed in her own house just for fun) and thinking of her
brother who is at Susquehanna Boys' Academy, an excellent
preparatory school in Maine, remembering him unclearly . . . he
has long manic hair and a squeaking voice and he looks like one
of the popular teenage singers of 1968, one of those in a group,
The Certain Forces, The Way Out, The Maniacs Responsible.
The girl in her turn looks like one of those fieldsful of girls who
listen to the boys' singing, dreaming and mooning restlessly,
breaking into high sullen laughter, innocently experienced.

2. The mother. A midwestern woman of Detroit and suburbs.
Belongs to the Detroit Athletic Club. Also the Detroit Golf Club.
Also the Bloomfield Hills Country Club. The Village Women's
Club at which lectures are given each winter on Genet and Sartre
and James Baldwin, by the Director of the Adult Education Program at Wayne State University. . . . The Bloomfield Art Associa-
tion. Also the Founders Society of the Detroit Institute of Arts.
Also. . . . Oh, she is in perpetual motion, this lady, hair like
blown-up gold and finer than gold, hair and fingers and body of
inestimable grace. Heavy weighs the gold on the back of her hairbrush and hand mirror. Heavy heavy the candlesticks in the dining
room. Very heavy is the big car, a Lincoln, long and black, that on
one cool autumn day split a squirrel's body in two unequal parts.

3. The father. Dr. _____. He belongs to the same
clubs as #2. A player of squash and golf; he has a golfer's um-
brella of stripes. Candy stripes. In his mouth nothing turns to
sugar, however, saliva works no miracles here. His doctoring is of
the slightly sick. The sick are sent elsewhere (to Dr. Berg?), the
deathly sick are sent back for more tests and their bills are sent

to their homes, the unsick are sent to Dr. Coronet (Isabel, a lady), an excellent psychiatrist for unsick people who angrily believe they are sick and want to do something about it. If they demand a male psychiatrist, the unsick are sent by Dr. _____ (my father) to Dr. Lowenstein, a male psychiatrist, excellent and expensive, with a limited practice.

4. Clarita. She is twenty, twenty-five, she is thirty or more? Pretty, ugly, what? She is a woman lounging by the side of a road, in jeans and a sweater, hitch-hiking, or she is slouched on a stool at a counter in some roadside diner. A hard line of jaw. Curious eyes. Amused eyes. Behind her eyes processions move, funeral pageants, cartoons. She says, "I never can figure out why girls like you bum around down here. What are you looking for anyway?" An odor of tobacco about her. Unwashed underclothes, or no underclothes, unwashed skin, gritty toes, hair long and falling into strands, not recently washed.

5. Simon. In this city the weather changes abruptly, so Simon's weather changes abruptly. He sleeps through the afternoon. He sleeps through the morning. Rising he gropes around for something to get him going, for a cigarette or a pill to drive him out to the street, where the temperature is hovering around 35°. Why doesn't it drop? Why, why doesn't the cold clean air come down from Canada, will he have to go up into Canada to get it, will he have to leave the Country of his Birth and sink into Canada's frosty fields . . . ? Will the F.B.I. (which he dreams about constantly) chase him over the Canadian border on foot, hounded out in a blizzard of broken glass and horns . . . ?

"Once I was Huckleberry Finn," Simon says, "but now I am Roderick Usher." Beset by frenzies and fears, this man who makes my spine go cold, he takes green pills, yellow pills, pills of white and capsules of dark blue and green . . . he takes other things I may not mention, for what if Simon seeks me out and climbs into my girl's bedroom here in Bloomfield Hills and strangles me, what then . . . ? (As I write this I begin to shiver. Why do I shiver? I am now sixteen and sixteen is not an age for shivering.) It comes from Simon, who is always cold.

III. WORLD EVENTS

Nothing.

IV. PEOPLE & CIRCUMSTANCES CONTRIBUTING TO THIS DELINQUENCY

Nothing.

V. SIOUX DRIVE

George, Clyde G. 240 Sioux. A manufacturer's representative; children, a dog; a wife. Georgian with the usual columns. You think of the White House, then of Thomas Jefferson, then your mind goes blank on the white pillars and you think of nothing. Norris, Ralph W. 246 Sioux. Public relations. Colonial. Bay window, brick, stone, concrete, wood, green shutters, sidewalk, lantern, grass, trees, blacktop drive, two children, one of them my classmate Esther (Esther Norris) at Baldwin. Wife, cars. Ramsey, Michael D. 250 Sioux. Colonial. Big living room, thirty by twenty-five, fireplaces in living room library recreation room, paneled walls wet bar five bathrooms five bedrooms two lavatories central air conditioning automatic sprinkler automatic garage door three children one wife two cars a breakfast room a patio a large fenced lot fourteen trees a front door with a brass knocker never knocked. Next is our house. Classic contemporary. Traditional modern. Attached garage, attached Florida room, attached patio, attached pool and cabana, attached roof. A front door mailslot through which pour *Time Magazine, Fortune, Life, Business Week, The Wall Street Journal, The New York Times, The New Yorker, The Saturday Review, M.D., Modern Medicine, Disease of the Month* . . . and also. . . . And in addition to all this a quiet sealed letter from Baldwin saying: *Your daughter is not doing work compatible with her performance on the Stanford-Binet.* . . . And your son is not doing well, not well at all, very sad. Where is your son anyway?

Once he stole trick-and-treat candy from some six-year-old kids, he himself being a robust ten. The beginning. Now your daughter steals. In the Village Pharmacy she made off with, yes she did, don't deny it, she made off with a copy of *Pageant Magazine* for no reason, she swiped a roll of lifesavers in a green wrapper and was in no need of saving her life or even in need of sucking candy, when she was no more than eight years old she stole, don't blush, she stole a package of *Tums* only because it was out on the counter and available, and the nice lady behind the counter (now dead) said nothing. . . . Sioux Drive. Maples, oaks, elms. Diseased elms cut down. Sioux Drive runs into Roosevelt Drive. Slow turning lanes, not streets, all drives and lanes and ways and passes. A private police force. Quiet private police, in unmarked cars. Cruising on Saturday evenings with paternal smiles for the residents who are streaming in and out of houses, going to and from parties, a thousand parties, slightly staggering, the women in their furs alighting from automobiles bought of Ford and General Motors and Chrysler, very heavy automobiles. No foreign cars. Detroit. In 275 Sioux, down the block, in that magnificent French Normandy mansion, lives _____ himself, who has the C_____ account itself, imagine that! Look at where he lives and look at the enormous trees and chimneys, imagine his many fireplaces, imagine his wife and children, imagine his wife's hair, imagine her fingernails, imagine her bathtub of smooth clean glowing pink, imagine their embraces, his trouser pockets filled with odd coins and keys and dust and peanuts, imagine their ecstasy on Sioux Drive, imagine their income tax returns, imagine their little boy's pride in his experimental car, a scaled-down C_____, as he roars around the neighborhood on the sidewalks frightening dogs and Negro maids, oh imagine all these things, imagine everything, let your mind roar out all over Sioux Drive and DuMaurier Drive and Roosevelt Drive and Ticonderoga Pass and Burning Bush Way and Lincolnshire Pass and Lois Lane.

When spring comes its winds blow nothing to Sioux Drive, no odors of hollyhocks or forsythia, nothing Sioux Drive doesn't already possess, everything is planted and performing. The weather vanes, had they weather vanes, don't have to turn with the wind, don't have to contend with the weather. There is no weather.

VI. DETROIT

There is always weather in Detroit. Detroit's temperature is always 32°. Fast falling temperatures. Slow rising temperatures. Wind from the north northeast four to forty miles an hour, small craft warnings, partly cloudy today and Wednesday changing to partly sunny through Thursday . . . small warnings of frost, soot warnings, traffic warnings, hazardous lake conditions for small craft and swimmers, restless Negro gangs, restless cloud formations, restless temperatures aching to fall out the very bottom of the thermometer or shoot up over the top and boil everything over in red mercury.

Detroit's temperature is 32°. Fast falling temperatures. Slow rising temperatures. Wind from the north northeast four to forty miles an hour. . . .

VII. EVENTS

1. The girl's heart is pounding. In her pocket is a pair of gloves! In a plastic bag! Airproof breathproof plastic bag, gloves selling for twenty-five dollars on Branden's counter! In her pocket! Shoplifted! . . . In her purse is a blue comb, not very clean. In her purse is a leather billfold (a birthday present from her grandmother in Philadelphia) with snapshots of the family in clean plastic windows, in the billfold are bills, she doesn't know how many bills. . . . In her purse is an ominous note from her friend Tykie *What's this about Joe H. and the kids hanging around at Louise's Sat. night? You heard anything?* . . . passed in French class. In her purse is a lot of dirty yellow Kleenex, her mother's heart would break to see such very dirty Kleenex, and at the bottom of her purse are brown hairpins and safety pins and a broken pencil and a ballpoint pen (blue) stolen from somewhere forgotten and a purse-size compact of Cover Girl Make-Up, Ivory Rose. . . . Her lipstick is Broken Heart, a corrupt pink; her fingers are trembling like crazy; her teeth are beginning to chatter; her insides are alive;

her eyes glow in her head; she is saying to her mother's astonished
face *I want to steal but not to buy.*

2. At Clarita's. Day or night? What room is this? A bed, a regular bed, and a mattress on the floor nearby. Wallpaper hanging in
strips. Clarita says she tore it like that with her teeth. She was
fighting a barbaric tribe that night, high from some pills she was
battling for her life with men wearing helmets of heavy iron and
their faces no more than Christian crosses to breathe through,
every one of those bastards looking like her lover Simon, who
seems to breathe with great difficulty through the slits of
mouth and nostrils in his face. Clarita has never heard of Sioux
Drive. Raymond Forrest cuts no ice with her, nor does the
C_____ account and its millions; Harvard Business School
could be at the corner of Vernor and 12th Street for all she cares,
and Vietnam might have sunk by now into the Dead Sea under
its tons of debris, for all the amazement she could show . . . her
face is overworked, overwrought, at the age of twenty (thirty?)
it is already exhausted but fanciful and ready for a laugh. Clarita
says mournfully to me *Honey somebody is going to turn you out
let me give you warning.* In a movie shown on late television
Clarita is not a mess like this but a nurse, with short neat hair
and a dedicated look, in love with her doctor and her doctor's
patients and their diseases, enamored of needles and sponges and
rubbing alcohol. . . . Or no: she is a private secretary. Robert
Cummings is her boss. She helps him with fantastic plots, the
canned audience laughs, no, the audience doesn't laugh because
nothing is funny, instead her boss is Robert Taylor and they are
not boss and secretary but husband and wife, she is threatened
by a young starlet, she is grim, handsome, wifely, a good companion for a good man. . . . She is Claudette Colbert. Her sister too
is Claudette Colbert. They are twins, identical. Her husband
Charles Boyer is a very rich handsome man and her sister, Claudette Colbert, is plotting her death in order to take her place as
the rich man's wife, no one will know because they are *twins.* . . .
All these marvelous lives Clarita might have lived, but she fell out
the bottom at the age of thirteen. At the age when I was packing
my overnight case for a slumber party at Toni Deshield's she was
tearing filthy sheets off a bed and scratching up a rash on her

arms. . . . Thirteen is uncommonly young for a white girl in Detroit, Miss Brook of the Detroit House of Correction said in a sad newspaper interview for the *Detroit News*; fifteen and sixteen are more likely. Eleven, twelve, thirteen are not surprising in colored . . . they are more precocious. What can we do? Taxes are rising and the tax base is falling. The temperature rises slowly but falls rapidly. Everything is falling out the bottom, Woodward Avenue is filthy, Livernois Avenue is filthy! Scraps of paper flutter in the air like pigeons, dirt flies up and hits you right in the eye, oh Detroit is breaking up into dangerous bits of newspaper and dirt, watch out. . . .

Clarita's apartment is over a restaurant. Simon her lover emerges from the cracks at dark. Mrs. Olesko, a neighbor of Clarita's, an aged white wisp of a woman, doesn't complain but sniffs with contentment at Clarita's noisy life and doesn't tell the cops, hating cops, when the cops arrive. I should give more fake names, more blanks, instead of telling all these secrets. I myself am a secret; I am a minor.

3. My father reads a paper at a medical convention in Los Angeles. There he is, on the edge of the North American continent, when the unmarked detective put his hand so gently on my arm in the aisle of Branden's and said, "Miss, would you like to step over here for a minute?"

And where was he when Clarita put her hand on my arm, that wintry dark sulphurous aching day in Detroit, in the company of closed-down barber shops, closed-down diners, closed-down movie houses, homes, windows, basements, faces . . . she put her hand on my arm and said, "Honey, are you looking for somebody down here?"

And was he home worrying about me, gone for two weeks solid, when they carried me off . . . ? It took three of them to get me in the police cruiser, so they said, and they put more than their hands on my arm.

4. I work on this lesson. My English teacher is Mr. Forest, who is from Michigan State. Not handsome, Mr. Forest, and his name is plain unlike Raymond Forrest's, but he is sweet and rodent-like, he has conferred with the principal and my parents,

and everything is fixed . . . treat her as if nothing has happened, a new start, begin again, only sixteen years old, what a shame, how did it happen?—nothing happened, nothing could have happened, a slight physiological modification known only to a gynecologist or to Dr. Coronet. I work on my lesson. I sit in my pink room. I look around the room with my sad pink eyes. I sigh, I dawdle, I pause, I eat up time, I am limp and happy to be home, I am sixteen years old suddenly, my head hangs heavy as a pumpkin on my shoulders, and my hair has just been cut by Mr. Faye at the Crystal Salon and is said to be very becoming.

(Simon too put his hand on my arm and said, "Honey, you have got to come with me," and in his six-by-six room we got to know each other. Would I go back to Simon again? Would I lie down with him in all that filth and craziness? Over and over again

a Clarita is being betrayed as in front of a Cunningham Drug Store she is nervously eyeing a colored man who may or may not have money, or a nervous white boy of twenty with sideburns and an Appalachian look, who may or may not have a knife hidden in his jacket pocket, or a husky red-faced man of friendly countenance who may or may not be a member of the Vice Squad out for an early twilight walk.)

I work on my lesson for Mr. Forest. I have filled up eleven pages. Words pour out of me and won't stop. I want to tell everything . . . what was the song Simon was always humming, and who was Simon's friend in a very new trench coat with an old high school graduation ring on his finger . . . ? Simon's bearded friend? When I was down too low for him Simon kicked me out and gave me to him for three days, I think, on Fourteenth Street in Detroit, an airy room of cold cruel drafts with newspapers on the floor. . . . Do I really remember that or am I piecing it together from what they told me? Did they tell the truth? Did they know much of the truth?

VIII. CHARACTERS

1. Wednesdays after school, at four; Saturday mornings at ten. Mother drives me to Dr. Coronet. Ferns in the office, plastic

or real, they look the same. Dr. Coronet is queenly, an elegant nicotine-stained lady who would have studied with Freud had circumstances not prevented it, a bit of a Catholic, ready to offer you some mystery if your teeth will ache too much without it. Highly recommended by Father! Forty dollars an hour, Father's forty dollars! Progress! Looking up! Looking better! That new haircut is so becoming, says Dr. Coronet herself, showing how normal she is for a woman with an I.Q. of 180 and many advanced degrees.

2. Mother. A lady in a brown suede coat. Boots of shiny black material, black gloves, a black fur hat. She would be humiliated could she know that of all the people in the world it is my ex-lover Simon who walks most like her . . . self-conscious and unreal, listening to distant music, a little bowlegged with craftiness. . . .

3. Father. Tying a necktie. In a hurry. On my first evening home he put his hand on my arm and said, "Honey, we're going to forget all about this."

4. Simon. Outside a plane is crossing the sky, in here we're in a hurry. Morning. It must be morning. The girl is half out of her mind, whimpering and vague, Simon her dear friend is wretched this morning . . . he is wretched with morning itself . . . he forces her to give him an injection, with that needle she knows is filthy, she has a dread of needles and surgical instruments and the odor of things that are to be sent into the blood, thinking somehow of her father. . . . This is a bad morning, Simon says that his mind is being twisted out of shape, and so he submits to the needle which he usually scorns and bites his lip with his yellowish teeth, his face going very pale. *Ah baby!* he says in his soft mocking voice, which with all women is a mockery of love, *do it like this—Slowly* —And the girl, terrified, almost drops the precious needle but manages to turn it up to the light from the window . . . it is an extension of herself, then? She can give him this gift, then? *I wish you wouldn't do this to me,* she says, wise in her terror, because it seems to her that Simon's danger—in a few minutes he might be dead—is a way of pressing her against him that is more powerful than any other embrace. She has to work over his arm, the knotted corded veins of his arm, her forehead wet with perspiration as she pushes and releases the needle, staring at that mixture of liquid

now stained with Simon's bright blood. . . . When the drug hits him she can feel it herself, she feels that magic that is more than any woman can give him, striking the back of his head and making his face stretch as if with the impact of a terrible sun. . . . She tries to embrace him but he pushes her aside and stumbles to his feet. *Jesus Christ*, he says. . . .

5. Princess, a Negro girl of eighteen. What is her charge? She is close-mouthed about it, shrewd and silent, you know that no one had to wrestle her to the sidewalk to get her in here; she came with dignity. In the recreation room she sits reading *Nancy Drew and the Jewel Box Mystery*, which inspires in her face tiny wrinkles of alarm and interest: what a face! Light brown skin, heavy shaded eyes, heavy eyelashes, a serious sinister dark brow, graceful fingers, graceful wristbones, graceful legs, lips, tongue, a sugar-sweet voice, a leggy stride more masculine than Simon's and my mother's, decked out in a dirty white blouse and dirty white slacks; vaguely nautical is Princess's style. . . . At breakfast she is in charge of clearing the table and leans over me, saying, *Honey you sure you ate enough?*

6. The girl lies sleepless, wondering. Why here, why not there? Why Bloomfield Hills and not jail? Why jail and not her pink room? Why downtown Detroit and not Sioux Drive? What is the difference? Is Simon all the difference? The girl's head is a parade of wonders. She is nearly sixteen, her breath is marvelous with wonders, not long ago she was coloring with crayons and now she is smearing the landscape with paints that won't come off and won't come off her fingers either. She says to the matron *I am not talking about anything*, not because everyone has warned her not to talk but because, because she will not talk, because she won't say anything about Simon who is her secret. And she says to the matron *I won't go home* up until that night in the lavatory when everything was changed. . . . "No, I won't go home I want to stay here," she says, listening to her own words with amazement, thinking that weeds might climb everywhere over that marvelous $110,-000 house and dinosaurs might return to muddy the beige carpeting, but never never will she reconcile four o'clock in the morning in Detroit with eight o'clock breakfasts in Bloomfield

Hills . . . oh, she aches still for Simon's hands and his caressing breath, though he gave her little pleasure, he took everything from her (five-dollar bills, ten-dollar bills, passed into her numb hands by men and taken out of her hands by Simon) until she herself was passed into the hands of other men, police, when Simon evidently got tired of her and her hysteria. . . . *No, I won't go home, I don't want to be bailed out,* the girl thinks as a *Stubborn and Wayward Child* (one of several charges lodged against her) and the matron understands her crazy white-rimmed eyes that are seeking out some new violence that will keep her in jail, should someone threaten to let her out. Such children try to strangle the matrons, the attendants, or one another . . . they want the locks locked forever, the doors nailed shut . . . and this girl is no different up until that night her mind is changed for her. . . .

IX. THAT NIGHT

Princess and Dolly, a little white girl of maybe fifteen, hardy however as a sergeant and in the House of Correction for armed robbery, corner her in the lavatory at the farthest sink and the other girls look away and file out to bed, leaving her. God how she is beaten up! Why is she beaten up? Why do they pound her, why such hatred? Princess vents all the hatred of a thousand silent Detroit winters on her body, this girl whose body belongs to me, fiercely she rides across the midwestern plains on this girl's tender bruised body . . . revenge on the oppressed minorities of America! revenge on the slaughtered Indians! revenge on the female sex, on the male sex, revenge on Bloomfield Hills, revenge revenge. . . .

X. DETROIT

In Detroit weather weighs heavily upon everyone. The sky looms large. The horizon shimmers in smoke. Downtown the buildings are imprecise in the haze. Perpetual haze. Perpetual motion inside the haze. Across the choppy river is the city of Windsor, in Canada. Part of the continent has bunched up here and is bulging outward, at the tip of Detroit, a cold hard rain is forever falling on the expressways . . . shoppers shop grimly, their cars are not parked in safe places, their windshields may be smashed and graceful ebony hands may drag them out through their shatterproof smashed windshields crying *Revenge for the Indians!* Ah, they all fear leaving Hudson's and being dragged to the very tip of the city and thrown off the parking roof of Cobo Hall, that expensive tomb, into the river. . . .

XI. CHARACTERS WE ARE FOREVER ENTWINED WITH

1. Simon drew me into his tender rotting arms and breathed gravity into me. Then I came to earth, weighted down. He said *You are such a little girl,* and he weighed me down with his delight. In the palms of his hands were teeth marks from his previous life experiences. He was thirty-five, they said. Imagine Simon in this room, in my pink room: he is about six feet tall and stoops slightly, in a feline cautious way, always thinking, always on guard, with his scuffed light suede shoes and his clothes which are anyone's clothes, slightly rumpled ordinary clothes that ordinary men might wear to not-bad jobs. Simon has fair, long hair, curly hair, spent languid curls that are like . . . exactly like the curls of wood shavings to the touch, I am trying to be exact . . . and he smells of unheated mornings and coffee and too many pills coating his tongue with a faint green-white scum. . . . Dear Simon, who would be panicked in this room and in this house (right now Billie is vacuuming next door in my parents' room: a vacuum cleaner's roar is a sign of all good things), Simon who is said to have come from a home not much different from this, years ago, fleeing all the carpeting and the polished banisters . . . Simon has a deathly face, only desperate people fall in love with it. His face is bony and cautious, the bones of his cheeks prominent as if with the rigidity of his ceaseless thinking, plotting, for he has to make money out of girls to whom money means nothing, they're so far gone they can hardly count it, and in a sense money means nothing to him either except as a way of keeping on with his life. *Each Day's Proud Struggle,* the title of a novel we could read at jail. . . . Each day he needs a certain amount of money. He de-

vours it. It wasn't love he uncoiled in me with his hollowed-out eyes and his courteous smile, that remnant of a prosperous past, but a dark terror that needed to press itself flat against him, or against another man . . . but he was the first, he came over to me and took my arm, a claim. We struggled on the stairs and I said, "Let me loose, you're hurting my neck, my face," it was such a surprise that my skin hurt where he rubbed it, and afterward we lay face to face and he breathed everything into me. In the end I think he turned me in.

2. Raymond Forrest. I just read this morning that Raymond Forrest's father, the chairman of the board at _____, died of a heart attack on a plane bound for London. I would like to write Raymond Forrest a note of sympathy. I would like to thank him for not pressing charges against me one hundred years ago, saving me, being so generous . . . well, men like Raymond Forrest are generous men, not like Simon. I would like to write him a letter telling of my love, or of some other emotion that is positive and healthy. Not like Simon and his poetry, which he scrawled down when he was high and never changed a word . . . but when I try to think of something to say it is Simon's language that comes back to me, caught in my head like a bad song, it is always Simon's language:

> There is no reality only dreams
> Your neck may get snapped when you wake
> My love is drawn to some violent end
> She keeps wanting to get away
> My love is heading downward
> And I am heading upward
> She is going to crash on the sidewalk
> And I am going to dissolve into the clouds

XII. EVENTS

1. Out of the hospital, bruised and saddened and converted, with Princess's grunts still tangled in my hair . . . and Father in his overcoat looking like a Prince himself, come to carry me off. Up the expressway and out north to home. Jesus Christ but the

air is thinner and cleaner here. Monumental houses. Heartbreaking sidewalks, so clean.

2. Weeping in the living room. The ceiling is two storeys high and two chandeliers hang from it. Weeping, weeping, though Billie the maid is *probably listening*. I will never leave home again. Never. Never leave home. Never leave this home again, never.

3. Sugar doughnuts for breakfast. The toaster is very shiny and my face is distorted in it. Is that my face?

4. The car is turning in the driveway. Father brings me home. Mother embraces me. Sunlight breaks in movieland patches on the roof of our traditional contemporary home, which was designed for the famous automotive stylist whose identity, if I told you the name of the famous car he designed, you would all know, so I can't tell you because my teeth chatter at the thought of being sued . . . or having someone climb into my bedroom window with a rope to strangle me. . . . The car turns up the blacktop drive. The house opens to me like a doll's house, so lovely in the sunlight, the big living room beckons to me with its walls falling away in a delirium of joy at my return, Billie the maid is *no doubt* listening from the kitchen as I burst into tears and the hysteria Simon got so sick of. Convulsed in Father's arms I say I will never leave again, never, why did I leave, where did I go, what happened, my mind is gone wrong, my body is one big bruise, my backbone was sucked dry, it wasn't the men who hurt me and Simon never hurt me but only those girls . . . my God how they hurt me . . . I will never leave home again. . . . The car is perpetually turning up the drive and I am perpetually breaking down in the living room and we are perpetually taking the right exit from the expressway (Lahser Road) and the wall of the restroom is perpetually banging against my head and perpetually are Simon's hands moving across my body and adding everything up and so too are Father's hands on my shaking bruised back, far from the surface of my skin on the surface of my good blue cashmere coat (dry-cleaned for my release). . . . I weep for all the money here, for God in gold and beige carpeting, for the beauty of chandeliers and the miracle of a

clean polished gleaming toaster and faucets that run both hot and cold water, and I tell them *I will never leave home, this is my home, I love everything here, I am in love with everything here.* . . .

MAGAZINES CONSULTED

Ann Arbor Review—115 Allen Drive, Ann Arbor, Mich. 48103
Ante—P.O. Box 29915, Los Angeles, Calif. 90029
Antioch Review—212 Xenia Avenue, Yellow Springs, Ohio 45387
Approach—114 Petrie Avenue, Rosemont, Pa. 19010
Ararat—Armenian General Benevolent Union of America, 109 East 40th Street, New York, N.Y. 10016
Arizona Quarterly—University of Arizona, Tucson, Ariz. 85721
The Atlantic—8 Arlington Street, Boston, Mass. 02116
Ave Maria—National Catholic Weekly, Congregation of Holy Cross, Notre Dame, Ind. 46556
Carleton Miscellany—Carleton College, Northfield, Minn. 55057
Carolina Quarterly—Box 1117, Chapel Hill, N.C. 27515
Chelsea—Box 242, Old Chelsea Station, New York, N.Y. 10011
Chicago Review—University of Chicago, Chicago, Ill. 60637
Colorado Quarterly—Hellums 118, University of Colorado, Boulder, Colo. 80304
The Colorado State Review—360 Liberal Arts, Colorado State University, Fort Collins, Colo. 80521
Commentary—165 East 56th Street, New York, N.Y. 10022
Cosmopolitan—1775 Broadway, New York, N.Y. 10019
The Critic—180 N. Wabash Avenue, Chicago, Ill. 60601
December—P.O. Box 274, Western Springs, Ill. 60558
The Denver Quarterly—Denver, Colo. 80210
Descant—Dept. of English, TCU Station, Fort Worth, Tex. 76129
Epoch—159 Goldwin Smith Hall, Cornell University, Ithaca, N.Y. 14850
Esprit—University of Scranton, Scranton, Pa. 18510
Esquire—488 Madison Avenue, New York, N.Y. 10022
Evergreen Review—64 University Place, New York, N.Y. 10003
Fantasy and Science Fiction—347 East 53rd Street, New York, N.Y. 10022
For Now—Box 375, Cathedral Station, New York, N.Y. 10025
Forum—University of Houston, Houston, Tex. 77004
Four Quarters—La Salle College, Philadelphia, Pa. 19141
Generation, the Inter-arts Magazine—University of Michigan, 420 Maynard, Ann Arbor, Mich. 48103

Georgia Review–University of Georgia, Athens, Ga. 30601

Good Housekeeping–959 Eighth Avenue, New York, N.Y. 10019

Green River Review–Box 594, Owensboro, Ky. 42301

The Greensboro Review–University of North Carolina, Greensboro, N.C. 27412

El Grito–2214 Durant, Suite 2, Berkeley, Cal. 94704

Harper's Bazaar–572 Madison Avenue, New York, N.Y. 10022

Harper's Magazine–2 Park Avenue, New York, N.Y. 10016

Hudson Review–65 East 55th Street, New York, N.Y. 10022

Impulse–Rockland Community College, Suffern, N.Y. 10901

Intro–Bantam Books, Inc., 271 Madison Avenue, New York, N.Y. 10016

Kansas Quarterly–Dept. of English, Kansas State University, Manhattan, Kans. 66502

Kenyon Review–Kenyon College, Gambier, Ohio 43022

Ladies' Home Journal–641 Lexington Avenue, New York, N.Y. 10022

The Laurel Review–West Virginia Wesleyan College, Buckhannon, W. Va. 26201

Lillabulero–P.O. Box 1027, Chapel Hill, N.C. 27514

The Literary Review–Fairleigh Dickinson University, Teaneck, N.J. 07666

Mademoiselle–420 Lexington Avenue, New York, N.Y. 10022

The Malahat Review–University of Victoria, Victoria, British Columbia, Canada

The Massachusetts Review–University of Massachusetts, Amherst, Mass. 01003

McCall's–230 Park Avenue, New York, N.Y. 10017

Midstream–515 Park Avenue, New York, N.Y. 10022

The Minnesota Review–Box 4068, University Station, Minneapolis, Minn. 55455

The Moonlight Review–P.O. Box 1686, Brooklyn, N.Y. 11202

Mundus Artium–Dept. of English, Ellis Hall, Box 89, Ohio University, Athens, Ohio 45701

New American Review–1301 Avenue of the Americas, New York, N.Y. 10019

The New Mexico Quarterly–University of New Mexico Press, Marron Hall, Albuquerque, N. Mex. 87106

The New Renaissance–9 Heath Road, Arlington, Mass. 02174

The New Yorker–25 West 43rd Street, New York, N.Y. 10036

North American Review–Cornell College, Mount Vernon, Iowa 52314

Northwest Review–129 French Hall, University of Oregon, Eugene, Ore. 97403

Panache—153 East 84th Street, New York, N.Y. 10028

The Paris Review—45-39, 171 Place, Flushing, N.Y. 11358

Partisan Review—Rutgers University, New Brunswick, N.J. 08903

Perspective—Washington University, St. Louis, Mo. 63105

Phylon—223 Chestnut Street, S.W., Atlanta, Ga. 30314

Playboy—232 East Ohio Street, Chicago, Ill. 60611

Prairie Schooner—Andrews Hall, University of Nebraska, Lincoln, Nebr. 68508

Quarterly Review of Literature—26 Haslet Avenue, Princeton, N.J. 08540

Quartet—346 Sylvia Street, W., Lafayette, Ind. 47906

The Quest—P.O. Box 207, Cathedral Station, New York, N.Y. 10025

Ramparts—1182 Chestnut Street, Menlo Park, Calif. 94027

Readers & Writers—130-21 224th Street, Jamaica, N.Y. 11413

Redbook—230 Park Avenue, New York, N.Y. 10017

Red Clay Reader—2221 Westminster Place, Charlotte, N.C. 28207

Sewanee Review—University of the South, Sewanee, Tenn. 37375

Shenandoah—Box 722, Lexington, Va. 24450

Southern Review—Drawer D, University Station, Baton Rouge, La. 70803

Southwest Review—Southern Methodist University Press, Dallas, Tex. 75222

The Tamarack Review—Box 159, Postal Station K, Toronto, Ontario, Canada

The Texas Quarterly—Box 7527, University of Texas, Austin, Tex. 78712

Trace—P.O. Box 1068, Hollywood, Calif. 90028

Transatlantic Review—Box 3348, Grand Central P.O., New York, N.Y. 10017

Tri-Quarterly—University Hall 101, Northwestern University, Evanston, Ill. 60201

The University of Windsor Review—Windsor, Ontario, Canada

The University Review—University of Kansas City, 51 Street & Rockhill Road, Kansas City, Mo. 64110

Venture (for Junior High)—910 Witherspoon Bldg. Philadelphia, Pa. 19107

The Virginia Quarterly Review—University of Virginia, 1 West Range, Charlottesville, Va. 22903

Vogue—420 Lexington Avenue, New York, N.Y. 10017

Washington Square Review—New York University, 737 East Bldg., New York, N.Y. 10003

Western Humanities Review—Bldg. 41, University of Utah, Salt
      Lake City, Utah 84112
Woman's Day—67 West 44th Street, New York, N.Y. 10036
Yale Review—26 Hillhouse Avenue, New Haven, Conn. 06520